SABER'S GUILD

LAURA NAPOLI

Saber's Guild

IMPORTANT IN-FUR-MATION

If you are new to my work, please note that this is the seventh book in the series. While I tried to make it readable on its own, I recommend starting with The Tails of Little Flower for the best experience.

Parents: This series is intended for adult and mature young adult readers due to scenes with both sex and violence. If you're unsure whether this book is suitable for your child, I recommend reading it yourself first.

Detailed trigger warnings and other in-fur-mation can be found on my website at https://heatingcats.com

To my fans: from the bottom of my heart, I thank you! I would love to hear from you. Please consider leaving a review or sending me a message, even if you threw my book in the freezer until the characters learned to calm down. (Yes, that's happened.)

1

ELLIE: RISING HEAT

*E*llie dug her claws into her palms, trying to control her instinctive need to mate. "Thank the gods Marsee came up with a way to get me out of there. It's been all I could do not to jump between Marcus and Jer for the last hour. Moons, your partner smells yummy. I can see why you picked him."

"I could go back in there and call him out," Myra teased as she unclipped her scanner. "It would be a more enjoyable trip back."

"No. While I appreciate your offer to share, that would be a scandal, and the last thing I want to do is give anyone more ammunition to use against us. Now, come on. Let's go before I bite the first male I see."

She turned to grab her drone but yelped as she found herself face-to-face with a pair of female Saber guards.

"This way," Tamarin said. "We've cleared a path to get you to your ship safely, assuming you don't want to stay. There are guards waiting if that's the route you want to go."

Her mind blanked as her instinct purred at the idea of mating with a guard. She couldn't remember why they were flying back or even that she'd been asked a question as her mating instinct took over.

"Ship," Myra answered for her, handing her a drone with some force. "She needs to go back to Saber. It's her third heat, and she has a rare blood type, which they're out of here."

Ellie blinked down at the drone in her paws as her instinct backed off some with the reminder. "Ship," she agreed, then looked up at Tamarin. "How did you know?"

"We weren't sure what was going on, as your medical record has been locked to all but the Senior Council, but when you logged your flight plans, we figured it could only be for one of two reasons," Tamarin replied. "Kendra had me sniff you out this afternoon. He removed your implant?"

"I see Marsee was right about your noses," Ellie said and then blinked. "I wasn't supposed to say that. Ugh. My mind is a mess."

"It's alright. We figured she'd tell you, and I'm personally glad you know. It makes things easier for everyone. Now, come on. If you're having a hard time thinking, we'd better hurry."

They sped straight to the ship as fast as their drones would go. Tamarin led them down deserted streets, save for more guards, and then through parts of the platform she'd never seen before. The speed and novelty snapped her out of her haze, and to her relief, they made it to her ship without incident.

She turned to Tamarin before boarding. "Thank you for your help tonight, but please, I don't want anyone to know where I'm going or why. Not yet, anyway."

"Your privacy is safe with us, Senior Guild Master. Your flight plan has been scrubbed, and your pilots have been replaced with members of our guard who are used to this duty. No one will know where you're going unless you tell them. On my oath and life, I promise."

Ellie nodded and turned, looking for Myra. She found her staring out the observation window at the ocean beyond, her tail clenched tightly in her paws. "Myra?"

Myra sighed and turned back to face her and the guards. She let go of her tail, but her friend's normally calm mask was gone, stripped away by deep furrows of worry and indecision.

"We'll protect them, too," Tamarin said. "They'll be safe. We won't let anyone harm them. The Senior Guild Master needs you. You protect her. We'll protect them."

Myra nodded and brought her emotions back under control. "Thank you."

"It's my honor. Safe flight."

Ellie grabbed Myra's arm and pulled her onto the ramp to her ship as she could feel her instinct flaring again. It wanted one of those yummy guards and didn't want to wait the four standard days it would take to return Saber. She slammed the door shut behind them the moment they were inside.

After taking several deep breaths to regain her control, she hit the comms. "Pilot, we're ready to go."

"It'll be a few minutes, ma'am. There's a transport unloading at the moment."

"Understood. Lock the doors, and don't let me back off, no matter what I say or do. We have to go back to Saber."

"Yes, ma'am."

She growled at Mrya, who had unclipped her med scanner and was waving it in her face again. She shoved Myra's scanner aside and forced herself to take her seat but fumbled with the harness, struggling to remember how it worked. "Why is this so difficult?" she huffed.

"I could sedate you if it's too much," Myra said as she helped her clip in.

"No," Ellie growled out. "I'll manage." After taking several more deep breaths to control her instinct, she pulled up the message she'd already prepared for Marsee, tweaked it a bit, and sent it off. Moments later, the pilot informed them they were taking off, but she had them wait in orbit before jumping.

"What are you waiting for?" Myra asked.

"I sent Marsee a message, and I want to see if she replies or has any questions before we jump. A few minutes won't matter now that I'm safely away from temptation, and I might not get another chance."

When the messages from Agate and Marsee arrived within moments of each other, Ellie smiled and relaxed. Her life's work was safe and in good hands. Marsee had risen to her challenge. She fired off a quick reply and then told the pilots they could jump.

"How did Marsee take the news?" Myra asked.

"*Guild Master* Chenzira is on her way over to the Guild to continue prepping for the meeting with Agate," she replied, a moment before the universe flickered out of existence.

"You promoted her to Guild Master?!" Myra squeaked once the universe reappeared. "She's barely an adult!"

"Myra, in another week, she may very well be *Senior* Guild Master, and she's earned it. She saved the Guild and the Consortium last night and on far better terms than any of us had any right to hope for. You have an amazing daughter, but that's not surprising considering who her mentor is. Now, where did you hide those toys? I am about to explode."

Myra snorted at her audacity but left to retrieve the toys she'd stored earlier.

Ellie followed right behind and rubbed up against her. "Sorry, I couldn't help it. You're even starting to smell good, not right, but good. This is going to be a very long four days, and I apologize in advance."

"Not if I can help it," Myra said.

"Huh?" she replied as she peeked in the bag, wondering what Little Flower had provided.

Myra reached out and rubbed the side of her face. "Ellie, you're my oldest and dearest friend. Do you honestly think I'm going to let you suffer for four days?"

Ellie started purring instantly, which surprised her. She'd never reacted to a female before, but then no one but Peter had ever touched her during a heat before either.

Myra started purring, too. "I'm a Healer, and Healer's orders say you need to play with some toys. Things that go *buzz* in the night."

Ellie chuckled and padded towards her room on all fours, her tail held to the side and her lower regions twitching with anticipation. *Maybe this won't be a difficult trip after all.*

Myra followed and locked the door behind her, not that there was any risk of her pilots walking in. They never came to this part of the ship while she was onboard. Myra rubbed up against her as she walked past and set the bag of toys down on the bed.

"Oh, that feels so good. It's been so long I'd almost forgotten."

Myra turned and rubbed up against her again, sniffed her backside, and licked.

Ellie groaned, and her legs nearly buckled out from under her as a wave of feeling washed over her.

"You smell and taste good, too," Myra told her. "But I see what you mean about not quite right. Huh. How odd."

"You're not going into heat, too, are you?" Ellie asked, frowning with concern.

"No, my implant is fully functional. I checked. Let's just say I'm going to be having a very awkward conversation with Kendra when I see her next."

Ellie looked closely at Myra, ears back and terrified, as she confirmed her suspicions. "You're using your instinct?! Myra! You know that's not safe!"

"You don't think I'm going to let you have all the fun, and it's perfectly safe. It's fully under control, and it...it wants to attract a strong mate for you. I had the idea from the conversations I had while trying to figure out why Marsee went into her pseudo-heat. It doesn't feel the same as a true heat, more like what I've been able to do with Jer, but if this gives you a better chance, then I am willing to do just about anything to keep you alive, and frankly, I could use a bit of a distraction myself."

Ellie didn't argue further. If Myra was able to talk with her instinct on, she was clearly still in control. Her own control, on the other paw, was rapidly deteriorating. She rubbed up against Myra's side again and returned the favor. Myra's groan did all sorts of things to her insides. "

Well, if I am going to die, at least it's going to be fun," Ellie said. "Now, what did Little Flower leave us?"

Myra dug through the bag. "I'm not sure what half of these are, but the Hue-mans are quite inventive. I suppose it's not surprising, seeing as they come into heat every couple of weeks. Let's see what this one does." She pulled out a case and opened it to reveal an oddly shaped wand. "Built-in sanitation? Huh. That's a nice touch." Myra found the power button, and it started vibrating. "Buzz buzz!" she said and turned to Ellie with a seductive grin.

Ellie grinned back and spun her backside around so it was up in the air and facing Myra, her tail held to the side with anticipation. A moment later, her claws scraped on the metal floor as they curled under her. "Blessed moons! I've been investing in the wrong department," she said, then stopped talking as even the memory of words left her.

Myra didn't stop until she was nothing more than a puddle of twitching goo.

"Myra, you have the touch of a goddess," she said when the ability to speak returned to her.

Myra grinned. "I should hope so. I am a Senior Healer with a specialty in reproduction, after all. Are you feeling better?"

"I am a melted, twitching pile of furry goo, well, fuzzy goo, and I can see why Jer followed you all the way out into the middle of nowhere. If I had the power, I'd promote you to Senior Guild Healer for that. Now, as soon as my limbs remember how to work, I'm returning the favor."

From experience, she knew her need to mate would continue to grow stronger until it was unbearable, and it wouldn't stop until her body encountered enough of the right scent and released her eggs. She'd been stuck in that state during her first heat while the healers tried to figure out what was going wrong.

Peter had smelled right, but the biological changes that occurred with their first heat hadn't happened. It had been fun at first, but then it had turned excruciating. Her instinct, stuck in the need to mate and terrified by the pain, hadn't backed off. She hadn't been able to speak, but she'd maintained enough control of her instinct to be able to respond to yes or no questions and allow the healers to approach and sedate her.

They'd been able to save her life and figure out what had gone wrong. Her second heat had been successful, but she'd miscarried halfway through her pregnancy. They hadn't allowed her to try again. She'd nearly died along with her cubs, and a third heat was almost always fatal. One in a hundred survived.

The urge to rub was stronger than she'd experienced with either of her previous heats, so she was hopeful she would produce a viable egg, but she knew it was unlikely she would survive another miscarriage.

Myra walked over to the pile where she'd tossed her harness at some point and pulled out her scanner. "Everything still looks normal, and I'm already seeing three eggs that look mature and several more forming. We should have plenty to choose from at this rate."

Ancient Gods, please just give me one healthy cub. While she was hoping for half a dozen or more, she wouldn't be greedy. One would be enough.

"You're a little dehydrated, though. Have something to drink before you nap," Myra continued.

Ellie padded out of the room at a fast trot and returned with a large pitcher of juice and two cups. She would do anything and everything Myra said if it meant a healthy cub.

Drink consumed, she dug into the bag to see what else they had to play with and found one of her favorites. The urge to mate was already returning, so rather than nap, she turned to Myra with a purr and held up the wand. "Your turn. Buzz buzz!"

2

MARSEE: RED FIN

*D*etermined to protect her mentor's legacy, Marsee stormed down the hall and made it as far as the end of the hallway before feeling like she'd stumbled into a thick wall of anxiety. Her paw shook as she reached for the switch to call the lift, and she just stared at it rather than pushing the button.

"What's wrong, Marsee?" Aris asked and gently touched her shoulder. "You're terrified."

"Everything," Marsee whispered. "Everything changes if I push that button. If she…" She couldn't even handle the thought of Ellie dying. "If *I*…"

"If you step forward, you'll be protecting your mentor's life work but putting your family at further risk," Aris answered for her.

Marsee swallowed hard and nodded even though it wasn't a question, eyes still fixed on that switch.

"What would happen to your family if someone like Rip got ahold of the Guild?" Aris asked her a moment later when she still didn't move.

She growled at that thought and slammed the switch to call the lift. She sensed Aris's approval, but when the lift arrived, the wave of anxiety hit again. She couldn't make herself step onto the lift.

Aris frowned at her, not with disapproval but with worry. She carefully examined the empty lift and then peered over the railing to the Commons before giving an amused snort.

"I don't see what's so funny?" Marsee muttered, annoyed by her reaction.

"Your instinctive loathing of the Press. There's a swarm of them waiting for you down below."

Marsee groaned at the thought of an interview on top of everything else and peered down over the railing. She focused hard, trying to see if she could hear what they were saying or sniff out their emotions.

"You somehow always manage to sniff them out before we do," Aris continued, tail spiraling as she looked down over the railing with her. "We're not sure how you do it, but we think you're picking up on the hum of their camera drones."

"I'd rather eat another slime eel than give an interview. They've kept their distance. I wonder what's changed."

"Well, either they're hoping to catch a random Councilor for their thoughts before the meeting, or they found out about Ellie. Shall we take a more discrete route to the Guild tonight?"

Marsee's anxiety vanished with that blessed idea. Added to the swirling scents, the sudden change in her emotions made her dizzy enough to wobble.

Aris grabbed her harness and pulled her away from the railing before peering at her with worry again. "Are you alright?"

She shrugged. "That depends on your definition of alright. My emotions are a mess. They're so strong and change so quickly that it makes me dizzy. Is that normal?"

"For some. It's better than the alternative, I suppose. Some people bottle up their trauma until it explodes at some random moment in the future, usually over something unimportant. Balance issues are also common for the…type of injuries you've had. Come on. We'll take the back door. The stairs and swim will be a good workout for you. I doubt we'll have time tomorrow."

She squinted with suspicion as Aris took to the stairs and started climbing. The main exit was several flights below, not up, but she followed her guard without hesitation as they climbed up nearly a dozen flights through multiple gravity zones at a pace that made her legs scream with the effort, but it was exactly what she needed to forget her nerves. Panting hard, she trotted after Aris down a narrow maintenance hallway that ran halfway around the platform before they stepped through a static shield into one of the Water Sprite tunnels.

Without a drone, she had to swim, and by the time they made it back down to what was labeled the main floor, she was exhausted, but she wasn't going to admit it. Rather than taking the exit, Aris hit a security panel on the wall, and a section of the wall vanished, revealing another tube that went down another half-dozen floors.

"Welcome to Platform Operations," Aris said at the bottom. "This is where all of the life support equipment is located. You need authorization to access, which you have, but the general population, including the Press, doesn't."

"I'm surprised you didn't hide us down here," Marsee said.

"We considered it, but I have a feeling you wouldn't have lasted very long."

She was about to ask why when Aris hit the switch to activate the door. A wave of sound nearly deafened her.

Aris grinned at her and swam through. Marsee pinned her ears flat and followed after. They passed a few Sprites who all wore Platform Operations badges and harnesses filled with tools. They flashed their respects but didn't stop them as they continued on. While she'd seen images of this area as part of her training, she hadn't recognized the scale of the machinery. Massive pieces of equipment filled what appeared to be all six floors below ground.

"How does anyone work down here and not go deaf?" Marsee signed. It was far too loud to talk without yelling.

Aris shrugged. "You get used to it after a while, and the Sprites don't need to hear to communicate. I bet they'd love those hearing aids of yours, though."

She considered putting them in at the reminder, but thankfully, they didn't stay in the space long. Aris led her to another door where they stepped through into a dry hallway. Marsee sighed with relief as the door slid shut. Amused, Aris's tail curled, but she said nothing and kept walking past several well-marked but empty offices and then back into another Water Sprite tunnel, where they swam back up several floors.

"Are you actually leading me out of here, or are you just trying to find the most convoluted route around the platform until I give up and decide the Press is less effort?"

Aris's tail corkscrewed with amusement, but rather than replying, she shifted aside so that a clearly marked sign in five of the six official languages was visible above her.

"Arboretum. Emergency Exit. Unauthorized use will activate alarm."

Aris apparently had authorization as the door slid open without the blare of an alarm. "Command will be notified regardless," Aris explained. "But I imagine they already know we're here. If they don't, we have a bigger problem."

Aris swam up and carefully peered through the hatch before swimming through. Marsee followed and found herself mostly surrounded by a hedge of flowers. Aris shoved aside what looked like a rock to uncover the security panel and shut the door. When it shut, there was no indication there was even a door, as it had been textured to look exactly like the rest of the dirt floor.

Once shut, Aris peered around the hedge before motioning her out, but Marsee stopped and froze. Not only did she recognize where she was, but she also recognized the two Water Sprite Guards who were in the middle of an animated conversation in the grotto - one too fast for her to follow.

"Marsee?" Aris asked.

The two guards stopped talking and turned to face them. Tanner flashed silver and purple, recognizing her, but the other guard stared at her in as much shock as she was staring at him.

"Marsee, what's going on," Aris asked again, but she barely heard the guard as memory of that day flashed in her brain. They were in the same grotto she'd been in when she was kidnapped, and he was the guard who approached her with the note.

"Marsee!" Aris snapped.

She ignored Aris, her attention focused entirely on the Sprite. "It was you!" she growled at him.

Aris had her stunner out in an instant but didn't fire as Tanner swam between them, hands up to stop them, and rapidly flashed, "This is my son. On my life and oath, I swear he wasn't involved. Please!"

She ignored Tanner. "You're the one that handed me the note! Aren't you?" she demanded.

Shame rippled across his skin before he gently placed an arm on his mother's arm and moved her aside. "Yes. I was, but please, let me explain. I promise I didn't know what was going on, and I never meant for you to get hurt. I had seen both Snapper and Rip swim by before you swam out of your suite. So when Snapper approached and informed me that he had a message for you from Rip, I didn't think much of it and swam it over. He stunned us both, or maybe Rip did. I never saw who actually fired the weapon. He stunned me before I could react. I'm sorry I didn't recognize the threat and that I failed to protect you. I owe you everything for saving my life. If you demand mine in return, it's yours."

The only emotion she sensed from him was shame, but she glanced at Aris for confirmation.

"As far as we can tell, he's telling the truth," Aris replied. "Kendra, Avery, Stinger, and all of the Seniors have questioned him. The comms were tampered with, so we don't have footage."

She frowned, not at Aris's words but at something Red Fin had said. "Stunner? I wasn't shocked? I remember something pushing into my back before the pain hit."

Red Fin shook his head. "The stunner hit your side, not your back. It causes your muscles to seize and can feel like something pushing you at first before your brain registers the pain."

She'd purposely lied to see what he would say. She glanced at Aris again, who shrugged. "I honestly can't tell much difference between the pain of being shocked and a stunner, but he's right. At close enough range, the stunner can hit with enough force to knock you over, bruise, burn, or even kill you."

"Please, I know my son," Tanner said. "He wouldn't have hurt you."

"Mama," he said and looked back at her with sadness. "I thank you for believing in me, but I did hurt her. I failed to protect her, and she nearly died because of it. You know as well as I do that I might be arrested and executed tomorrow for that failure alone."

Marse frowned at that statement and the grief she could smell from Tanner, although it remained off her skin. If he was telling the truth as he appeared to be, then he was as much a victim as she'd been. Her father had informed her that Red Fin had been tortured to try to make Petra give a false statement against Wind Rider.

No one moved, waiting for her to speak. "My father said you were injured trying to protect Petra?"

He turned, lifting his arm so she could see the scars that started on his side and wrapped around his back, and that was enough to convince her.

"I can't say what the Seniors will decide, but you'll receive no demands for arrest or additional reparations from me," She signed when he turned back around. "I know what the placement of those scars means, and as far as I'm concerned, you've already suffered enough."

Tanner flashed her relief and gratitude, but Red Fin only flashed surprise, matched by the stunned expression on his face.

"Why are you surprised?" she asked, wondering if it had anything to do with her knowing about their mating practices.

"You were so angry at me a moment ago. I…"

"Ask anyone," she interrupted. "My emotions are a mess these days. I was caught off guard. I thought Snapper was the one who delivered the message, not you. My father said Snapper confessed to that crime. That he knocked you out and then delivered the message."

All three guards expressed their surprise.

"Snapper does have similarly colored ear fins," Aris said. "Half the time, that's the only way I can tell you all apart."

Marsee peered at Red Fin, whose own ear fins were yellow and green. "Why *is* your name Red Fin if your ear fins are yellow and green? Or am I mistranslating your name?"

Humor bubbled across Tanner's skin, and Red Fin flashed a bit of embarrassment, tinged with grief before his ear fins changed to bright red.

Marsee pinned her own ears back in surprise. "Ellie told me you couldn't change the color of your ear fins."

"We can, but it's one of the first things we learn to control," Tanner said in her language. "It's considered…childish? No. That's not the right word."

"Rude," Red Fin corrected. "Crass. Uncivilized. Our ear fins only change color with intense anger. The closest insult to your language would be to call someone…hot-headed."

That confused her more. "Why would you want a name that's an insult?"

"For a number of reasons," he replied. "My father used to call me his little red fin because I would get so angry at the injustices of the world. When he…died. I was so angry my fins were red for weeks. It was right before my name day, and I chose it as both a warning to others and to honor my father. After taking my oath of adulthood, I swam right to the Guard and joined."

"What happened to your father?" she asked.

For the first time, grief and anger flashed on both their skins, and Tanner turned away.

Red Fin looked at his mother, sighed, and turned back to her. "He was murdered by someone as bad as Rip. Someone who tried to impinge upon his honor. It took me years to clear his name and bring him justice.

She nodded and was about to ask another question when Tanner and Red Fin's comms went off. "Squads one through twelve, return to station."

Tanner and Red Fin looked at each other, then back at her. "If you'll excuse us," Tanner asked.

Marsee nodded, and the two bolted at speed. They were barely out of sight before Aris's comms went off. "Squads two through twenty-four, return to station."

This was followed immediately by a different tone. "Tamarin, return to station and bring Avery with you."

"What's going on?" Marsee asked.

"I don't know," Aris replied. "Probably prep for tomorrow. I'm sure Avery will inform us if we need to know. Come on. I believe someone is waiting for you at the Guild."

She squinted her eyes at Aris. "You're lying. You're worried. Tell me."

Aris sighed and looked in the direction Tanner and Red Fin had gone. "I honestly don't know, but whatever it is, it's bad. The tones indicate it's an order issued by the Senior Council, and they wouldn't leave the city unprotected if there wasn't a very good reason."

She frowned. "Should I go back to the room?"

Aris shook her head. "No. They know we're out and would have informed me if there was a threat to you."

"But…?"

Aris didn't answer, but her worry deepened into grief.

"Answer me, Aris," she ordered.

Aris sighed. "Our squad is running dark. That means no outside communication that could give away our position unless they've detected an immediate threat. That they informed us of the return to station, means they wanted to let us know that we won't have backup for the foreseeable future without making it obvious. The second alert was just for our squad, and based on the tone and message…" Aris paused again, and her grief bloomed. "I believe Avery is being arrested."

"Avery?! Why?"

Aris looked at her and snorted. "Because of what he did to you and Stormy, of course."

"But I didn't press charges, and neither did Stormy."

"It doesn't matter any more than it does with Red Fin. Stormy was a minor at the time, and Clear Seas has the right as both his father and Senior Councilor to order his execution. We're honestly surprised it hasn't happened already. I lost that bet days ago."

She frowned. "Why would they recall everyone, though? A few guards could easily bring Avery in, even if he resisted."

Aris's grief and worry deepened. "Because, unless there's something else going on, they're going to execute Kendra and/or Stinger and install new Seniors, or at least temporary Seniors. Unless there's an emergency, doing so requires a quorum of at least a dozen senior-ranked guards."

"Do you think they're involved?"

Aris shrugged. "I don't believe so, but it doesn't matter what we think. Both gave their oath that they would ensure that things like this wouldn't happen under their command, and Kendra is Avery's mentor. She gave a life oath to your father and uncle that he could be trusted. If the Seniors have found anything against him, they're both dead. Now, come on. I've changed my mind. We're flying over."

Aris's mask slammed down, indicating the conversation was over. Marsee followed Aris back inside the emergency exit and through another door where dozens of small ships were parked. Aris led her over to one of the ones reserved for the Guard and checked it over before letting her on.

"We couldn't have just done this in the first place?" Marsee asked as she clipped into her harness.

Aris's tail curled. "If we had done that, you wouldn't have gotten your workout in this evening or learned where the back door was. Of course, if you hadn't been terrified of the press, we'd have been there already."

"Guards…" Marsee muttered under her breath. "They're almost as bad as the moons' forsaken Council."

Aris's tail spiraled as she took off and flew out the small bay door on the back of the platform.

As they flew to the Guild, Marsee unclipped her tablet and sent her sister a message.

"Can you look into the history of the Honor Guards Red Fin and Tanner and find out how Red Fin's father died?"

"Sure, why?" Little Flower asked.

"I need to know if we can trust them."

3

QUINN: OATH BOUND

Grinning widely with his tail curled tightly behind him, Quinn held out the box with the successfully gathered cobra-chicken egg to Nazari. It was a rare victory, even if it bent the rules significantly, but it was one he would take.

"I'm not sure if that counts as cheating or not," Nazari said, shifting her cub to one arm so she could take the box from him. "A grav-belt? Seriously?"

"You never stated *how* I had to get the egg, just that I needed to do so unharmed."

She snorted at him, but her tail curled. "Well, it was an inventive solution. I'll give you that, but I doubt it will work a second time. You do know they can fly."

"I'll take that bet," he replied and started to follow her in, but two steps later, his tablet blared with an urgent alert.

Quinn pulled off his tablet and read through his orders, signed by all six members of the Senior Council, then sighed as he scanned the lengthy list of guards he'd been ordered to arrest. His heart broke as he found name after name that he knew.

As Kendra's Second and District Senior for Council City, he regularly traveled to the other districts. He had trained and worked with these people for years, many for his whole life, and he struggled to maintain his composure, knowing there was a crowd watching.

Citizens from four of the six species had gathered that morning to watch what had become a daily spectacle. His record was abysmal, but the challenge had brought the community together and eased the tensions and lack of trust he'd sensed from the local residents at the mere presence of a guard.

That didn't mean he wasn't aware of the threat. Many of his guards were visible and appeared relaxed as they joked and bet with locals, but he knew it was all a well-practiced act. Every one of his guards was nervous and on edge, as was the entire contingent of guards hidden throughout the community, all on high alert for an attack.

When he finished scanning the list, he scrolled back up and frowned as he re-read the orders. The Seniors had linked tickets with arrest details, but they were still marked as Senior's Eyes Only. He didn't know what they had done to deserve arrest, but he knew the Seniors well enough, especially Marcus, to know they wouldn't arrest without evidence.

Interestingly enough, none of the guard's mentors or District Seniors had been listed, and he wondered if that would come later, as many of those were even closer friends, and they had all taken an oath to ensure that those under their command conducted themselves with honor. It wasn't the first time he'd brought members of the Guard in for infractions over the years, even a few of his own proteges that he hadn't been able to save, but to have so many at once...

Steeling his heart behind decades of training, he fired off messages to the various District Seniors to have the orders executed before looking up from his tablet again and letting out a loud whistle.

Every guard within earshot, both visible and hidden, instantly flocked to his side and followed him into the arena. Once everyone was in, he shut the door. He couldn't guarantee privacy, but it was the best he could do without a proper barracks.

"Lark, I need to head back to Council City to deal with an issue. You're in charge here. Once I leave, close the air space. No one enters without my explicit approval, and that includes members of the Guard."

"Yes, sir," Lark replied. "Has something happened?"

He nodded and, after a moment of hesitation, held out his tablet, watching her closely as she read.

A moment later, her legs buckled, and she sat down hard, shaking her head. "No...No, I don't believe it. She wouldn't be involved. This has to be a mistake."

Her reaction was genuine. There was no hint of a lie or smell of guilt, only grief and confusion, but the others around her began to smell of worry and concern.

"I'm sorry," he said, taking his tablet back before explaining it to the rest. "I have been sent orders, signed by all six members of the Senior Council, to arrest over a hundred guards, one of which is Lyrik, Lark's littermate," he added for Nazari's benefit. She was the only one in attendance who wouldn't know Lyrik.

He scanned the guards, looking for signs of anger or threat, but all he smelled was grief and resolve. "Today will be a dark day for the Guard and Consortium. No matter your feelings for those arrested, remember your oath. You are here because these people need you. You were chosen because you're the best this planet has to offer. You're their only protection against people who have shown they have no honor and will stop at nothing to get what they want."

Lark visibly recoiled as if struck.

"Can I trust you to honor that oath?" His question was to Lark, but everyone else answered.

"Yes, sir!"

He examined the crowd, then refocused on Lark, who hadn't answered. Tears streamed down her face, and her fists were curled tightly as she looked away, struggling to contain her grief.

"Can I trust you?" he asked again, this time softly and with compassion.

She took several deep breaths, lifted her head, and squared her shoulders. Her eyes met his, still glistening with tears, before she spoke.

"Yes, sir." Her voice cracked, and her jaw shook with the pain of those two words, but there was no lie, only heartbroken resolve.

He focused on her for a moment longer before nodding. "Dismissed."

The rest of the guards all bolted for their assigned duties — all except for Nazari, who still held the box with the egg in it, and Lark, who hadn't moved from where she sat.

Lark wiped the tears from her face before climbing to her feet. "Do you have any other orders, sir?"

"No. Take whatever time you need to compose yourself, then do your best not to worry about it until we know more. I don't know why she's been arrested. It could be that she's only wanted for questioning or even protection from someone targeting her."

Lark nodded, although he could tell she didn't believe him any more than he believed himself. He watched as she walked away, tail dragging on the sand behind her.

"Are *you* alright?" Nazari asked quietly.

"No, but I gave an oath, and if they broke theirs, then it's my responsibility to see that they're brought to justice. I only pray that this means the Seniors have sniffed out everyone involved and that this can all end today without further bloodshed. Inform the Trauma Center that the ships are grounded and have them reroute patients to Sand Dune."

"Yes, sir," Nazari replied.

By the time he landed in Council City an hour later, everyone had been arrested and was either in holding locally or confirmation had been received that they were in transport.

Before entering the Council Building, he supervised the unloading of a ship that arrived at the same time he did. He sensed anger and resentment from the prisoners as they were dragged off and disappointment, grief, and resolve from those bringing them in. Several had resisted arrest and were rather scuffed up.

Two were dead.

He sighed as the bodies were unloaded. He had healers brought in for the others and their injuries treated before taking statements from those involved in the deaths, then arrested everyone involved. They, thankfully, didn't resist.

Once they were in custody, he retreated to the privacy of Kendra's office and wrote up his report to the Seniors. His rank entitled him to his own office, but he preferred to be out in the main office with the others where he could keep an ear on everything.

When his report was sent off, he called Lark.

She took one look at him, and her ears drooped. He could tell she was bracing for news she didn't want to hear.

"I'm sorry," he said softly. "Lyrik is dead."

Lark's training to control her emotions did little good as tears started to fall again. "What happened?" she signed, unable to speak as she struggled to contain her grief.

"She…resisted arrest," he replied. "I'll send you what footage I was able to retrieve."

She frowned, and her face hardened as she picked up on what he wasn't saying. She was growling by the time she finished watching, and he didn't blame her.

"I don't know what the Senior's found, but I intend to investigate this. Something doesn't smell right. Why wasn't their camera on the whole time?"

He flicked an ear back slightly. "They *claim* they forgot. I've arrested them both and informed the Seniors. I acknowledge your right as her next of kin to perform your own investigation and bring forth charges. Do you want me to put Keeta in charge so you can take some time off to grieve and begin your investigation?"

Lark took a deep breath and closed her eyes for a moment but then shook her head. "No. I gave an oath. The people here need me. I'll grieve tonight when my shift is over. Somehow, I have a feeling today is only going to get worse."

He nodded, honestly expecting no less from her. The loss of friends and family was a constant risk in the Guard, and there were times you couldn't stop to grieve, or others would die, too, but the loss of a littermate was something else entirely. Only the pain of losing a child was worse.

He'd barely disconnected with Lark when another message arrived. This time from Kendra.

Quinn,

I have received orders to confine myself to my office. By the time you read this, I may already be dead. I'm honestly surprised it's taken them this long. The Senior Council knows what I ordered you and Avery to do at Little Flower's trial, and I took full responsibility for it. I pray that's enough to protect you and everyone else involved.

Whatever happens, I want you to know how very proud I am of you. You've come so far from that angry and belligerent cub that was dropped in my lap all those years ago, and I can't think of anyone better suited to lead the Guard in my absence.

Assuming this is my goodbye, I have one last order to give you. Protect the Senior Guild Master at all costs. I don't know what will happen at the meeting, but I'm expecting violence and another attempt on the Seniors, as I'm sure you are. If they're successful, they'll come after her next. While you're at it, if you can, bring Myra into the Guard. I have a feeling we're going to need her skills.

Live your life with honor, and may the General protect us. With all my love, Kendra.

Quinn leaned back in his seat, rubbed at his face, and reread the message, frowning as he tried to figure out what Kendra was really trying to tell him. There really wasn't anything that he didn't already know, including the reason for Ellie's unexpected return.

He'd been worried for his mentor since word of Avery's failure had arrived, and with the Guard so badly compromised, he'd known there was little chance she would survive. While he was grateful to have her farewell, they had already said goodbye before she left, and they both knew any communication she sent would be monitored by the Senior Council.

He was honestly surprised he hadn't been arrested, too, and not just for his treasonous actions at Little Flower's trial. Members of his own district's guards had been involved. While none of them were his direct reports or his proteges, he'd given an oath just like she had.

Is she trying to protect me? No. If they've implicated her, this would do more harm than good. A warning? No. She wants me to do something. I just know it, but what?

Kendra's comments about Myra worried him. He was honestly surprised that Myra hadn't lost control already after what had been done to her family, but he was relieved that she was no longer on the Water World. If something happened to her family at the meeting, they had a better chance of saving her here.

If she's anything like Nazari, Myra's going to be formidable. Is that it? No. There's more. What is it? Think Quinn!

He rubbed at his scruff and read the message again. The last line caught his attention, and he looked over at the bookcase where the key was hidden. He hit the privacy screen and locked the door before pulling down the book, but the key wasn't there. Frowning, he examined the room with his senses and smiled at a memory from his childhood. Kendra's most recent scent was in several locations, but only he knew the significance of their placement.

He was surprised she remembered after all these years. He walked over and pulled down another small, nondescript book of little importance to anyone but him. Lost in memory, he rubbed his paw over the cover, then opened it to find the key inside.

Placing the book back on the shelf, he quickly located the keyhole in the desk, and a few minutes later, the trick needed to open the hidden drawer. There on top was a letter with his name on it.

Quinn, if you're reading this, then I'm either dead or about to be, or you're snooping where you don't belong. If it's the latter, put this letter back and start running laps, because if you aren't when I find out, you'll regret it.

If it's not Quinn, then oh, are you in for a surprise. The documents contained in this drawer are the last known words of General Marsee Chenzira, written over ten thousand years ago. Make of them what you will.

I pray they give you the answers you need to save our people and that we've already averted war, but I haven't been the Senior Honor Guard this long not to fear otherwise and be prepared.

Marsee, if you're the one reading this, I have believed in you since the day I first met you. You probably don't remember, but I was the guard who interrogated you the day you bit your classmate's tail. When you stood there, full of righteous indignation and conviction, a tiny cub glaring down none other than the Senior Honor Guard, I knew.

I've watched you over the years. I watched as you struggled through challenges foretold millennia ago, and I knew. I watched you rise to those challenges and do what no one has ever done before, and I prayed I was wrong, but in my heart, I knew I wasn't.

Perhaps you've already done what you needed to do to stop the horrors foretold in these documents. I don't know any more about what's to come than what's in this drawer, but if this is only the beginning, I know you'll do what needs to be done to save our people because you are an Honor Guard. You have always been an Honor Guard, one worthy of her name, and I salute you.

Quinn, stop snooping and get back to work.

He chuckled and pulled out the pair of protective gloves included inside. He smiled at that memory, too. He'd been belligerent about needing to learn to handle the old documents, claiming there was no need to go sniffing around in dusty old books, but then that had all been an act to hide the fact that he couldn't read.

The next document was the one Kendra had shown him before. He read it again, thinking about all that had occurred because Kendra had followed the General's orders. The next one was also protected, although it was in far worse condition, torn and faded to the point of nearly being unreadable, but what he could read made his paws shake.

Ancient Gods!

It wasn't the General's writings but someone who knew her and was with her towards the end. They didn't know if she was foretelling the future or lost in the terrors of the past. Either way, it was horrific.

He set that aside, praying it *was* nothing more than a memory, and found several documents he recognized as part of their training manuals. Most of their training was to handle one-on-one fights and crowd control, but once a decade, the Guard held war games where they practiced large-scale maneuvers in the event some unknown species ever attacked. He hadn't realized they came from the General herself, and he wondered at their significance. He made a note to add them to that evening's training as a refresher, if given the chance, and set those aside, too.

Lastly, he pulled out a small book. He carefully flipped it open and recognized it immediately. It was the General's journal on the senses. Kendra had already shared a digital copy with him, but holding it in person hit hard. It almost felt like the General was there in the room with him.

Had she seen him all those millennia ago? Were they on the path of war, or had it been averted when Marsee killed Rip?

A page had been marked, and he opened it, gasping as he realized his copy was incomplete. There was another note tucked inside. It simply read, "General's Eyes Only. You're not ready for this, Quinn, but I have a feeling you'll know when she is."

Curious, he read for a bit anyway, struggling with the ancient script, but before long, he closed the book, unable to make any sense of what the General was describing. It was as impossible to read, if not more so, than when he'd been a cub. The words themselves made sense, but together, they meant nothing. He didn't have the context. He wondered if Kendra even understood it.

Far too unnerved, he carefully put everything back the way he found it and sat for a moment, fiddling with the key, trying to take it all in and determine if he had missed anything else with Kendra's message.

Like so many, his heart was broken for those he'd arrested and for those he might still lose, although one tiny part of him purred at an impossible thought. He allowed himself to dream for a moment, then squashed it, knowing his duty and oath would come first. Then, with a heavy sigh, he replaced the key back in the book where he'd found it, knowing whoever followed him would be able to find it. With both their scents on the book, it would stand out like a sore tail.

Eventually, he turned off the privacy screen and glanced at the time. It would be hours on the Water World before the meeting started, and then it would take nearly another two before the broadcast reached them.

He made his way back out into the main office to watch the broadcast, curious if anything was being reported yet, but they were still rehashing the same information they'd been broadcasting for days. The other guards in the room picked up on his unease as he tried to decide where he needed to be.

Would they go after New Hope or try to rescue those who had been arrested, both or neither? Have they identified everyone? No. We can't assume that.

His thoughts returned to what he'd read and, more specifically, the General's orders. *"Do as she would do, and always honor thy oath."*

He hadn't realized he'd spoken it aloud until everyone in the room turned to look at him.

"Who?" one of his guards asked.

He didn't answer that question, at least not right away. His mentor might be sure that Marsee was their future general, but he'd always been skeptical of prophecies and legends, especially ones so old. Outside of the few documents hidden in Kendra's desk, he wasn't aware of any other mention in the history books of General Chenzira.

At least he'd never found any. But he had held her journal and seen her words, written in the same ancient script, and for a moment felt her presence.

What would Marsee do? he wondered. *Not sit around and wait,* he decided. *She would stop at nothing if there were lives to save.* He already had just about every guard on duty out patrolling the city or guarding those in holding.

Holding...

That word shoved him hard. It was a feeling he'd learned to trust, even if he didn't quite believe it.

"Call me if someone so much as twitches a whisker wrong," he ordered, then bolted out of the station and down to the holding cells. The Seniors might not have informed him of what everyone had done, but they were brought in for a reason, and if he could sniff out what was planned or who was leading it, they might be able to stop it before it happened.

4

JER: BROKEN HONOR

Jer scowled as he read the message Kendra had sent to Quinn for the fifth time. While the other Seniors were worried about her signature, he was far more concerned about Kendra's desire to bring Myra into the Guard. Outside of the brief moment when she'd walked off the ship, he'd seen nothing to indicate his partner was losing control, and her anger at him had been more than justified.

"I don't like it," Clear Seas said. "Who is this General she's referring to?"

"I have no idea," he replied.

"Could it just be a saying within the Guard?" Sammianna asked.

"Not one I've ever heard them use," Marcus replied. "I still think it's a coded message to warn Quinn."

"About what?" Jer asked. "She's already implied that she thinks we're going to arrest her, and it's not exactly a secret that Myra and Ellie are returning to Saber, although I am honestly surprised the press hasn't gotten their paws on it yet."

"Could Quinn be our mystery guard?" Sammie asked.

"We've found no motive. Outside of a handful of fights as a cub, Rip had nothing on him," Jer replied. "Besides, he's next in line already and has nearly as much authority as she does. Everything else feels like a goodbye, and her desire and reasons to protect Ellie are valid."

"Why does she want your partner in the Guard, though? Leverage?" Apakna asked.

"I have no idea," he replied, although that was a lie. "Perhaps her skills as a Healer?"

"I expect she's trying to tell Quinn that she's worried about Myra's control," Marcus said. "I know I am. Frankly, I'm glad she's off the planet."

"She seemed perfectly fine tonight," Sammie said. "Jer, have you seen any issues?"

He shook his head. "Outside of her anger at me the day she arrived, she's been fine. If Kendra was worried, she would have said something."

"She did," Marcus replied, and everyone turned to look at him.

"She did?!" He growled at his brother. "Why didn't you tell me?"

"I didn't want to worry you. There was an incident the night Little Flower went into heat. Kendra says she watched Myra go non-verbal in the Trauma Center while talking with Rowena. The incident lasted several minutes."

He swallowed hard. "Gods no…"

"She recovered, and as far as I know, there haven't been any further incidents, but it might be best if Myra did join the Guard," his brother replied. "Quinn has been able to help Nazari. Perhaps he can help her, too — if it's not already too late."

"You knew Myra was going non-verbal and let her get on a ship with Ellie?!" Clear Seas snapped, flickering orange with anger.

"I couldn't exactly say no and explain why in the middle of the restaurant," Marcus snapped back. "I honestly don't know why Ellie's leaving, but it wasn't a sudden emergency like she said, and I didn't leave her unprotected. Kendra notified me of the flight plans earlier in the day. She wanted guards to go with her, and I picked them out myself. Ellie doesn't know, but there's a half-squad on the ship with her."

"Is Ellie having issues?" Apakna asked.

"Not that I've heard," Marcus replied. "I asked the same question. Kendra didn't know why Ellie was leaving either, and in case you haven't looked, the message Ellie received was from Marsee. It simply stated that she needed to leave now. As far as I can tell, it came from Marsee's account. I had Lowell confirm as soon as she left."

"You looked?" Wind Rider asked.

"Of course I did," Marcus replied. "I needed to make sure she wasn't being blackmailed before the meeting. If Ellie is having issues, leaving the planet is the best option. It could be nothing more than a distraction to make her enemies think she's left. I suppose we won't know until she reappears. Either way, the safer she feels, the easier it will be for her to maintain control, and the guards will be able to contain the situation if it becomes a problem for either of them."

Jer sighed, wishing he could tell everyone what was going on, but Ellie had asked that the others not be informed.

Before he could come up with a plausible excuse, Clear Seas' skin flashed solid red, getting everyone's attention. "Is that so?" Clear Seas demanded. "Or did you order the guards to kill them once they were in jump, so that none of us could stop you?"

"Of course not!" Marcus replied, ears pinned back with shock that immediately shifted to anger. "Whatever their status, I am not going to risk a war with you over the lives of two people, and I'll remind you, *they* are not the most pressing issue we have right now. Kendra is."

Clear Seas scowled at Marcus for several moments but eventually calmed his skin. "Do we have enough evidence to arrest Kendra based on her message?"

"Everything we have against her is circumstantial," Sammianna replied. "It could be nothing more than a goodbye, and even if it is something, we're better off keeping her alive so we can find out who this general is. Of course, how she reacts when Jer shows up could change everything. As far as I'm concerned, our plan stands."

Murmurs of agreement went around the table, and they all turned to face him.

"Walk in the light of the full moons, Little Brother," Marcus said.

Jer took a deep breath. The blessing his brother used was one their people reserved for the most dire of circumstances, one where they didn't expect the other to survive, but then the odds were not in his favor.

He nodded and swam out before his nerves got the best of him.

Surprisingly, his instinct had been quiet these past few days, even though the risk of another attack increased by the moment. Still, he felt it watching from the back of his mind, poised and ready for an attack. He did nothing to contain it, knowing it was the one advantage he had.

Two guards floated outside of the Guard Station when he arrived. They saluted but didn't stop him as he placed his palm on the access panel.

The door slid open to reveal a packed room of more than two contingents of Saber's guards. All, save the squad monitoring the feeds, were standing at attention and waiting for him as ordered. They had been that way for over an hour. No one had even so much as speculated why they'd been called in. Avery and Tamarin stood in front.

As one, they all saluted and then pivoted to face Kendra's office, where a pair of Contingent Seniors stood on either side.

Similar orders had been sent to all five Senior Honor Guards, purposely crafted to make it appear like they were being arrested so that they could see how they would react. The only difference with the orders sent to Kendra was that they'd included orders for Avery's arrest as well.

Outside of the message Kendra had sent, they had all followed orders.

It took every ounce of self-control he had to walk past the packed room to Kendra's office and hit the switch. He didn't bother to knock, but he did leave the door open. It was both a calculated risk and the one chance he had to save his life if she tried something.

He found Kendra sitting by her window, looking out at the dark sea, with her tail wrapped loosely around her front feet. He stared at her from the doorway as her gaze shifted to watch him back through the reflection. There was no sign of threat in her posture, and the fierce mask she normally wore had been stripped away to reveal a deep melancholy and resignation. It was the defeated posture of someone who knew they were going to die.

"I am not involved in this," she said quietly but didn't turn around to face him. "Nor are my District Seniors or any of the guards I brought with me. I give you my word, Senior Councilor, but I will not fight you if you're here to call for my execution."

He flicked an ear back, both at her claims and her phrasing. It made him wonder if there *were* guards that had been sent ahead of her, including Avery, that she didn't trust. The room was so silent behind him that it made his hackles rise, but he forced it down through sheer will and decades of training.

"I honestly don't know if I can trust you," he replied. "The rest of the Seniors do not, but they're leaving it up to me to decide what to do with you. You've protected my people and children in the past, yet your nephew and protege, whom you gave a life oath I could trust, left my daughter and Stormy unprotected, and they nearly died."

"I take full responsibility!" Avery cried behind him. "Please don't punish her for my mistakes."

He spun to face Avery with pinned ears and a low growl. "I will deal with you *after*, Honor Guard. Stand down."

Avery swallowed hard but backed off at the unexpected ferocity, as did many in the room. It was rare that he let his mask drop enough to growl at someone, no matter how angry he was, and they knew it.

He let his anger free for another moment before shoving it back behind his mask and turning back to face Kendra, who had turned to face him following her nephew's outburst. Her face was full of grief before she locked it down and shifted her stance to full attention.

"I, Kendra Arianna Hunt, swear that I will defend and guard the freedoms, rights, and lives of the people against all enemies and threats and place them before my family, the Guard, and the Council. Should I be found guilty of any crime, no matter how small, I fully acknowledge that my life will be forfeit. I also swear that any who are under my command will be held to the same oath, to the best of my ability, and with my life held as collateral should I fail to do so."

He tilted his head slightly, acknowledging her oath. "As a member of the Senior Council, I accept your oath and life as collateral against the honor of the Guard."

It was a traditional response, but she swallowed hard and braced to await the verdict she knew was coming.

"Regarding your admission of observing the private meetings of the Senior Council during Little Flower's trial and instituting plans to protect her and her people, knowing that doing so could be seen as treason, the Senior Council has unanimously determined that those decisions were just and in keeping with your oath, in light of the charges against the Council at the time, and all charges of treason have been dropped against you and those guards who were involved. *That* decision is final."

She closed her eyes and gave a deep sigh of relief.

"However..."

She swallowed hard before opening her eyes again.

"The honor of the Guard *has* been broken," he continued. "We have substantial proof that members of the Guard were involved in Rip's plot, along with other crimes, and that includes members of Saber's Guard."

Kendra sighed, realizing she'd just signed her own death warrant in front of a member of the Senior Council and two contingents of Guards. "I understand and fully accept my punishment," she replied, lifting her claws to her neck.

He raised a paw to stop her. "As far as we can tell, none of them were among your District Seniors or those currently here on the Water World. With regards to the life oath you gave that Avery could be trusted, the Seniors unanimously gave me the right to decide what to do with you, as my daughter was the most harmed by his actions."

Mask firmly in place, he glared at her, wondering if she would defend herself or Avery.

She said nothing and remained at full attention as she awaited his decision.

"I have decided to take you at your word that you knew nothing about this plot. I am giving you your life back in exchange for the risk you took in protecting my people."

Kendra's ears flicked back in surprise, but he continued before she could say anything.

"The Senior Council has already sent District Senior Bluestone orders to begin arrests. Councilor Surellis will...*deal* with them when he returns."

She nodded, but her eyes drifted behind him. "And Avery?"

He turned to face Avery and let slip his anger again. Not enough to growl, but enough to make Avery swallow hard and stiffen to attention even more than he already was.

"The Senior Council has found no evidence against Honor Guard Avery Hunt and has unanimously decided that his actions in leaving my daughter and Stormy Seas alone were not done with malicious intent."

Avery sighed with relief, and he heard Kendra's sigh behind him, but he raised a paw again.

"However, those actions caused both people to be severely hurt and nearly killed. As Marsee was the one who ordered you away, regardless of her legal ability to do so, for a just cause in finding the other missing people, and as neither has chosen to press charges, we find you not guilty of that negligent behavior. We are, however, putting you on probation."

Avery nodded his understanding. "Yes, sir."

"As my daughters have agreed to allow you to mentor them, if unofficially, and continue to guard them, we are making that mentorship legal and binding. Your life will be tied to theirs. Should you fail to protect them while they are under your guard or your squad's guard or fail to train them adequately to protect themselves, *you* will experience whatever injury or harm they incur due to your negligence, in equal measure, up to and including your death. If they choose to end the mentorship for any reason other than determining that your services are no longer needed, your life will be forfeit. This was a unanimous decision by the Senior Council and is final. Do you understand?"

Sammianna had been the one to come up with the idea, but they had debated for hours about whether they had the right to force a mentorship on anyone and if the current mentorship laws fit the added stipulations. Ultimately, they decided that it did, even if they rarely held mentors to the full extent allowed by the law. And, while his children hadn't taken the formal oath or joined the Guard, they'd decided that their acceptance of Avery's training was considered binding enough.

"Yes, sir," Avery replied. "I accept those terms willingly and without reservation. On my life and my honor, I will do everything in my power to protect them and ensure that they are trained to defend themselves as good or better than I can do myself."

It was a modification of the formal mentorship oath, but Jer nodded his acceptance of it and shifted his gaze to the others in the room. "Camera's off," he ordered.

Murmurs of surprise traveled around the room at that command, but they did as ordered and said nothing as he personally checked that everyone's camera was off before continuing. There were only two reasons he could legally order the guard's cameras off: for the requested privacy of an individual and to coordinate a council-ordered military action.

He sent them the Senior's orders, knowing no one would follow them otherwise, as he technically wasn't their senior, even if they provided guard coverage for his people, and then explained. When he was done and had answered the few questions that were raised, one contingent left to begin arrests while the other followed him out and down the hall to Stinger's office. Only Avery and a half squad remained to monitor the feeds.

He had no doubt the Water Sprites knew they were coming, but what he didn't know was how they would react to the show of force. He knew they all expected Stinger to be arrested, but a single squad should have been more than enough to handle that.

Like Saber's guards, the Water Sprites were all floating at attention, but he saw many of them reaching for their stunners when Kendra and her guards swam in behind him to circle the room with their own stunners out.

Stinger swam out of his office at speed. "Councilor, what in the bottomless depths going on?" he flashed in Water Sprite. His words were laced with both anger and confusion, but he stopped just outside his office door and raised a paw to stop his own guards from reacting to Kendra's guards, who all raised their stunners at him.

Jer frowned at the rudeness of the question, trying to determine if it was intentional or simply an emotional reaction to their show of force. "Senior Honor Guard Stinger," he replied in both Saber and Sign, "the Senior Council has found evidence that members of both the Sea Patrol and Honor Guard were involved in Rip Current's attempted coup. As such, by unanimous decision of the Senior Council, the Sea Patrol has been stripped of the right to arrest or be involved with prisoner transfer, and those in league with Rip Current will be executed, following questioning, and pursuant to their oath."

Stinger's anger disappeared, followed by the ripple of a disappointed sigh, but there was no other sign of emotion, nor was there movement from anyone in the room, although surprise flickered the skin of many.

Jer had expected people to attack immediately at his announcement. When nothing happened, he unclipped his tablet and began reading names. Most were in Rip Current's district or scattered around the planet, but there were many in Council Platform and nearly a dozen in the room. To his astonishment, no one resisted arrest. Perhaps because they knew how overpowered they were, which had been the whole point. Once collared, they were dragged off to cells for questioning, where Clear Seas would handle their interrogations.

Stinger remained floating by his door, expressionless as his guards were dragged off.

"Honor Guards Tanner and Red Fin, swim forward."

Both guards did but stopped when he raised a paw. "The Senior Council has investigated the both of you at length for your involvement in my daughter's kidnapping, the attack on the Senior Guild Master, and involvement with the protest riot the day before. The only evidence we found was circumstantial at best. By unanimous agreement, the Senior Council finds you both not guilty and restores your rank and authority. Additionally, Honor Guard Red Fin, for your efforts in protecting Senior Councilor Wind Rider and her daughter Petra, the Senior Council promotes you to the rank of First Contingent Senior."

It was one step below District Senior and one of the newly vacated spots. That decision hadn't been finalized until Aris had shared her camera footage with Marcus that evening. It was Marsee's leniency that had decided them.

Tanner flashed her relief and pride as she hugged her son tightly. The rest of the guards cheered and flashed their agreement while Red Fin floated there in stunned surprise.

"I thank you, but I don't deserve it," Red Fin finally said after the applause died down. "I failed to protect your daughter, and as far as Petra goes, there was nothing I could do to protect her."

Jer raised a paw to stop Red Fin. "You did far more than nothing. You offered your life in exchange for Petra's and her mother's. As for failing to protect my daughter, well, failure does not mean a lack of honor, only an opportunity for improvement."

Red Fin nodded, although he didn't look convinced.

Jer turned to face Stinger. "Senior Honor Guard, Stinger."

The room quieted, and Stinger snapped to attention.

"You gave your oath to Senior Councilor Surellis, stating that you were not involved and that you were ultimately responsible if any of your guards were found guilty."

Stinger took a deep breath and nodded. "I did. I swear I had no idea any of my guards were involved or how deep this went. I knew something was happening in Rip's District, but not what. I should have done more, including going to Clear Seas with my suspicions, even though I didn't have evidence." He turned to face Kendra as the slightest hint of white crept along his skin. "Regardless, I expected this. There are letters in my desk for my family. Please see that they're delivered. I'm ready now unless you wish to question me further, too."

Kendra didn't move, and Stinger eventually turned his attention back to Jer.

"The Senior Council argued for a long time about what to do with you," Jer said. "Ultimately, it was Rip who decided your fate. Late last night, we found evidence that he intended to bring you down, too, and install someone else as Senior Honor Guard. As such, we're not holding you to that oath and instead only punishing those involved."

Stinger took a deep sigh of relief, although he managed to keep the emotion off his skin this time.

Jer dismissed the rest of the guards, save for Kendra, and nodded towards Stinger's office. Once inside, he activated Stinger's privacy screen. "You should be aware that we don't know who Rip had in mind to replace you. It could be someone we've already identified or not. There were people in all five guards involved, and they are currently being arrested. At the moment, though, that doesn't matter."

After informing Stinger and Kendra of what they planned at the Council meeting in the morning, he swam back out with Kendra and made a split decision regarding her letter. "I'm sure you're aware that Ellie and Myra left the planet last night."

"I am, and I know why. I'm honestly glad we don't have to deal with that on top of everything else and that they're both safely away from this mess."

"As am I. I want guards watching them the moment they land. I know it's outside of my jurisdiction, but Ellie wanted it kept from the rest of the Seniors, and I haven't informed Marcus."

"Already done," she replied. "Which I'm sure you already know. If you haven't seen my orders, I would be concerned about your investigation."

He tilted his head, acknowledging that point, and decided to press the issue further. "Who's the General?"

She snorted. "I wondered how long it would take you to ask about that and debated even sending it. It's not anyone, well, not anyone alive. That phrase is a bit of a good luck charm that goes all the way back to the Psychosis Wars, or so my father told me. Legend states that anyone who was with our last general would always survive whatever battles they faced. Hopefully, you've sniffed everyone out, but we're all prepared for the possibility of another attack, if not outright war. I know it's superstitious, but when you face down death every day, you take whatever luck you can find wherever you can find it."

He raised a brow, not entirely convinced, but it would be easy enough to ask another random guard for confirmation. He nodded and started to swim off to rejoin the Seniors.

"Councilor, wait," Kendra called out after him.

He turned to face her, brow raised again.

"Thank you for trusting me. I promise I will do everything I can to restore the honor of the Guard, including stepping down if that would relieve your concerns."

He stared at her for several long moments as he carefully considered his reply. "I honestly don't know if I can trust you, but I trust you more than anyone else right now, even after what your nephew did, and that's the only reason you're still alive. Consider yourself on probation, too."

She tilted her head, acknowledging his words, and he swam off. It took everything he had to turn his back to her and swim away. He didn't look back until he reached the end of the hall. She was still floating there, watching him. He didn't move or drop his gaze until she turned and swam away.

He silently prayed to the Ancient Gods that he had made the right decision in trusting Kendra and the rest of her guards. The lives of his family and people depended on it, but far too many of his decisions had hurt them anyway, and he wondered how much more they would have to endure because of his decisions today.

Would they be at war by the end of the day? he wondered.

"May the General protect us, indeed."

5

KENDRA: HABITAT

*C*onflicted and rather surprised that she was still alive, Kendra watched as Jeran swam away. His mask was back in place, and there was surprisingly still no sign of a waiver, but his tense body language told her he was expecting her to attack.

He didn't trust her, not even a little bit. None of the Seniors did, and it was no surprise why. Her heart broke at the friends she would lose, although she was beyond relieved that her nephew had been spared.

At the end of the hall, Jeran turned and glared back at her. She expected anger, but all she sensed from him was disappointment and worry. With a heavy sigh, she turned and swam off.

Bentley should be arriving in Rip's district soon, she thought, picking up her pace. The guards in the outer office glanced in her direction as she entered but immediately resumed their duties.

"Report," she demanded.

"Bentley's two minutes out," Avery replied, "but we have a problem. Either they were informed, or they already had plans. They ditched their cameras and tracking devices outside the city while we were arresting the Sprites, and they're currently swimming at full speed towards the Habitat. We're tracking them via heat signature on the satellite. Bentley will arrive about the same time they will."

She frowned. They had orders to run dark, as several of the guards currently posted at the Habitat were on the list.

"How many?" she asked.

"Three squads," he replied.

She frowned, not liking the odds. Bentley's contingent outnumbered the Sprites four to one, but the Sprites could kill with a touch if they got close enough.

The ships were nearly on them, but as she watched, the heat signatures vanished.

"Where'd they go?" Bentley asked.

The ship slowed and spun, scanning the surroundings, but there was little to see. The area for the Habitat had been specifically chosen due to its lack of complicated terrain and impact on other species. Only a few small fish swam by. There was evidence of a rift and seismic activity, but unlike the Trench, it was shallow and easily viewed.

She slammed her comms. "Squads two through six. Alert Level Three. Finish your current assignments, then secure the Council and Platform."

"Ma'am," came several replies.

She scanned the banks of monitors, looking for any sign of an attack, then frowned again. "Where's Aris?" There was only one guard on Marsee's door.

"With Marsee at the Guild," Gretta said. "She went back out shortly after returning from dinner." Gretta adjusted one of the side monitors to show a camera positioned outside Ellie and Agate's office. Aris was floating outside, and she could see Agate and Marsee deep in conversation. As she watched, Marsee looked up and out the dark window and frowned with worry.

"Squad Seven. Secure the Guild," she ordered.

"Ma'am."

She turned to Avery. "Go with them."

"Ma'am," he replied and bolted for the door at a full run.

She returned her attention to Bentley's contingent as they continued to scan the area, and she considered where else they might attack. "Where are Clear Seas' children?"

"Stormy's home, but the older two are on duty," another guard called out. The side monitor shifted to show their locations.

She frowned. There were already several squads in and around the Trauma Center to protect the victims that hadn't been released yet, and Temperate was reasonably safe in his ship, but there was only a half-squad stationed around Stormy and Clear Sea's home, by Clear Sea's own order and against her recommendation. He'd insisted that the guards be used to secure the rest of the potential targets first.

She took a deep breath and closed her eyes to clear her thoughts. Then, when she felt fully grounded and calm, she flipped the switch that wasn't there in her brain anymore. *What are they up to? Where are they hiding? Who are they targeting?* Like the rest of her Guard, she no longer had an instinct and couldn't access the knowing, not the way she'd been able to before, but she'd learned that sometimes a thought would come through from her subconscious if she allowed herself to enter that same state.

She allowed herself to think of each potential target, then gasped as her thoughts shifted to Carrie, Snapper Fish's daughter. Her eyes snapped open.

"Bentley. They're camouflaged and hiding their heat signature somehow. Use your ship and stun their last known location with a wide beam."

"Ma'am, a ship's stunner could be fatal," he replied.

He was one of the few with high enough rank to question her orders, and it was right that he did so, but several in the room still stiffened in shock that he even dared.

"I know that," she replied. "But they've abandoned their post and have already been found guilty by the Senior Council for crimes against the Consortium. Do it. I take full responsibility for any deaths."

"Yes, ma'am," he replied, and a moment later, the ships spread out and began opening fire.

The very first shot caught someone. Their body spasmed, half hiding them again in a cloud of dirt that they'd used to cover themselves, but when the dust settled, their bluish-grey body lay on the ocean floor.

Several others in hiding bolted, and the nearest ships opened fire. Several shots hit a pair of unfortunate Sprites at the same time, and based on the heat signature that reappeared and then slowly dimmed, they were dead.

The ships left them where they floated and continued in a wide search pattern until they had cleared a fairly substantial area.

When their shots failed to uncover anyone else, Bentley and half the contingent left their ships to secure those they'd found. While the other guards checked for signs of life and restrained those who were still living, she watched as Bentley slowly pivoted, examining the area with his senses. The sounds of his deep breathing came over the comms. By the time he'd completed a full circle, the incapacitated guards had been restrained and secured.

Bentley turned as one of his guards approached.

"Only one squad and four are dead," the guard stated.

Where are they going, and where are the rest? Three squads were only a small fraction of the guards and patrol they had orders to arrest.

"This was a distraction. Secure the Habitat," Kendra ordered. "Then move on to the East Sea Barracks."

"Ma'am," Bentley replied, whistled, and motioned his guards back on the ship.

Two minutes later, they arrived at the Habitat, but all they found were the guard's discarded comms and tablets.

Bentley woke the Senior Healer as he stormed into her suite without knocking. Although flustered by his sudden appearance and rough questioning, she appeared not to know anything about the missing guards.

After Bentley's squads confirmed that the Habitat was secure, they boarded their ships and took off for the East Sea Barracks. There, they found the local command station empty save for a pair of dead guards and the boards ripped out.

She swore under her breath as Bentley broke the contingent up into squads to secure the rest of the barracks and sea patrol.

"Five credits, they won't find anyone," the guard nearest to her muttered. "Alive, that is."

She grunted. "I'll take that bet simply because I'd rather not have the alternative. I'll be in my office. Inform me when they…"

"Command, Alert Level Five. This is Temperate Seas. There's been an attack at the Guild. I repeat…"

TEMPERATE: WINDING PASS

Temperate hovered his ship just above the Trench and peered down into the darkness that the lights on his ship did nothing to illuminate. With an hour still left on his shift, exhaustion and nerves made his tentacles twitch. Everyone was on edge with the coming council meeting, and his shift had been far too quiet, although no one dared mention it. Even Old Bessie hadn't made an appearance, and she'd been pestering the travel lanes and outer communities all week.

The tracking beacon they had on her hadn't left the Trench all night, and it registered again on his display at a depth that made his lungs ache to even think about.

"She's deep, and it's not like her to stay so still," his squadmate said over the comms. "She's usually far more active this time of night."

"Well, this is where they dumped what was left of Rip," he replied. "Councilor Chenzira was worried that it would give the poor thing a stomach ache. I wouldn't be surprised if it did."

"Great. That's all we need, a Leviathan with a stomach ache," his other squadmate replied. "I don't care what the Senior's order. I am *not* taking a healer down there to treat her."

His skin bubbled with humor. "I doubt that's anything we need to worry about. I imagine it would be difficult to get a healer to volunteer to risk it in the first place." He called in the squad's status before turning his ship to follow along the edge of the Trench for a bit before turning back towards Council Platform. The other two ships of his squad followed, matching his slow pace.

"Command, this is Squad Four. We have a sighting of an unidentified Leviathan. Requesting backup."

"Copy. Squad One, you're closest. Assist," came the reply from Command, along with Squad Four's current position."

"Copy," Temperate said. "What are we looking at? Juvenile?" Most juveniles were tagged by the Sea Patrol in the district where their nesting grounds were located, but they still tagged a few dozen every year.

"Negative. Elder by the size of her. She's at least as big as Old Bessie."

He frowned. The adult Leviathans rarely shared territory, and it had been decades since they'd found an untagged Elder.

A few minutes later, they were pulling up alongside Squad Four, but his proximity sensors showed nothing. He flipped over to the satellite footage, hoping to pick up a heat signature.

"Where is she?" he asked.

"She ducked into Winding Pass. I didn't dare follow without backup," the squad leader replied.

"Did you tag her?"

"Negative. We tried, but our stunners did nothing, and we couldn't get close enough to harpoon her."

Of course not, he thought, as one of his tentacles twitched. *Is this a trap?*

He typically didn't work the evening shift but had traded shifts so he could attend the council meeting in the morning. Prior to the past couple of weeks, he'd never questioned the honor of anyone he worked with, but now he found himself questioning everyone, especially those he didn't know well.

On top of that risk, Winding Pass, while it sounded peaceful, was anything but. It was the preferred hunting ground for several of the larger predators, not just the Leviathan. Tight corners, thermal vents, and blind canyons made navigating the currents, even in daylight, treacherous. At night, they would be deadly.

He considered taking to the air, but that wouldn't give him any better of a scan than the satellites. If there was indeed an untagged Elder in the area, it was a risk he needed to take to protect the people.

If it's a trap... I'm as good as dead, anyway.

That thought decided him.

"My ship is the fastest, so I'll take bait, but we'll go slow. There's no rush."

"Copy," the others called out and spread out in their standard bait and chaser formation.

Swallowing down his fear, he switched the flight controls to immersive. The autopilot was good, but it couldn't handle the rapidly changing currents that made Winding Pass so dangerous, not the way he could instinctively feel them.

A static shield built into his safety harness enveloped him as a visor dropped down over his head. The shield wasn't designed for protection but to capture his slightest movement and connect his skin to the sensors embedded in the ship so he could feel the currents and creatures around him.

The walls of the ship disappeared as the visor activated, and his harness shifted to allow free range of movement while still keeping him in place. It now felt as if he were in the ocean directly, not inside one of the most technologically advanced ships for his species.

Flexing his tentacles, he spun the ship, making sure everything responded — and did it ever! The ship matched every twitch and bunch of his tentacles. He'd trained for months on a simulator on the off chance his Squadron Commander would let him fly it or one of the ones on order. His old ship, the replacement to the one that had been destroyed a week prior, had the technology, but he'd never had a chance to use it before it was damaged while rescuing Senior Councilor Apakna's uncle.

With a deep breath, he bunched his tentacles and swam forward. The currents were far more turbulent than he expected, and his heart raced with both the thrill of the challenge and the fear he hadn't fully overcome from his two prior accidents. The sensors picked up dozens of heat signatures that both appeared on his visor and as warmth and texture on his own skin as he wove through rock formations and the twisting canyon walls. Many of the creatures were big enough to be dangerous, but all were hidden in caves, tunnels, and behind foliage, and none of them took the bait.

The lack of visible creatures calmed his fears about a trap as everything hid when a Leviathan was in the area. As they traveled, the water temperature rose from underground thermal vents, making the heat sensors useless. He turned them off to focus on visible light, and the world around him shifted to a brightness similar to his natural vision during the day, only with more of a blueish hint to account for the fact that it was night.

While they went slow, it wasn't long before they were on the other side, where the pass connected back up with the Trench and, beyond that, nothing but the open seas. Aside from the turbulent waters and relatively smaller predators, they found nothing in the pass itself.

He scanned the Trench down as far as his sensors would go and found nothing big enough to be an Elder Leviathan. "She's either swum back out to sea or found someplace to hide," he flashed.

He split the squads again and sent them in opposite directions to scan the Trench. He stopped when they reached the section where Old Bessie was lurking.

"Bessie would have reacted if another Elder had come this way," his squadmate said, and he had to agree, so they turned around and sped up to catch up with the other squad, but their search proved fruitless.

With his shift nearly over, he was about to order his squad back to base when his comms blared with an alert.

7

MARSEE: DARKNESS AND DANCING RAINBOWS

Marsee sighed as she looked out Agate's window, worried about Ellie and Avery, emotionally exhausted by her meeting with Red Fin, and knowing it would be far worse in the morning.

She startled as Agate gently touched her arm.

"Sorry, I didn't mean to scare you," Agate flashed, then switched to Saber. "Are you alright? You seemed..." Agate paused, trying to find the right word.

"Distracted, worried. Scared — if I'm being honest," Marsee replied. "Forgive me. My thoughts drifted, and I didn't see what you said."

"There is nothing to forgive," Agate replied. "We can stop here if you want. I seriously doubt we'll get this far tomorrow."

"No," Marsee said, refocusing her attention on the task at hand. "I need to know everything, and I have no time to learn it. Now, explain this to me like I'm a cub. These numbers don't make any sense. They seem far too high for..."

She stopped as Aris bolted into the office without warning. "We need to move now."

"What's going on?" Marsee asked as Aris swam over to grab the drone that Marsee had left just inside Agate's office.

"I don't know. I was ordered to move you to a secure location," Aris replied. "Grab your stuff. We're going back to the ship now."

Panic and fear made her throat nearly close up, and she froze solid. It wasn't until Agate grabbed her by her harness that she snapped out of it.

"I've got her, Honor Guard," Agate said and bolted towards the door, ignoring Marsee's surprised yelp.

They were halfway across the main hall before Marsee recovered from her panic enough to speak. "No. Not the ship," Marsee said and tried to wiggle out of Agate's grasp and swim in the other direction.

Aris stopped her drone and looked back at her. "Why not?" she demanded.

"I don't know, but the thought of getting on that ship terrifies me," Marsee replied, honestly not sure why she was so terrified. "Temperate's...what if..." Panic nearly enveloped her again, and she was finding it hard to breathe. Something was horribly wrong. She just knew it.

"The apartments?" Agate suggested. "Trench is big enough to fight off anyone, and it's a maze down there. It'll be easier for us to defend on our own."

Aris frowned, looked at her, and nodded when she didn't argue.

Agate took off, swimming so fast that the sudden motion made Marsee dizzy, but it snapped her out of her panic. Aris punched her drone hard to follow after them.

While she trusted Agate, she couldn't help but yelp as Agate careened around the first corner without slowing, terrified they would crash into the wall, but Agate didn't hit the wall, and she didn't stop. She spun and dove, twisting and turning, sometimes going completely upside down as she used the walls and ceiling for increased momentum.

The sound of Aris's drone fell behind them, and Agate paused and looked back as she realized it.

"Keep going," Aris yelled, "I'm right behind you."

"Grab my harness, Honor Guard," Aris said. "I can go faster than you on the drone, even with the weight of both of you."

Aris nodded, and the moment she had a firm hold on Agate's harness, they took off again.

Marsee kept her eyes closed to combat the wave of dizziness that followed. The Guild Master hadn't been joking, as she somehow managed to increase speed, and long before she expected it, they came to a screeching stop. Agate didn't even knock before barging straight into Trench's room.

He was hunched over a project and looked up, flashing surprise, then worry. "What's wrong?"

"I was ordered to move Marsee to a secure location," Aris replied. "Marsee didn't want to go back to the ship, so we came here instead."

Trench nodded and swam over to peer out his door before shutting it. Then, to Aris's surprise, Trench moved a large shelf aside to reveal another door, reinforced, which he closed over the sliding one and locked with a spin of a wheel and several loud clanks.

Aris frowned at Trench. "What's with the door?"

It wasn't quite illegal, but manual doors like this, which members of the Guard and Council couldn't breach, were rare. Even the ancient doors in the old part of the Compound had been upgraded to allow access, and while there were manual locks, it was only to secure the compound from storms and predators in the event of a power outage, not to keep anyone out.

Trench snorted. "I would think by now, Honor Guard, that you would realize our people are not as honorable as we would like you all to believe. This building outdates your people's arrival to our planet by centuries, in a time when we were at war, and its defenses were never removed. I chose this suite specifically because of its defenses."

He swam over to the far wall, moved aside the empty display case where her cloak had once hung, and hit another switch to reveal a small, dark tunnel where it had once stood. "Agate knows the way out. You're welcome to go or stay, whichever makes you feel more comfortable."

She peered down into that dark space. She'd thought she'd overcome her fear of the dark with her training the past few days, but something about it seemed even worse than getting on the ship, and once again, panic nearly swallowed her whole.

Before she could speak, Aris did. "We'll stay here unless there's a reason to leave. Close the door." Aris swam in front of her, pulled her into a hug, and purred. "Breathe. Marsee. You're safe. You're not in the cave, and we won't go down there unless we absolutely have to."

Trench did as requested and turned back to them. "I'm sorry. I should have realized you'd fear the tunnels and darkness. Please forgive me."

"It's not the…" she started, then shrugged. "Oh, maybe it is. I thought I was past my fear of the dark. The guards have been working with me on that. It's not your fault. Thank you for showing us a way out if we need it."

"It will take time," Aris said and leaned back to peer in her eyes, then turned away to begin securing the small space, although there wasn't anything more than a small attached waste room.

Once she had confirmed they were secure, Aris opened her tablet and began tapping away at it.

"What's going on?" Marsee asked when Aris frowned and reclipped it to her harness.

"I don't know," Aris replied. "No one is answering my calls, which means they're either too busy or it's not safe to answer. We'll wait here until we get further orders. I did get a message from Thatcher. Your sister and cub are safe. Additional guards were sent to secure your suite."

Marsee couldn't sniff anything but worry from her guard and sighed, wondering if the rest of her life would be like this, hiding from those who wanted to hurt her, always a victim, a target, weak, terrified, and helpless.

"You're safe here, Translator," Trench said, picking up on her mood. "I won't let anyone hurt you, and it would take a Leviathan to get in here."

She nodded and decided to ignore what she couldn't do anything about. "What were you working on?" she asked instead.

He smiled and flashed a bright blue. "I'm not sure of the word in your language, but they're for my great granddaughter when she's born. Would you like to see it?

"Congratulations, Grandpa, and I would love to."

He swam over to his desk, picked up a small item, and motioned her over to the display case. "The effect will be best over here under the light."

She swam over, and he handed her the item. She examined it with curiosity. It was an articulated, jeweled fish, expertly made and stunning in its detail and color. The style reminded her of Sea Turtle's drum.

When she was done examining it, he took it back from her and held it under the light in the display case. It sparkled with a brilliance that rivaled the drum, lighting up the room in a rainbow of colors that danced on every surface.

"There will be a dozen different fish and creatures when I'm done, and they will be strung together off of a similar light source that will hang above her sleeping net. The current will make them swim. Our children are fascinated by color and movement and will mimic whatever colors they see before they learn to speak."

She spun to watch the dancing rainbows, for a moment forgetting about her fears. "They're not the only ones fascinated. It's beautiful. I thank you for sharing, and I know she'll love it."

He flashed his happiness at her compliment and, rather than returning it to the desk, hung it off of the hook that had once held her cloak, leaving the room basked in a rainbow of dancing colors.

She watched for a few more moments, then turned to Agate. "Well, if we're stuck here for the foreseeable future. I suppose we should get back to work. About those numbers…"

"Explain it to you like you're a cub?" Agate asked.

"No. I think my brain is too numb for numbers right now. We'll revisit them tomorrow. Let's move on to the next item. That one has lovely pictures to go with it if I remember correctly."

Agate chuckled but humored her.

8

AVERY: GUILD INVASION

Avery swore as his eyes fluttered open to the vague shape of a Sprite floating above him. He scrambled back, reaching for his stunner as he tried to blink clear his vision.

"You're safe, Honor Guard," the Sprite said. "I'm not going to hurt you. I'm Temperate. Clear Sea's son."

"Forgiveness," he replied formally, then rubbed at his eyes. "My vision is still foggy. The others?"

"I don't know. My squad is checking on them now."

"Did you catch who did this?"

Temperate flashed his regret. "There was no one here when we flew over and saw you."

Avery's vision finally cleared somewhat, and he looked down at his chest at the spot that still hurt and frowned as he saw his comms unit was off. He hit the switch to activate it, but nothing happened.

"Come any closer, and you'll regret it!" a voice yelled.

Avery shot up and spun in that direction to see one of his guards pointing a stunner at a Sprite he recognized.

"Drop your weapon!"

"It's not a weapon! It's a hypo!" The Sprite flashed as he backed off, dropping the hypo. It took him a second to recognize the Sprite.

"Snapper Fish? What are you doing here?"

"He's on my squad, Honor Guard," Temperate said behind him.

He spun to face Temperate, "You're joking! Who had the unmitigated gall to put him on your squad?"

"That would be me," Temperate replied. "No one else would take him, and so far, he's been behaving."

"I know you have no reason to believe me, but I am on your side," Snapper Fish said. "If you would feel more comfortable, you can collar me. I won't resist."

Avery glared at Snapper, but he couldn't detect any signs of deceit, and apparently, neither did the other guard, as she lowered her weapon. The others, he noticed, were all starting to wake. Relieved, he reached over and activated Temperate's comms. "Command, this is Avery. My comms have been disabled."

Kendra responded immediately. "Report. Are you hurt?"

"I'm fine, and the others appear to be recovering. We were ambushed. I saw at least half a squad before I was stunned. I recognized two of them. Both were Water Sprite guards."

"Copy. Backup is already on the way and will be there shortly. Marsee is secure. Track and neutralize the threat — by whatever means necessary."

"Yes, ma'am," he replied and disconnected.

The landing pad contained two ships and half a dozen shuttles, including Marsee's — all standard issue for the Guild, with their colors and designations. Marsee's stood out as it was a rather old model, marked with the rental colors of the Ship's Guild and parked in the area reserved for the Senior Guild Master. The drones they'd used to swim over were nowhere to be found.

After completing a full circle, he motioned for Temperate to follow him and swam over to where the guards had fired from. He found hints of their scent on the surfaces where they'd been camouflaged, but he found no other scent trail. The current from the ships had washed it away. He checked the door, but there was no sign of their scent on the door switch either.

"They didn't go inside, at least not via this door," he said as another guard approached, rubbing at her head.

"How can you tell?" Temperate asked.

"Sharp noses," he replied. "The only scent on the door switch is Aris's."

Before backup arrived, the others had recovered. He split them up to explore the surroundings to try and find a trail, but before he could resume the search himself, the sounds of ships approaching caught his ears.

These were all marked with Guard colors. He conveyed his orders to the pilots using sign language. The ships hovered long enough for the guards inside to swim out, but the moment they were clear, the pilots began a search pattern. He directed the guards to fan out, then resumed his own search, stunner out in the event of another attack.

A good ten minutes later, he heard a distant whistle. He responded, then started to swim back in the direction it had come from, but Temperate grabbed his harness and dragged him over. He had to admit it was faster, especially since his chest was still throbbing from the stunner.

The Guild complex was massive, but like most traditional Water Sprite buildings, there were only a handful of entrances as it was built into the side of a small mountain.

Most people used the main public entrance, but there were two secured entrances on either end of the complex in addition to the reserved rooftop landing pad, which Aris had used, and the warehouse, which had a much larger entrance and landing pad on the other side of the mountain, along with a dedicated shuttle bay for residents and visitors.

He found several guards floating near an open tunnel door that was hidden behind a large clump of seaweed. Hints of the Water Sprites that had passed through colored the edges of his vision where they'd brushed against the opening and seaweed. The tunnel was small, barely big enough to fit an adult female Saber.

Going in after them would be a death trap.

He turned back to Temperate. "Any chance you've got some decent scanners on that ship of yours? Can we see where this tunnel leads?"

Temperate nodded, grabbed Avery by his harness again, and bolted for his ship. Within seconds, they were on board, and Temperate was clipping into his harness.

Avery whistled as he clipped into his own. "This is some ship."

"It belonged to my Mentor after my brother blew up my last one," Temperate said as he took off.

When they were at a good altitude to get a scan, Avery activated the sensors and used his access to pull up a detailed schematic of the Guild, then overlayed the two. When that was in place, he accessed the Guard's positioning satellites and triangulated Aris's position among the various heat signatures.

He recognized the location. "They're in Trench's apartment," he said, then panned out, looking for movement or a large collection of heat signatures. The warehouse was bustling, but the rest of the complex, save for the apartments, which were all on the same level as Trench's apartment, was empty.

"There," Temperate said, pointing to a spot on the map. They were moving slowly. Slow enough that he'd missed it at first.

Avery zoomed in, confirmed they were in a tunnel and not one of the well-marked halls, and then panned back out. "Where are they heading?" he muttered under his breath.

"They've already passed the spot where it heads down to the apartments, so I'm guessing they're going here." Temperate tapped on another spot on the map.

Avery grinned, realizing their prey would be trapped.

He flashed Temperate's flood lights in a signal to have everyone meet up with him, then ordered Temperate to land near Marsee's ship.

He swam out with Temperate behind him again. "They're currently heading towards the Senior's offices. Lucky for them, we'll be there to meet them. Temperate, I want you to take to the air. Keep a fix on them. I'll call you once we're in place and connect to your scanner. If they change directions before we get there, text me. If they're smart, they're monitoring the comms, so stay off them if you can. I need a volunteer to swim down the tunnels after them and keep them from escaping."

Every hand went up.

He nodded his approval and picked the smallest of them. "You'll fit the best in there. Shoot at the first sign of motion. Don't wait to confirm their identity. They can see better than us in the dark, and I'd rather stun a friend than have you get killed."

The guard nodded and took off.

He motioned to two others. "Guard the tunnel. Make sure no one sneaks in behind him."

They bolted as well.

He pointed to three squads. "Secure the other entrances. Don't let anyone out until you've confirmed their identity, then begin a sweep."

The squads took off.

"The rest of you are with me. If something moves, shoot it. If you notice something out of place, alert."

Then, praying his nose and the scans were accurate, and that this wasn't a trap, he let his squads inside.

They swam hard for Agate's office, which thankfully wasn't far from the entrance, and he again split the squads. One taking Agate's office and another Ellie's. They quickly scanned the room, but he couldn't find an exit. Then, remembering Kendra's office, he swam into the small attached waste room that the Sprites used. It was nothing more than a cylindrical tube where a strong current pulled the waste away. He examined the space. His senses picked up an opening in the floor, but he couldn't find a switch.

He placed a pair of guards in the hallway in case they came out of another office and signaled to his squad to take up positions around the room, hidden behind furniture and out of sight of the waste room. As they moved to follow his orders, he unclipped his tablet and contacted Temperate. Temperate fed him the scans immediately.

He kept his ears swiveling to catch the slightest sound while he watched the heat signatures slowly approach.

When the guards were close, he signaled for them to get ready, then ducked behind the desk he was using for a shield, stunner out. The heat signatures approached, then moved past them and stopped.

There was the slightest sound of a click, then the slight whir of the fan that drove the current in the waste room slowed and stopped. He heard the sounds of a door sliding open, and his brain filled in what he couldn't see.

He waited, slowing his breathing and stilling his body, until the door of the waste room slid open.

And fired.

A dozen shots hit their target all at once. The guard nearest the door grabbed the stunned target and dragged him out of the way as his guards fired again, catching someone coming up out of the floor. The guard nearest the door yanked that person out of the hole and fired again, then cautiously leaned down and fired several times in both directions.

Avery watched as one of the fleeing blobs on his tablet stopped moving. Another blob in front kept swimming while the rest were trapped on the other side of the opening, which, from the sounds of things, the other squad had fully under control.

He watched the fleeing guard, wondering if he should send someone after, when there was a brief flash of heat on his tablet, and the guard stopped moving. A second blob cautiously swam forward, then started pushing the Sprite back towards them.

He left the room to check on the other squad, but as expected, they had everything under control. Once the Sprites were sufficiently collared and restrained, he split everyone up into quarter squads to assist with securing the rest of the Guild.

It took nearly two hours to check every room and confirm that everyone they found was supposed to be there. When he was sure the Guild was safe, he swam down to Trench's apartment with a squad of guards, leaving the remaining squad to secure the route out.

He banged on the door. "Aris, it's Avery. Threat neutralized."

He heard several loud clanks and something moving aside before the door slid open. Aris had her stunner up, and Marsee was hidden behind both Agate and Trench in the far corner of the room. Aris dropped her weapon when she confirmed the situation was safe. He smelled relief, but nothing showed on her face as she turned to the others.

"It's clear," Aris said. "Marsee, we're going now."

Marsee sighed and turned to Trench. "Thank you for your hospitality. Hopefully, the next time we meet will be under better circumstances."

"You are welcome here anytime, Translator," he replied.

"Thank you," she said and turned to Agate. "Until tomorrow?"

"Until tomorrow, Translator. Pleasant dreams."

His nose informed him that Marsee was slightly annoyed at the formal use of her title, but nothing showed on her face as she grabbed the drone he handed her and swam out into the hall. Aris followed closely behind.

To his surprise, Marsee didn't ask about the situation as she followed him up to the landing pad. In fact, she didn't speak until he started heading towards her ship.

"Not that way," she said quietly.

He turned and looked back at her, and to his surprise, for the first time since retrieving her from Trench's office, he smelled fear from her. "Why not?"

"I just…I don't know, but I don't want to get on that ship."

He didn't argue. Instead, he turned to several of the guards who had followed them out. "Impound every ship that was on this platform when we arrived, tow them to the shipyard, and give them a full workup. Assume they've all been compromised."

"Sir!" the guards replied and took off to follow orders.

He examined the ships that were hovering above the Guild and motioned one down.

Marsee sighed with relief when she recognized Temperate and punched her drone hard for his ship. He, Aris, and a half squad followed her on, and Temperate returned them to the platform, parking in the same spot Ellie's ship had been parked only a few hours earlier.

Knowing why she'd left, he braced himself for the residual scent of desire as they walked off, thankful that the half-squad he had with him was all female, but it was unnecessary. The air filtration systems had done their job removing any sign of Ellie's heat from the air. Everything else was covered by the thick scent of cleaner from a nearby bot that was sanitizing the floors.

A few minutes later, they had Marsee secure in her suite. He stared at the closed door for a moment, listening to Marsee talk to Little Flower in the Hue-man's strange high-pitched language and, for the first time, taking a breath to process everything that had happened that evening, then focused on Aris. "Report."

She gave a rapid-fire report.

He frowned when she was done, then glanced at the door again.

"If you had gone to the ship or taken to the tunnels, you'd have been dead," he said quietly. "There was an ambush waiting for us on the landing platform. They stunned us all before we could react and took to the tunnels. I'm assuming they were attempting to capture or kill Marsee and Agate. You should also be aware that arrests are being made across all five guards and the Sea Patrol. Unless you have prior authorization from me, do not allow anyone outside of our half-squad to approach them."

Both guards frowned but nodded.

"Yes, sir," Aris replied. "The alert earlier… Did they arrest Kendra?"

"Surprisingly, no."

He glanced at Marsee's door again, where he could still hear voices, and left without elaborating.

After picking up a new comms unit from the armory, he returned to the Guard Station. Kendra looked over as he entered, then motioned him back to her office, where she activated the privacy screen and, to his surprise, hugged him.

While she had raised him since he was a cub, she had kept her distance from the moment he'd joined the Guard, treating him as she did everyone else. If anything, she was more distant and harsher with him than she was with any other guard, but he knew it was because she didn't want anyone to believe he'd earned his rank through favoritism. She'd told him to expect as much the day he took his oath.

The last time she'd hugged him was right before he'd left for Earth, and she'd been furious with him from the moment she'd arrived on the planet for his failure to protect Marsee and Stormy.

He held her tight, knowing it might be years before another hug happened again, and frankly, he was just as relieved to see her alive and to have the threat of the Council's decision over with.

The hug didn't last long, and, as he half expected, she leaned back, grabbed him by the shoulders to peer down into his eyes, and then slapped him upside the head. "That's for getting shot."

"Yes, ma'am," he replied, unable to keep the grin off his face.

"Imputant, cub," she muttered and then walked over to lean against her desk. "Report."

He did as ordered and waited through the silence that followed.

"We've arrested everyone locally on the list," she finally said. "Quinn managed to…convince a few people to speak, and he sent us a warning. The rest of the missing guards were pretending to be members of the Press. We found an entire squad waiting in the main entrance of the platform, and another had the gall to swim right in the back door of the Council Building."

"The press?!"

She nodded but frowned at him. "Your reaction is stronger than I expected. Why?"

"Marsee's been avoiding the press like the plague. Aris said she couldn't even make herself take the lift down tonight, and that was before either of them realized the press was there."

It was Kendra's turn to raise a brow. "If she so much as frowns at somebody going forward. I want to know about it immediately."

"Yes, ma'am," he replied and was about to leave before she raised a paw. "Quinn also informed us that Lyrik is dead. She resisted arrest."

He sighed with grief. Lyrik had been on his squad for decades. "Do we know what the charges were yet?"

She shook her head. "The Senior's haven't released them. Do you trust Lark?"

He nodded. "I trusted Lyrik, too. I honestly can't believe she's involved in this. She was as committed as the rest of the squad in rescuing and protecting the Hue-mans. She considered it part of Luke's legacy. The only reason she switched squads was to spend time with her new grandcubs. She told me she fully intended to return if and when the Hue-mans decided they wanted a Guard."

Kendra pursed her lips and frowned. "I can't believe half of the people on the list were involved, but I know Marcus well. He wouldn't have ordered their arrestes if he didn't have evidence."

"Could it have been fabricated like the evidence against Clear Seas?"

She shrugged. "I imagine they've been checking for that. Regardless, no one has requested an Advocate, at least as far as I know. Lark has formally requested a review into the death of her sister as the arresting Seniors had their cameras off."

He frowned again. "That's not like them. Something smells rotten in that district."

She nodded. "Agreed. Quinn has already arrested them. They didn't resist, but they refused to talk. That'll have to wait, though. We have more important things to worry about than one dead guard. You are officially off duty until morning, with orders to return to your room and sleep. I want you rested for tomorrow. Take a sedative, if necessary, and put something on that burn."

He frowned and looked down at his chest. He'd honestly forgotten about it. "Yes, ma'am."

When he looked back up, he found her staring at him with an unreadable expression.

He raised a brow in a silent question.

Her eyes squinted at him ever so slightly. "While I thank you for standing up for me today. I order you not to do so in the future."

He frowned with confusion. "I couldn't stand there and let them kill you for my mistakes."

She shook her head. "You swore to protect the people before the guard *and* your family. Your feelings towards me do not matter. Corruption stained the honor of our guard under my watch. The Council should have demanded my execution for that failure, but they didn't, likely for the same reason they didn't get rid of Stinger. I will do everything in my power to restore that honor, including walking to my execution, if necessary. You cannot protect me. Don't even try. I don't want my failure to bring you down, too."

He sighed. "I don't know if I can do that."

"You must, and you will," she growled. "That's an order. From this moment forward, you and your half-squad will focus entirely on protecting Marsee and her family. You will make her and Little Flower a force to reckon with, and you will sniff out anyone who tries to hurt them. In this, you cannot fail."

"I will give my life to protect them," he promised.

"You'd better. Because if you don't, I promise you will welcome your last breath." She dropped her voice down to subvocalize below what the cameras could pick up. "We might have won the battle today, but war is coming, and I have no doubt this was just the opening volley. No matter what else happens. She *must* survive. Is that understood?"

He swallowed hard at the threat he saw in her eyes. "Yes, ma'am."

9

TEMPERATE: BETRAYAL

It was well after midnight by the time Temperate parked his ship in the shuttle bay of his father's home. He yawned as he entered the house. He was exhausted, but he doubted he would get much sleep.

His father's light was on in his office, but he didn't interrupt. Instead, he turned and swam to the kitchen for a late-night snack before bed. He doubted his father would sleep tonight, either, and he was honestly surprised that he was home at all after what had happened at the Guild.

Halfway down the hall, his father called his name, and he stopped and turned around.

"I need to talk with you."

His father's expression was a hard mask, one he knew well and one that was never a good sign. He swallowed hard and followed his father back into his office. His father shut the door behind him but paused before turning around.

"What's wrong, Papa?"

"I…I am sorry, son. I have some bad news."

Fear made his breath hitch. "Is everyone alright?" he flashed.

His father took a deep breath, paused, and then tried again. He had rarely seen his father at a loss for words, and the sight made him sick with worry.

"We found evidence against Snapping Turtle. I will be ordering his execution in the morning."

Temperate shook his head in horror and disbelief. "No, not him!? I can't believe it. He wouldn't hurt us."

"I didn't want to believe it either, but the evidence is quite clear. He's been abusing Blue for some time. There are multiple flags on Blue's medical record…"

"That doesn't mean it was abuse," Temperate interrupted. "Blue would have told us if something was wrong, and he is a bit of a klutz. I've seen him swim into walls on more than one occasion."

"True, and if it were that alone, I would most definitely side with Snapping Turtle over the evidence we found in Rip's home, but there's more. In addition to a number of other crimes, we have multiple deleted transcripts of conversations with Rip where he shared private information about our family and plotted with him to remove me from office. We've tracked some of that information back to Melody."

His skin flashed mottled white and black with fear and grief. His relationship with Melody had been strained since he'd decided to remain a pilot, but he'd been hopeful he'd be able to win her back once things calmed down some.

"No! Papa, you can't. She's pregnant with my daughter!"

His father raised a hand. "She is not your daughter yet, and you know I would wait until she was born, as is the law, if that were necessary. We have no proof that Melody knew where that information was ultimately going, and sharing information with a parent about someone you're considering a partnership with would be both normal and expected, but I can't guarantee that she's not involved. She could be playing you for information. I did confirm that she's pregnant, but it will be a few weeks before we'll know if the child is yours. As it is, I imagine she may not want anything to do with our family after tomorrow, or she may decide to end the pregnancy, as is also her right, and for that, I am deeply sorry."

"You're not arresting her?" he asked for confirmation as his heart started beating again, although grief still tore at his heart.

"Not at this time. There's still a lot of evidence to dig through. Either way, you can't say anything to anyone, including her. That's an order from the Senior Council."

"You're sure Snapping Turtle was involved?"

His father nodded. "Believe me, more than anything, I wish I was wrong, but the evidence speaks for itself. I can show you if it would help."

He nodded. He trusted his father, but he needed to know what Snapping Turtle had done. He had been a close family friend for his entire life and his father's unofficial mentor after Temperate's grandfather had died. He'd never liked Rip, although he'd never been able to figure out why, but he'd never had reason to mistrust Snapping Turtle. It was one of the reasons he felt comfortable going after a relationship with Melody. He'd known her since they were both children and, like him, she had little interest in following in their father's paths, or so he'd once thought.

Could she be playing me?

His father opened his tablet and handed it over a moment later. As he read, his grief turned to the anger of betrayal mixed with disbelief as he read through page after page of evidence.

"Are there others involved?" he finally asked.

His father nodded. "Far too many. I can't tell you who. I shouldn't have even told you this. We agreed to keep it secret from our families, but I felt you should know so that you can protect yourself tomorrow. I don't know how Melody will react once her father is arrested."

"Protect myself?" he muttered. "If she attacked, I doubt I'd be able to hurt her, even in self-defense. I love her. How are you going to do it? Snapping Turtle's practically your mentor!"

His father sighed, and a hint of his own grief slid through his control, but it was tinged with anger. "I honestly don't know, but he betrayed us and broke the law." His father let his emotions free for a moment longer before tucking them back behind his mask.

"I…" His father paused. "Are you entirely sure that you do not want to be my heir?"

"I will do my duty if the people ask it of me, but yes, I am sure. Even as angry and betrayed as I feel right now, I couldn't kill or even order Snapping Turtle's execution, and not just because of my feelings for him or his daughter. That's not who I am."

His father nodded. "I know, and I love and respect you for understanding that about yourself. Whatever happens tomorrow, know that I am proud of you and have always been proud of you and the path you've chosen."

"Thank you. I feel the same way about you, Papa."

His father took a deep breath. "That being said. You should also know that I intend to publicize Stormy's rank tomorrow."

That caught him by surprise, enough for it to flash on his skin. "I thought you were waiting until after the meeting. Did something change?"

His father nodded again but didn't explain. "I know you were planning to attend the meeting, but…"

"You don't want me to go."

"No. Personally, I would prefer you to be as far away from Council Platform as possible tomorrow, but if you're willing, I have a favor to ask you from Wind Rider."

Once again, surprise flashed across his skin. "Wind Rider?"

"Petra is not doing well with her recovery, both physically and mentally. Wind Rider was hoping that you'd wait out the meeting with Petra on their ship. As far as we've been able to determine, the pilots, guards, and her Senior Healer are all clear, and if something happens, you'll be able to leave the planet with her."

He swallowed hard with guilt. He hadn't checked in with Petra since she was released from the Trauma Center, but he frowned with confusion. "I didn't realize she was still on the planet. The press said she had jumped days ago."

His father nodded. "That was intentional to protect Petra. A ship did leave, but she wasn't on it. We expected that she might need to testify for the meeting, and Wind Rider didn't feel comfortable having her a planet away."

He felt torn between being there for Melody if she needed him and his friendship with Petra, but he nodded. It wasn't often a member of the Senior Council asked a favor of anyone. There were far too many strings attached to the implied reciprocity, but this he could easily do. "Of course, I'll go over. Are you sure you don't want me at the meeting?"

"I'm sure. If someone has a question for you or Petra, I'll call you. I doubt they will, though. The evidence is quite clear against Brandon, and everyone involved in Petra's kidnapping is already dead."

He nodded to his father and sighed as the weight of his grief threatened to overwhelm him again. "Is there anything else?"

"No," his father said. "Nothing I can tell you anyway."

He nodded and swam out. No longer hungry, he swam to his room but stopped in surprise when the light flickered on, and he found the room occupied. Stormy was curled up in his sleeping net, sound asleep, with his signed copy of the Adventures of Super Stormy tucked protectively under one arm. Swimming over, he gently shook his brother awake.

Stormy's large eyes fluttered open and blinked up at him. "Hey."

"Hey to you," Temperate said, gently taking the book from Stormy and placing it on the table beside the net. "What are you doing here?"

Stormy's skin flashed a multitude of emotions: fear, worry, grief, and a hint of embarrassment. "Have you spoken to Papa?"

He nodded. "I have."

Stormy's skin darkened with added grief. "I'm sorry. I hope Melody isn't involved and that she understands, for your sake."

It took him several deep breaths to keep the grief and betrayal from flashing on his skin. "Thank you. I understand your fear, worry, and grief, but why are you embarrassed?" he asked when he felt sure his emotions wouldn't tinge his words.

Stormy's embarrassment deepened. "I'm scared about tomorrow. What if they kick Papa out or something happens to him, and they vote me in? I'm not ready to be a Senior Councilor."

He chuckled. "You might be the most annoying, snot-nosed little blubber fish of a Senior Councilor we've ever had, but you're ready. It doesn't matter how much training you have. It's your heart that matters. Everything else can be learned, and I'll help you in any way you need if that happens, but that's not really why you're embarrassed, is it?"

Further embarrassment flashed on his little brother's skin, proving him right. "No. I had a night terror and couldn't fall back to sleep. I was hoping maybe I could stay here. I don't really want to be alone tonight, but if you want to be by yourself, I understand."

His heart melted. It had been years since he'd been awakened by his little brother from a night terror — not since he'd moved out. Stormy had never wanted his parents to know he was too scared to sleep alone and so had always come to him instead. "Of course, little brother. I doubt I'll be getting much sleep tonight anyway, and I think I could use the company, too."

Stormy shifted over so he could climb into the net and then wiggled a bit, trying to find a comfortable position.

He wrapped an arm protectively around his brother. "You've grown a bit since the last time you slept here."

"Trying to kill someone will do that," Stormy replied in Hue-man.

He sighed, not sure how to respond to that statement. Instead, he reached over with his other arm and turned off the lights. Then, using a tentacle, he pushed gently against the wall to rock the net.

His brother soon fell back to sleep, but as expected, he couldn't sleep. Worry, grief, and guilt kept him awake. His little brother might very well be sworn in as Senior Councilor in the morning, all because *he* wasn't strong enough to bear the weight of responsibility.

He was still awake, an hour or so before dawn, when a flash of light crossed his closed eyes, and he opened them to find his father peering in through a small crack in the door. His father's expression was unreadable, and they just stared at each other for several long moments.

"I love you, Papa," Temperate flashed.

"I love you, too, my son," his father replied, then swam away.

10

MARSEE: GUILD MASTER

Marsee jumped as Little Flower's high-pitched alarm blared and startled her awake.

"Five more minutes, Papa." Little Flower groaned and snuggled in close, tightly grabbing the arm she was still using as a pillow.

Marsee pinned her ears at the aggravating sound of the alarm and thwapped her sister's tablet hard with her tail to shut it off.

"Thanks," her sister mumbled.

"You're welcome, but as much as I would love to stay here all day and snuggle, today would not be a good day to be late," she replied, then she tried to extricate her arm.

Little Flower squeezed tighter, refusing to let go, so Marsee took her tail and used the very tip of it to tickle the bottom of her sister's feet until she started giggling.

"That's not fair!" Little Flower complained and tried shoving her feet under Marsee's body to get them away from her tail.

Marsee shifted to tickling her sister's side instead. "Well, it's this or dump you on the floor. I need to pee."

"Fine," her sister muttered and let go so she could get up.

After using her sister's awkward raised waste hole, she decided to use the sonic shower, even though they'd be right back in the water.

The vibration on her new fur still tickled, but it was a welcome distraction from the nerves that were threatening to overwhelm her. She chuckled at the reminder of the prank Ellie had pulled on her father, but that only reminded her of Ellie, and her worry for her Mentor threatened to overwhelm her.

Little Flower followed after and hugged her as they traded places. Marsee leaned in, purring, feeling instantly better with her sister there, but far too soon, Little Flower let go and climbed into the shower herself.

While her sister showered, Marsee threw on her carry harness and checked for urgent messages, of which there were thankfully none, then started preparing breakfast.

A few moments later, Little Flower left the waste room and began the arduous task of climbing into the special swimming clothes that were designed to keep her warm. Marsee was half tempted to order a set for herself as she was perpetually cold any time she left the suite, even with her cloak and fur that was finally starting to regrow, but that thought only lasted for half a second as her brain spiraled back to worry about the coming day.

"You seem quiet this morning," Little Flower said. "Did something happen last night?"

Marsee nodded but didn't explain.

"Are you alright?" her sister pressed.

She set her knife down and turned to face her sister, but it took several tries to form the words that had been swirling in her brain. "I... Last night..." She paused, took a deep breath, and squared her shoulders. "I know we talked the other day about sitting with the other victims, but that was before Ellie, and last night there was an incident. I didn't bother asking what had happened, but we were ordered to move to a secure location, and there were dozens of Sea Patrol and Guard ships outside the Guild when we left. I'm...I'm tired of feeling like a victim, of hiding. I don't want to leave you alone today, but I..."

Her sister gave her a knowing smile. "Marsee Chenzie Butt Chenzira, I want you to swim into that chamber with every bit of ferocity you have in you. Claim your proper place, not as a victim, but as a survivor and as Ellie's chosen heir. Make a show of it. Remind people what happens when they cross a Chenzira. I know I intend to." Little Flower bared her tiny fangs.

"You are positively feral," Marsee replied. "It's what I love best about you."

"And here I thought it was because I'm so adorable," her sister replied with mock hurt.

"You are especially adorable when you bare your fangs. There is nothing I enjoy more than watching people several times your size cower in fear of you."

Her sister snorted and resumed pulling on her outfit, then woke and changed Hope.

Marsee had their breakfast ready by the time Little Flower was done wrangling a new poop sack on their grumpy child. They ate in silence and were nearly done eating when there was a knock on the door. She answered it to find her father waiting outside. He walked in and hugged her. "Good morning, Guild Master Chenzira. How are you feeling?"

She flicked an ear back in a shrug. "I am a giant tangle of knotted emotions, but I'll manage. Mostly, I'm worried about Ellie and want this whole mess over with."

He hugged her again. "Me too, Kitten. Me too."

Before she could sit down to resume eating, there was another knock at her door. She grabbed the last bite of food off her plate, then walked back over to open the door again. GrandFather and Henry waited outside. She let them in, too.

"Are you ready to head over?" GrandFather asked as he scooped Hope up and brought her to the sink to wash her sticky paws.

"Just about," Little Flower replied and began to pick up their breakfast dishes.

Marsee grabbed her cloak off the hook beside the bed and stared at it for a moment as her resolve from earlier faltered. Then, with a half growl, she flung it on with determination, clipping it in place with a loud snap. She looked up to adjust it in the mirror but stopped and stared at the image she saw reflected back.

Her father walked over and wrapped his arms around her. "Are you okay?" he whispered.

"I don't know. I don't even know who I am anymore." She shifted her gaze to his face. "I left home nothing more than a Journeyman Crafter just, what, a little over two standard weeks ago? It feels like a lifetime. Now, I'm a guild master with a pile of other titles. I have two new claws, a giant gaping hole where my instinct used to be, and a whole host of new abilities that I'm barely able to grasp."

She tilted her head to look at the side of her face and lightly touched her short fur. "Even my fur is coming in differently. The scars are growing in white." She leaned back against him and let out another heavy sigh laced with jagged nerves. "And in another week, I could find myself voted in as Senior Guild Master. What happened to Marsee? I don't even know if she's still in there."

"She is. Marsee is the foundation on which everything else is built. It was Marsee I saw the other night, making the decision to help others before herself, and it's Marsee that I see in front of me now. One that is stronger, wiser, and far more grown up than she was before, not those other titles. You amaze me every day with your resilience and compassion, and I know you have no reason to believe me, but I am so very proud of you and everything you've accomplished."

"Thanks, Papa," she replied, hugging his arms back, and took another deep breath. "Well, come on. There's another Leviathan we need to slay."

She turned and took Hope from GrandFather, then walked out the door before her nerves won out rather than climbing back into bed to hide under the pillows like she really wanted to do. All four of her normal guards were waiting outside her door, plus two others she didn't know. She took a deep breath but said nothing as she walked off, keeping to her sister's slower pace.

By the time they made it to the exit, there was an entire squad of guards around them. She nearly turned around again when they stepped through the outer shield and found another squad of guards, Water Sprites this time, waiting for them — one of which she knew.

Avery picked up on her hesitation. "Is there a problem, Translator?"

She knew he was referring to the fact that RedFin was present, but that wasn't what had stopped her. It was the sheer number of guards. Her father slammed his expression tightly behind his mask as he waited for her answer.

She shook her head, then squinted at Red Fin and the shiny new badge on his formal harness. "You weren't Contingent Senior when I saw you last night? Were you promoted?"

"Yes, ma'am," Red Fin replied. "I don't believe I deserve it, but apparently, the Senior Council believes I do. My mother says I'll grow into it. Personally, I'm hoping I don't make a fool of myself on my first day. If you would prefer different guards, I can call them over."

She grinned. "I have a feeling I know exactly how you feel right now, and I would be honored to have your protection, Contingent Senior Red Fin."

Her father relaxed, but the guards were on high alert as they grabbed their drones, and she understood why. In addition to the ever-present risk of another attack, a massive crowd was forming outside, with more people swimming in from every direction.

Protesters? she wondered, but then she realized that they were there to support the victims when she saw what they were flashing or signing: mostly demands for justice for those harmed, but some were calling for Clear Seas to step down. She snorted when she realized something else.

"What is it?" her father asked.

"Look at the crowd, Papa. Only the Hue-mans are stopping to talk with the protesters. The rest of the Council is reeking with fear, but they're not. They're the smallest among us, but they're the only ones not afraid. Even the guards watching them are nervous."

"We're used to this," GrandFather replied. "The best way to prevent war is to make friends."

She nodded at his wisdom and took off.

When the protesters saw their party approach, the Sprites all flashed silver and purple and bowed as they gave her and her entourage room to swim through the crowd.

She nodded her head back in acknowledgment but didn't stop until she was in the building. She doubted her guards would have even let her based on how tightly packed they were around them.

Little Flower, GrandFather, and Henry swam into the council chamber, and her father left to join the other Seniors, but Marsee stopped, unclipped Hope's carry sack, and handed Hope over to Tamarin, who clipped the sack to her own harness so that she and Thatcher could escort Hope down to the nursery but still keep her hands free.

They would remain there to guard over Hope and any other children that might be there. Tamarin had informed Marsee the day before that it was one of her favorite duties. Avery and the others would take up positions inside the council chamber where they could assist if necessary but still be hidden.

She thanked Red Fin, and he and his squad left to escort another group of councilors through the crowd. Tamarin and Thatcher swam off, and the remainder of her personal guards vanished into the shadows as they'd said they would, but she knew they were still watching.

She took several deep breaths to calm her nerves and was about to make her way in when a tiny flash of blue caught her attention. She turned to see Stormy swimming over to see her with his mother following close behind.

"Translator!" he signed a moment before tackling her in a hug. Then, seeming to remember where he was, he pulled back and tried to put on a serious, grown-up expression.

"Good morning, Stormy," she signed back.

"You look so much better than the last time I saw you. I hope you're feeling better, too?" he asked.

"I am. Very much so. Thank you. How about you?"

"Honestly, I'm kind of nervous, but at least this time, I don't have to worry about being tackled by the guards when I enter," he replied with a grin and a slight nod in the direction of the two massive Water Sprite Guards flanking the entrance.

Marsee curled her tail in humor, and she sniffed humor from the guards, although they remained professional and showed no outward signs of their amusement. "Do you want to know a little secret?" she asked, leaning in slightly.

He nodded solemnly.

"I'm a little nervous, too. Shall we swim in together?"

He nodded again. So, heads held high, they made their way into the chamber side by side, with Stormy's mother following a respectful distance behind them.

More guards floated outside the witness seating area. Marsee stopped her drone and waited while Stormy and his mother were checked in. She looked through the growing crowd for Temperate and Petra but didn't find either, and she wondered if they were coming or if their parents had kept them away on purpose.

"I thought Temperate was going to be here. He said he was planning on attending last night."

Jewel shook her head. "He was, but he's...not feeling good this morning."

Marsee sniffed out the lie but understood. Clear Seas hadn't officially named an heir, which meant Temperate was next in line, and if something happened today, they needed to keep him safe. "Please let him know that I hope he feels better."

"Thank you, Translator," Jewel replied and motioned her son in to take their seats.

Marsee bowed to the other victims, then turned to face the entrance to the main part of the Council Chamber. She took a deep breath and let it out slowly before forcing herself to enter.

She'd seen footage of the massive amphitheater, but it did nothing to prepare her for seeing it in person. She'd only been in the smaller chamber reserved for the local council. She paused just inside to look around and get her bearings. The massive space made her feel tiny and insignificant — a feeling she was starting to loathe.

Like all the chambers, it had its own flair, celebrating the culture and uniqueness of the hosting species, and like everything else she'd seen of Water Sprite culture, the room was opulent and ornate. Jeweled carvings, flowers, and other greenery decorated the space, making it feel like they were still outside. Unlike the Guild, the ceiling was closed off, but it had been painted with a beautiful mural depicting the various creatures of this world and was so lifelike it was hard to tell there was a ceiling there at all.

There was no need for ramps or stairs in the water, as people could swim up to their desks. Nor were there dry booths like there had been in the Local Chamber. Rather than the raised and angled stadium seating of New Hope or Council City, every member of the Council and major guild had their own booth, delineated by intricately carved archways that were covered in life. In the front of each booth, there was a podium and seating for each Councilor or Guild Senior, based on their species needs, and behind them, additional seating for their Junior Councilor and any Staffers they brought with them.

There was no sign that the chamber had recently been renovated to make room for the newest members of the Consortium. The Hueman section looked just as ancient as the rest, but there was still a hint of fresh paint in the air that made it through her mask.

The booths took up most of the circular area of the chamber, save for a section reserved for a bank of monitors and the section at the front where the Senior Council sat. Here, a platform jutted out, more ornate than the rest of the chamber. On it were the six desks of the Senior Council and, behind them, their entrance to the chamber. Above each desk hung that world's flag, and above that, an enormous monitor, which typically showed the agenda or whoever was speaking but now only displayed the opening preamble of the Charter.

We, the sentient species of the Consortium, do hereby promise to lead our worlds through peace and diplomacy, to reject war and crime, and to ensure that all species can live their lives happy, healthy, and free.

She stared at that monitor, feeling like every word cut into her soul with the promise that had been broken. Even as people realized she was there and the Water Sprites flashed their respects and bowed to her, she continued to stare.

The murmurs of those in the chamber ceased as she refused to acknowledge the Sprites. Her anger at what had been done to her and her family and friends by a member of this very Council raged in her soul, and she did nothing to hide it.

With a disgusted snort and shake of her head, she turned in the direction of the Guild box and deliberately paced her drone to be fast enough to make her cape ripple behind her but not so fast to make it seem like she was rushing.

Dramatic flair, she thought. *Oh, who am I kidding? It'll be a success if I manage not to run my drone into the wall or get tangled in my seat today.*

The memory of Ellie tangled in her sleeping net in the Trauma Center nearly made her snort out loud, but it took the edge off her fear, and the gods blessed her with just enough coordination to avoid running into the wall with her drone.

"Good Morning, Guild Master Chenzira," Agate deliberately signed with a nod and flash of respect before shifting over to deliberately give her the highest-ranking seat.

Marsee caught brief flashes of surprise and murmurs as people picked up on her new title. The one challenge with sign language was that it was difficult to keep anything secret, but then Agate fully intended to make sure everyone knew of Marsee's promotion.

"Good morning to you, Guild Master Agate. Is there anything new I should know about?"

"Not since last night, ma'am," Agate replied with a flash of formal deference that further indicated Marsee was higher ranking, then turned and introduced her to the others in the booth that she didn't already know. Several Guild Masters with projects tentatively scheduled for the afternoon session were already in attendance, along with their Senior Staffers. She nodded to Iruki, who was seated directly behind her as her own Senior Staffer.

Iruki nodded back but said nothing.

Marsee brought her sense of scent into the foreground but only sniffed out nervousness from the Staffer and many of the others in the booth.

When the introductions were complete, Marsee took her seat and looked out at the growing crowd of councilors and victims as they arrived. She saw several people sign their curiosity about where the Senior Guild Master was since she was neither in the guild booth or with the other victims. Several expressed concern, and the Water Sprite Councilor, directly to her side, turned and asked if something had happened to Ellie.

"She had to leave for an unrelated family emergency last night," she signed back, knowing that many in the chamber were still watching her.

"I hope everything is okay," the Councilor replied, flashing his concern.

"As do I," Marsee said but didn't give further information, and the Councilor, recognizing that this was a public and recorded venue, didn't press her.

"Congratulations on your promotion," he said. "It is well and truly deserved. I was very surprised by the decisions you made. I think very few would have taken the route you chose, especially considering how this Council nearly harmed you and your family only a few months ago. I'm sorry to say that I voted against your family that day, and I was against your father's promotion. It's clear I misjudged you and your parents, and I hope you can forgive me."

Marsee tilted her head, acknowledging the apology. As far as she could tell, he was telling the truth. "There's nothing to forgive. My parents made their own decisions to offer themselves up as a sacrifice, which, frankly, you had little choice but to accept, and the precedent regarding punishment was already set. I'm just thankful my sister is so tenacious and fearless."

He flashed his amusement. "She will make an excellent Senior Councilor someday."

"We shall see. I don't think her heart lies in that direction," Marsee replied.

"Ahh, I take it she's far more interested in the Guild? She is quite the artist."

"Honestly, no. She joined the Healer's Guild this past week. She wants to be a Trauma Therapist."

"Really?!" the Councilor replied and flashed his surprise. "That is unexpected, but then again, considering the trauma your family and her entire species have been through, perhaps not."

The lights in the chamber flickered, warning that the meeting was about to start.

She nodded the point to the Councilor and turned to face the chamber.

11

MARSEE: RIPPED COUNCIL

The chamber quieted as everyone stood to float in respect. Marsee's attention shifted, not to the Seniors as they entered, but to the two guards floating on either side of their entrance.

Based on his badge, the first was Stinger. The other guard was Kendra. It was exceptionally rare for the guards at that entrance to be of a different species than the host guard, and from Marsee's understanding, Kendra rarely attended council meetings. She wondered what that meant and made a note to ask Avery later. What was obvious was that both were on high alert.

She shifted her attention back to the Senior Council and gasped at what she saw. Their masks were all on tightly, far too tightly. She could see the tension in her uncle's and father's measured pace. Like the guards, they expected something to happen. She shifted her hand near her stunner and scanned the rest of the chamber, looking for any sign of a threat.

Clear Seas, the last to enter, swam forward past his desk and out onto the platform as the other Seniors settled into their seats. He placed his hand on the small podium in front of him, and the monitor above changed to show the agenda in all six written languages.

Item 1: Rip Current: Sentencing for crimes against the Consortium (Multiple). Verdict: Guilty on all accounts by unanimous decision.

Her own desk changed to show a detailed view of the docket item, but she barely gave it a glance.

"This Council is now in session. Please be seated," Clear Seas signed.

She was too far away to sniff out what he was thinking, and like the others, his mask was on tight, but she'd seen his expression before. It was the look of a Senior Councilor who was resolved to act on decisions that he did not want to make. She'd seen that same look on her uncle several times now, and it made her heart race with fear. She took several calming breaths to control her emotions, immensely grateful that she wasn't on the receiving end of that look this time.

Murmurs went through the Council at his silence and expression but quieted as he remained floating there unmoving long after everyone had taken their seats. While his tentacles shifted slowly to keep him in place, he appeared as solid and unmoving as a statue. Nothing showed on his greyish-blue skin, but from one instant to the next, everything about him shifted from resolve to barely controlled fury.

"This past week, our Consortium and millennia of peace and prosperity were nearly destroyed by a member of *this* Council." His disgust was as evident as if it were flashing on his skin.

"A Leviathan was found hiding among us, disguised as a friend, a peer, and a trusted advisor. This *diseased* individual murdered, tortured, and raped our people. We welcomed him into our homes and hearts, and he turned around and tried to destroy us all with his greed and lust for power. He kidnapped and tortured our beloved Translator. He beat the Senior Guild Master within an inch of her life and then tried to blame it on Senior Councilor Wind Rider and her daughter. He practically tore the wings off of a future Nest Mother and threatened every hatchery on Flyer if Wind Rider did not confess to orchestrating *his* crimes. He forced Petra to confess to kidnapping the Translator by torturing a child in front of her. He orchestrated the kidnapping of two members of this Council and their infant child. He planned their deaths and tried to frame Guild Master Nardal for those crimes. He attempted to kill the partner of Senior Councilor Apakna and attempted but failed to kidnap the nephlings of Senior Councilor Sammianna."

Clear Seas took a deep breath, almost a sigh, "But his crimes go further back than the events of the past two weeks. His very acceptance as a member of this council was a crime. We found his journal where he admitted to staging the shuttle accident that killed his father."

Murmurs rippled through the crowd but quieted quickly.

"He tortured and killed dozens of others who found out his plans and tried to stop him, including his own brother. He even dumped his unconscious nephew in the Trench. He convinced me that those who were protesting were terrorists so that I wouldn't speak with them. He purchased and brought hundreds of sand spinners, one of the deadliest crawlies on Saber, to the Hallowed Eve Festival in New Hope and tampered with the command relay so that help would not arrive in time. Those actions caused a member of this Council to be seriously injured and put nearly every high-ranking individual in the Consortium at risk, along with dozens of nearly extinct species. He convinced others to tamper with my son's shuttle, nearly killing him as he defended this community from the Leviathan, and came very close to killing my youngest son by his own hands in front of me, and this is only a *small* fraction of the crimes he's committed as a *trusted* member of *this* Council."

He paused as additional murmurs traveled around the room again, but they stopped immediately when Clear Seas continued.

"Three members of the Senior Council, myself, Senior Councilor Surellis, and Senior Councilor Chenzira all witnessed as Rip Current attempted to kill both my youngest son and Translator Chenzira before she was able to capture and subdue him, and before we were able to arrive to assist. We found him guilty and executed him on the spot for his crimes before he could escape again and harm someone else. We were fortunate in finding thirty-seven others alive, but we have since identified well over a hundred additional victims of his crimes over the past forty years, of which the following have been confirmed so far."

He read through a long list of names and the crimes committed against them and waited for the murmurs to die down again.

"Even with the seizure of his estate, the funds recovered would do little to compensate for the lives lost and hardships endured. The Senior Council struggled to find a way to adequately compensate everyone for his actions. For those whose reputations were damaged or property seized in wrongful convictions, the Council has reversed those decisions and repaid with interest on those accounts, but that only accounted for a few individuals and does nothing to bring back the lives that were lost."

He turned in her direction and flashed his gratitude. "Fortunately, we can all thank the generosity, kindness, and honor of Translator Chenzira for a solution. My people gave generously to her in an attempt to make up for the harm that was done to her. Her first thought was not of her own comfort or reparations but a desire to ensure that everyone was adequately compensated. To do so, she created the Leviathan Fund, a new scholarship in their honor. Each year, funds will be distributed to the victims or their families on the basis of the crimes committed against them, both those already identified and those to come. Translator Chenzira, on behalf of the Senior Council, I can't even begin to thank you for your generosity and compassion."

He bowed low to her, and the entire Council, in turn, rose and bowed to her as well.

She nodded back in recognition, embarrassed but not surprised.

Clear Seas waited until everyone had settled before continuing, but his countenance hardened again. "Every conversation we've ever had with Rip, every decision we've made based on his misinformation and misdirection, and every life we've taken on his word alone is now suspect. For nearly forty years he's sat in this very chamber, as both a Junior Councilor and Councilor, and plotted against us, against our best interest, and waited for an opportunity to strike. He very nearly succeeded. It will take months, if not years, to untangle the mess that he left behind and to right the wrongs that he committed. I challenge all of us to do some soul searching and cleanse ourselves of the darkness that he left behind before it spreads and infects us all."

Clear Seas said nothing for several moments. "Thanks to the information provided by Snapper Fish, we located a secret room in Rip's family home. There, we found thousands of files. He was gathering information on all of us, every member of this Council, or in a position of power across every guild in the Consortium. Whether to use it as blackmail or to bring us down, I do not know, and perhaps may never know, but far too much of what we found was damning and is proving to be true."

Murmurs traveled through the chamber at this, and Clear Seas let it go on until it quieted on its own, his gaze never wavering. If anything, it hardened more.

"Rip Current was not the only Leviathan. We have more than ample evidence to convict many in this room of crimes equally as heinous."

Marsee shifted her paw to her stunner again, but no one moved as Clear Seas continued.

"The Senior Council is giving you all *one* chance to come forward, clear of repercussions, save only that you step down from the Council and any future role in our government, to say if he was blackmailing you, and provide us with the information to correct whatever harm was done, before we charge anyone with the crimes we have already uncovered. We want to make things right and correct the problems he forced us into because this isn't just about righting those wrongs but protecting our future and regaining the trust of the people. So, I ask you now. Look deep inside yourself and decide whether or not *you* have been compromised and are still worthy to hold the seats you now hold. Show your strength and honor by admitting you were wrong, and let us begin the hard work of restoring honor to this institution."

Clear Seas paused and made a point of looking around the chamber at everyone. He even looked at her but nodded in respect before moving on to the next person.

No one moved.

The crowd outside roared, and after a minute or so, someone changed the monitors to show the crowd's reaction. Anger flashed red on every Water Sprite's skin, along with demands for the entire Council's execution. Clear Seas let it play for a moment before raising a hand.

"Do you see what Rip has done to us, to you? He's stripped us all of our honor. Who among you has a shred of honor left? Who here is brave enough to admit their crimes and stand before the people for judgment?"

It was nearly ten minutes before the first person swam down, head hung low in shame. To her surprise, the crowd cheered. She'd expected more hate and jeers, but they seemed pleased by their admission. This apparently gave others the strength to do the same, as a few minutes later, the next person swam down. When all was said and done, nearly thirty councilors floated in front of the head podium. Half were Water Sprites, but there were others from four of the five other species. Only the Hue-mans remained free of representation in that group.

Then again, Rip had targeted Damon and the other males instead of the Council, Marsee thought. *Likely, there just hasn't been time to gather evidence against them.*

"It takes a great deal of courage to admit when you're wrong, and I respect you for doing so. Please follow the guard out and begin writing up your statement. We will question you later," Clear Seas ordered.

When the sad procession of disgraced councilors made their way out of the chamber, Clear Seas held up his tablet. "Guards, arrest the following individuals. For the crimes of child abuse, inciting a riot, false arrest and imprisonment, collusion and accessory to murder, lying under oath, and treason, Water Sprite Councilor Snapping Turtle."

Honor Guards swarmed Snapping Turtle before he could react, collared, and dragged him down before the Council. Surprise was the only emotion she caught from him as they dragged him past her booth. The look Clear Seas gave Snapping Turtle was so sharp and full of anger and betrayal that Marsee wondered what their relationship was. Snapping Turtle said nothing. He didn't try to defend himself or deny the charges and simply sighed.

Clear Seas glared at him for a moment longer before reading the next name, and the next, and the next, until she lost count. Many she knew either by reputation or personally. Some fought their arrest or tried to escape. Others denied the accusations, claiming that this was nothing more than a seizure of power, but overall, it went smoothly. Far smoother than she expected. Overpowered as they were by the guards, there was little they could do to resist, but she was surprised that Clear Seas didn't acknowledge their accusations.

When it was all said and done, more than a quarter of the Council floated before Clear Seas, surrounded by several contingents of guards. Once again, only the Hue-man Council remained untouched.

Marsee was shocked, as was everyone else, by what she heard: murder, rape, blackmail, bribery, abuse, treason, and so much more. Growing up, the Council had always been seen as the best of them, but her faith had been rocked hard at her sister's trial and torn to shreds by Rip. Now, she wondered how she'd ever trust the Council again.

The crowd outside clearly felt the same as their jeers and yells echoed through the chamber long after Clear Seas raised a hand for silence. Eventually, he gave up and started signing over them anyway.

"The Senior Council has enough evidence to prove without a shadow of a doubt that these people have committed the crimes indicated. Outside of the evidence where minors were involved and their names redacted for their privacy, that information is now publicly available, as are the crimes found for those in the Honor Guard and Sea Patrol. Those members have already been arrested and, pursuant to their oath, will be executed after thorough questioning. The councilors before you were given a chance to redeem themselves but chose not to, and as such, it is the unanimous decision of the Senior Council that, after thorough questioning, these individuals will also be executed for their crimes against the people. This decision is final. Guards remove them from the chamber."

At those words, pandemonium erupted as many of the accused now tried to fight back and escape, even though bound and collared, but the Honor Guard quickly controlled the situation. More than half were stunned or shocked into submission and dragged off.

Clear Seas gave everyone time to recover their composure before continuing. "For everyone else in this room, you have fifteen minutes to decide what your fate will be. Come clean about your crimes for the same level of immunity in exchange for information, although we reserve the right for any of the guilds to demote or remove members from their positions, should they deem it warranted."

Two more Councilors, along with a few Junior Councilors and Staffers, came forward, and they were promptly dragged off.

When the fifteen minutes were up, Clear Seas took a deep breath, almost a sigh, and began reading out more names.

"For the crimes of theft and treason, Senior Guild Staffer Irukandji."

She didn't recognize the name at first but then jumped in surprise as Iruki let out the Sprites equivalent of a scream and flashed bright red with rage from the seat behind her. She spun, trying to unclip her stunner as Iruki lunged for her, but squeaked in surprise as Agate suddenly grabbed her, a mere fraction of a moment before Iruki made contact and yanked her out of the way.

Aris and Avery suddenly appeared from wherever they were hiding and swam hard in her direction as more guards swarmed in, stunners out but not firing. Her attention was entirely on Iruki as the Sprite continued to chase after them, dodging guards that tried to stop her.

Suddenly, a blue orb of a stunner flashed in front of her and hit Iruki squarely in the chest, stopping her instantly.

Before she could even react to that, one of the Water Sprite Guild Masters caught Avery by his tail as he swam past. Avery's back arched as he screamed with pain, but a moment later, another shot was fired, and that person was stunned as well, although Avery slumped, unmoving.

She turned in the direction of the shots to see who had fired and found Little Flower floating above her seat, stunner still in hand and poised to fire again if necessary, as she scanned the room looking for additional threats.

Others in the room bolted, trying to take advantage of the distraction, and the guards who had swarmed to protect her now bolted after those trying to escape. She heard more screams and saw flashes all around her as Agate shifted her grip and spun, trying to find a safe place to take cover in the chaos.

"Agate!" someone yelled out, and Agate spun so fast that Marsee yelped with surprise again.

Aris was waving them back over to the guild booth.

Agate bolted to Aris's side. Then, at Aris's instructions, Agate dragged her to the back of the Guild box with Thatcher and several other guards now forming a wall around her.

Through a space between their bodies, Marsee watched as Aris restrained and collared Iruki and the person who had attacked Avery before finally checking on Avery. She injected him with something, and Marsee sighed with relief as he sat up, although it was clear from his still-arched back that he was in a lot of pain. He brushed off Aris's attention, nodding sharply in Marsee's direction, then turned and signed "thank you" to Little Flower before following Aris.

"Are you alright?" he asked.

"I'm fine. You?"

His back was still arched, and he held his tail wrapped tightly around his side. "Fine," he lied. But pain or not, his focus remained on the room around him.

Once the others had been caught and dragged out, Clear Seas called out for the room to settle in both Saber and Sign, and only then did Agate release her.

"Thank you," she told Agate.

Avery wouldn't allow her to return to her seat until he growled the remaining Guild Masters and Staffers back several rows of seats in the booth. They bolted quickly. Once her seat was secure to their satisfaction, most of her guards shifted to the perimeter of the booth, stunners out and scanning for threats, but Avery claimed Iruki's now empty seat directly behind her.

Marsee leaned back in her seat. "I'm not sure this is helping my case any," she whispered to him. "Look at Saber's Council. They're all ready to drag me out of here, too."

"If they have a problem with me guarding you after what just happened, they can take it up with me," he whispered back. "Don't let them get to you. Show them you're stronger than your instinct. Every one of them is clutching their tails right now, and they weren't the ones attacked. I wouldn't be surprised if half of them go to Kendra for help after the meeting."

"Seriously?" she asked.

He nodded. "It happens more often than you think. Almost every member of our council steps down when they start having issues, and that would include your grandfather."

She turned around to look at him at that. "How would you know about that? He retired long before you were born."

"I make it my point to know everything about those I guard and mentor, including family history."

She raised a brow but returned her attention to Clear Seas, who called out again for everyone's attention.

This time, he got it. After another heavy sigh, Clear Seas continued reading out names. No one else tried to resist after that, and another forty people across all of the guilds were dragged out of the room, including several others in her booth. Thankfully, none she knew well, but many she had met or knew by reputation. She wondered what they had against her and her family. Whether it was personal or if Rip had corrupted them with false information, too.

Once the arrests were complete, Clear Seas continued, his expression changing to one of defeated resolve as he took in the far emptier chamber. "We have only begun to review the information that Rip Current collected, so we extend the same offer to the rest of the Consortium and give everyone else one standard week to come forward. The council seats will remain vacant until elections have occurred, and I ask all of you to consider them in the decisions you make here today and going forward. Our entire society depends on our integrity to function, something our colleagues have chosen to abandon. We have been voted in by the people with a level of power and authority that *must* be held in check by our honor. We are not royalty. We are servants to the people and tasked with a level of responsibility that *must* supersede our own desires."

"To the people, to the best of our knowledge, the councilors remaining before you are innocent and honorable, but it is up to you now to decide whether the people you elected, including myself and the other Seniors, should remain in office. Your trust has been badly broken, and we recognize that. To move forward with any further decisions would be unjust. When the vote has been received, we will continue with the planned agenda, or if more than half of the Council is voted out, reconvene when a majority has been reelected."

Tablets around the room dinged and buzzed with the required vote as he submitted it.

Marsee gladly voted yes to reelect her uncle as her representative. While her illness had strained their relationship, there wasn't anyone she trusted more to lead her people. Like her father, he would honor his oath. He had always honored his oath, even at the expense of himself and his family, and she knew he would continue to do so, even if that meant killing her. But she knew, too, from the expressions of Saber's remaining council, who continued to watch her and not the rest of the Council, that he was the only chance she had.

MARSEE: HONORED

The Council burst into surprised conversation, but Clear Seas held up a hand to silence everyone. "No one will be allowed in or out of the Council Building until a majority decision has been reached in each district."

Several people hit their podium lights to speak, the majority of which were from the Ice Planet, but Clear Seas raised his hand for silence again.

"I expect you are all concerned about how long it will take to get a response from our constituents, as were we. Thankfully, recent advances in our technology now allow us to give priority access to the networks on a case-by-case basis. This access comes at a cost, as it requires pausing all other communication to free up resources. Due to the severity of this vote, results will be gathered on each of the planets and sent in priority batches every fifteen standard minutes. We believe this will have minimal impact on regular communication, and we expect results from the Ice Planet to begin arriving in about four hours."

The lights all went off.

"While we wait for the results, would Councilor Henry Curtis, Staffer Stormy Seas, and Crystal Current please come forward?"

Murmurs ran around the Council at Stormy's title. Even she was surprised. She wondered, as many did in the room, if Clear Seas was officially naming his heir. That certainly seemed to be the consensus among the Water Sprite Council.

Henry swam down out of his Council seat while Stormy and Crystal, a young Sprite only about twice Stormy's size, swam out of the witness area. Crystal looked confused as she swam forward to float next to Stormy.

Clear Seas turned and motioned to someone out of Marsee's line of view, and half a squad of guards swam forward in unison in three rows of two. Five of the six species were represented. Water Sprite and Flyer in the front. Two Sabers were in the middle, carrying a large flat box between them, and they were followed by a Digger and an Ice Giant.

The slow procession made its way behind Clear Seas, stopped, and pivoted in unison without so much as a visible command. Then, after a beat or two, the two Sabers lifted and opened the box. She couldn't see what was in it until the press drone shifted to take in an aerial view. Five glittering medals lay inside on black fabric that shimmered in the light. Next to them was another box, which she couldn't quite make out.

"Five?" Agate whispered.

Marsee glanced at Agate, then refocused on Clear Seas as he shifted to float in front of Crystal.

"It has been brought to my attention that your grandmother, Fast Current, was never honored for her sacrifice in hunting for a specific food source that the Hue-man species needs for their survival. That element has only been found in one location in the known universe, the nesting grounds of the Leviathan. This Council not only awards Fast Current the Consortium's Medal of Honor, but her name has also been added to the memorial in New Hope so that she may be honored each Remembrance Day, along with the others who gave their lives to rescue the Hue-mans."

Clear Seas turned, picked up one of the jeweled medals, and placed it over Crystal's head. The Council began to applaud, but Clear Seas raised his hand to stop it.

"As I mentioned earlier, your grandfather, Gentle Current, found out what his brother was doing and tried to stop him, but Rip killed him. Your father tried to find out what happened to your grandfather and the other missing people and find out why your grandmother was not honored. His protests and demands were ignored by this Council, by me, because of Rip's influence. I failed in my duty to listen to the complaints that your father and the other protesters submitted because I believed them to be violent and acting without honor. I even went so far as to accuse your father of kidnapping the Translator and had the entire Guard and Patrol out looking for him. Yet in his final moments, he chose to protect me and this Consortium over himself and his uncle and ultimately gave his life to protect the Translator. He kept her warm long enough for help to arrive while he suffocated as his lungs dried out and burned."

Clear Seas turned and picked up two more medals and placed them over her head. "I know a medal does nothing to bring your family back, but their images will be added to the Hall of Honor outside of each Council, and I've ordered that your father's image be placed directly across from my office so that I and whoever follows me, will always be reminded of the harm this Council caused by not listening to its people."

Murmurs traveled around the chamber at those words but soon changed to applause as Clear Seas flashed the silver and purple and bowed low. Marsee noticed that while the Water Sprite Council bowed and flashed the silver and purple, many also flickered with a color she'd only recently learned meant shame.

Clear Seas waited for the applause to die down before shifting over to float in front of Henry. "Councilor Henry Curtis, you traveled on the back of a horse nearly fifty leagues out into the Wilds of your new world, unequipped to fend off the dozens of predators that could have easily killed you, to chase after Damon Minor, who had kidnapped Little Flower, GrandFather and Hope on the orders of Rip Current. If I hadn't seen the video of you riding Buster, I'm not sure I would have believed it was even possible. Had you arrived even a few minutes later, both Little Flower and GrandFather would have died, and who knows what would have happened to Hope. So, it is with our thanks that we award you with the Medal of Honor for that selfless and dangerous act."

Clear Seas laid the medal over Henry's head and bowed as he did with Crystal. Then, he nodded to her father, who began playing a video of Henry riding.

"This video was not the one Councilor Curtis provided for evidence, but one taken by a guard after Buster incredibly allowed a group of Saber cubs to ride on his back." The video changed again to show one of the cubs riding.

"It is obvious to me from these two videos, and from what you were able to accomplish, that you are able to communicate with this creature far more than we have ever been able to communicate with any domesticated species. It has also come to my attention that Buster attempted to warn both you and GrandFather about the sand spinners, killed the one that stung GrandFather, and then continued to locate and clear out other sand spinners for nothing more of a reward than a handful of dried star fruit, a task which I'm told the local Honor Guard would have struggled in managing safely themselves. I have also been informed that the guards protecting New Hope at the time gave him the rank of Honorary Honor Guard for those actions. This Council permanently acknowledges that rank, not just for his actions that day but since. What this means for sentience for the species as a whole has yet to be decided, but for now, this Council has decided to grant the horse known as Buster and his species protected status. At no time may this species be hunted or used for food, and it should be assumed that this species is sentient or nearing sentience and should be treated as such."

This caused all sorts of murmurs throughout the Chamber, but Marsee felt it was fitting. She knew she'd willingly give her life to protect that horse, and not just because he meant so much to her sister.

"As we have no idea what Buster would want in the way of reward for his selfless acts and would likely have little need for a medal, we've invented one specifically for him."

Clear Seas turned and grabbed the smaller box, then displayed it to the Council. Whatever it was, it was in the same general shape as the rest of the awards, although looked nothing like it.

"This...award, for lack of a better word, has been made out of the grains horses eat and the star fruit Buster so clearly enjoys. As this is temporary, a more permanent plaque and display have been shipped to New Hope for installation in the Barn so that all who visit can learn about his heroics. Included in that display is a dispenser for dried star fruit along with a lifetime supply. While we may never be able to communicate our thanks to him, hopefully this will show it instead."

Henry chuckled and accepted the box. "I'm quite sure Buster will appreciate this," he signed. "Even if he doesn't understand what it's for."

Clear Seas smiled and flashed a bit of relief before grabbing the last medal in the box and turning to face his son.

Stormy straightened out as much as his tiny tentacles would allow and plastered a very serious expression on his face.

Marsee personally thought it was adorable, even if that was not the look he was going for.

"It's not very often that a Senior Councilor has the opportunity to both reward and thank someone for disobeying their direct orders, but here we are. Stormy, I have never been more proud of you in my life. I ordered you to stay home and wait for your mother. Senior Council Chenzira even placed an Honor Guard in our home to watch over you. Instead, you somehow managed to sneak out from behind the back of that guard to follow Rip Current down into the very depths of the Trench to save my life and that of Translator Chenzira. In the process, you also prevented Deep Current from becoming a meal to the Leviathan, located the Translator, braved the Leviathan a second time, and then managed to break into this very chamber, past half a squad of guards to bring the Translator help and ensure that Rip Current did not escape. And if that wasn't enough, not two days later, you attempted to take on Rip Current directly in order to save the Translator's life, an act which very nearly killed you but gave her enough time to recover and capture him."

Clear Seas hung the medal over Stormy's head and then hugged him tightly before floating back, flashing the silver and purple and bowing.

The entire chamber bowed and cheered, while the Sprites also flashed silver and purple as the honored returned to their seats.

While they swam back, Clear Seas closed the now empty case but didn't dismiss the guards. He turned back around and waited for the applause to fade naturally before resuming.

"Translator Chenzira, please come forward."

Surprised and embarrassed, Marsee swam down in front of Clear Seas. She neither wanted nor expected a reward. She'd had more than enough already.

Clear Seas nodded to her, then shifted his gaze up to the Council.

"Less than a day after being released from the Trauma Center and still recovering from her injuries, Translator Chenzira left the safety of her ship to find people she wasn't even sure were missing. In the process, she located them and then caught and killed the Leviathan hiding in our midst. She saved my son's life and the lives of thirty-seven other people, including the daughter of Senior Councilor Wind Rider. Even though I saw her do it, I'm still amazed she managed to survive and fight through the charge of someone Rip's size, but she did — not just once but multiple times. She did what trained Honor Guards could not, as we witnessed here today, and what I seriously doubt I could have done. I know full well how painful and incapacitating our charge is."

His gaze shifted back to her, and he shook his head slightly. "I honestly don't have words adequate enough to express my gratitude for what you did for me, for my son, and for the people of this Consortium. I have never felt more hopeless or helpless in my life than I did in that moment, and I will forever be in your debt for saving my son's life when *I* should have been there protecting you."

He looked like he was about to say something else, but then his entire body language changed, making him appear vulnerable and small, but his focus remained entirely fixed on her, and while it didn't show on his skin, she could sniff a mix of surprise and horror at what he saw.

She tilted her head in confusion, wondering what horrified him so much. She swallowed hard when her first thought was that he was horrified by her loss of control, but she didn't smell fear on him like she had when she'd first spoken to him about her illness.

Instead of responding, he shifted closer, picked up her paw, and traced one of the new white lines in her short fur. His gaze shifted up her arm, and his skin rippled with a heavy sigh.

His voice was quiet, melodic, and melancholy as he shifted from sign language to Saber rather than letting go of her paw. "As if the trauma and mental anguish of what Rip did to you wasn't enough, I see you now carry the permanent and visible reminder of his actions in your very fur."

He continued to examine the jagged white lines that now covered her body and then reached up and shifted her head to better look at the ones on her neck and face.

She let him, not sure what he intended, as she sensed no hint of malice from him.

His gaze shifted back to her eyes, and he looked at her with immense sadness before blinking and shifting back, well out of reach — not as if he was afraid of her, but as if he suddenly realized what he was doing and where he was.

On her trip to the Water World, Ellie taught her that the Sprites didn't touch or hug others unless they considered each other close friends or family, and Agate had expressed that same sentiment when meeting Little Flower. This made sense when everyone could kill with a touch, and she sniffed a hint of embarrassment from him that shifted back to confusion.

"Please accept my apologies for being so informal, Translator."

"There is nothing to apologize for," she replied.

He actually snorted, and a hint of disbelief crossed his skin. "Every time I think I begin to understand you, you somehow manage to baffle me. After everything that has happened to you, after being attacked only a few minutes ago, yet again by one of my people, how is it that you can float there and let me touch you without even the slightest flinch? You treat my people with such kindness when all you've been shown is hate. I can understand your desire to want to help the other victims and applaud your compassion, but I don't understand your other decisions. You could have demanded anything from this Council, and we would have had no choice but to honor it. You saved my people from decades of hardship, keeping only enough to live comfortably and provide for your family. You allow and excuse my familiarity when, from my perspective, you have little reason to even trust me."

He motioned to the chamber. "Rip Current's actions, sadly, I understand. Half of my council chose greed and power over their oath. My Honor Guard and Sea Patrol are riddled with corruption and dishonor. You have no such oath to bind you. You were given more power than any single person in the Consortium has ever held, and you gave it all away. Why?"

Her nose told her this was entirely unplanned and that he truly wanted to know.

She smiled at him as she considered her words. "Rip believed I wanted power when I accepted Ellie's offer of mentorship, but I didn't. I wanted to believe in myself as much as she believed in me. I wanted to make a difference in people's lives the way she had made such a difference in mine. I believed in her vision of the future, of how we're stronger when we work together, and I still do. The people of this world reacted with overwhelming love that far exceeds what Rip did to me. Sure, I drooled over a ship or two. Who wouldn't think about all you could do or buy with that kind of credit? But it brought me no joy. During my darkest moments, when I didn't think I would recover from my injuries, it was the children of your world that kept me alive, not the credits or the power that came with it. Their drawings made me smile and laugh when all I wanted to do was cry and give up. Stormy's especially. Those draw-ings and the love behind them are worth more than all the credit in the universe. Your son risked his life to save mine. How could I turn around and hurt him, hurt any of them? How could I keep all of that credit when so many others were hurt just as bad, if not worse than I was? How could I turn around and buy a ship when it would mean a Trauma Center wouldn't get built or buy a library of books when schools went unfunded? To do so would make me no better than Rip."

He nodded the point.

"As for trusting you..."

She swam slowly forward, knowing that approaching the Senior Council uninvited could get her killed, but he didn't stop her, nor did any of the guards. There was no fear in his scent, only curiosity.

She reached out and gently took his hand in hers and placed it on her chest, directly above where her heart was and switched to Saber as she held it there. "I don't flinch from you because I can see the good in you and your desire to protect the people of this Consortium from those that would hurt them. I see that in the actions of your children, in their kindness and compassion, and in their desire to help others. I see it in your people, in Deep Current and Fast Current, who gave their lives to protect me and my sister's people. I see it in the actions of those who floated outside my window and begged your gods to remove the darkness that had infected them, even though they hadn't hurt me. I see it in Guild Master Agate, who risked her own life to save mine only a few minutes ago. I see it in those outside this building demanding that justice be served."

She took a deep breath as the crowd roared in response and waited until they calmed to continue. "But most importantly, I see it in you, a Senior Councilor, who is willing to admit when they're wrong, as you just did with Crystal, one who is prepared to do the impossible to ensure that justice is served, and one willing to give up power and authority to restore honor to this institution. That's something Rip would never do. I don't flinch from you because *you* have earned my trust."

She let go of his hand, seeing that he was very close to losing his composure, and held out her arms, offering a hug to show everyone how much she trusted this particular Water Sprite and wanting to give him cover to bring himself back under control.

Clear Seas flashed his surprise, then accepted her offer and hugged her tightly.

She could sniff how overwhelmed he was by her show of trust, but she was nearly as overwhelmed by his trust in her. He knew her secret, had seen the worst of her, and no longer feared her.

"Thank you," he whispered, but she didn't pull away until he did.

He took a deep breath and tilted his head in respect towards her. "Thank you for that trust... but I don't deserve it, least of all from you."

The Council murmured around them.

He took another deep breath and shifted back to sign language, although he didn't fully pull himself behind his mask.

"Only a few months ago, you stood before us translating our words as we very nearly took your ability to have children from you for a crime you did not commit. *I* very nearly took that from you, and I wish to formally apologize for a decision that was neither fair nor just, even if it was precedent. Who we are as a people has changed since that original ruling millennia ago, although we obviously still have far to go. Perhaps it made sense all those years ago, but not now, and never again. You appealed that precedent, calling me out for my unjust actions, and I'll admit that it took me far too long to realize I was wrong. The Senior Council has since found unanimously in your favor. Never again will the children of someone found guilty of a crime be held accountable for the actions of their parents. I asked you once if there was anything I could give you in reparation, and you declined. I ask you again."

She smiled at him, knowing by that question that this was for more than just the precedent that he was apologizing for. He was apologizing for nearly killing her and her sister at the Trial, too.

She shook her head. "No. There's nothing I need or want. It's enough that you've made the change, and I accept your apology. I understand why you made the decisions you did at the Trial and your concerns that softening the consequences might cause others to be hurt in the future. It is your responsibility to protect the people of this Consortium, and far too often, there's never a right decision, only the best decision we can make with the information and wisdom we have at the time."

"Again, your compassion and understanding astound me," he replied, tilting his head in acknowledgment.

He shifted his gaze up to the Council, and his body language changed again, finally returning to the power and presence of a Senior Councilor, although not to the hardness of before. "For those not familiar with the cloak the Translator wears, it was given to her by Guild Master Trench in the hopes that it would help to protect her and her family. This cloak was given to him in recognition of the sacrifice made by his older brother, who died protecting his village from an actual Leviathan nearly two hundred and fifty years ago, and I have confirmed that it was the last cloak ever given. Since that time, we have been able to track and chase off the Leviathan, thanks to the technological advances provided by our membership in the Consortium, and it is with the greatest of honor and my undying gratitude that this Council permanently awards Marsee Bet Chenzira the cloak and title of our first and only living Leviathan Slayer in recognition for the sacrifice and service she has provided. Among my people, there is no greater honor."

Clear Seas flashed silver and purple and bowed low for a very long time. When he straightened, he crushed her in another hug as the room continued to cheer around her. "Thank you for saving my son," he whispered.

She hugged him back. "It was my honor."

13

MARSEE: ELECTED SENIORS

To no one's surprise, the Hue-man Council had reached a majority decision by the time she returned to her seat. Interestingly enough, her father was the only one who did not get a unanimous vote, based on their unique ranked voting system, and she had a feeling he was the dissenting vote based on the look Clear Seas briefly gave him before turning to the Hue-man Council and having them all rise and give their oath again.

"Councilors of Little Earth, I would now like you to submit your recommendations for Senior Councilor."

Murmors traveled around the chamber again at this announcement, but within moments, the vote was in, and only two names appeared: her father's and Councilor Jordan Ross's. That surprised her as she expected GrandFather to be nominated. Her father honestly seemed surprised by his nomination, but he accepted it, as did Jordan, after some thought.

"Councilors, would anyone like to speak for or against either of the nominees?"

Her father hit his switch first, and Clear Seas raised a brow. She really wished she was close enough to sniff out what they were both thinking. It was nearly unheard of for other members of the Senior

Council to speak at a Full Council meeting, but as this was a vote for Senior Councilor, any member of the Council could speak, especially those nominated.

"Senior Councilor Chenzira, you have the floor."

Her father rose from his seat and turned to face his council. "Councilors, it has been my honor and privilege to be your Senior Councilor, and I will continue to do so should you elect me, but I believe you are ready to chart your own destiny. Over the past eight months or so since you all arrived in what is now New Hope, I have witnessed incredible growth, compassion, talent, and creativity from every one of you, and I would gladly cast my vote for any of you, but one, in particular, has shown her talent for bringing our community together, and that is Councilor Jordon Ross. From the very first day in New Hope, she commandeered the kitchens and claimed them as her domain. The organizational skills necessary to safely feed what on any given day is well over ten thousand people of every species is one I've rarely seen outside of a Digger Staffer. Her creativity in finding substitutes for those foods you lost has proven popular with the other species and added multiple avenues for exports far sooner than I think anyone expected, and her compassion for every individual who enters her domain has helped your people recover from the trauma they've experienced. I've not heard a single bad word about you, Councilor Ross. You treat everyone as if they're family. But these past two weeks, I've seen you excel, both in your coordination of the search efforts for my missing family and in your outreach since arriving here. I have heard from hundreds of individuals about the trade agreements you've proposed and signed, not just with those in the Council but with various Guild Seniors and even local individuals. Without your tireless efforts, New Hope wouldn't be close to sustainable yet, but you've not only made us sustainable but profitable, nearly a decade ahead of schedule. The entire Consortium could benefit from your guidance and expertise." He bowed his head slightly in respect. "I release the floor."

Jordan nodded, and her father sat back down.

"Councilor Ross, would you like to reply?"

Jordan stood and looked around the chamber for a moment before speaking. "The day you rescued us, my life was at an all-time low. I was homeless. The local government had swept up what little shelter I had and thrown it all in the trash. I was nearly thrown in the trash along with it. I didn't have a credit to my name and hadn't eaten in three days. I don't even want to think about what I had to do to earn that meal. I didn't know where to go or what to do. There were no homeless shelters in my district anymore, winter was fast approaching, and I had no friends or family left. When the asteroid hit, I was actually disappointed to have survived and wondered why god hated me so much."

She turned in the direction of Flyer's Council. "I just sat there as the ashes of my world fell around me. When a Flyer appeared and swooped down on me, I didn't even bother to run even though I was fairly certain I was going to be lunch, not that there was much left of me worth eating. I was skin and bones at the time. Imagine my surprise when I woke in the Agency, my injuries treated, with a bed and a warm blanket to call my own and more food than I had eaten in weeks. I honestly couldn't believe it. I thought I'd died and gone to heaven. For most of the people here, our time in isolation was a challenge, the food horrendous, and the living arrangements...bare. For me, it was a blessing. When you have nothing, even the smallest kindness can mean the world, but it was nothing compared to what was provided for us in New Hope. Senior Councilor, you didn't just save us, you and your partner and your daughter welcomed us into your very home. Something none of our leaders would have ever done. Yes, it was a council verdict, but I have no doubt that you would have done the same if Little Flower had simply asked. We arrived angry, broken, and scared, and you gave us everything you had. I have seen your light on and you working from before the first rays of dawn to well after midnight, even while caring for your injured daughter and new granddaughter. You could have taken time off to care for them, but you didn't. You kept working for us, to build us a home and a future, even when that made your family a target, just as you had from the moment word of the Cataclysm reached you. You have been fighting for us from that very first day, and you haven't stopped once. You ensured that we were educated and cared for, that all of our needs were met, and yet at least one of us couldn't see that, and so many others that were in this room only an hour ago decided, along with Rip Current, that you were grasping for power when that was the last thing you wanted. Your family was targeted, tortured, and nearly killed because of that mistaken belief, and I'll be *damned* to the darkest depths of hell if I allow anyone to do that again on my watch."

Murmurs traveled the Council at the intensity of her conviction.

"We left a world filled with crime and hate and greed and arrived in one where we have been shown nothing but love and compassion. If my people vote for me, then I will willingly bear that responsibility, but know this. My vote is for you, Senior Councilor Jeran Chenzira, and I will continue to vote for you as many times as I have to, to prove to the people of this Consortium that you not only deserve this position but that you did not accept this position out of greed or avarice, but solely to protect my people, and you did so at great risk and harm to yourself and your family."

Jordan took a deep breath, and if she was going to say something else, but she didn't, as GrandFather rose out of his seat next to her, then Little Flower, and a heartbeat later, the entire Hue-man Council rose behind them.

Her father honestly looked like he was about to cry at the show of support, but he shoved his emotions back under his mask and nodded.

"I think the Hue-man Council has spoken quite clearly," Clear Seas both said and signed, getting everyone's attention. "But we'll put it to an official vote, anyway."

When the vote was in, it was nearly unanimous. The only vote for Jordan was from her father. Clear Seas turned to her father and had him rise to give his oath as Senior Councilor.

"Jeran Frederick Chenzira, do you accept sole responsibility for the species of Little Earth, to see that they flourish and grow and that their rights are honored and protected, to represent them in the Full Council for the remainder of your term, or until you are voted out or step down of your own choice, even at the expense of yourself and family?"

He shifted his gaze hers for a long moment before replying in both Saber and Sign. "I do."

His voice was soft, quiet, and full of regret. In those two words, she heard not a pledge, but an apology for the harm that had been done to her and that might still be done in the future. She smiled sadly at him and nodded her understanding and respect.

He took a deep breath before shifting his gaze away from her and refocusing on Clear Seas.

"Will you provide fair and unbiased counsel to all six species as a senior member of the Full Council, and will you uphold the articles of the Charter to the best of your ability?"

"Always," her father replied. His voice was no louder than it was before, but this time, it was full of accusation as his gaze traveled around the far emptier room.

"Then it is this Council's unanimous and final decision to welcome you as Senior Councilor for the people of Little Earth."

There were no handshakes or applause as her father took his seat, but she noticed he let out a heavy sigh as he settled down into it. Then, with another deep breath, he tucked everything back behind his mask and resumed the expected calm of a Senior Councilor.

Clear Seas watched her father take his seat, then turned to face the Council again. He shifted the monitor back over to the results of the other votes and stared at his tablet for several moments. His expression didn't change, but there was a definite sigh before he began reading names.

"The following districts have reached a majority decision. For those districts that have voted no, please leave the building immediately. Your personal belongings will be packed and delivered to your home. For Council Platform, the people have voted yes to reelect. For Coral Ridge, the people have voted no. For Wind Swept Bay, the people have voted no. For..."

Surprising no one, the Consortium was in an uproar. She could hear the jeers outside as former councilors left the building one after another, as a majority was reached in their district over the next several hours.

When the final vote was in, there was barely enough left on the Council to continue with the session. The Water World, which had the majority of people involved in the coup, barely had a third of their council left, the Ice Planet a little less than half, and both Flyer and Saber were down a quarter. Digger didn't vote anyone else out, but far more had been involved than Marsee would have ever expected. Only the Hue-man Council remained untouched.

As with the Hue-man Council, Clear Seas had the remaining councilors give their oath again and then called for a re-vote for Senior Councilor. Several nominated others for the position, but no one put their own names in, and all of the councilors nominated, save for the Current Senior Councilor, refused the position.

After everything Rip had done, she guessed that no one dared show a desire for the position, or perhaps no one wanted to deal with what came next. She wondered if she could execute a friend and colleague, even knowing what they had done.

Eventually, the Seniors were all sworn back in, and while they didn't show it, she had a feeling they were all disappointed.

14

MARSEE: UNEXPECTED ADVOCATES

Clear Seas waited for Apakna to take her seat again before moving on to the next agenda item. "Outside of those already identified and sentenced, three others were working with Rip Current and previously arrested for their crimes: Master Pilot Snapper Fish, Master Tech Brandon Hollow, and Apprentice Builder Damon Minor. Guards, bring forth the accused."

Marsee was surprised that they were even bothering to bring them before the Council after having passed judgment earlier, but she supposed that maybe they weren't unanimous on their decisions regarding their specific cases.

Out of a side door, the three were led in. A full squad of honor guards surrounded each of them.

Once they were in place, Clear Seas read off the long list of charges, from theft, tampering with evidence, framing a Senior Councilor, inciting violence, and arresting without cause on Snapper Fish's part to destruction of property, kidnapping, and attempted murder on Damon Minor's, and both murder and attempted murder on the part of Brandon Hollow.

"Each of the accused has already pleaded guilty to these crimes and has declined an Advocate for their defense. Is there anyone who wishes to provide witness or speak on their behalf?" Clear Seas paused but not for very long, obviously not expecting anyone to do so. "Then it is…"

"I do!"

Murmurs and flashes of surprise rippled through the chamber. Marsee couldn't see who had spoken from where she was sitting.

"Come forward and state your case," Clear Seas ordered, his expression and normally melodic voice flat. Every one of the other seniors stiffened, as did both guards behind them.

The Council gasped as Former Senior Councilor Tabor swam forward.

Marsee looked over at her sister. Little Flower was fuming, arms crossed and scowling at Tabor, and Marsee didn't blame her. It was all she could do to keep from growling, too. While Tabor had stepped down of her own choice, it was in response to Little Flower's accusation of being denied her rights.

Is she trying to get back at Little Flower for publicly embarrassing her? Marsee wondered. Either way, as a former Senior Councilor, her words would have significant weight with the other Seniors, even if she'd stepped down in disgrace.

Normally, only a Councilor could advocate at a Full Council trial, but Clear Seas allowed it. She guessed that precedent had been set when her uncle had advocated for Little Flower. There was no question that Tabor understood the law after being a Senior Councilor for decades, but she wondered what the people thought when the only Advocate for a criminal was one herself.

Clear Seas took his seat and nodded at Tabor to begin.

"Distinguished Councilors and Honored Guests, I am not here to deny that these crimes were committed or that the accused did not commit them. By their own statements, they did. I come before you instead to beg the Council to consider leniency in their sentencing."

Murmurs of surprise traveled through the Council. Clear Seas let it go on for a moment before raising a hand to stop everyone.

"It is my belief that the reasons behind these actions should be considered. In the case of Snapper Fish, his own daughter was being held hostage and found among the victims. In addition to the other forms of abuse she incurred during that time, medical records state she was emaciated from months of being held and provided inadequate food to survive. Up until she was taken, Snapper Fish's record on the Sea Patrol was exemplary, so much so that he was being considered for a position in the Honor Guard. Only a few moments ago, this very Senior Council offered leniency towards those being blackmailed in exchange for information. The moment Snapper Fish was captured, he immediately began working with the Senior Council to provide information, with no regard for his own safety. He openly and freely admitted his crimes before even being asked and then provided the Council with information that led to uncovering the other crimes that occurred. In addition, he's provided the Council and Guild with information on how he was able to modify the Archives, and I believe his abilities are more than adequate to have allowed him to modify the logs without making it obvious. As evidence, I submit his academic record from the Guild."

She paused briefly to send that information to the Seniors, but they didn't put it up on the monitors. "Having viewed that record, I was curious as to why he would have impersonated the Senior Guild Master, as that was not recorded in his expulsion, so I spoke with him. I have a transcript of that conversation here, and I will read one portion of it. 'I found the security flaw in the code used by both the Guild and Archives and spent weeks trying to figure out a solution for it. When I had both the flaw and solution documented, I presented it to my mentor, but nothing was done with it, so I presented it to the Senior Guild Master. The response I had at the time from her stated that they'd looked into it and determined it was not the risk I believed it to be. And so my work was denied. I decided to prove it to her and made use of those flaws to make several statements that I considered to be so clearly not from her that they would cause those people to bring it to her attention. Instead of being rewarded for finding something that could be so easily manipulated and for which, to this day, has not been fixed, I was expelled. After years of being unable to find work in my chosen profession due to that expulsion, I made use of that very flaw to change my identity so that I could move on with my life. I joined the Sea Patrol as a way to help my community. I never used it again until Rip found out and tried to use it as blackmail, and he took my daughter before I could notify the Senior Council. I know I should have come forward anyway, but I was a coward and terrified that he would harm her if he even suspected I told someone.'"

She set her tablet down and looked up at the Senior Council again. "It is my belief that his intentions were good and that he deliberately made those changes in the Archives in such a way as to try to save this Council, and Senior Councilor Clear Seas in particular, from what Rip Current was attempting to do. I ask that the Council give Snapper Fish the same leniency given to your peers, and I ask you to consider what you would have done to protect and save your own child."

Tabor paused for several moments as the Council murmured.

Clear Seas let it go on for far longer than she expected before asking for silence and then nodded for Tabor to continue.

"As for Damon Minor, I would remind the Council that he is not considered a legal adult among his people based on the current rules of their charter. However, prior to the Cataclysm, he was. We have no way to verify anything that happened prior to the Cataclysm, but he states that he was both partnered and had a young daughter, which would make him a legal adult in our society, yet that status has been denied to him. As proof, I submit the only skin drawing that he did not have removed, which he claims is a drawing of his partner and daughter."

Tabor displayed the image on the monitor, and Marsee looked over at Damon, who swallowed hard at that image. She wished she were closer so she could sniff out what he was really feeling, but she had a feeling that if they weren't underwater, he'd be crying. The skin drawing had the same feeling of love as the one she'd drawn of Little Flower and Hope and that Little Flower had drawn of her.

"He has tried repeatedly to regain his legal status so he could learn the skills he was most interested in, but that was denied as joining the Ship's Guild requires a mentor or adult status. He's requested the right to leave New Hope and make his way on his own, but that was also denied. All of these facts are public record, as they were made during multiple Local Council meetings. In addition, he was denied friendship, partnership, and family due to something he could not change until he was able to communicate with us. He was even denied the request to adopt one of the orphaned children and subsequently denied even the ability to interact with them. By his own statement, he could not afford to remove the skin drawings on Earth, and by the time he was able to remove them here, the damage was already done. He was judged by the actions of his youth and not by his actions within the community and laws he now lived. Up until Rip Current took advantage of this fact, his work record was also exemplary. He never once missed a shift, never complained about the work he was given, and, based on his statements, took jobs that no one else in the community wanted, hoping that people would see his hard work and give him a chance. He indicated that on multiple occasions, he tried to learn new skills and work with other teams but was denied because the others did not want to work with him or eventually left because he felt so uncomfortable being where he was not wanted. I have verified this and have statements from multiple team leads on this fact, as well as statements from several Masters who were teaching in the Guild at the time. However, at the suggestion of Senior Councilor Chenzira, he returned to those guild classes and worked hard to prove himself in the hopes that someone would sponsor him, and yet even though he showed existing skills, he was denied a promotion due to the fact that he was on a watch list, a fact he had no knowledge of or any way to change. As a juvenile without legal guardians or parents, Damon Minor was a ward of his Local Council and had no way to fight those charges, and it is my belief that the actions he took were not ones of intentional malice but of a child acting out from months of emotional abuse and neglect, whether that was the intention of his Local Council or not."

The Council gasped at this, and Clear Seas had to yell for silence. Even after yelling, it took several minutes for the Council to come to order.

"Nearly every Hue-man rescued reacted with violence during

their time in captivity at the Agency, proving the damage that isolation sickness has on their species. However, Damon Minor is one of the few who did not, not until he was further isolated among his peers from within his own community. It is my belief that his Local Council has proven to be an unfit guardian for him and likely for the other males of his species, who, outside of GrandFather and Henry Curtis, have not been granted adult status. While Henry clearly proved his honor to this Council, risking your life should not be the only way in which someone can prove their adulthood. As no one was killed, their injuries fully recovered, and the damage Damon did to the property of Marsee and Little Flower Chenzira restored, I am asking the Council to forgive Damon Minor for his crimes, as I believe they were done in self-defense, and as the result of an advanced case of untreated isolation sickness. I also ask the Council to grant me guardianship and parental rights so that he may be shown the love and compassion he has clearly been lacking from his own species and current guardianship. I also ask the Council to consider that the other Hue-man males be assigned guardians outside of the Hue-man Council, as they have all proven incapable of moving past their own biases."

Marsee gasped in astonishment and glanced over at her sister again. She looked angry enough to kill, and most of the Hue-man Council looked just as livid. However, GrandFather crossed his arms, leaned back in his seat, and smiled. That was not the reaction she was expecting at all. Damon had nearly hung him from a tree and denied his granddaughter critical medical care. She didn't expect forgiveness from him, not after everything she'd learned about their history.

The reaction of the Senior Council was just as interesting and unexpected. Clear Seas was evidently annoyed, although nothing showed on his skin. Wind Rider seemed amused. Apakna actually snorted, and Sammianna appeared confused. Her uncle was as calm as ever, but the very tip of his tail twitched in much the same way she'd seen her Uncle Ammond twitch one of his claws when he was thinking hard. Her father looked relieved.

Whether anyone besides her even noticed, she didn't know

because the roar of anger from the crowd outside made everyone jump.

Clear Seas let the anger go for a significant length of time as he maintained eye contact with Tabor.

Tabor didn't back down.

Eventually, Clear Seas raised a single finger and got instant silence from the crowd. He then motioned for Tabor to continue.

"I was not aware of Brandon Hollow's expected presence today, so I have not had much time to prepare, but from what I read a few minutes ago, it would appear that he, too, was forced into committing crimes to protect his family, and once they were protected, gave this council a full admission of his crimes. Many of which this Council would have been unlikely to find. Like Snapper Fish, I recommend considering that with your decision. Thank you. I relinquish the floor."

Clear Seas gave a curt nod to Tabor. "Does anyone wish to respond to these requests or allegations?"

Several councilors indicated their desire to speak. GrandFather hit his button first.

"Councilor GrandFather Chenzira, you have the floor."

GrandFather floated up and looked around the Council, then glanced back at Little Flower and the rest of his council before speaking.

"My people have a long history of racism, bigotry, hatred, and abuse. My granddaughter spoke of that at our sentience trial. When Damon Minor arrived on this planet, he was covered in skin drawings that represented all of those things. I personally told Senior Councilor Chenzira that I did not trust this man and that if anything happened to me or to others with my skin color, Damon should be the one to investigate first. Were we still on Earth and I met him, I would have run for my life. Right or wrong, my survival depended on my ability to instantly judge a person. Because of the color of my skin and my preference in partnership, I was seen as…less than even our domesti- cated animals. Many believed that by choosing a partner of the same sex or with a different skin color, that I was committing a crime before our gods. I don't even know if you have a word for this. My own grandfather was born a slave. For those that don't know that sign, it meant he was owned by others, and they could do whatever they wanted to him, beat, rape, kill, force him to mate, and then sell his children and partner. I have been arrested for doing nothing more than driving our equivalent of a ground crawler, one I was legally licensed to operate, and for sitting in non-violent protest against the abuses done by our equivalent of the Honor Guard and Council. Before the Cataclysm, many of our people still thought that people with lighter skin should be allowed to own those who were born with darker skin, and we had no idea if those beliefs came with those rescued. What's more, nearly every Hue-man councilor you see before you today has indicated on public record that they have experienced abuse, sexual assault, or rape in their lives back on Earth. At a minimum, the females of our species were seen as being worth less than their male counterparts, paid less for doing the same work, and prevented from working in the fields of their choice. For a long time, I felt it poetic justice that the only males who had the right to vote were a gay black man and a giant cat. No offense to the Sabers, but you do look like the felines of our world."

This actually caused several in the Council to chuckle.

"But everything former Senior Councilor Tabor says is also true, in as much as we can verify it. I will never know if what Damon says about his personal history is true, and I will likely never trust him because of what he did to my family, but *if* what he says is true, then he did no more than any of us did in the Agency, and we judged him unfairly before we ever took the time to get to know him or give him a chance to change. I know I personally avoided him as much as possible once word of his skin drawings came out. How many healers were kicked, bitten, or had things thrown at them during our time at the Agency? How many of us would have been willing to kill for even a small chance at freedom? The only difference between myself and him is that he had a way to act on his hatred, whereas I and others did not. I believed his actions to be based on racism, not his desire for freedom. I have been struggling hard to come to grips with his actions and my own bias and desire for reparations against those like me and my granddaughter, which may very well have fueled his anger and caused him to treat us both with more violence than he originally intended. I'm sure every member of my council expects me to demand his death, but I came to the same conclusion as Senior Councilor Tabor, and I don't want those old biases to poison our chance at a good future, to turn potential friends into enemies. Over the past several months, I have seen what love, friendship, and forgiveness can do, and I have come to know and respect former Senior Councilor Tabor. If she believes that she can bring Damon Minor out of his isolation sickness and turn him into a respectable adult, then I am willing to give her that chance. As for the two others, I have no comment. I release the floor."

All of the other lights flicked off save one, Little Flower's. She sat there glaring at her grandfather, and for a moment, Marsee wondered if she would shoot him with her stunner. She was *that* angry.

Clear Seas had to wait for several minutes before she turned to look back at him. "Councilor Little Flower Chenzira, you wish to speak?" he signed.

She nodded, but it was nearly another minute before she could get her emotions under control enough to do so.

"I am not as forgiving as my grandfather," Little Flower finally signed. "I've thought about what Damon Minor claimed, and perhaps his actions in destroying our property could be considered the result of advanced isolation sickness, but I don't believe his other actions were. They were done with consideration and planning. I believe he should pay for his crimes. I was completely defenseless. I couldn't even walk on my own and had only been released from the Trauma Center hours before, following brain surgery. Yet he had no problems with hitting me in the head and kicking me hard enough to do serious damage to my internal organs. He intended to kill my grandfather and do who knows what with my child, and let's not forget that he poisoned my father, myself, my grandfather, and my infant daughter prior to that. If he'd wanted to leave so much, he could have just taken a ground crawler and left. It's unlikely anyone would have stopped him or gone after him. I would have given him the right to leave if that's what he wanted, but I was on medical leave from the Council and didn't know about his requests. He never once attempted to ask me, yet he felt justified in kidnapping me to get what he wanted. As GrandFather said, every female member of my council has experienced sexual assault, abuse, or rape in their life. Violence against us was common. If we said no to a sexual advance, we were more than likely to be killed for denying a man what he believed was his right. We didn't even have the right to end our partnerships for a very long time, even in an abusive relationship. When we finally did earn that right, the males of our species started saying that their anger was *justified* because we wouldn't show them affection, yet by their very actions, they pushed us away. Would you want anything to do with someone who drew the symbols of hate and war and bigotry on their very body? Would you want to partner with someone who saw you as nothing more than breeding stock or a trophy? What would it take for you to trust them, to allow them around your children? I may have attacked Healer Brice in my anger and destroyed my room, but I wasn't trying to hurt her, not really. How could I? Without teeth or claws, without a stunner? I couldn't even defend myself from one of my own kind. I was trying to get her to react, to tell me why I was stuck in that awful room, to do anything besides sit there and stare at me. Every night since Damon kidnapped us, I've had nightmares of that day. I close my eyes and see my grandfather dragged off to be hung from a tree. I don't know how my grandfather believes it wasn't racially motivated when the very method by which he was nearly killed was how so many people like him were killed in the past."

She glanced over at her grandfather briefly before continuing.

"We fought wars to stop people like him. Millions died to earn our freedom, and you want to let him go? I've been attacked twice in less than a year by the males of my species. I don't feel safe around him and likely never will as long as he's free, but if the Senior Council does choose to grant *former* Senior Councilor Tabor her request, I ask that he be banned from ever returning to New Hope. I don't want him near me or my family ever again. I don't want him to poison our people with his beliefs, and I hope that *former* Senior Councilor Tabor understands that I will hold her personally responsible for any actions he might commit in the future. *She* might think he's salvageable, but *I* do not."

Little Flower glared at Tabor, who nodded, and then at Damon, who sighed and hung his head in shame. Her sister took a deep breath before continuing.

"As far as Snapper Fish is concerned, I have seen the evidence that proves, while he was involved in the kidnapping of my sister, he left her in the suite unharmed. There is no evidence that he knew what Rip was ultimately doing. I believe he was a forced and unwilling accessory to those crimes, and as he has been very cooperative with the Senior Council, I agree that leniency should be extended. However, I do feel that he should pay substantially for his crimes and not be given full immunity, as he has hurt others and, in several cases, his actions ultimately led to peoples' deaths."

Several people murmured in surprise at her leniency, and Marsee looked back at Snapper, who seemed just as surprised. She honestly wasn't sure how she felt at the idea of Snapper being free. She'd never even considered that a possibility.

"When it comes to Brandon Hollow," her sister continued. " His actions over the course of twenty-five years resulted in the deaths of several people, including a member of this very Council. He has had ample opportunity over the years to find a way to come forward to save his family but chose instead to do what Rip Current wanted. In his case, I do *not* recommend leniency. I release the floor."

She sat down, crossed her arms, and glared at the Senior Council.

"Does anyone else wish to speak on behalf of the accused or victims?" Clear Seas asked. After several long moments, when no one else hit their lights, he continued. "Councilors, please submit your recommendations on sentencing. This court is in recess until all recommendations are submitted, and the Senior Council makes their decision."

15

MARSEE: FINAL VERDICT

"Well, that was rather unexpected," Marsee said to Agate after the Seniors had left the room.

Agate snorted. "That seems to be a regular occurrence today."

Marsee nodded the point and swam down to meet up with her sister and GrandFather once they'd submitted their recommendations and left their seats. Little Flower wouldn't even look at GrandFather and swam past them both and out the chamber door. A cloud of anger surrounded Little Flower, and to Marsee's senses, it was nearly as bright red as the Water Sprite's anger.

GrandFather sighed as he watched her go. "I suppose you're mad at me, too," he said when he swam up to her.

She examined him but couldn't decipher his emotions. She gave up and shrugged. "I'm living proof of the power of love, but I think it will be a long time before I am ready to forgive either of them. Do you honestly believe that Damon's salvageable?"

"Honestly, I have no idea, but I'm willing to give him that chance, just as you and Little Flower were both given," he replied.

Marsee frowned, wondering if anyone else had been listening who understood Hue-man but considered his words and eventually nodded before swimming out to find her sister.

It wasn't difficult to sniff her out, and Marsee found her floating on an archway overlooking the square. The crowd outside continued to protest while children played in the park, oblivious to what was going on inside. Avery and several other guards stayed close to her as she left the chamber, but she waved them off and swam up to her sister alone. They backed off, giving her a semblance of privacy, but more importantly, kept the press away.

"Hey," she said.

Her sister didn't look over at her, just let out a heavy sigh.

Marsee swam up behind and hugged her. Little Flower leaned back and rested her head against Marsee's chest, and they stayed that way for a long time.

"Thank you for saving my life today," Marsee said. "I think you even impressed Avery."

Her sister grunted but didn't say anything.

Marsee waited until her sister was ready to speak.

"I don't know if I want to swear, cry, or throw something right now," Little Flower said. "I will never be able to get the image of him beating GrandFather and dragging him towards that tree out of my mind or the absolute terror and helplessness I felt when he grabbed Hope out of her crib. Tabor might think he's redeemable, but I don't, and I will never be able to trust him."

"Never is a long time," Marsee replied.

Little Flower spun around and glared at her. "You're taking GrandFather's side, too? I can't believe it!"

"I am not taking his side. I wouldn't expect you to trust him. I don't trust him either. Nor do I trust Snapper Fish, yet you recommend leniency on his part. Besides," she replied with a mischievous grin and attempted to lighten the mood. "I've tried to kill you multiple times, and yet now I get to eat you whenever I want."

"It's not the same, and you know it!" Little Flower snapped.

"Isn't it, though? How is Damon's psychosis any different than mine?"

"You were trying to fight it. You didn't mean to do those things," Little Flower said.

"Most of the time, that was true, but not always. I wanted to tear Rip Current to shreds for what he did to me. I freely gave myself over to that hatred, and it nearly killed me. I almost lost myself to the darkness then, and again later, as my guilt over the joy I felt with those actions made me try to kill myself, but it was your love and your light that pulled me out of my hatred and darkness. You and I are both proof that love can change people for the better."

"I am not forgiving him!" her sister yelled.

"I'm not asking you to forgive him," Marsee replied back. "But if I know my father, he will give Damon that chance, just as you gave Snapper Fish, and you're going to have to learn to live with it, just as I will."

"That thought terrifies me," Little Flower whispered as she slumped against Marsee again.

"I'm not worried," Marsee said, wrapping her tightly in a hug.

"You're not?" Little Flower asked, leaning back to look up at her. "Why?"

"Because you've got that stunner to protect us, and we're going to train until we're both so skilled at defending ourselves that no one will ever dare to attack us again."

Her sister nodded and looked away, lost in thought. "Are you mad at me about Snapper Fish?"

"No," Marsee replied. "Of course not. I trust you. You wouldn't have recommended leniency if the evidence didn't back it."

Moments later, an announcement indicating the session would resume in fifteen minutes was blared over the speakers in all six languages.

"They've made a decision already?" Little Flower asked and then sighed.

"So it would seem. Come on, we'd better take our seats, and I need to find a waste room before the session starts up again. It's been a rather long morning."

"I'll meet you there. I need another minute or two," her sister said.

Marsee crushed her in another hug and left. Avery directed her to the nearest waste room, and by the time she returned, her sister had already entered the chamber. Marsee made her way up to her seat and waited.

"How is she?" Agate asked.

"Justifiably upset and terrified. I can't say I'm any different."

Agate nodded, but before she could respond, the session started again.

"We have reviewed the evidence provided by Former Senior Councilor Tabor and the suggestions on sentencing by the Council," Clear Stated once everyone was seated again. "The Full Council was in no way unanimous and ranged the full spectrum, nor was the Senior Council unanimous on all decisions, but we have come to a majority. Snapper Fish, please rise."

Snapper Fish floated up from his seat.

"Under normal circumstances, the charges you pled guilty to would warrant a death sentence, but that does little to repair the damage caused by your actions. Many of the actions you performed were under the direct orders of your councilor. Refusing such would have placed you in severe legal trouble, and with the added consequence of your kidnapped daughter, it meant you had little choice but to follow those orders. We agree with Councilor Little Flower that there is little evidence that you knew what Rip Current ultimately intended with the Translator and the others he ordered you to arrest, and after speaking with Master Tech Lowell, we are in agreement that you could have removed the evidence that ultimately proved my own innocence. The Former Councilor is also correct that you have provided us with vital information in this investigation without prompting, knowing full well that information would prove your guilt. To deny you what we have given our peers would put us above the law. You are being removed from your current position in the Sea Patrol and returned back to the position you had as a Master Pilot prior to Rip Current's influence. Your record in that position was exemplary, and there are far too few pilots with the skills necessary to chase off the Leviathan. Additionally, you will be placed on a watch and your wages as Master Pilot will be garnished for ten years and added to the Leviathan Fund, or until such time as you complete twenty thousand hours of community service. This decision is final. You may leave."

Snapper Fish was so astounded to realize he wasn't going to be executed for his crimes that he didn't move for several moments. As he made his way out of the council chamber, one of the victims bolted from her seat and swam in front of him, stopping him from leaving. No one moved, not even the guards. Whoever she was, she was scrawny and covered in visible scars.

His daughter? she wondered. *Or one of his victims?*

"I am beyond sorry," he flashed and hung his head as his skin shifted to the mottled color of shame.

The child stared at him for a moment, let out a ripple of a sigh, and swam up to him.

He looked up at her approach and then flashed bright blue with happiness when she held her arms out for a hug. He shifted forward and hugged her gently as if afraid he might break her. After a long moment, they swam out together, holding hands, followed by a pair of guards.

At least someone will be happy with the Council's leniency. Her heart broke at the thought of all the families that would grieve over those soon to be executed, but she was still conflicted by the thought of him being free, even if he was being watched. *Unintended consequences,* she thought and shook her head.

Agate placed her hand on Marsee's arm, and Marsee looked over to see concern and sympathy in the Guild Master's expression. "He deserved far more than that for what he did to you and Ellie," Agate said softly.

She flicked an ear back dismissively, not really sure what to say.

Before she could figure it out, Clear Seas continued. "Brandon Hollow, please rise."

Brandon floated up, tail tucked tightly around him, and she guessed that if they hadn't been underwater, it would have been fully poofed in fear.

"Brandon Hollow, by your own admission, you have admitted to tampering with several shuttles and ships over more than two decades, which has resulted in the death or serious injury of nearly a dozen people, including Rip Current's father and my own son, Temperate Seas. You claimed that your family was being threatened, yet when we investigated, your *former* partner informed us that she ended the partnership due to verbal abuse directed at her and her children several months prior to the incident in which you claim Rip Current first found and blackmailed you for. Further investigation into that original incident has found probable cause that it was not an accident but a deliberate attempt to kill Councilor Chenzira, resulting instead in the death of his partner's parents, Bethany and Terrance Chenzira, who borrowed the councilor's shuttle following routine maintenance, which you performed. This Council unanimously finds you guilty of murder, with your execution to occur within one standard day."

Marsee sat there in shock, realizing that what she'd always been told had been a freak accident during a storm had been murder. Rip had tried to claim that her father had killed her grandparents, and while she'd told Clear Seas, his comments had led her to believe it was all a lie, and she hadn't given it another thought.

Why did he try to kill Papa? she wondered, but before she could even think more than that, Brandon let out a ferocious snarl, somehow managed to snap the cuffs restraining him, and bolted straight towards the Senior Council. He didn't get far before the guards caught up to him. The Sprites attempted to stun him into submissions, but he continued to snarl and fight back through the pain.

It was only then that Marsee realized there was only one way he was still able to fight back. He was already gone, lost to his instinct.

Moments later, the guards must have decided he was too much of a risk to keep alive. She shook with remembered pain and fear as she watched his body writhe as not one but several guards pumped him full of electricity. Urine and feces clouded the water as he lost control of those muscles and died.

One of the guards checked for a pulse and then signed, "dead," before dragging his lifeless body out of the chamber. Someone from maintenance appeared a moment later and cleaned up the remaining mess, but she wasn't seeing any of it.

"Are you all right?" Agate asked, placing her hand on Marsee's arm again.

She jumped in surprise at the touch but managed to control her fear and not lash out. "No. Not really," Marsee replied, taking deep breaths to control her reaction.

Avery leaned forward. "You're safe," he whispered.

This day had shown her that she was anything but safe, not from those who hated her family, not from her father or uncle, who were watching her, and most certainly not from Saber's Council, who was also watching her. But the ridiculously inaccurate comment was enough to snap her out of her panic.

She snorted at him but didn't reply as the meeting started up again.

"Damon Minor, please rise," Clear Seas called out in Saber to get everyone's attention again and then repeated it in sign.

Damon untangled himself awkwardly from the netting and floated up, looking absolutely terrified. She was pretty sure she saw him shiver.

"As the former Councilor reminded us, you are *not* considered a legal adult in our society, even though you likely qualified as such on your former world. The Senior Council agrees that the withholding of adulthood, as has been done by the Hue-man Council, is biased and unjust in that it does not provide the Hue-man males with any other means of obtaining adulthood outside of exceptional measures and waiting a length of time nearly a sixth of the length of your formerly known lifespan. As such, this Council has decided to adjust the provisions in the Consortium's Charter such that anyone earning a Journeyman's rank or the equivalent in *any* guild will be granted the rights and responsibilities of adulthood and will be awarded to anyone who currently has that rank. Additionally, as several guilds currently do not allow membership until adulthood, we are banning the restriction of membership to a guild based on age. We are also removing the restriction of owning a home for any of the rescued Hue-mans, regardless of age, should they wish to live on their own outside of New Hope. Should *any* existing member of the Hue-man species wish to leave New Hope prior to earning their adulthood, those arrangements will be made, and housing equal to or better than what has been provided in New Hope will be given. It is this Council's opinion that Damon Minor attempted all possible legal recourse available to him and was summarily denied those accommodations due to being placed on a watch he was not aware of, lasting more than the standard six months, and for which he had no way to rectify. Further, after speaking with Senior Healer Hyacinth, we are in agreement that the isolation and treatment by the other members of his species led to an advanced case of isolation sickness and that the Hue-man Council's treatment was abusive."

Another round of murmurs went through the room as people wondered what this meant for the Hue-man Council as they'd all just been found guilty of a crime.

Clear Seas raised a single finger and had immediate silence. "The Senior Council also fully understands the harm that was done to those same councilors in the past and their reasons for requiring the males of their species to prove they can be trusted, and as such, has chosen not to punish the members of the Hue-man Council. Instead, as was suggested by Former Senior Councilor Tabor, we are granting the Hue-man males who have reached physical maturity the right to request a different legal guardian, and if so, one will be appointed by the Senior Council. We are also requiring that the still un-adopted Hue-man children be found parents among the other species, with the restriction that they must remain in New Hope for a minimum of nine months of a standard year until they earn their adulthood, unless granted permission by the Council. Those adoptions and guardianships will be reviewed by the Senior Council before being awarded. In the case of Damon Minor, we are awarding full custody and parental rights to Former Senior Councillor Jennette Tabor. However, as people were harmed by Damon's illness and damage done to property, reparations are still in order. Damon Minor, we are requiring that community service be performed for the benefit of New Hope in the amount of five thousand two hundred and eighty-two hours, which is the estimated value of the damage done to the property of Marsee Bet Chenzira and Little Flower Chenzira. This community service must be done under the supervision of an Honor Guard, and at no time are you allowed out of your home or in New Hope unless you are being supervised by a guard or Former Councilor Tabor or her partner until such time as you have completed your community service *and* earned your adulthood. This decision is final. This Council is now in recess and will reconvene in one standard hour."

While the others, including Agate, made their way out of the chamber for the recess, Marsee sat and watched as Tabor swam over to Damon and looked down at him for several moments. Damon looked completely dumbstruck by the outcome, just as Snapper Fish had.

"Why?" he asked Tabor. "I hurt them, and I deserved to die. I want to die, to be with my family again. Why are you doing this?"

"Because I know what isolation, loneliness, and grief can do to a person," she replied. "My family welcomes you with open arms and hopes that you can find happiness with us. Starting today, you will be judged solely on your actions going forward. My understanding is you want to be a pilot?"

"I do," he replied.

"Well, come on then. There's no time to start like the present."

Damon's face lit up with a huge smile, and he followed her out.

Marsee looked over to where her sister was sitting.

Little Flower had watched the exchange as well and continued to watch long after they'd exited the chamber, but Marsee couldn't tell what her sister was thinking, and she was too far away to sniff. She continued to sit and watch as GrandFather swam up to her sister. They spoke for several minutes. She could have listened in, but she chose not to, giving them their privacy.

Little Flower nodded and leaned into GrandFather's side as he hugged her.

It would be a long time before either of them felt safe again, but they were both healing and who knew, perhaps the Council's compassion might result in a far better outcome for everyone. Certainly, the other Hue-man males now had opportunities they didn't before, and they were all learning.

Darkness, hate, and greed were not exclusive to the Hue-mans. If the other species still suffered from it after millennia of trying to snuff it out, how could any of them expect the Hue-mans to get it right in less than a year?

The councilor in the booth next to Marsee had not left and was talking with their junior councilor. Marsee glanced over as the flash of light caught her attention.

"I think where the Hue-mans are concerned, we should all learn to expect the unexpected," the councilor stated, then swam off.

She had never seen a more true statement in her life.

When the others had all left the council chamber, save for Little Flower and GrandFather, Marsee finally swam down.

"That was a bit of an eventful session," GrandFather signed.

Marsee snorted. "Indeed. Did you know about Brandon?"

Both Little Flower and GrandFather shook their heads.

"Not about your grandparent's involvement. That wasn't in the evidence released earlier. Are you okay?" Little Flower asked.

"Surprised, but I never knew my mother's parents. They died right before I was born. I was always told they died in a bad storm. As far as I know, my parents never questioned it. I'm glad my mother wasn't here, though. She's going to be furious with Papa for not telling her. How are you doing?"

"I'm just as furious with him," Little Flower replied and swam off, leaving both of them behind.

Marsee sighed and watched her swim off, followed by Aris and three other guards. Then, taking a chance, not sure if she was allowed to, Marsee swam over to the Senior's entrance. Neither guard said or did anything to stop her as she swam up and knocked.

Clear Seas opened the door a moment later and motioned her in. "What can we do for you, Translator?"

"I was hoping to speak to my father and uncle for a moment," she replied.

"Of course," he said. "Would you like privacy?"

"No, I'll only be a moment. I know you're busy," she said and then turned to her father, who swam out of his chair and crushed her in a hug.

"Thank the moons, you're okay," he whispered. "That was far too close. If Agate hadn't..."

"I'm fine," she said. "Why didn't you tell me about Iruki or my grandparents?"

Her father looked embarrassed and rubbed the back of his head, but it was her uncle who spoke.

"We were worried that others would realize that we had information on the rest of the Council and didn't want anyone to figure out what we had planned. Brandon's arrest was known, but as far as the Council knew, it was only for tampering with Temperate's shuttle. As for Irukanji, we were worried that you would react in fear and give it away before the Council was in session. We didn't know if the others planned to attack or not, but figured if they had any sense that they were going to be arrested, they would either attack or attempt to run, as many obviously still did."

Marsee nodded her understanding. "Why did Brandon target you, Papa?"

Her father sighed. "More unintended consequences, I'm afraid. His daughter had psychosis. Hers was the first test I ever had to witness. Once again, my actions and decisions have hurt you. I'm sorry you never got to meet your grandparents, and I'm honestly very glad your mother is not on the planet right now."

Marsee snorted. "Yeah, she's not going to be happy with you for hiding that information when she finds out. You might want to bring a few guards with you for protection when you go home."

He chuckled in return. "I doubt that will help. I'm hoping it will be enough to know we caught him and that he's dead. How's your sister doing?"

"She's just as livid, and I'd watch out for that stunner of hers. She's quite good with it, in case you haven't noticed."

"I saw," he replied dryly, and she noticed a hint of humor on the other's faces and Clear Sea's skin, who were all trying to appear like they weren't listening. "And you?" he asked.

"Terrified, but I understand why you did what you did. I just pray there aren't more…unintended consequences," she replied, and then thanked everyone for letting her interrupt and swam out to find her sister.

As the door slid shut, she heard Wind Rider ask, "How much do you want to bet Little Flower does shoot Jer before the week is up?"

She chuckled as she swam out into the main chamber.

GrandFather was already back and waved her over. "You do not want to go out there," he said. "The press is circling like vultures. Little Flower's hiding in your father's office while the guards are growling everyone away."

"What's a vulture?" Marsee asked, taking the wrapped package of food he handed her.

"They were carrion birds, like the harbingers, only far uglier," he replied. They spent the rest of the hour talking about vultures and other extinct creatures from Earth and ignoring what had happened that morning. When Little Flower returned, she ignored them both and swam up to her booth.

TEMPERATE: RECESS

emperate floated in a transport cart in the common area of Petra's ship, along with Sun Chaser, Wind Rider's Senior Guild Healer, and a pair of Flyer guards who refused to leave them alone.

The Council had broken for recess, but he just sat there, staring at the monitor, unable to get over how many people had been involved and how many of them he'd known his entire life. Far too many were family, people he'd once trusted.

"Thirty-four," Petra muttered under her breath.

"Hmm?" Temperate asked. He'd been so lost in thought that he wasn't sure he'd translated her words correctly.

"Thirty-four nest mothers were involved," she repeated. "I had to get permission to leave the planet from *them* because our species is dying out. They *knew* what I'd be forced to do, and yet they still made me go before them. They sat there and bickered for hours that the risk of letting me fly was too dangerous. The potential loss of my genetic diversity was too valuable for the species to risk. The males, I can almost understand. Leaf and Willow believed I wanted the power and prestige that comes with being a Nest Mother, but I didn't. I just wanted to fly, even if it was only for a few years. Now, I can't even stretch my wings, and thirty-four of our Nest Mothers will die. If the loss of my genetic material could lead to our species' extinction, what will happen with the loss of thirty-four? What will the people say when I refuse a mating flight now?"

"I thought your mother changed that rule," Temperate replied.

Petra snorted. "She did, but that won't change people's beliefs. They'll think I'm being selfish for not doing my duty, assuming I'll ever be able to fly again."

"You will," Sun Chaser said. "That I can promise. I've seen and treated far worse. The timing is unfortunate, but you'll recover, assuming you do your exercises."

Petra snaked her head around and hissed at Sun Chaser with such venom that even the guards reacted.

"Sounds like quite the trade," Petra spat. "I'll fly again as long as I allow you to torture me for the next year. And what does that get me? Not my freedom but a lifetime of servitude. The moment I'm cleared to fly again, I'll be expected to allow some male to rape me for the survival of our species."

"It's not like that," Sun Chaser said.

"The law states that if I feel like it's rape, then it's rape. But that doesn't matter. My only value to society is how many eggs I can produce, and I don't even get to keep them unless they're female. If I'm so lucky, I'm then expected to teach my daughters that it's their duty to the people that they allow a male to rape them and produce as many eggs as possible. I am as much a slave as GrandFather mentioned *his* grandfather was, whether the Council has changed the rules or not. I was tortured and nearly killed because people couldn't believe I'd want to do anything else with my life. I didn't even realize how wrong our society was until Marsee mentioned Little Flower's concern for me. I didn't have a word for what I am until today. I am not a Nest Mother. I am a slave, bound to other people's expectations and desires. I will be forced to mate, to give others the children *they* desire, and be expected to give up every hope and dream I might have or face the consequences of being ostracized by my people. I don't think you can understand the guilt I feel for even wanting something different, for not doing my *duty*."

With those words, Petra climbed off her nest of pillows with a grunt and hiss of pain and started to walk away.

"I feel the same way," Temperate said softly.

Petra stopped and looked back at him with disbelief.

"Stormy will be my father's heir because I'm not strong enough to take on that mantle. I've spent most of my life running from the expectations of my people and will always feel guilty about leaving that responsibility to my younger brother. But it doesn't matter what your people think any more than it does mine. You need to live your life true to who you are, if not for yourself, then for the next person who wants a different life. Fight for your dreams. Don't let anyone take them away from you. If you want to fly, you fly, and don't let anyone or anything take your wings from you."

"If only it were that easy," she replied, lifting her bandaged wings. "Rip may have chained me and snapped my wings like a twig, but the real chains have been there my whole life, and I don't have the key." With that, she turned and walked away.

Temperate watched until she entered her room.

Sun Chaser let out a heavy sigh the moment the door slid shut. "She's right," he said. "Our people won't understand her. They'll give her time to heal and recover from her trauma, but with the loss of so many Nest Mothers, they'll expect her and every other Nest Mother on the planet to make up the difference. There's a decade-long waiting list for eggs now as it is, and her genetic line is the most fertile. Her mother just laid two female eggs, which hasn't happened in my lifetime, if not half a millennia."

Temperate's skin flickered orange. "And you see nothing wrong with forcing her to mate?"

"I didn't say that," Sun Chaser replied. "But in many ways, we are in much the same predicament as the Hue-mans. With the loss of so many today, some districts won't even have a Nest Mother anymore. Marsee's hypothesis on the reason our numbers are so low is intriguing, but we have studied the length of flight, age, elevation, temperature, stress, and every other factor we can think of. I find it hard to believe that the changes that have been made will, in any way, affect our clutch sizes, but at this point, I'm willing to try anything, and I'll be quite happy if I get to say I was wrong."

He cooled his skin and flashed his understanding, then turned his attention to the monitor again. The press was still scrambling to dig through all of the evidence and recover from the unprecedented and unexpected events of the morning, but a swarm of reporters were trying to get interviews from anyone they could, and the guards were badly outnumbered trying to keep them away. Most of the people leaving the chamber were ignoring the press, but when his brother and mother appeared, the swarm ignored all protocol and broke through the wall of guards to descend on his brother.

The guards swarmed to protect them as his mother pulled him back inside the doorway. But to his surprise, Stormy wiggled free and swam up. "Please stop. I will answer your questions, but please, back up so that others may pass."

To his surprise, the Press did, but the Guards didn't move from in between them.

"Does your title as Staffer mean that your father has chosen you for his heir?" someone called out.

"No," Stormy replied. "I don't believe my father will pick an heir, but I have started training to take the position if the people decide they want me to lead them someday. That training is available to any of our citizens, and I, in no way, expect the people to vote for me simply because I'm my father's son. I want people to vote for me because I've earned the position and their trust, not because of my genetics."

He had to chuckle. The press was so stunned by his brother's response that it took them a moment to ask another question.

"Did you know about everyone being arrested today?" the next reporter asked.

"No," he replied. "Not everyone. I knew that there were others involved, but my father didn't tell me who, except in a few cases where he was worried for my safety."

"How do you feel about your brother having to work with Snapper Fish after what he did."

Temperate gasped as he hadn't made that realization yet and wondered if Snapper would return to his home district or stay in Council Platform. Although not in the same squad, he'd flown with Snapper on several occasions.

Stormy didn't answer for several seconds. "I honestly don't know, but I have seen the evidence on his case, and as much as it scares me, I would have probably voted the same way. He was given the same chance that everyone else was given, and we'll have to live with the others in our communities, too. I pray that they appreciate the chance they were given and live the rest of their lives with honor."

"There's still a lot of evidence to dig through, and on its own, not everything warrants a death sentence," another member of the press called out. "Several were only arrested for bribery or theft, and many claimed that they were innocent of the charges against them. How do you feel about the Seniors not bringing these cases to trial?"

Stormy was silent again for several moments before answering. "Councilor Little Flower once said that every decision we make has unforeseen consequences. Those in the Guard or elected to the Council are supposed to be the best among us. How can they pass judgment on crimes when they themselves are criminals? For that reason alone, those in the Guard and the Sea Patrol with the authority to arrest take an oath that their life is forfeit if they commit any crime, no matter how small. An argument could be made that the Council's oath to put the people before themselves and their families is equivalent. They broke their oath. They knew what they had done but attempted to keep their power instead of putting the people first. I have a great deal of respect for those who came forward, especially for former Councilor Haisley, who was the first to swim forward. It's not easy to admit when you've been wrong, and I pray her family remains safe."

"And what about those who say they were innocent? Your father had evidence fabricated against him. Who's to say the others didn't, too?"

"I am quite sure that the Seniors have taken that into consideration, and if something should come up during their interrogations, they will take it as seriously."

"My understanding is that you are attending school with Snapper Fish's daughter and have been seen hanging out with her. Is there more going on?"

Stormy blinked and flashed his confusion. "More?"

"As in a relationship?"

Stormy stared at the reporter for several moments, and Temperate had to chuckle at the expression on his brother's face.

"I've...never even given that a thought. Yes, I've been spending time with her. I don't blame her for what her father did. What she has been through is horrible and unimaginable. I thought she could use a friend."

"Your compassion is surprising," another reporter said.

"Is it?" Stormy asked, flashing a hint of anger. "You find it odd that I would care about someone who was tortured and starved for months?"

The reporter spluttered to take it back. "No, of course not. It's just that people were harmed because of her, including your father. I would think you'd want to keep your distance from her and her family."

"*No.* People were harmed because Rip *abused* her. That distinction is important. She is not a criminal. She is a victim, and anyone who thinks otherwise should go stuff themselves down an active lava tube. *This* interview is over." With that, Stormy swam off, bright red with anger, with his mother and several guards following closely behind.

Temperate's skin bubbled with humor at the stunned reaction of the reporters.

"Your brother has an attitude, I see," Sun Chaser said. "Has he been hanging out with Little Flower?"

His chuckle turned into nearly hysterical bubbles of laughter. "No. That attitude is all his. He's a snot-nosed, little blubber-fish, but his heart is in the right place."

17

MARSEE: FINDING THE ZONE

When the rest of the Council started returning, Marsee returned to her booth. She didn't want to talk to anyone and pretended to focus on her tablet. In reality, her nerves were shot, and she was doing all she could to remain calm.

Suddenly, there was a lull in the conversation, enough to get Marsee's attention. She looked up but couldn't tell who everyone was looking at.

"What's going on?" she whispered to Agate as murmurs started up again.

Agate leaned over and tapped on one of the grids on her desk that showed each of the Councilors and Guild Masters. "Stormy just swam into his father's booth but didn't take the spot that would normally be reserved for his Junior Councilor or Senior Staffer. Everyone is wondering what that means."

Stormy sat quietly in his seat, looking forward and pretending to ignore everyone.

"He's neither yet. Clear Seas would have…"

"Neither of Stormy's older siblings joined the Council," Agate interrupted. "For that matter, neither did Clear Seas, although he was twice Stormy's age. Gentle Seas announced he was making Clear Seas his Junior Councilor on the day Clear Seas gained his adulthood, and that was it. That's typically how we do it."

"So what do you think it means?"

Agate didn't answer for several moments, then shrugged. "I honestly don't know. Perhaps he's waiting for his father to make it official, or it has more to do with his age and lack of experience. He is quite young to be an adult of our species, although he is older than your sister."

Their conversation ended as the Seniors returned.

Thankfully, the afternoon session was far less eventful as it returned to the more mundane tasks of running the six worlds, and she had come well-prepared for her role in the afternoon session. Clear Seas said nothing about his son's presence, although Marsee caught him looking in Stormy's direction on several occasions. There was little debate, likely because everyone was still in shock from the morning's events, and they ended several hours early.

As the Council made their way out, Marsee made plans to meet up at the Guild with Agate after the evening meal to review the next day's items, but that still left her with several hours of free time. She watched as Agate swam off, but didn't leave her seat, then sighed. "I suppose I have to face the press now."

"No, not tonight anyway. The Guard moved the press back after several incidents during the break, and I don't think they're going to press their luck again today."

Marsee sighed with relief, wondering what had happened, but didn't bother asking as she climbed out of her net. Avery was right. The one member of the press that they saw in the halls bolted at the sight of them.

After collecting her child and the rest of Avery's squad, they made their way out the back door to avoid the crowd and press that was still in the park outside, intending to return to the suites for a nap before having someone deliver the evening meal, but Little Flower was pensive and positively reeked of fury.

"Change of plans. We're not going back to the suite," Marsee said, stopping everyone.

"Where are we going?" her sister asked.

"To the firing range. You're going to shoot off some of that fury, and then we're both going to train in the Arena until we drop from exhaustion, or it's time for dinner, whichever comes first."

She caught a look of approval from Avery.

Little Flower nodded, fists still curled, changed directions, and swam back the way they'd come. A few minutes later, with Hope handed off to Tamarin, they entered the range and grabbed an open lane. They were all open.

Marsee practiced under Avery's tutelage but also watched as her sister ran through the entire program multiple times. At first, her sister's shots went wild as her emotions flared, but eventually, she settled down into the same calm she'd had before. When her sister finally completed a set without errors, they stopped.

"Better?" Marsee asked.

"Some," her sister replied, and they left to make their way to the Arena.

Marsee sniffed mixed emotions from Avery as they left the firing range, so she stopped and turned to face him. "What's bothering you?"

"I'm sorry I wasn't able to prevent the attack from happening in time," he replied. "If your sister hadn't been there, we would have both been hurt or worse. I was not in a good position to safely fire without possibly hurting you if I missed, and I didn't recognize that the others intended to attack until it was too late. I knew they were angry, but I couldn't tell why."

"Well, lucky for us, Little Flower was there, and no one was seriously hurt. Have you been checked over by a healer?" She knew he hadn't, outside of Aris's brief scan in the chamber.

"I'm perfectly fine," he replied.

She doubted that as she could easily sniff the burns on his skin now. "Well, make sure you put some nano cream on that tail. You don't want it to get infected and fall off."

He scowled, but Tamarin chuckled.

"Yes, ma'am," he replied after a glare in Tamarin's direction and redirected his attention back to scouring the area for threats.

They were nearly at the Arena entrance when Marsee heard the distinctive buzz of a press drone. Apparently, their reprieve was up. Thankfully, they made it inside before the press could catch up with them. Aris and Thatcher remained by the door, even though it was locked to the Press.

Like the shooting gallery, the Arena was empty. Avery pushed them both hard, although he made sure they remained well hydrated and didn't let up until they were both lying collapsed on the ground, trying to recover. While they did, Avery made a run through the course, proving he wasn't seriously injured, and then called out to make another attempt at the maze.

"Do you think he's figured out the trick yet?" her sister asked as they waited in the dark.

"Nah, not if he's still trying," she replied. "Should we tell him?"

Her sister snickered. "And spoil all his fun?"

Sure enough, while he'd improved his time, he was clearly still trying to use his memory to make it through the maze. When he exited and saw them snickering, he fumed and ordered them up for more laps.

Laughing, they climbed to their feet and took off at a jog.

"You think my performance is funny? Well, I think your pace is pretty funny, too. Pick it up," he snapped at her. "Your reaction time was far too slow today. Your stunner should have already been unclipped, and you should have been able to identify that Iruki was a threat without being informed."

Her humor vanished in an instant, and she took off. He was right. She'd recognized that Iruki wasn't acting normally towards her, enough to try and sniff her out, but had dismissed the threat. She had let others protect her, and if Agate and her sister hadn't been there, she would be dead, but she'd just floated there in shock. Her instinct had always snapped her out of her fear before, but she didn't have that now.

Avery didn't back off and kept pushing her to run faster as he easily kept pace with her. It reminded her of her father's test, but unlike then, it motivated her to dig harder, to push herself past what she had done before. She wasn't running in fear of her father; she was running in fear of everyone else who wanted to hurt her family.

Her feet dug into the dirt, spraying gravel along the arena wall with every step, her focus singularly on placing her feet and maintaining her breathing. She pushed her screaming muscles out of her mind. They didn't matter. She needed to be strong to protect her family, and the only way that was going to happen was if she gave everything she had to her training and recovery. She lost track of the others around her, only briefly noticing Little Flower as she passed her with each lap.

She ran until Avery quite literally dragged her to a stop.

"That's enough," he said. "Walk it off. Any more, and you're going to hurt yourself, but that was much better. You still have a long way to go to build up your strength and endurance, but you found the zone. Remember what that felt like and try to find it every time you train. You'll progress much faster if you can."

Marsee nodded, now too exhausted to even speak. Her body, reacting to the stresses she put it under, made her legs feel weak and wobbly as she practically crawled around the arena for her cool-down lap. She was still panting after a lap, so Avery had her complete another lap at a walk before letting her have a drink.

When she collapsed on the ground, Avery ran over and finished the last lap with Little Flower, pushing her hard, too. Her sister's running was improving. She wasn't any faster, but she was falling less and had nearly doubled the length of time she could keep running before dropping down to a walk.

While she waited, Marsee watched the others in the obstacle course and found Tamarin with Hope, climbing one of the rope bridges. Hope was having little difficulty making her way up, and Marsee remembered the time her sister had climbed the bandala tree.

Climbing must be instinctive for their species, she realized.

Tamarin picked Hope off the ropes before she got out of arms reach and brought her, laughing and upside down, over to a low balance beam, where she watched as Hope crawled up on it and then stood, making her wobbly way over it.

Hope made it halfway before losing interest, crawling off, and running over to another obstacle.

Little Flower finished her lap and flopped down beside her. "Okay, I think I'm done for today," she said, still breathing hard.

"That's good. Hope's not. I think she's going to be an Honor Guard when she grows up."

"What makes you say that?"

"Watch," she replied.

Hope had started making her way up the climbing wall. Her little hands and feet had no problems finding purchase on the bumps and cracks of the wall, and she was flexible enough to reach holds that surprised Marsee. It was one of the few obstacles she'd tried but avoided because it hurt her new claws too much.

"She likes to climb, just like her mother."

"So she does," her sister replied.

"Is that instinctive for your species?" Marsee asked as Tamarin plunked Hope off the top and set her back on the ground.

"Probably. We descended from a type of creature called a monkey. I have no idea which species. GrandFather probably knows. They lived in trees. Our people like to climb everything. Trees, the side of a cliff, buildings…Honor Guards."

Marsee snorted as Hope was now climbing up Tamarin's leg, using her fur for handholds, while Tamarin winced and tried to peel her off rather unsuccessfully.

"Tell her, 'Resistance is Futile,'" Little Flower said.

Marsee looked at her sister, confused, but shrugged and did as requested, simply because her sister was amused. "Another quote?"

Little Flower nodded. "I'll explain later."

Tamarin looked up, noticed they were done, and started walking over with Hope now clinging to her side.

"So my daughter has joined the Guard, has she?" Little Flower asked when Tamarin arrived.

"The earlier you start, the better," Tamarin replied. "She's a natural at the climbing obstacles, the ones she can reach anyway."

"And apparently, Honor Guards, too," Marsee said as Hope took advantage of Tamarin's momentary distraction to keep climbing up onto the guard's shoulder.

Tamarin's tail curled, although she winced again as Hope grabbed her ear for balance.

"Well, I, for one, am good with it. I want her to be able to defend herself," Little Flower said.

"If she's anything like her parents, there won't be a safe ear in the universe," Tamarin replied, then tried to remove Hope's hand from her ear but eventually gave up and flattened the other ear to match.

Marsee grinned, having a hard time keeping a straight face at Tamarin's abused expression.

"Well, I suppose it could be worse," her sister said.

Tamarin raised a brow as if asking how.

"You're lucky she likes you. She's apparently inherited another natural defense from our species' ancestors," Little Flower replied.

"Oh? What's that?" Avery asked.

"The monkeys of Earth were known to fling their poop at their enemies."

Both Tamarin and Avery snorted.

"Your father will never live that down," Aris said, from the balcony. "We had bets on how long it would take him to figure out what was going on with the showers. Sadly, I lost that bet, too."

"I told you he was far too trusting to believe it was anything other than a technical issue," Tamarin replied.

"I wonder if we could use that defense on the Press or if that would be considered an act of war?" Marsee asked.

"Self-defense, definitely," her sister replied. "I'm honestly surprised Aris managed to get me to Papa's office unscathed."

"Me?" Aris said. "I had nothing to do with it. Marsee, you should have seen your sister. When they refused to back off or clear a path for us to get through, your sister unclipped her stunner and shot the nearest member of the press."

"You did not!" Marsee exclaimed.

"I did. They refused the direct orders of both a member of the Guard and the Council. As far as I'm concerned, it was self-defense. How was I to know what their intentions were? Perhaps they only wanted an interview, but they could have been trying to get close enough to shock me. They had us outnumbered and surrounded and were refusing to let us pass. I will give an interview when I'm good and ready and not a moment before, and most certainly not when being held against my will."

"Are you pressing charges?" Marsee asked.

"Nah," Little Flower replied. "Not unless someone presses their luck again. I considered that a warning shot."

"Well, they certainly took your warning," Aris said. "There was stunned silence, and then everyone bolted. I have never seen the Press disappear as quickly as they did."

"Hopefully, it will last a little longer," Marsee said. "I'm starving, and there's nothing left to eat in the suite. Do you think we can sneak over to Fire Sticks?"

The guards chuckled, but it was Avery who responded. "You must be tired. Thatcher left and picked up an order half an hour ago. I'm surprised you haven't sniffed it out already."

She sniffed deeply, and her stomach grumbled in response. A moment later, she was bolting for the ramp as fast as she could run. Laughter followed her, but she didn't care. She was halfway through the first wrapped package before the others caught up.

"You know, Avery," Tamarin said as she grabbed her own package. "If you really want Marsee to put some effort into her run, you just need to stay a few steps ahead of her with a package of fire sticks."

"Nah," Avery said after a moment of consideration. "I'm stupid, but I'm not *that* stupid. We've already been warned not to get between her and her food. If I tried something like that, I have a feeling she wouldn't even bother with the stunner. She'd gut me first and ask questions later."

She grinned wickedly and grabbed another stick.

"How about that," Little Flower said. "He can be trained."

It was a good ten minutes before any of them could stop laughing at Avery's scowling and abused expression long enough to speak, much less keep eating.

"You're going to pay for that tomorrow," Marsee said to her sister in Hue-man when she could finally breathe.

Little Flower shrugged, completely unphased by the potential consequences, and kept eating.

18

MARCUS: GUILTY AS CHARGED

Marcus swam out of the council chamber and slumped into his customary seat at the table in the Senior's conference room along with the others. At lunch, by consensus, they'd focused on the afternoon session, but now that session was over, and it was time for all but Jer to fulfill their sworn oath and interrogate and execute those found guilty. By further consensus, they'd decided to each focus on their own citizens.

Jer had offered to share the load, only having expected to have to execute Damon, but they'd given him what they had deemed the riskier task of arresting the guard and patrol instead. No one spoke, each lost in their thoughts.

Marcus had prayed before the meeting opened that more would come forward and admit their crimes so that they could grant leniency, but far too many of those he'd considered life-long friends had not. He didn't know how to reconcile his grief and rage. How do you process the knowledge that friends and colleagues you'd known and worked with, shared meals over, and invited into your home weren't your friends and actually wanted you dead? They'd all been blindsided at how deep the plot had gone, and this purge only accounted for a fraction of the files they still needed to dig through.

"Putting this off won't make it any easier," Clear Seas said eventually. He wasn't even making an effort to control the emotions rolling across his skin, and the twisted, sickening colors matched Marcus's mood perfectly. Clear Seas didn't so much as twitch a tentacle to move out of his seat, though.

"I don't see you swimming very fast," Apakna stated.

"I was waiting for you," Clear Seas replied.

"Ah," Apakna responded but didn't move either.

"Do we give the other members of the Sea Patrol and Guard the same leniency as Snapper?" Jer asked.

"No," Wind Rider said. "None of them came forward with additional information like Snapper did or tried to work around Rip's blackmail, plus far too many of them tried again last night."

"The guards took an oath knowing that what they were doing was a death sentence if they were caught, as did those members of the Sea Patrol with the power to arrest," Clear Seas replied.

"I think we should base it on each person's testimony," Sammianna said. "If any of us believe there's just cause for someone's case to be reviewed before execution, I'd rather be safe than kill and find out later we made a mistake. We've gone through an awful lot of evidence in a very short amount of time."

Murmurs of agreement went around the room, but still, no one moved.

Marcus took a deep breath and forced himself out of his seat and over to the exit. Someone had to go first, or they'd all sit there and never leave.

The others watched him but still didn't move, and he stared at the door switch for several long moments before making his shaking paw hit it. Once open, he took a deep breath and swam out. He heard the others mutter and follow after, but he didn't look back. He was afraid if he did, he'd never be able to turn back around.

He made his way down to the holding cells, which were lined with guards, two at every door. There weren't even enough cells to hold everyone who had been arrested. Many were being held in small groups in various conference rooms, commandeered offices, and guard buildings.

Kendra was waiting for him. She nodded in acknowledgment, and he followed her over to the first cell.

He'd purposely put *her* first, knowing she would be the hardest. He stared at that closed door for several moments, reminding himself about what she'd done to his family and to others, and let his rage build enough that he was able to hit the switch.

He swam in, followed by Kendra and the two guards at the door, but all of his rage vanished the instant he saw her.

She sat in the cell's sleeping net and looked up at him with fear in her eyes. "For what it's worth, Marcus. I am sorry."

"I am, too," he replied. "Trisha Westrose, you have been found guilty of crimes against the Consortium with the sentence of death. Do you have anything to say in your defense or changes you'd like made to your will?"

She swallowed hard but shook her head and handed him two folded stacks of paper. "My statement and letters to my family," she explained.

He took the stack, never taking his eyes off of her. He knew her family and had met her partner and cubs on several occasions. She was one of his oldest and dearest friends, someone he'd once offered partnership to when he was young, but she'd chosen another and then chosen to side with Rip.

"Why Trisha?" he finally managed to ask.

"Why what? What do you want to hear, a reason that will change your mind so you don't have to kill me? Because we both know that's not going to happen. I did the things I've been found guilty of and then some. The full list is in that stack of papers. Why do you think I turned down your offer of partnership? You were too good to be dragged down by the likes of me. I was in trouble long before you offered partnership, and I knew someday I'd pay for my crimes."

"Why would you hurt my family, though? Did I do something to hurt you? What could have been so bad that you sided with Rip?"

"Marcus, love, the rules don't bend for you. For you, the world is black and white, full of precedent and laws, but real life isn't like that. Rip was good for my district. I didn't know he knew about those items, or I might have come forward, and I didn't know what he planned. Not really. There was no love lost between him and your family. He wanted things to change, and so did I. I swear I never thought he'd hurt your niece, pressure you and Jer to step down, but not hurt her. But Rip was right about one thing. Your family does have too much power. Even if Marsee handed much of that back, it's thrown everything out of balance, and you're far too honorable to even see it. Not everyone knows you the way I do. I tried to convince Rip that you'd step down at the end of your term and that Jer would after a decade or two, once the Hue-mans were back on their feet and ready to advocate for themselves, but he came from a feudal society and couldn't conceive that anyone would willingly give up power, especially not after the Senior Guild Master made Marsee her heir, not unless someone made them."

"Rip wasn't blackmailing you?" Marcus asked for confirmation.

"No, he wasn't. Marcus, I did what I did of my own free will. I believed it was for the good of my people and I stand by those decisions even if it was against the law and a few people got hurt in the process. Do what you need to."

"People didn't just get hurt, people died, Trisha."

"People die every day. Their deaths meant a better future for my district. You were willing to sacrifice your life for Little Flower's people. Is it any different if I'm willing to sacrifice someone else's life for mine?"

Marcus sighed. Arguing the nuances of morality would make little difference. There was little he could do now. The Senior Council had reviewed and passed guilt on everyone they'd brought in today. Whether she was telling the truth about knowing what Rip intended didn't change the other crimes she'd committed. Innocent people had died because of it. He looked down at the stack of papers and read through her statement, which detailed far more than he'd been aware of.

Out of everyone, he wished he could save her, wished she'd lied, denied everything, or blamed Rip for blackmail so he could have an excuse to reconsider her case. But he had no grounds to do so now, and doing so because of his feelings for her would put him above the law.

He folded and stuffed the papers through the straps on his harness and swam over.

She looked up at him, full of conviction and fear. He was honestly surprised she wasn't struggling with her instinct or that she'd even been able to admit her crimes.

He reached over and caressed the side of her face one last time.

She closed her eyes and leaned into it.

"For what it's worth, I never stopped loving you," he said softly.

She opened her eyes and peered up at him, then took a breath as if she were going to speak, but before she could, before she could shatter his heart again, before he lost his nerve or control of his own instinct, he snapped her neck.

Her body slumped against his, and he caught it, holding her in death as he'd only dreamed of doing in life, watching as the light dimmed and faded from her eyes.

"I'm sorry," he whispered. It took every ounce of self-control he had to keep his tears in check.

He stayed there holding her long after her heart stopped beating. Not until he was sure his mask was firmly back in place did he gently lean her body back into the net and let go.

Unclipping his tablet, he recorded the time of her death and clipped it back to his harness before turning to face the guards. Their expressions were completely unreadable and professional, but he wondered what they thought.

He nodded to one of the two guards that had been outside. "See that her body is prepared and sent home."

"Yes, sir."

With a nod to Kendra, she turned and swam out of the cell.

He followed her to the next...

and the next...

and the next.

Some tried to beg for their lives, others refused to speak or perhaps couldn't, and some were fully gone, lost to psychosis, and killed by the guards before he could enter, but in the end, it didn't matter. The result was the same.

19

TEMPERATE: PLEA

emperate watched the press for a bit and then checked his tablet for a message from Melody but found nothing.

Petra returned right before the meeting started and said nothing about their prior conversation or the fact that he was still there. She collapsed on the pillows again with a groan and winced as Sun Chaser checked her wings and sprayed them with something.

His tablet dinged dozens of times throughout the afternoon session. Most were from the press, requesting an interview, which he ignored, but by the time the meeting was over and Melody hadn't sent anything, he sighed, figuring he wouldn't hear from her ever again.

Petra looked over at the flicker of light. "What is it?"

"Nothing important," he replied.

She squinted her eyes at him. "You don't lose control of your skin over nothing. What is it?"

"The father of the person I wanted to spend the rest of my life with was arrested today."

Petra sagged with sympathy and then winced as the motion jostled her wings. "I'm sorry."

He shrugged, although it was laced with grief. "Our relationship was strained before. She doesn't want me to be a pilot because she's worried about the risk. Granted, I've been in two accidents in the last two weeks, so she's not wrong about that, but I was hoping for some sort of message, closure at the very least."

"You still care about her?"

"I don't know what I feel. She told her father about things I told her, and that was used against us. I don't know if she's involved or if her father was using her for information."

"That does make it harder."

"She's pregnant, too," he added.

"Ooof. I'm sorry."

He shrugged again.

"You should talk to her. Maybe she's waiting for you to call her."

He looked over at Petra. "But what if she's involved?"

"What if she's not?"

He sighed again. "She still might not want anything to do with me because of my father. Every time she'll see me, she'll be reminded that my father killed hers."

"What did her father do?"

"Child abuse against her older brother, treason, and several cases of bribery, among other things."

"If he abused her older brother, then maybe he abused her, too," Sun Chaser said.

That thought hadn't occurred to him, and he gasped, instantly worried for her.

"You should at least try," Petra added. "Make sure she's okay and hear her side of the story before you decide."

He scratched at his ear fins. "I don't know."

Neither said anything else as they watched the recap. Finally, his worry for Melody overrode his concern for his own safety, and he unclipped his tablet and, after multiple failed attempts at trying to figure out what to say, he simply sent, "Hey. If you want to talk, let me know."

He waited a moment to see if she would reply and then closed his tablet with another sigh. He was about to tell Petra that he was going to head out now that the meeting was over when his tablet rang with a call.

He checked it and was surprised to get a call, not from Melody, but from her brother. "May I?" he asked, nodding to the monitor.

"Do you want privacy?" Petra asked.

"No. I think it's best they know there are others listening."

He answered the call and put it on the monitor. "Blue?"

"Temperate, I'm so glad you reached out to Melody. I don't know what to do. I've tried reaching out to your father, but he's not answering, and the guards won't let me anywhere near the Senior's offices or where they're holding Papa. I've looked over everything they had on Papa. I don't know about the rest, but I promise he never abused me. Every incident is a result of my own lack of spatial awareness. I'm a floating accident. You know that. I promise. I am not lying to try to protect him. If they're wrong about that, they might be wrong about the rest. Please. Call your father. Give me a chance to investigate."

"How do I know you're not involved, too? Papa showed me messages that Melody sent to her father about my schedule and plans to have my ship in the shop for maintenance."

"I'm so sorry about that!" Melody called out from somewhere else in the room and then swam around so he could see her. "I know you have no reason to believe me, but I had no idea how that information would be used. I can't believe Papa would do anything to hurt you. Maybe Rip accessed his account and saw it. I promise. The thought that I had anything to do with your accident makes me sick, and I figured you'd never want to talk to me again, which is why I didn't reach out to you. Please? If you have any feelings left for me, please try."

He frowned but nodded. "I will call Papa and let him know about Blue's denial of abuse. I don't know if it will help, but I'll do that."

"Thank you!" she replied, relief and gratitude flashing on her skin.

"Thank you," Blue said as well and hung up.

He took a deep breath, rubbed at his ear fins again, and then called his father.

20

APAKNA: CHALLENGED

*A*pakna was the last to swim out of the Conference room. Even Jer had left. She knew what she had to do, but she didn't know if she had the strength to do it. It wasn't that she hadn't killed before, but these were her friends, her peers. Sighing, she deactivated the ice current, knowing that, eventually, the temperature would get uncomfortable enough to force her to leave.

It was another several minutes before she finally forced herself to swim out, but stopped as she saw her uncle waiting by her door.

"Now is not a good time, uncle."

"Now is the only time," he replied. "If I wait, it'll be too late. We need to talk."

She scowled at him but shoved past him into her office, where a blast of cold air hit her the moment she stepped through the shield. She leaned against her desk and crossed her arms as she continued to scowl. "Make it quick."

"You can't do this, Api. Their cases need to go before the Council."

"They do not. Every decision was unanimous, and they were given a chance to come forward," she replied.

"At least a dozen of those arrested claimed you're the ones behind the coup, and after what Rip told me..."

She growled. "I can't believe it. You're siding with him?!"

"I am not siding with him. I'm trying to keep you from making things worse. Half of the crimes listed aren't worth a death sentence, and you know it. I am officially requesting the right to Advocate for everyone who claims they're innocent or whose crimes would not normally warrant death, removed from the Council and punished, sure, but not executed."

She scowled at him, trying to figure out how to salvage the situation, and furious that he would even question her authority and a unanimous decision. "We have a mountain of evidence against everyone we arrested today and thoroughly investigated each case. If we allow them to come before the Council, all it would do is sow more distrust. The people need to see that we will come down hard on anyone who breaks the law. We can't be above it."

"Is that so? Or are you afraid of what they might say? *Are* you protecting Jer and Marcus, like Rip said, or perhaps your own crimes?"

"If you thought I committed a crime, why did you vote for me?"

"Who else could I vote for? No one else came forward to accept the nomination."

"I didn't see you put your name in," she countered, "or even accept your nomination."

"I couldn't. No one could. If any of us had, we would have been voted out immediately."

She narrowed her eyes. They'd argued this same point for hours. "No. No one wanted to deal with the consequences of executing their friends. Tell me truthfully. Could you do it? If you think you can, I'll step down now and let you take my place."

To her disappointment, he didn't take her up on her offer, although she doubted he would. It was not in his nature.

"What did they do, Api? Jer and Marcus. Tell me the truth."

"That information has been marked as Senior's Eyes Only to protect the people of Saber. I assure you, we are fully aware of what Rip intended to bring forth and determined that Marcus and Jer were justified in their actions."

"So there was something?"

She scowled at the trap she'd fallen into.

"Api, you can trust me. What's really going on?"

"Uncle, I would tell you if I could, but I can't. I won't. I won't put other people's lives at risk. You need to trust me on this."

He shook his head. "And what about those who claimed they were framed like Clear Seas was? It's their right to have their cases investigated before the Full Council, and you know it."

"We've been looking hard for any evidence of that, which, I might add, is the only reason *you* weren't arrested. Did you know that Rip deleted dozens of your conversations?"

Surprise flashed across his face. "No. I never even went back to look. I don't even know why he would. Nothing we ever discussed was criminal in nature."

"I know, but some of it could have been seen as treasonous if we hadn't dug further. I assure you, Uncle. I do not take this responsibility lightly. And I promise you, if any of them have any sort of proof that the evidence against them was fabricated, we will look into it further and, if necessary, bring it before the Full Council."

He sighed but nodded. "I suppose that will have to do. Thank you."

She gave a single curt nod, and he left.

The moment he was gone, she slammed the privacy screen back on and roared out her frustration, grief, and anger. Then, before she lost her nerve, she left her office to perform her sworn duty, more than anything, wishing he'd taken her up on her offer.

2 1

MARSEE: TANGLED MESS

"N o," Marsee growled at Avery. "You'll go with Tamarin and Thatcher to escort Little Flower and Hope back to the suite. Then you're going to swim your furry little butt over to the Trauma Center and have the Senior Healer check you over. If you don't, I'll have Tamarin drag you in by your tail."

Tamarin snorted, but Avery scowled. "You have no authority to order me around. The risk to you is far too high. I can't call in any additional guard right now, and I'm not leaving you unprotected because of a minor burn that can wait. I assure you, I'm fine."

"The risk to me is far less than it was last night, seeing as the Seniors just arrested over a thousand people involved in the coup. Aris is perfectly capable of escorting me the few blocks over to the Guild, and don't lie to me. You are *not* fine. Your tail is bothering you enough that you can't sit still, and you're still short of breath from your workout earlier, even if you've been trying to hide it."

Tamarin snorted again.

Avery turned his glare on Tamarin.

"Don't look at me like that," Tamarin said. "She's right, and you know it. I wasn't going to call you out on it because you obviously didn't want her to know how badly you were hurt, but you do need treatment, more than I can give you with some pain meds and nano cream."

Avery's scowl deepened, and he lashed his tail, proving it still worked, even if it did hurt. "I am not that badly hurt, not enough to risk leaving Marsee unprotected."

Tamarin's expression shifted from amused to full guard. "Your performance on the course was several minutes shy of your current average, and admit it, you pulled Marsee to a stop, not because she needed to stop but because you were having trouble keeping up with her. If you can't recognize that your performance has been severely impaired, I'll have to assume your mental faculties have been impaired, too, and relieve you of duty."

Avery flattened his ears and opened his mouth to argue.

Tamarin tilted her head slightly.

"Fine," Avery growled.

Marsee squinted at Avery, then glanced at Tamarin. "Make sure he actually goes."

Tamarin's tail curled, although her facial expression didn't change. "Oh, he'll go. He knows I'm not bluffing."

Avery was not impressed. "Who exactly is the Senior Guard in this squad?"

"Marsee," the other three guards replied without hesitation.

Marsee couldn't tell if they were joking or not, as they were far too amused by the whole situation.

"She is the only living Leviathan Slayer," Little Flower added sweetly, having finished putting her fins back on. "I believe Clear Seas stated that 'among his people, there is no greater honor,' and that 'she did what trained honor guards could not?'"

Avery scowled at Little Flower to hide that he was upset about his failure. "If you're sufficiently done rubbing it in, we can go now."

Little Flower grinned wickedly and wiggled her fingers. "Not really. I do so love a challenge."

"Little Flower..." Marsee chided. "You can pick on him *after* he gets treated for his injuries."

"Spoilsport," Little Flower replied but stood, took Hope back from Tamarin, and flopped her way over to the exit.

Tamarin and Thatcher followed, tails curled tightly behind them.

She raised a brow at Avery, who didn't follow right away, but he turned back to Aris and gave her a pointed look before storming out after Little Flower.

She snorted and turned back to Aris, who was shaking her head, not at Avery but at her. "

What?"

"I've been on Avery's squad longer than you've been alive, and I wouldn't have dared pull rank like you just did. Tamarin didn't even dare until you called him out on it."

"Even though he's hurt?" Marsee asked.

She nodded. "Your life is more important than his — than any of ours."

"Why?"

Aris honestly seemed surprised by the question. "Our oath, of course."

Marsee shook her head. "My life doesn't matter. You should be focusing on protecting Little Flower and Hope. The Hue-mans can't afford any further loss of genetic diversity."

"Your life matters just as much as theirs, if for no other reason than watching you and Little Flower yank on Avery's tail every chance you get."

Marsee snorted. "Is that why you keep me around?"

"Can you think of a better reason?"

She tilted her head, considering the question. "Honestly, no."

Aris's tail spiraled. "Come on. It sounds like the Press has stopped hovering outside, which I'm sure had everything to do with your sister. Let's go before they regain their nerve."

She nodded and followed Aris out.

It was still light out, but based on the color of refracted light, the sun was setting on the world above. Marsee expected Aris to cut across the guard complex, but instead, she took Marsee through the still heavily populated Market Square. People gave them space to get through, but the Sprites all flashed silver and purple.

They were nearly out of the square when Aris suddenly pulled her to a stop.

"What is it?" Marsee asked.

Aris didn't respond. Her attention was fixed on a group of children near a small playground, mostly Water Sprite, but there was one small Saber cub in the mix, being carried by a larger Water Sprite child and chased by the others as the one carrying the cub ducked and weaved around a swarm of others, many of whom where bright red with anger.

Suddenly, the cub yelped.

Aris bolted for the children. "What's going on here?"

Marsee followed right behind.

The Sprites all turned to face Aris, saw that she was a guard, and turned pure white with fear.

Aris ignored the scared Sprites and swam over to the cub, still being held by the older Sprite. "Are you alright, child?"

Parents, Marsee assumed, came swarming towards them. The Water Sprite children, all except for the one holding the cub, bolted and ducked under their parent's tentacles.

"I'm fine, Honor Guard," the cub replied. "We were just playing. Honest."

"Playing? You yelped. Did they shock you?"

The cub shook her head. "No. I was pretending. I have to yelp if a member of the red team touches me before the other team can get me to safety. That's how they know which team wins."

The cub's mother, one of Saber's Councilors, based on the badge she was still wearing, swam up. "It's alright, Honor Guard. They *were* just playing."

"Councilor Goodwin," Aris nodded in greeting and relaxed at the Councilor's comments.

Goodwin turned to Marsee. "You are quite popular, it would seem. The children saw my cub and her similar coat and instantly invented a game called 'Save the Leviathan Slayer.'

Marsee raised a brow. "Save the Leviathan Slayer? Tell me you're not serious?"

Goodwin shrugged. "If my translation is correct. I'm still learning sign. The 'Traitors' are currently up by three points, but my credit is on the 'Honor Guards.'"

"And I thought the toys were bad," Marsee muttered under her breath.

Goodwin chuckled.

The older Sprite let go of the cub and swam forward. "I'm sorry, Leviathan Slayer. We'll stop playing. We didn't mean to insult you. Please forgive me. It was my idea."

She raised a paw to stop the child. "No insult has been taken. Quite the opposite, in fact. I couldn't think of a better way to honor Guild Master Agate for the risk she took today in protecting me. I'll be sure to let her know of your respect. Go on back to your game. No one is in trouble."

The Water Sprite children cautiously came out of hiding, and Marsee moved back to give them room to resume their game, and was about to leave when Goodwin stopped her.

"If I could have a moment of your time, Leviathan Slayer."

The parents all moved off, giving them plenty of space and privacy. Marsee raised her brow at the Councilor.

Goodwin paused briefly and glanced at Aris before answering. "You're...looking better than I expected."

"The healers here took good care of me," Marsee replied and decided to deflect. "How are *you* doing? I imagine today was not easy for anyone on the Council."

Goodwin let out a heavy sigh laced with grief and anger. "*That's* an understatement, but I'll be honest. I'm not surprised about half of them. I never had any proof that they were doing anything wrong, but I've always wondered how many of them kept getting reelected. I'm personally far more worried about who's left."

"Oh?"

Goodwin paused again. "If...*I* were you, I wouldn't come home until your watch is up. There are a number of people still left on our

Council that vehemently oppose your uncle at every turn. They may have voted him back in today, but I doubt they were happy about it, and they will be looking for any opportunity to bring him down."

"Who?" Aris demanded before she could.

"I am not going to name names without proof of any wrongdoing," Goodwin replied. "That would be libel, but I am keeping watch on them, and I am on your side. I pray every night that your…discovery really works as well as it seems to." She turned back to watch the children. "My older sister…*died* when she was about your age, and my daughter is an only cub."

Marsee took a deep breath, understanding immediately. "I'm sorry for your loss."

"Thank you, but I never met her. She died before I was born."

Marsee was silent for a bit. "How did you know it was me? I thought that was restricted to the Seniors."

Goodwin grinned ever so slightly. "I didn't for sure until just now."

Marsee sighed.

Goodwin looked back at her. "Don't worry. I won't tell anyone, but I imagine most of the Council has come to the same conclusion, if for no other reason than the fact that you survived. Does it really work?"

Marsee examined Goodwin with her senses and realized the Councilor wanted desperately for her to say yes.

She flicked an ear back. "I suppose only time will really tell, but as you say, I survived. Healer Rowena told me she believes sign language cuts through the haze because our ability to communicate via body language is older than our ability to speak."

"Rowena?! She's been here? Have you had any problems since…"

Aris answered before she could. "We've been with her the whole time. There were some minor issues, but those were all attributed to her injuries and the fact that she didn't know she'd been rescued at first. She's been tested by several members of the Council and Guard, including Kendra, and if there had been any issues, we would have seen them today."

Goodwin sighed with evident relief, but then she frowned. "Is that why your mentor wasn't here today?"

Marsee snorted and looked at Goodwin with disbelief. "Have you met my Mentor?"

The councilor chuckled. "Fair point. Is she alright, though?"

Marsee nodded. "There was a family emergency. I'm not at liberty to say more than that."

Goodwin nodded, then sighed as her cub yelped. "There goes another five credits. Oh well. I'm just glad she found some friends. Thank you."

"For what?" Marsee asked, confused as she had nothing to do with the cub.

"For being brave enough to share your experiences with the Council. There are quite a few in my district alone who owe their lives to you."

Marsee nodded and glanced at Aris, who had a knowing smile on her face, before looking back at the Councilor. "If you'll excuse me, Councilor? Guild Master Agate is expecting me."

Goodwin tilted her head. "Of course. Have a good night, Leviathan Slayer."

Marsee grabbed her drone and bolted as quickly as she could without appearing to be fleeing from the Councilor, but once outside the Market, she sighed. "Please tell me, I read Goodwin correctly."

"She appeared to be telling the truth," Aris said, then stopped her drone and faced Marsee. "Do you see it now, how much you matter to people like Councilor Goodwin? Her daughter has a much better chance of surviving now because of you."

Marsee nodded. "That may be, but my orders stand. If it's between me and Little Flower or Hope, or any of the Hue-mans, for that matter, you protect them first."

Aris nodded and grinned. "Spoken like a true Honor Guard. Now, come on. It's getting dark, and I'm in no mood to play another round of Save the Leviathan Slayer."

Marsee groaned. "Why do I have a feeling that's going to be a regular drill in the Guard from now on?"

Aris chuckled but didn't reply as she returned to scanning the area for threats.

A few minutes later, they were outside the public entrance to the Guild. To her surprise, the doors were locked, and a large sign had been taped to the front, stating they would reopen in the morning. She'd never known the Guild to be closed or locked, even in the small city of Sand Dune, where she'd had most of her training. Someone was always posted at the public entrance.

Aris frowned at the sign, too, and had her wait by the desk while she confirmed the hall toward the offices was secure.

Marsee ran a paw along the top of the counter, the last place she'd seen Iruki before the meeting.

"When did you know Iruki was involved?" Marsee asked quietly.

"When Clear Seas called out her name," Aris replied, then checked the door to the warehouse on the other side of the counter. The sounds of beeping machinery caught her attention, and she saw someone moving a large shipping container before the door slid shut again.

"And you didn't pick up on her threat before that?" Marsee asked.

Aris shook her head. "The problem with being able to sense people's emotions is that you can't tell what they're really thinking. They could be angry at you or angry for you. While Iruki's skin showed rage, she was also terrified, and I suppose rightly so. Instinct or otherwise, it's in our very nature to fight for survival. Everything happened so quickly that I honestly couldn't tell if Agate was kidnapping you or Iruki was attacking. I didn't even know that Iruki wasn't her full name."

"Neither did I," Marsee admitted.

She wondered what she'd done to incur such wrath with Iruki or if Rip had twisted her full of lies, too. She turned and looked back in the direction of the Council Building, not that she could see it, wondering if Iruki and the others were dead yet and wondering what it would do to the Seniors. Would her father and uncle survive killing their friends and coworkers, or would they struggle like she had after killing Rip?

"I don't know how they're going to do it," Marsee said softly.

"They're Senior Council. They'll do what needs to be done to protect the people, even at their own detriment, just as you did for Stormy. It's why they were voted back in. But if they can't, the Guard will assist."

Marsee sensed sadness from Aris. "I take it there were people you cared about brought in?"

Aris let out a heavy sigh. "I knew most of them. I've been with the Guard for a little over eighty years, and with Kendra as my mentor, I've been all over Saber and the five planets. A few were close friends, people I thought lived with honor. One used to be a member of our squad until just recently. I honestly can't believe she was involved, but it would appear your sister was right. I wonder if we have the right to call ourselves the Honor Guard anymore."

Marsee considered. "Your oath is to the people, is it not?"

Aris nodded. "Our oath is much the same as the Council's. Only we have the added stipulation that if found guilty of any crime, we can and will be executed."

"Rip was a twisted, evil person, but he preyed on the belief that my family had too much power, and in that regard, he was right. I know my father and uncle would never abuse that power..."

"Your family's honor has never been in question."

"To you perhaps, but not to others. If you believed that the Senior Council was acting without honor, what would you do? And would removing them not be honoring your oath to the people, even if it was treason?"

Aris sighed and nodded the point. "That doesn't justify the means in which those actions occurred. When the Senior Council intended your sister and her people harm, Kendra acted to ensure that they couldn't. I, along with several squads of guards, were sent to the Agency to protect them, with orders to bring the Seniors in for trial if they attempted to go forward with those plans. That could very well have been considered treason, but Kendra was justified in those actions because the Council was under trial in the first place. There are procedures and protocols on how we're supposed to handle situations like this. Kidnapping and torture is not one of them."

"And what if you felt like those procedures and protocols weren't being followed or honored?"

"I, as a citizen, have the right to step forward at any council meeting and bring forth charges against any member of the Council, just as young Stormy did. Your father arrested Rip Current on nothing more than the words of a child and was duty-bound to investigate. If he didn't, or if the people voted him out and he didn't step down, then and only then would the Guard have had the right to remove your father, by force, if necessary. If Rip or the others felt that your father and uncle were abusing their power and had proof, they could have brought it forth at any time, but I don't think he did. If he had that proof, he wouldn't have tried to fabricate it."

She frowned. "He knew far more than he should have about me, like the flag on my medical record. Even just bringing it forward, whether I denied something happened or not, would be enough to tarnish my family's reputation."

"And without proof or your word, it would be considered libel," Aris replied.

Marsee nodded the point and swam off.

Agate wasn't in her office yet, so she continued on to Ellie's, intending to wait there. Aris took up guard outside the office, but Marsee didn't swim in, stopped in her tracks at the sight of Ellie's vacant desk. She'd been able to forget her worry about Ellie with her stress and nerves of the day's meeting and everything that had happened, but the sight of the empty seat hit her hard.

"What's wrong?" Aris asked gently, picking up on her mood.

Marsee gave a slight snort. "What isn't?" she replied. "I'm worried about Ellie and terrified about being good enough to honor her legacy if she doesn't survive."

"I'm not," Aris said.

Marsee looked up at the guard with a raised brow.

"Ellie is one of the most stubborn and tenacious people in the known universe, your sister aside. She survived what Rip did to her for hours. She'll have no problem surviving a failed heat. But even if she doesn't survive, you'll make an excellent Senior Guild Master.

Will you make mistakes? Absolutely. Nobody's perfect, but you have your mentor's tenacity and your parent's honor, and that's more than enough."

"Thanks," she said and finally swam in. With a heavy sigh, she sat in Ellie's seat and pulled out her tablet to begin working.

Agate arrived a few minutes later and stopped short in the open doorway.

Marsee looked up as Agate flashed a heavy sigh and swam in.

"I'm pretty sure I had the exact same expression a few minutes ago," Marsee stated. "And thank you again for saving my life earlier today."

Agate's skin flashed a rainbow of emotions. "I can't believe Iruki was involved or that she would try to attack you, or any of the others for that matter."

"Neither can I. Have you reviewed what the Seniors had on them? I haven't been able to bring myself to look yet."

"I have. We have a mess to unpack," Agate replied with another heavy sigh.

"I was afraid of that." Marsee tilted her head as a thought occurred to her. "Clear Seas said Iruki was stealing. Was that why she was working the front counter? I thought that was odd."

"She was in charge of the warehouse until about a year ago when I promoted her to my Senior Staffer after my former Senior retired. She told me she missed working with the public and that it was a welcome break from staring at reports all day. She often covered if someone needed a break and no one else was available. From what was posted, she was stealing inventory and re-selling it. We'll need to do a full inventory of the warehouse, which I've already ordered, and review every report she touched, starting with what we need for tomorrow."

Marsee groaned. "I think it would have been far less painful if you'd just let her zap me."

Humor bubbled across Agate's skin. "You're probably not wrong there. I could oblige if you're really interested."

She pretended to consider the offer for a moment and then shook her head. "I'd say yes, but I really don't want to lose my fur again. It itches something fierce coming in, and with my luck, it would turn green this time."

Agate grinned. "I hear green is quite popular, but let me know if you change your mind."

Chuckling, they went to work, but it wasn't long before Marsee found herself seriously considering taking Agate up on her offer.

2 2

MARCUS: LOSS OF CONTROL

Marcus sighed as he watched as the body of another close friend was dragged out by a pair of guards. He was only about halfway through his Council, and he wasn't sure how he was going to finish.

He moved to follow after, but Kendra raised a paw to stop him and then shut the door. "Councilor, you need to let us take over now or take a break and continue tomorrow."

He looked up at her, surprised, trying to understand why she would stop him. The longer he waited, the greater chance someone else would get hurt.

She reached down and lifted his paw, and to his further surprise, it was shaking. "You're starting to lose control."

Am I? he wondered. He didn't feel like he was. He felt numb. He'd pushed his instinct and emotions down harder than he had ever pushed before. It was the only way he could keep going. If he hadn't, he would have stopped with Trisha. He didn't feel out of control, but then he hadn't even known his paw was shaking. He stared at it, willing it to stop, but it didn't.

"Please, sir. Let me finish the rest for you. It's what I'm trained to do, and I don't have the emotional attachment you do."

Marcus nodded, recognizing that it wasn't a request. If he said no, she would kill him. He supposed it didn't matter. Whether he did it himself or watched, the result would be the same. He would be responsible for their deaths. He knew, though, that if he stopped, he would never find the resolve to finish.

To his surprise, she didn't test him, but she did insist that he wait until his paw stopped shaking, then led him through a breathing exercise. When they were done, his paw was steady again, along with his resolve. She examined him closely for a moment before stepping aside.

It was close to midnight before he was done with the last of them. His legs held long enough for the guards to carry out the body before he sat hard. He closed his eyes and focused on his breathing again. He heard the door shut and the beeps as Kendra both locked and overrode his authority to open it. He half expected her to kill him right then and there for his slip earlier, but nothing happened.

Eventually, he opened his eyes to find her sitting in front of him with an unreadable expression.

"Are you ready?" she asked.

He took a deep breath but nodded.

She reached over and gently but firmly grabbed his head.

He felt his instinct stirring with the threat. *Better this than we hurt someone later,* he thought.

"Turn it on," she ordered.

He honestly wasn't sure what would happen, but to his relief, it felt no different than normal.

"Can you understand me?" she asked.

"Yes," he replied, and to his surprise, she removed her paws.

They sat there staring at each other in silence for some time. "For what it's worth, I am proud of you, Councilor."

He raised a brow in question.

"Not many would have been able to do what you did."

"I gave an oath," he replied.

"And I have seen lesser people crumble under the weight of that oath."

He nodded the point.

"You can turn it off now."

He did, thankfully without issue, and let out a sigh of relief.

She raised a brow at his reaction. "You were worried?"

"Of course," he replied. "Weren't you?"

"Not particularly," she said. "If there were issues, you would have reacted when I locked the door or when I grabbed your head, especially since you don't trust me."

"Fair point," he replied and stood, thankful to see his legs no longer shook.

She stood as well and unlocked the door.

Without another word, he made his weary way back to his office, where he found Jer waiting for him.

"It's over?" Jer asked as he set the large stack of papers he now had to review and record down on his desk to deal with in the morning.

Marcus nodded, but he couldn't pull his eyes away from the stack as the tremor in his paw returned, and his body began to shake uncontrollably.

Jer walked over and grabbed him tightly in a hug.

He leaned into the embrace as he fought hard to regain control. He couldn't even make himself warn his brother.

"It's alright, Big Brother. Let yourself grieve. I've got you."

The sob he'd buried broke free, and tears streamed down his face. Jer held him tightly as he cried and shook from the grief he'd kept locked down through the ordeal, still unable to pull his gaze from the stack. It was a long time before he could regain control. When he did, Jer insisted on escorting him back to his suite and refused to let him spend the night alone. He didn't argue.

They both chose to ignore Kendra and the squad of guards, who followed them discreetly. More guards were stationed outside his suite when he arrived. He ignored them, too.

Once in the suite, he walked straight to his bedroom, not really seeing any of it, and sat down on the edge of the bed, staring down at his paws.

Jer followed right behind, then unclipped his carry harness, tossed it over the back of a chair, and stretched.

The sounds of his brother's back snapping and popping made him cringe. He hadn't really understood what his niece had meant about wondering if she'd ever get the feel of Rip off her claws or how a sound could be so triggering, but he did now.

He'd killed before, many times, but those deaths hadn't hurt. They hadn't been his friends, his peers, his love. They hadn't betrayed him. Most had already been lost to their psychosis, so he'd seen it as a mercy.

He wondered if he'd ever forget the feeling of Trisha's neck snapping or the image of her face as her soul departed from her eyes, and he wondered how many more times he'd have to fulfill his oath before this was all over. He still had the guards back home to deal with, although thankfully, there was no emotional attachment there. He made a vow to do for Kendra as she had done for him.

Jer walked over and sat down in front of him, lifting his head. "They made their choice, and they died painlessly, which is far better than they deserved."

"It doesn't make it any easier," he whispered.

"No, it doesn't, but then no one else on your council had the courage or integrity to step up and do what needed to be done," Jer replied. "I think, perhaps, because none of us would have survived. Now, you know the drill."

Marcus snorted. "Don't you think Kendra tested me before I left the last cell? She made me stop performing the executions halfway through as it was, not that I couldn't still feel it every time."

"I'm sure she did, but that was before you allowed yourself to feel," Jer replied. "Unless, of course, your hesitation is because you feel like you're going to lose control."

He rolled his eyes at his brother's teasing but turned his instinct on. "You've developed such an attitude, Senior Councilor. I think I liked you better when you were a cub."

Jer chuckled. "If you think I have an attitude, you should try working with my council sometime." He shook his head. "I honestly can't believe they re-elected me, although I wonder if they would have if we'd waited to hold the vote until after sentencing Damon."

"They had more than ample opportunity to vote you out after," Marcus replied. "Of course, we could have removed them and you from office, but I doubt that would have gone over well either."

"Well, all but Henry," Jer replied. "Turn it off."

Marcus did with a yawn as the last reserve of his energy faded with his instinct.

Jer reached over and unclipped his harness. "Come on, big brother. You need your rest. Morning will be here soon enough, and Senior Councilors don't get snooze buttons."

Marcus snorted. "Who told you that nonsense?"

"Papa," Jer replied with a grin. "The day after I was elected."

"What does he know? He was never a Senior Councilor or even Acting Senior," Marcus said, shrugging out the harness.

"Are you planning to tell him he's wrong?"

"Have you lost your ever-loving mind, Jer? Tell Papa he's wrong? If you think I hit hard…"

Jer frowned at him. "When did Papa ever hit you?"

"Jeran Frederick, I love you, but you are so clueless sometimes. How do you think I knew how to help you, or why Papa stepped down so soon after I passed my Junior Advocates test, or why I never ran for Senior Councilor even before you had issues?"

Jer blinked at him. "You're serious? *You* lost control?"

"Once, but not during the test, about a few months after. I don't think anyone knew besides Papa. Senior Councilor Edent never said anything to me about it, and she was ruthless when it came to psychosis."

"What happened?"

"I fell in love, and she chose someone else. No one was hurt, and I never even made it out of our house before Papa stopped me."

"I'm not sure what surprises me more, that you lost control or fell in love," Jer teased, his tail curling in amusement.

"Watch it, cub," he growled, but Jer's tail only curled further.

"So who was it?" Jer asked. "Do I know her?"

When Marcus failed to answer, and a sob escaped his control, realization crossed Jer's face, and he pulled him in for another hug. "Oh, I am so sorry."

When he finally pulled himself back together, he climbed onto the bed.

Jer curled around him, purring, holding him together like he'd done for Jer only days before, and for much the same reason. Tears slid silently down his face again, this time unchecked.

"Why didn't you let me do it?" Jer asked.

"Because as annoying and clueless as you are sometimes, cub, I couldn't bear the thought of losing you, too."

2 3

MARSEE: ICE GIANT TRANSPORT

It was midnight before Marsee called it quits, with plans to meet up again in the morning. The Seniors had thankfully adjusted the start of the meeting to after the noon meal to allow everyone time to recover from the day's events, so they still had several hours to finish up their adjusted reports.

Aris took her down a different path through the Guard Complex and around the Council Building. Guards were out in force as they approached the rear of the building. Several ships were parked out back, but she wasn't particularly paying attention.

She had the niggling feeling that she was missing something important about the reports they'd reviewed, but she couldn't figure out what. So it was with some surprise that Aris suddenly raised a paw to stop her. Only then did she refocus on her surroundings and realize what was happening.

The ships were being loaded with bodies.

Clear Seas floated outside the door, his face an unreadable mask and his skin emotionless, but he was rubbing at his hands. Marsee recognized that motion. She found herself doing the same often, not from the pain of her injuries but from trying to get rid of the feeling of killing Rip out of her claws.

They watched until the last of the bodies were carried out, and the ships flew away. Clear Seas watched the ships, but she watched him. Only when he thought he was unobserved did his mask slip and grief show on his skin. With a heavy sigh, he turned to swim back inside but caught sight of her floating there and stopped short.

She nodded her head in respect to him for having the strength to see that justice was served. Considering how conflicted she felt after killing Rip, she could only imagine what he was feeling now.

He didn't move for several moments, and she wondered what he was thinking. He was too far away to sniff out. But then, without a word, he turned and swam inside.

A few minutes later, they pulled up outside the platform. Marsee hung up her drone and stepped through the shield, grateful that the lobby was empty, save for a pair of guards on patrol.

As they waited for the lift, Marsee's tablet dinged with an updated agenda for the following day. Half a dozen items had been pushed to the end of the meeting or dropped entirely, while others had been moved forward.

Busy reading through the details, she barely noticed as Aris directed her onto the lift when it arrived. She was in the process of typing up a reply to Agate when the lift stopped, and the door opened.

With her attention still focused on her tablet, she misjudged the opening, bouncing her shoulder off of the edge of the door. That was a common occurrence, which she barely noticed, but she also missed the fact that the lift had stopped just short of the floor. She tripped over the small ledge as she stepped through and her tablet was knocked out of her hands as she stumbled and nearly fell. She would have if Aris hadn't caught her.

"You're supposed to go through the doorway, not the wall," Aris teased.

Marsee snorted at her, "Now you tell me." She picked up her tablet, checking it for signs of damage. Relieved to find it unbroken, she clipped it to her harness and kept walking, but she only made it a few steps when she stopped and gasped.

"What is it?" Aris asked, instantly on alert and scanning the halls for monsters.

Marsee ignored her as she followed her thoughts, connecting piece after piece, and pulled out her tablet again to confirm her suspicions.

Realizing that Marsee wasn't reacting to an external threat, Aris calmed and waited for her.

"Aris, how many guards *are* available right now? Can you call in a squad you trust?" Marsee asked without looking up.

"Why?" Aris demanded, reaching for her stunner again.

Marsee looked up at the motion and noticed that Thatcher, guarding their suite, had her stunner out as well and was scanning for threats.

"We have some investigation to do, and I want backup. Have them meet us at the terminal. Thatcher, stay here and let Little Flower know I'll be a while."

Marsee clipped her tablet back on her harness and started trotting towards the terminal as Aris called in her orders, then ran to catch up.

To her surprise, not only was a squad waiting for her when they arrived, but Kendra was leading them. She'd expected Kendra to be busy and for Avery or others to appear, but she didn't know any of these guards. She wondered how they arrived so quickly.

"What's going on?" Kendra demanded.

"It may be nothing but an exhausted and overactive imagination, but my...crawly senses are tingling," Marsee replied. "There's a guild shipment scheduled to go out in a few hours. In light of what happened today, I want to confirm that what's on that shipment is actually what's supposed to be going out. I have a feeling Iruki was up to far more than stealing and reselling a few items. I wanted backup in case someone tried to stop me from finding out."

Kendra nodded. "That's a reasonable precaution. Do you want us hidden or visible?"

She considered. "I could really use your help locating and checking the containers against the manifest, so...visible. I'm also not sure exactly which ship it would be or where it would be parked. I know it's being shipped to the Ice Planet and scheduled to depart tomorrow morning, scratch that, this morning, at ten."

Kendra pursed her lips but pulled out her tablet and, a moment later, took off at a fast trot.

Marsee had to run to keep up. They bypassed the public terminal and went through a door marked staff only.

Kendra used her authorization to access another lift system, and a few moments later, they were on the top of the platform.

A cold wind whipped her cape hard the moment they stepped out. Several Sprites were about in transport carts, but most people were off-worlders. It didn't take long for people to notice them and stop what they were doing to watch.

Kendra led her to the far side of the terminal, where a massive cargo ship was being loaded. It was nearly as big as the ones Ellie had commandeered to build New Hope after the Trial. A stack of shipping containers was piled haphazardly off to the side, with more being delivered.

She sensed nervousness from just about everyone at their approach. Even though she knew anyone would be nervous with a squad of guards bearing down on them, especially in light of recent events, she wasn't letting her guard down this time. She'd learned that lesson the hard way with Iruki.

One male Ice Giant broke away from the group and started walking towards them. She'd never paid particular attention to how big the males were before, but he towered above her. She shifted to stand on two feet to make herself appear taller.

"Is there a problem, ma'am?" he asked in his language.

"That's yet to be determined, Ship Master," she replied in his. She didn't often get to speak Ice Giant and hoped she was pronouncing everything right. "Your manifest, please."

He handed over his tablet, and she confirmed they were loading the shipment she expected, but there was far more on the ship than just the manifest she wanted to check. She tapped a claw on her tablet as she considered, then copied the manifest to her own tablet before passing off the Ship Master's tablet to Kendra. "Check every container," she ordered.

Kendra shared the manifest with her guards, who split up, half making their way onto the ship, while the rest, including Kendra and Aris, followed her over to the stack yet to be loaded.

She scanned the first container's manifest to confirm that it matched what was on her list, then opened it. At first glance, it appeared to be the scrap wood listed on the manifest, but she wasn't taking any chances. She started digging, but after only going down a few inches, she found a tray or something under it. Shifting to the side of the container, she found the edge and lifted it aside with Kendra's assistance.

She didn't even have to say anything.

Kendra hit the comms on her harness. "Command, this is Kendra, code 3A, platform surface, north quadrant. Requesting backup and authorization."

"Granted. On my way. Squads Saber Three and Four assist. Sprite One on standby," a voice replied. By the tone, she guessed it was a Water Sprite, although they spoke Saber.

Several sharp 'yes, sirs' replied immediately, which gave her a pretty good idea who it was.

Marsee waited, taking Kendra's lead as she wasn't sure what the protocol was at this point. A minute later, sounds of a ship breaking through the surface roared through the night air, followed by another from the other side of the platform. No one moved as the first of the ships landed nearby. Two squads of Saber guards swarmed off as the second, far smaller ship landed next to it.

Kendra flashed several signs that Marsee didn't know. One squad bolted for the transport ship while the second formed up behind them.

She heard the sounds of a ramp extending and turned to face the second ship. Moments later, a Water Sprite exited in one of the mobile carts. Lit up as the platform was, she had no problems identifying the Senior Honor Guard. She stepped forward to meet him.

"Translator, what's going on?" Stinger asked.

"Smuggling," Marsee replied. "I had a feeling more was going on than what was entered for evidence against Irukandji and the others arrested from the Guild today. Among other things, several reports weren't adding up. I decided to come here and check the cargo before it shipped and asked Aris to call in backup, just in case. This container was the first we opened. The manifest states it should be scrap wood."

Stinger peered inside to see an entire pod full of high-end tablets. Sitting on top were seven standard units.

If she had to guess, they were the ones that she'd handed to Iruki to recycle. One she recognized as her father's old tablet because of a scratch in the case that she had put there during a fit of anger the week before.

The briefest hint of a sigh crossed Stinger's skin before he turned. "Ship Master, you and your crew are under arrest for smuggling, and your ship and cargo impounded."

"I swear, I knew nothing about this," the Ice Giant replied as one of the guards cuffed him. "I just load the cargo and take it where it says to."

"Then you have nothing to worry about," Stinger stated. "Until then, your cooperation is appreciated."

"Yes, sir," he replied, allowing the guard to lead him off without further resistance.

Guards began dragging others off of the cargo ship. Once everyone loaded, the guard ship took off.

Marsee sighed as the ship dove below the surface. "Well, let's see what else we can find," she said, then began digging through the next container.

As she expected, every item on the recycled materials manifest was full of high-value items, buried under a layer of whatever scraps the container was supposed to hold.

At first glance, the other containers all appeared to be what was on their manifests, but she knew differently. Every item was marked as lower quality than what was being shipped. A guard might not recognize it, but she did.

It took several hours to document and move the evidence. When that was complete, Kendra disconnected the ship's navigation system, which contained the flight logs, and essentially scuttled the ship. With that in hand, they boarded Stinger's ship and returned to his office. Guards were still about everywhere, and she saw several more bodies being carried off, but she did her best to ignore it.

Kendra and Stinger began interrogating those brought in while she and Aris reviewed the flight logs, which she correlated with her guild reports, manifests, and the evidence the Seniors had released.

By the time the interrogations were complete, Marsee was grabbing at what little fur she had on her scruff. "This is far bigger than Iruki."

"That's an understatement," Aris replied. "You need to stop hanging around your uncle."

She snorted. "What I can't tell is if this goes all the way up to the Council in these districts or not. They signed off on the trade agreement, but that doesn't mean they knew anything about what was happening."

"Agreed. What we have is circumstantial at best. It's enough to warrant a deeper investigation, though."

She nodded and made her way into Stinger's office, where he and Kendra were deep in conversation. She reviewed what she'd found with both Senior Honor Guards, and they shared the results of their own investigation, along with random bits of information they'd been gathering since everything had started.

By the time they finished recording everything, the first rays of early morning sunlight were starting to shine through the window of Stinger's office.

"This is all new to me," she said. "What's the protocol now? Do I inform the Senior Council, or do you?"

"Typically, it would be the Senior Honor Guard in charge, but..." Stinger started and hesitated.

"None of us are in the Senior's good graces right now," Kendra finished. "I think it would be best if you presented it. Besides, this was your investigation from the start. Both Stinger and I have reviewed all of the evidence the Seniors uploaded, and neither of us realized the true extent of what was going on. Good work, Honor Guard."

It was all Marsee could do to keep from snorting at the title or the praise.

"The Seniors are all in their conference room," Stinger added.

"How do you know that?" Marsee asked, surprised that he'd anticipated her question and had the answer.

"Comms chatter. It's all in code, so you wouldn't have recognized it," Stinger answered.

Marsee nodded the point. She had stopped paying attention to the constant noise hours before. Grabbing her cloak, which she had taken off earlier, she flung it back on, clipped her tablet in place, and swam out before her nerves got the best of her.

2 4

TEMPERATE: SQUAD MATES

Temperate swam through the far emptier halls of the Sea Patrol. Like the Guard, it had been gutted. The press had barely mentioned those in the Guard and Sea Patrol who had been arrested and executed, focusing only on those in the Council and guilds. He supposed that made sense. The general public wouldn't know most of the others, but he did. So many of those he had worked with, considered friends, and trusted to watch his back were now gone, including a member of his own squad. Those who remained were silent, grieving, or angry. No one spoke or even acknowledged him as he swam past.

His squadron commander looked up at his knock on the door and motioned him in. "I have a bit of a problem."

Temperate snorted at the understatement. "Do I even want to know, or should I just hand in my resignation?"

His mentor gave a slight shrug. "Probably the latter. As I'm sure you've realized, we're down a total of fourteen squads. It's even worse in several of the other districts. I've promoted just about every junior pilot we have to fill those slots, but it's not enough. We'll run a modified flight plan and schedule for the foreseeable future while we get the Trainee's up to speed. We're dropping from four shifts down to three and combining several squads."

He flashed his understanding. He'd expected as much. "Who am I getting? Or am I being reassigned?"

"That's my problem," she replied and leaned back in her net. "I have one pilot who has been refused by every squad leader, and I imagine you can guess who that is."

"He's not returning to the East Sea District?" Temperate asked.

"No. They've flat-out refused him, as has every other Squadron Commander on the planet, and he's requested to stay here to be closer to his daughter, if at all possible. For whatever it's worth, he will be watched by a member of the Guard. It would give your squad an extra ship. I'm not ordering it. I'm asking. I honestly don't know who I can trust enough to foist him off onto. If you don't want him either, I'll find something for him to do, but he is a Master pilot, and you are currently down one."

He sighed. "I honestly don't know how I feel about the whole situation. I certainly don't trust him, but Little Flower did advocate for leniency, and she wouldn't have done that if there was any evidence that Snapper really knew what Rip intended."

"I honestly can't believe she did that," she said.

"Neither can I," he replied and sighed. "I suppose if Stormy can make friends with his daughter, I can work with him. I'll take him on a trial basis. I don't want him near my ship or anyone else's, and if he so much as twitches wrong…"

"You have my full authority to zap him if he so much as looks at you the wrong way," she replied. "If I were you, I'd place him as permanent bait."

He snorted again. "That reminds me. Have you spotted that rogue elder again?"

"No, and Bessie's been rather stationary lately, too. She hasn't left the Trench in several days. We can't get a good fix on her from the satellites either. She's too deep. So I don't know what's up. It's possible she was injured in a fight with the other elder and is hiding until she's recovered, but she'll need to hunt soon, and if she's injured, she'll go for an easy target."

"You're full of good news today, aren't you?"

She chuckled, then leaned for the comms unit on her desk. "Snapper Fish, report to my office immediately."

Immediately turned out to be about three minutes, and he was escorted by a member of the guard—not one he knew particularly well, but one who had a reputation. Obsidian was known for being as hard and cutting as his name, but he was normally stationed on Council Duty because of his rather impressive size. He wondered why this particular guard was here.

Snapper swallowed hard when he saw him there, but Temperate maintained the calm mask he'd spent several decades perfecting, or at least he hoped he did. He'd already reconciled the fact that he would likely see, if not work directly with Snapper, although he hadn't planned on having him on his squad.

His mentor leaned back in her net again and glared at Snapper Fish for several long moments. "I am not happy you're here, but I'm apparently stuck with you as no one else will take you. Temperate has graciously agreed to let you fly on his squad. You're on probation and will follow his orders without question. Is that understood?"

"Yes, ma'am," Snapper Fish flashed and turned to him. "Thank you for giving me a chance."

He grunted and swam out. Snapper and the guard followed him to the flight deck, where the rest of his squad was waiting for him. To say they were not impressed by their new squad mate was an understatement.

"I am not flying with that, that...traitor," his Wing Second flashed.

"Then you can find another squad," Temperate replied. "For better or worse, he's part of my squad now."

His second scowled and swam off.

Temperate sighed with disappointment and turned to the one remaining member of his original squad, a young Junior Pilot, talented but still inexperienced. He'd only been on the squad for a few months. "What about you, Waves?"

"I'm staying, sir. Someone has to keep an eye on him."

He snorted as Waves was half the size of Snapper Fish and unlikely to be able to do anything if Snapper tried something, any more than his brother had with Rip. "Well then, Congratulations on your promotion, Wing Second Rolling Waves." He turned to the guard. "What do you have for patrol and flight experience?"

"I started in the Patrol, two decades out of Cross Current before moving here and joining the Guard. For what it's worth, I volunteered for this mission and agreed to move wherever Snapper was stationed, as did the other members of my squad, but if you want someone else to watch this miscreant, there's a long list of volunteers to pick from, and I won't take offense."

He squinted at the guard. "Why did you volunteer? You were on Council Duty before, were you not?"

"As your Second stated, someone has to keep an eye on him, and my squad has a vested interest. One of the still missing guards is my younger brother."

Snapper swallowed hard at this.

"Are you going to be able to remain professional while guarding him?" Temperate asked.

"I took an oath, and I know what the consequences are if I don't, but I promise you this. If I have even the slightest inkling that he's up to something or hiding information, I will personally make his life as miserable as he made his daughter's and the Translator's as I drag him back to the Council for sentencing. He may have helped uncover the scum hiding in our ranks, but that's only because he's scum himself."

A slight flicker of fear crossed Snapper's skin before he controlled it, and the guard seemed pleased by that reaction.

"That may be, but I won't allow threats under my watch either," Temperate replied. "I expect you to be professional and work as a team. That includes protecting his back as you would any member of your squad. This is your squad now. Our lives and the lives of the people we protect depend on it. If you can't do that, assign someone else. If I see any signs that you're abusing or continuing to threaten him in any way, I will report you."

Astonishment flashed on both their skins. The guard nodded but didn't leave. Temperate turned to Snapper Fish. "I don't trust you, but my father would be dead now if you hadn't shared what you'd known. That is the *only* reason I'm giving you a chance to prove yourself and make amends. Don't fuck it up."

Snapper flashed his confusion. "What does that word mean?"

"It's a Hue-man swear. If you impress me enough with your flying today, I might just tell you the meaning. To your ships."

"Sir!" the three snapped and bolted in the direction of their ships, although the guard made sure Snapper was on his first before boarding his own. Temperate watched for a moment before boarding his own ship, wondering if he hadn't hit his head harder than he thought in his two prior accidents for agreeing to this in the first place.

Once he was strapped in, he powered up his ship and the comms. "Command, this is Squad One, reporting for patrol."

"Squad One, Copy. Safe Patrol."

As one, his squad rose up and flew out as if they had been flying together for years. The first half of the shift was fairly uneventful: one broken-down shuttle that needed to be towed in, a few ticketed off-worlders for flying outside of the travel lanes or not obeying speed limits, and chasing off one lazy, overgrown blubber-fish that had decided to take a nap against someone's front door and pinned them in.

It had taken all four of them nearly half an hour to shove the creature far enough away from the door for the citizen to be able to leave their home. It was one of the few creatures immune to their shocks. The thick layer of blubber provided it ample protection, and as it was twice their size and poisonous to just about every creature in their ocean, it had no natural enemies, so it didn't care the least that they were poking and prodding at it. It was comfortable, and it had absolutely no intentions of moving. The squishy texture made it nearly impossible to grab ahold of, too.

"They'd be cute if they weren't so big," the citizen commented after thanking them for the rescue. "They're friendly enough, at least."

He snorted. "This thing is more likely to sit on you than eat you. I recommend you put in an order for a second exit. I recognize this home is grandfathered in, but it is out of code, and the Council will cover the cost of the upgrade."

"Yes, sir," the citizen replied and thanked them again.

They had just swum back onto their ships when a call came in from Command. "Squad One, satellites are picking up a rather large heat signature heading slowly towards the Northern Corridor. There's no transponder, so I'm guessing it's our visiting Elder."

"Squad One, Copy. Requesting backup."

"Granted. Squad Two and Three, assist."

"Copy!" The other two squad leaders replied.

The coordinates and satellite imagery were sent to his ship, and he took off, punching the engines. His squad followed, and a minute later, they had visuals. He whistled. "She's as big as Old Bessie, that's for sure.

"Are you sure it's not Bessie?" Waves asked. "Those scars on her dorsal fin look the same."

He frowned and zoomed in on her. "You're right. They do look similar. Command, do you have a fix on Old Bessie?"

"Same place she was the other day. Her transponder hasn't moved," Command called back and sent him the coordinates. "But we can't get a heat signature on her. She's too deep."

He frowned at the information and then shrugged. "Well, we'll have to try and tag this one either way."

Just as he said that the Leviathan spotted them and screeched but then turned and swam back towards the Trench.

He swore under his breath. "If she makes it to the Trench, we'll lose our chance to tag her. Snapper, you're bait. Waves and Obsideon, you keep her distracted. I'll tag."

To his credit, Snapper didn't question being placed as bait and took off immediately, as did the rest of his squad, but the moment they started heading towards the Elder, she screeched again and picked up speed, swimming hard for the Trench, making it there, just before they did.

He muttered a few more Hue-man swears as he stared down into the darkness of the Trench. His sensors showed her diving deeper than their ships were rated to go, and eventually, she disappeared entirely.

"I have no idea what any of that meant," Obsidian replied. "but my sentiments exactly."

When the two other squads arrived, he split them up and had half fly in the opposite direction as they patrolled the edge of the Trench, hoping to draw her out. Eventually, they flew over the location indicated by Bessie's transponder. It was deep but just barely within reach of their ships.

He tapped on the controls. They really needed to know what was up with Bessie. Had she lost her transponder, was she dead, or were there two Elders in the area?

"I'll go," Snapper said.

He frowned. It was one thing to play bait when you had visuals on a creature, but another entirely when you were the one entering their domain. What's more, it was the same location where Marsee had been held and where they had dumped Rip's body. The place felt cursed, and every scale on his body said to leave.

"No. We'll all go," he decided. "The more eyes we have on this, the better."

Taking a deep breath, he dove. Surface light vanished immediately, to be replaced by the light of his ship, which automatically turned on. Even added to the other five ships, it did nothing to illuminate the gloom. His ship creaked and groaned with pressure as they dove deeper than he'd ever flown or swum, yet it wasn't anything compared to what Stormy had endured on his own.

Their sensors picked up nothing as they approached Bessie's transponder, and when they finally found it, Temperate swore again. It was resting on the same ledge where Stormy had found Deep Current.

"Well, that answers that question," Wave's commented. "At least we don't have two Elders in the area."

He grunted and unclipped his safety harness. "Command, I'm exiting my ship to retrieve the transponder."

"Copy," Command replied.

He took a deep breath before swimming through the static shield that kept the deeper pressure of the ocean out of his ship, but it was still excruciatingly painful. He grunted and swam hard for the transponder, wondering how Stormy had endured the pressure, but he forgot the pain as he picked up the transponder and examined it. He didn't have a swear strong enough to cover the fear and astonishment that hit him.

"What is it?" Obsidian asked as Temperate's skin revealed what he was really feeling.

He turned to face the ships and held up the two pieces of the transponder. "She didn't lose it. Someone cut it, and they left it here intentionally for us to find."

25

MARCUS: 2+2=6

Marcus woke with a groan as his brother tried to climb off the bed quietly and failed.

"You would have to be an early riser, cub," Marcus muttered. "You do realize I suggested the adjusted start to the meeting today so we could sleep in."

Jer chuckled. "Sorry. You know I can't sleep once the sun's up."

Marcus groaned and buried his head under his pillow, which only amused his brother more.

"You sound just like Marsee every time I had to wake her for school. She always insisted that school started far too early in the morning, but then, like you, she was often up half the night reading."

He snorted. "You know, I felt the same way as a cub. Maybe I should change that. I'm sure I could use the bump in ratings right now."

Jer chuckled again and made his way out into the common room.

With Jer out of the room, Marcus tried to drift back to sleep. His father might not believe in snooze buttons, but he did. Those few minutes always produced the most interesting dreams.

Long before his alarm went off, Jer started making a racket as he dug through the refrigeration unit.

Marcus nearly climbed out of bed just to claw his brother for making so much noise, but he had absolutely no desire to get out of bed and face the empty seats of his gutted council. As it was, if his brother hadn't been with him the night before, he'd have probably hidden in the depths of the Archives for the next century or three.

He felt the bed shift as Jer sat down next to him.

"Come on, big brother. You can't hide in bed all day. We have work to do, and breakfast is ready."

Marcus growled at him and thwapped his tail in warning, even though it had never done any good before.

"If you weren't always such a grump in the morning, I would be far more concerned about your growling," Jer teased. "Do I need to call Kendra?"

Marcus pulled his head out from under the pillow and glared at his brother. "You're clawing a very fine line this morning, cub."

"Perhaps, but that's nothing new. Now, come on. You have a Consortium to put back together."

"I quit," Marcus muttered, flopping back down on the bed. "I did the dirty work. Let somebody else figure out the rest."

Jer laughed. "Sorry, that's not allowed. If I can't quit, neither can you. If it would help, I could slap some sense into you, like you did with me." Jer lifted a paw and wiggled his claws with a wicked grin.

"Try it, and I'll consider it an act of war," Marcus growled but sat up anyway. His brother was obviously not going to allow him to hide in bed all day, and he was right. There was work to be done.

Jer looked up at the ceiling and pursed his lips. "It might be worth it. My one-person army is quite skilled with a stunner, better than *your* guards anyway."

Marcus snorted, but he couldn't argue the truth of that statement. "Are you appointing her as Senior Honor Guard then?" He was surprised as Jer appeared to actually consider it.

"Who knows? She is training with the Guard. Perhaps she'll decide to change guilds again. Regardless, I am moving forward with having our own guard stationed permanently in New Hope."

"You're going against your council's wishes?" Marcus asked, surprised.

"It's more than time for one, and after everything that's happened, we clearly need one. If anyone says otherwise at this point, I'll bring them in for questioning. I am not leaving my people or my family unprotected ever again."

Marcus nodded and made his way out into the common room. "Good. I never liked that decision, but I understand why they made it, and I respect you for honoring it. So, if not Little Flower, who do you intend for your Senior Honor Guard? Quinn's stationed there now, isn't he?"

"Avery, probably, unless Quinn decides he wants to move."

"Avery?!" Marcus exclaimed. "You're pulling my tail."

Jer shook his head.

"Why him?"

"Avery and his squad have been protecting my people from the beginning. More importantly, Marsee seems to trust him, and he's nearly lost his life three times now trying to protect her. Four, if you count his injuries when she tried to take her life."

"That may be, but he nearly got her killed, too."

"We all make stupid mistakes, brother. If we're lucky, we live long enough to learn from them, and he has added incentive now to keep my family safe and prove himself. Besides, half his squad is already stationed there."

"What if Marsee doesn't return to New Hope?"

"Then I'll pick someone else," Jer replied. "But I have a feeling she'll return once she's cleared to jump. Her watch is a formality at this point, and it'll take a month or two to build a barracks anyway."

Marcus grunted acknowledgment, stretched, and made his way into the waste room. He used the shower three times but still didn't feel clean, even though there was nothing on him. When that failed, he tried scrubbing at his paws in the sink, but that made no difference either. He knew it never would. Sighing, he stared at his reflection for several moments, honestly surprised to see the same face reflected back when he felt so very different this morning.

I wonder what history will make of me now? he mused. *Hero or a villain?*

They ate quickly, purposely ignoring the news and their tablets, and made their way back over to the conference room. Guards were out, but thankfully few others as it was still very early.

Everyone but Apakna was there, but no one was moving or talking when they entered, and the others all had the same haunted expression he knew was on his face. Even Sammianna looked haggard, and she'd had the least to kill. He took his seat with a sigh. "So is it done then?"

"Not even close," Clear Seas replied. "I didn't even get through a quarter of my council last night before I quit, and I have three who are demanding a trial before the Full Council."

"Our decisions were unanimous," Sammianna said. "Do they have grounds to warrant it?

Clear Seas shrugged. "All three are stating that they believed Rip intended to press charges against Jer and Marcus during the meeting, not kidnap, murder, and extortion, and are claiming that the evidence against them was fabricated."

Marcus's ears flicked back in surprise. "What charges were they intending to bring forward?"

"Marsee's medical flag," Clear Seas replied dryly.

Jer sighed with evident defeat.

Apakna walked in at that moment but didn't take her seat. Instead, she practically ran into the waste room, slamming the door shut behind her. Moments later, they heard the sounds of her being sick. No one said anything until she returned to the room and slumped in her seat, burying her head in her paws.

"Can I get you anything?" Clear Seas asked quietly.

Apakna sighed. "An extra large bottle of Fuzzle Knockers would be really nice. Three would be even better."

Jer snorted, but Sammianna frowned.

"I don't think attending the meeting drunk would be a good idea," Sammie said.

"And I don't particularly care," Apakna growled back.

"But your rankings are nearly low enough to trigger a revote now as it is," Sammie continued, frowning with worry.

"Perfect," Apakna said. "Clear, make it four bottles."

Clear Seas bubbled with humor. "Well, one glass won't hurt. I know I could use one."

Marcus turned and looked at Clear Seas, ears back with astonishment. "Seriously?"

"I'm with Apakna. If the people can't handle it or don't understand, then I look forward to being voted out and making this someone else's problem," Clear Seas replied. "Besides, it wouldn't be the first time I've attended a meeting drunk." Clear Seas swam back with the bottle and the Sprites equivalent to glasses for everyone. The bottle was already half empty.

"How much have you already had?" Marcus asked.

Clear Seas lifted the bottle and shrugged. "Not nearly enough." He poured out drinks for everyone except for Sammianna, as it wasn't safe for her species. As far as Marcus knew, they didn't have any form of recreational narcotic.

For all of his complaints, Marcus downed his glass in a single gulp, for once reveling in the burn of the beverage.

Apakna downed hers, lamented its empty state, and then grabbed the bottle and refilled her glass. No one tried to stop her.

"If I fall asleep during the meeting, Clear, I give you permission to zap me," Apakna said after downing that glass and pouring another. "I haven't been to bed yet. I just finished the last of them."

"Well, you're in luck. I'm completely drained," Clear Seas replied. "I don't think I could make a spark right now if my life depended on it. In case you're wondering, thirty-two."

"That many?" Jer exclaimed. "That's far more than the Senior Healer implied. How did Marsee survive?"

"I have absolutely no idea," Clear Seas replied. "Placement or species difference, perhaps? I can kill one of my own in three seconds. One. Two. Three." He took another swig of his drink. "Rip should have been able to easily kill Marsee, Stormy, and the three of us and still have charge left over."

"Well, he did knock out a number of people before," Marcus said.

"I could do that all day and not run out of charge," Clear Seas replied. "It's the difference between lifting my tablet and lifting you."

"I thought it took several minutes," Jer said. "That's what the Senior Healer implied."

"No, that's how long we can maintain a full charge without resting, typically. But, like with anything, the more you practice, the stronger you get."

Clear Seas looked down and rubbed at his hands. "I've seen the scars your daughter now carries far too many times. All of my people would recognize that she'd been shocked. Accidents happen fairly regularly, especially in our youth, but few would know what I know. Few would have ever seen it in person. She took a lethal charge, Jer. It should have killed her."

"We knew that," Jer said.

Clear Seas shook his head. "Jer, we watched him shock her for far more than three seconds, and he had multiple contact points, which makes it lethal at a lower amperage, especially when crossing the body as he did. I couldn't believe she was able to fight back at all, even if it had been a non-lethal charge. I had convinced myself that Rip hadn't been trying to kill her, but her scars tell a different story. Whether Rip intended it or not, she took a lethal charge on several occasions, not just that last time."

Clear Seas unclipped his tablet and pulled up footage from one of the executions. "The length could be from both duration or amperage, but it's this mark here where the scars originate. This only occurs above a certain amperage, which in my species is fatal. She has that same mark on all four contact points and both sides. And what's more, the length of the pattern is longer than I've ever seen on anyone, alive or dead. That's what made me forget myself yesterday. I honestly don't know why I didn't recognize it before. Perhaps it was the cast she was wearing or the lighting in the restaurant."

Jer reached over and poured himself another drink. Marcus didn't blame him one bit and considered grabbing another one for himself, even though he detested the taste.

"So what are we going to do about your councilors, Clear?" Marcus finally asked. "If they're telling the truth, we have no right to execute them, but if we let them go and they try to bring forward Marsee's medical flag, all of Saber will be harmed, and Marsee's reputation will be ruined."

Apakna looked up from her drink. "What are you talking about?"

"Three of my councilors said Rip intended to charge Jer with abuse and Marcus and Kendra for hiding it and are claiming the other evidence was planted," Clear Seas explained.

"Lowell didn't find any other altered evidence," Apakna replied.

"With Snapper Fish's account," Sammianna said. "That doesn't mean he didn't have someone else doing the same with the others."

"I'm more than willing to stay those executions until we can confirm if that evidence had been altered," Wind Rider stated.

"Wouldn't that invalidate all of our convictions?" Clear Seas asked.

Marcus let out a heavy sigh as he thought about Trisha but shook his head. "No one on my council denied their other crimes, although several claimed they didn't know what Rip was planning. I'll second a stay on those executions until an investigation into those claims can be completed."

"And if they were fabricated, what then?" Jer asked. "How do we protect Marsee or Saber?"

"I don't know," he replied. "If they're telling the truth, then we should be able to tell them the truth. I'm more concerned about who else knows and might use it against her."

There was silence for a moment until Wind Rider spoke. "Has anyone dared to watch the news or look at the boards this morning?"

"It's exactly as bad as we expected," Sammianna replied. "The press, as of an hour ago, was still digging through the evidence and reporting on what we found. My queue is buried in appeals and requests to review cases brought before the…removed councilors. The public boards are in an uproar, nearly split between those who believe us and those who don't. A fairly large number are in agreement with those who claimed that we were the ones attempting a coup. No one believes Marsee's statement about Ellie needing to leave for a family emergency since Ellie doesn't have a lot of family. Most seem to believe that we purposely kept her away, as we did with Temperate and Petra, and are waiting for her statement, although a few seem to believe we got rid of her, too, and put Marsee in her place. We might have to put out a statement there, although people were impressed with Marsee's performance yesterday, especially once the press reported on the full details of her contributions."

"As was I," Clear Seas replied. "I wasn't expecting her to take over from Agate, but she handled her part flawlessly, and I see no grounds to deny her promotion. She's certainly earned it."

"She's come a long way from the shy cub I once knew," Marcus said. "Ellie's done wonders with her. She'll make an excellent Senior Guild Master someday."

Clear Seas stared at him for a long time. "You've changed your mind about her? Haven't you."

He nodded. "I suppose that's the one good thing that happened yesterday. If she had been lying or somehow deceiving Rowena about not being able to use her instinct, it would have been apparent to everyone. Her instinct wouldn't have let her freeze when Irukanji attacked, certainly not for as long as she did. Plus, her instinct would have been to fight back with teeth and claws, not scramble for her stunner. She's changed, too, and I don't even know how to explain it. Her whole demeanor has shifted. The timid cub I once knew is no longer there."

"What she's been through would change anyone," Wind Rider replied. "I know it's changed me. I honestly don't know how she swam into that chamber yesterday. It took everything I had to swim through that door, and I haven't been able to get Petra to leave the ship since the moment she left the Trauma Center."

"Trauma affects people differently," Apakna stated. "Some people it destroys, others it hardens, like tempered steel, and after what she's been through, what's a few grumpy councilors?"

Marcus snorted. "It was far more than grumpy councilors, and she knew it, too. You saw her when she swam in. She didn't say a word, but her silent lecture was far more eloquent than Clear Seas speech."

"And here I was trying to be as loquacious as you," Clear Seas replied with mock indignation.

"That was your first mistake," Sammianna replied, causing everyone to burst out with surprised laughter, even him.

"Just out of curiosity, Jer," Clear Seas said when the laughter died down. "When did Little Flower become so good with a stunner? I only received notice of the requisition a few days ago. Has she been training in New Hope?"

"On Earth," Jer replied. "Her father was a guard and taught her how to fire a projectile weapon that they used to have. She told me back before the Trial that she was considering joining a competition team right before the Cataclysm. One of the first things I did as Senior Councilor was ask her if she wanted a stunner, but she declined it then. She and the rest of the Hue-mans didn't want weapons or guards in New Hope because of their past history of abuse with them. Needless to say, I'm changing that, too. I've already had more than a few people ask about requisitioning their own, and I've granted it. You should have a record of it in your queue by now."

Clear Seas looked away for a bit. "You know, part of me always wondered if she was exaggerating to make her species appear tougher, but no longer. Even with her injuries, she reacted faster than the Guard."

Jer glared at Clear Seas and looked like he was about to say something, but Clear Seas raised a hand to stop him.

"I mean them no harm, Jer. I certainly don't have the moral high ground to state that our species is any better, not anymore, and I'm honestly relieved that she has a way to protect herself. I'm curious, though, why none of Marsee's guards opened fire."

Jer flicked an ear back in a half-shrug. "I spoke with Avery last night while you were all...busy. He didn't have a clear shot and was worried about hitting Marsee. With her new heart, it could have killed her. I confirmed that with Hyacinth. As for Little Flower, she apparently beat the simulator without a single missed shot on her first attempt, and they're already working to make it more challenging for her. Avery believes she could outshoot anyone in the Guard."

"Was Avery injured?" Wind Rider asked.

Jer nodded. "He was receiving treatment at the time I called him and claimed he'd been shocked worse in training when I asked him, but the Senior Healer said otherwise. If it weren't for Little Flower, he'd be dead. She was keeping him overnight for observation but expects he'll make a full recovery."

Wind Rider nodded, and Sammianna flicked on the monitors to review what the press was reporting. It was even worse than what Sammianna had stated.

Fifteen minutes in, Clear Seas reached over and poured himself another drink, and his skin rippled with amusement as Marcus tossed his own glass over.

He'd just finished downing his glass when there was a knock at the door. No one moved.

"How much do you want to bet it's more bad news?" Wind Rider asked.

"I'm not touching that bet," Sammianna replied. "I'd lose either way."

Clear Seas snorted, and his skin rippled with amusement before he swam over and opened the door, flashing surprise, then concern.

Marsee shifted uncomfortably. "May I come in?"

"Of course," Clear Seas replied.

Marsee swam in and nodded to everyone. "Councilors, I'm sure the last thing you want to hear right now is more bad news, but..."

Apakna actually snorted.

"I told you," Sammie said.

"Oh, go curl up in your shell," Wind Rider muttered back.

Marsee stared at them, ears flicked back in disbelief at the insult flung at Sammie, then confusion as Clear Seas bubbled with laughter.

Marcus rolled his eyes, then let out a heavy sigh that came out almost in a growl. "What's wrong *this* time, cub?"

Clear Seas immediately shifted from humor to the bright red of anger and honestly looked ready to attack.

Jer snorted with surprised laughter and put a hand up to stop Clear Seas while Marsee looked at all of them with added confusion as Apakna reached over and poured herself another drink.

"Sorry, Kitten," Jer said and waived his other hand in Wind Rider and Sammie's general direction. "Ignore those two. They're worse than the Guard when it comes to bets, and I wasn't laughing at you. Your uncle has used that same tone and phrase with me at least once a week since I joined the Council. In this room, the rules of expected decorum are usually dropped. It's the one place we can be ourselves. Welcome to the club."

Clear Seas calmed his skin, realizing he hadn't insulted Marsee, and motioned for her to take a seat.

Marsee's tail curled, but he could tell she was nervous as she fidgeted in her seat and took a deep breath before starting. "As I'm sure you're all aware from your investigations, Iruki ran the warehouse until last year when she was promoted to Senior Staffer. In addition to what you found, we believe that she was involved in a fairly extensive smuggling operation."

"Who's we?" Clear Seas asked.

"Senior Honor Guard's Hunt and Stinger and Honor Guard Aris," Marsee replied.

"Why didn't one of the Senior Guards present this?" Marcus asked.

"Both Seniors stated that they felt it would be received better if I delivered it," she replied.

He grunted, acknowledging the point. "They're probably not wrong. Tell us what you know."

She spent the next hour reviewing everything they'd found. He was both impressed by the thoroughness of her investigation and horrified by how deep it went. Sammianna dug through the reports Marsee brought with her, double-checking the math as they grilled her on the evidence. She handled the interrogation like she'd been in the position for decades, not two days, and outside of her initial nervousness, she showed nothing of the easily intimidated cub he once knew.

His thoughts drifted back to the previous conversation, and he wondered if her change in behavior was related to her training, the experiences of the past few weeks, or her loss of instinct.

"Marsee, you've always struggled with math. How did you figure this all out?" he finally asked.

She looked around the room, hesitant for the first time since she entered. "Don't get me wrong, I'm still horrible at math, but Ellie knew that when she took me as her protege and has been attempting to knock some sense into me. Personally, I think it amuses her, as it gives her an excuse to hit me with her tail when my eyes inevitably glaze over."

She rubbed her head as if she had a headache, causing several in the room to chuckle.

"Thankfully, math had little to do with it, at first anyway. I think I might have found it sooner if I hadn't second-guessed myself. The first report I showed you, Agate, and I had actually reviewed the other night, and I struggled hard with it. I kept adding two and two together and coming up with six."

Sammianna snorted. "You really are bad at math."

Marsee grinned. "So my instructors regularly informed me. But it wasn't just the math. There was a whole list of things that didn't make sense. First, Iruki was still working at the front desk and in the warehouse after her promotion. Agate said Iruki enjoyed the break from staring at reports, but that's usually a position reserved for Apprentices. It would be nearly as unusual if Ellie staffed it. I didn't even realize Iruki was Agate's Senior Staffer until two days ago because I only ever saw her at the desk. Secondly, her increased guild rate would have more than made up for the added income brought in by what you found. Third, I couldn't figure out why she attacked me, as she'd shown no signs of negativity towards me in the past, and everything you posted stated she was mad at Ellie and Papa, not me. Fourth, it didn't make sense for Rip to advocate building a major shipyard. Why spend all that credit when you've already negotiated a lucrative trade deal that would be completely negated by the completion of that shipyard, and why build it right next to where you're doing something illegal?"

"We're pretty sure he was trying to lure you and Ellie out there," Marcus replied.

Marsee nodded. "That was my first thought, too, but it wasn't until I walked into Council Platform that it hit me, quite literally. I was in the middle of reviewing the updated docket for today when I tripped and bounced off the side of the lift door and dropped my new tablet."

Marcus chuckled.

Marsee scowled at him, and flickers of orange appeared on Clear Seas skin again.

"Marsee is a menace to stationary objects when there's a book or tablet in her hands," Marcus explained. "She destroyed a good dozen bookshelves in my library when she was a cub. I had to put guard railings up to keep it from happening again. I'm honestly surprised she hasn't walked off her tower balcony yet."

"I probably should warn your guards about that," her father mused.

She rolled her eyes but otherwise ignored their teasing. "The shipyard is months behind schedule, partly because people kept quitting, stating that the build was haunted by the ghosts of the two killed, but also because critical components kept arriving damaged. That's the whole reason we came in the first place. But then I wondered if it was all related. According to the evidence you posted, Iruki was marking inventory as broken when it wasn't and reselling it, which made me wonder if the parts sent to the shipyard weren't actually damaged or if they were damaged on purpose."

"Did you find anything," Sammianna asked. "Ellie stated she was looking into that several days ago."

"She never mentioned anything to me, but when Ellie and I went to the warehouse to get our new tablets, we found the entire shelf empty. Ellie went to find Padina to see what was going on. We found Padina and Iruki in Padina's office. They were looking at something on a tablet when we entered, and we scared them. At the time, I thought we'd just surprised them, but now I think they were actively talking about what they were doing."

"What time was that?" Wind Rider asked.

"About an hour and a half or so before I came here," Marsee replied.

Wind Rider wrote it down, and Marsee continued.

"When questioned about the tablets, they indicated that there was a manufacturing defect identified in the latest batch and that they were checking them over. Neither of us thought anything of it at the time, but when I dropped my tablet, I realized the entire shelf of tablets was missing, not just the latest batch. There are always several years worth of models available because most people can't afford the latest model."

"They could have been checking that the older models didn't have the same defect," Sammianna said.

Marsee nodded. "That was my thought initially, but there's more. Later, when Iruki brought up the tablets, she also brought a manifest for Ellie to sign. Ellie got a call at the same time and had me handle the manifest as a training exercise, which happened to be almost identical to the one Senior Councilor Wind Rider had me review. I realized last night that Iruki signed off on the manifest that Wind Rider had me look at, and I pulled up other manifests and saw that Iruki and then Padina signed off on all of them, so there was no reason for her to have Ellie do it. That's when I realized that the call Ellie had taken was with Padina as she was talking about more damaged shipments. I couldn't figure out why Padina would call if she knew Iruki was on her way up unless it was to distract her while signing the manifest, to make it seem like Ellie was involved. Iruki had seemed annoyed, but at the time, I assumed it was because of my questions, not because their plans had been foiled. Then, last night, when I arrived at the Guild, the door to the public entrance was locked, and when Aris checked the warehouse entrance before letting me in, I heard the sounds of equipment and saw shipping containers being moved about, which reminded me about the recycled materials shipment. On the spur of the moment, I decided to check to see what was actually in that shipment before it left because if she had been hiding something and thought I had found out and reported her for theft, it would explain why she attacked me."

"Well, math skills aside, I can't find fault in your reasoning or intuition," Sammianna stated. "That shipment you intercepted was worth a small fortune."

She nodded. "What do you want me to do about my report for the meeting later? The numbers are going to change fairly significantly from what people are expecting. Do you want me to present what we had before or these?"

Marcus replied first. "Update your reports, and if anyone asks, state that you reviewed everything that Iruki and the others had touched based on yesterday's events, but don't mention anything else about what you found. We'll take it from here."

She nodded again and stood. "Let me know if you need me to look into anything else."

After she left, they all stared at the closed door for several long moments. No one spoke.

"Bottomless crevasses," Apakna muttered. "How did she manage to figure that out? She only had a fraction of the evidence we do, and we couldn't figure out how it all went together."

"Like with Wind Rider and Petra, she's the only one that had all the relevant information," Marcus replied.

Apakna tilted her head, acknowledging the point, but sighed and poured herself another drink.

"What is it?" Marcus asked.

"There's one piece of information Marsee didn't uncover," Apakna said and downed the glass in a single gulp. "Or she was polite enough not to mention it."

"Oh?" he asked when she didn't elaborate.

"My uncle is the one that initially negotiated that trade agreement with Rip," she replied.

"There's no evidence that your uncle knew what was going on," Sammianna stated. "We already know that Rip wanted to put Iruki in Ellie's place, and I've read through your uncle's account going back years and found nothing of concern."

Apakna raised a brow at Sammianna.

Sammianna cocked her head slightly. "Based on your expression, I gather you're surprised?"

"I am. Why? Did you not trust me to investigate him fully?"

"Trust has nothing to do with it. While reading through Rip's journal, I realized that there was nothing negative written about your uncle. In fact, quite the opposite. Rip hated everyone, but he respected your uncle. That stood out as an exception and made him a person of interest. I read every bit of communication between your uncle and Rip going back to before Rip was in office. I found nothing that would indicate he knew what Rip was doing. I believe Rip was protecting the one friend he actually had. On top of that, Iruki didn't move from Rip's district to Council Platform until about a decade ago, when she took over the warehouse, which is around the same time that Marsee's evidence shows the first signs of smuggling. I see no grounds to arrest your uncle for Iruki's crimes. Padina and the other warehouse seniors are a different story."

"Do we arrest them now or wait?" Wind Rider asked.

"We wait till the end of the week and see if anyone comes forward," Marcus stated. "That goes for the pilots, too. We have no proof that they had any idea of what they were transporting. I suggest releasing them but impounding the ship and cargo and placing them under a watch with orders not to leave Council Platform. Let's see who they contact and if it leads to anyone else."

The others murmured their agreement, and after a quick break, they returned to the far more arduous task of dealing with the fallout from the day before. However, before they got very far, there was another knock on the door.

"Don't even ask," Sammianna told Wind Rider.

They all snorted, and Clear Seas swam over to the door again.

"Avery? What are you doing here? I would expect you to be watching Marsee."

"May I come in, sir?"

Clear Seas nodded, and Marcus noticed that his brother slammed his mask down hard.

Avery swam in and floated at attention. "I received a memorial transmission from Honor Guard Lyrik yesterday, which I only just read. There's information in the memorial that I believe you need. She was investigating Councilor Winthrope and two of his nephews who recently joined the Guard. It's not conclusive evidence, but there's definitely something going on in that district. I'm sure you know she was a member of my squad until just recently, and while I know you have little reason to trust me, I never once had reason to mistrust her. She's saved my life on more than one occasion, and I believe the evidence you had against her was fabricated to cover up what she found."

Marcus raised a brow. He'd seen a Memorium from her, too, along with Quinn's note about her death, but hadn't had time to look at it yet. It was fairly common for guards to donate some or part of their death benefits back to the community or Guard in general, and he had figured that was all it was.

Avery shared the information with them and waited in silence as they started reading it.

It didn't take long for Marcus's brow to raise. "Place Winthrope on a watch," he ordered Avery. "I want to know who he meets with and where he goes. I want an updated report daily. I'll order Quinn to bring in the two other guards for questioning, but keep this quiet with everyone else."

"Yes, sir," Avery said and left.

"Avery's right," Marcus said after the door shut. "This is all fairly circumstantial, but Lyriks death was suspicious. Her Senior and second failed to activate their cameras before arresting."

"Do you think that's our spy?" Sammie asked.

"It's quite possible, but regardless, there's not enough here to arrest Winthrope, even with everything else we found on him. What we do have is evidence that Clear Seas' councilors might be telling the truth. These records were all manipulated after we caught Snapper Fish. I'll have Lowell investigate."

There wasn't anything else they could act on with the evidence provided, so they set it aside and returned to dealing with the more urgent fallout from the day before.

Ten minutes later, there was another knock on the door. No one spoke, but Sammie shook her head at Wind Rider. No one laughed this time.

"The Hue-mans have a saying that bad things come in threes," Jer said when no one moved to open the door.

Clear Seas' skin rippled with a sigh, and he swam over to the door again, but he said nothing as Temperate swam in, carrying a small evidence box with him.

"What's wrong, son?" Clear Seas asked.

Temperate swam over and placed the box on the table before lifting out some sort of broken metallic object and setting it on the table next to the box.

He had no idea what it was, but Clear Seas evidently did, as his skin went solid white.

"My squad found this on the ledge outside of the lava tubes where Marsee was found," Temperate explained.

"What is it?" Wind Rider asked.

"It's a tracking beacon," Clear Seas answered before Temperate could. "We use them to track the Leviathan and keep them away from the population."

"We've confirmed that this one belonged to Old Bessie, the Leviathan that Stormy faced down," Temperate added. "And we've confirmed that it was cut, not broken."

"How in the bottomless depths did anyone get close enough to do that?" Clear Seas asked.

Temperate shrugged. "What we do know is that it happened before the meeting started. There have been reports of an untagged elder since my shift the night before."

"So it's possible that whoever did this has already been arrested?" Sammianna asked.

Temperate nodded. "It's possible, but it doesn't get rid of the threat of an untagged Elder."

"Make tagging her again a priority," Clear Seas ordered, "with a year's bonus for any squad that actually manages it."

"A year's pay?" Apakna asked.

"You're right," Clear Seas said. "That's not nearly enough. Make it two."

Temperate nodded and left.

When the door shut, they all turned and stared at the remains of the tracking beacon that still sat on the table where Temperate had set it. Eventually, Clear Seas placed it back in the evidence box and swam it over to the Pile before returning to his seat with a heavy sigh.

"Is it really that dangerous?" Apakna asked.

"More," Clear Seas replied. "My grandfather, as his first act as Senior Councilor, ordered the newly formed Honor Guard to tag every Elder they could using the newly acquired satellites. We lost half the guard in that effort, and we lose dozens more every year tagging the juveniles as they leave their nesting grounds."

"You lost half your Guard?" Sammie asked. "Why was this never reported on?"

"We don't want to scare people away. I don't think you can possibly understand the scale of these creatures and the danger they pose."

"I can," Jer said. "I thought Heela monsters were big, but the one I saw could have eaten our biggest transport ship in a single bite. The stunners on the Sea Patrol ships didn't do anything more than aggravate it."

"That's Old Bessie," Clear Seas said. "She was old in my grandfather's time. Like us, they never stop growing. Killing an Elder of her size would require the full charge of a contingent or more of our biggest guards. The one that killed Trench's brother was only a few years old, and twenty people lost their lives that day."

Marcus tossed his empty glass to Apakna as she started pouring herself another drink.

Everyone turned and looked at him. Clear Seas flashed his surprise. His brother had his ears pinned back, equally surprised, and Wind Rider groaned.

Apakna said nothing and tossed him his drink.

"Pay up," Sammianna said calmly.

"I don't think I've ever seen you drink that much in one setting," his brother stated as Wind Rider transferred credits.

"There's a first time for everything," Marcus replied. "You bet on me?"

Sammie nodded. "Wind Rider was convinced you wouldn't break enough to get drunk. Your aversion to any form of narcotic is well known, but if I've needed to resort to medicating my way out of this mess, I certainly can't expect you to do any less."

"You have a narcotic?" Clear Seas asked, flashing his disbelief.

"Not in the same way you do. It provides clarity, not obfuscation or incapacitation the way yours does. I believe the Sabers call it Bottled Digger. The only effect is a dulling of emotions. It's quite popular among our species."

"Why does that not surprise me?" Apakna asked.

They all laughed, and after another round of drinks, they got back to work.

Far too soon for his liking, his drink was gone, it was time for the meeting, and he had a splitting headache, which the pain blockers they kept in the room did nothing to help.

It was all he could do to maintain his mask as he swam out and took his seat, only to be faced with Trisha's now empty booth and the half-empty Council surrounding it. He wasn't a religious person, but he could have sworn he felt her presence glaring down at him. He knew he would probably never understand why she had done what she did, but it didn't make it any easier to bear.

Marcus, love, the rules don't bend for you. For you, the world is black and white, full of precedent and laws, but real life isn't like that. The sound of her words in his memory was nearly as clear as if he was still in the cell with her.

Perhaps not, but it's our job to enforce those laws and precedents, he mentally replied, trying to repair his broken heart and remind himself of what she'd done. *You knew the consequences and still chose to break the law, and you hurt my family in the process.*

I did what I thought was best for my people.

As did I.

He shook himself free of his imagination, and the weight of her presence lifted, but he nearly bolted out of the chamber a moment later, vowing never to drink again, when he heard a different voice in his thoughts, one not belonging to Trisha or even Ellie, who had first spoken the words to him.

It was not his own voice either, but similar and somehow far more primal.

No wonder they all died.

26

MARSEE: AUDIT

After leaving the Seniors, Marsee returned to the Guild and found Agate already in her office.

Agate looked up as she swam in. "You look exhausted. Couldn't sleep?"

"No. I haven't been back to my room yet. We have an even bigger problem than we thought. Do we have an inventory yet?"

"Some. Padina's still working on it," Agate replied. "Why?"

Marsee hit the privacy screen and slumped into the seat across from Agate with an exhausted groan. "Because the Guard impounded the transport ship last night. Every container was full of smuggled goods. I think we'll need to confirm the inventory ourselves."

"Bottomless depths." Agate's skin flashed defeat and grief. "I swear I had no idea what was going on."

"I know," Marsee replied. "I've been digging for hours. You can't tell anyone yet, by orders of the Senior Council."

"You think Padina's involved?"

Marsee nodded and caught Agate up on what she'd uncovered.

Agate's skin was solid black before Marsee was done.

"I don't know how we're going to keep the extent of this hidden for the next week," Agate said.

"We'll focus on items needed for today's session, overestimate the loss, and prepare for the worst," Marsee replied.

Agate nodded. "Well, come on. Let's go *help* Padina with the inventory."

No one noticed as they swam into the warehouse, which was as busy as always. Their first stop found more issues than expected. Agate was in the process of counting when Padina arrived, swimming hard in their direction.

"Guild Masters, I was informed you were here. Can I help you find something?" Padina asked. Her skin was blank, but it was obvious she was nervous.

"We're all set," Marsee replied. "We're just checking on a few items before the meeting. How's the inventory going?"

"We'll have it done in an hour or so."

"So soon?" Marsee replied, honestly surprised. The warehouse was massive. "I'm impressed. You must have been up all night."

Padina nodded. "We've had a full crew working on it. We have found inconsistencies. I can send you the preliminary report."

Marsee nodded, curious if the items on the transport ship would be on there. Padina must have known that the ship and cargo had been impounded by now, but they'd purposely kept the results of their investigation hidden.

Padina unclipped her tablet, and a moment later, both their tablets dinged.

"Thank you," Marsee replied. "I won't bother you any further. Your work on the inventory is far more important."

Padina frowned and looked like she was about to say something.

Aris shifted slightly, and Padina quickly changed her mind and left.

Marse waited until Padina was out of sight before opening her tablet and reading the report, then sighed.

"That bad?" Agate asked.

"Worse," Marsee replied and handed over her tablet.

Agate scrolled for a bit. "Well, the numbers here match what she has listed. That's something, I suppose."

Marsee nodded, and they moved on to the next item. An hour or so later, they returned to her office to adjust the reports again using Padina's finished tally, which, for the most part, matched their own investigation. The few discrepancies they found were all minor and could easily be accounted for as a simple counting error. However, over time, those discrepancies could easily add up.

Marsee sent the updated reports to the Senior Council, then leaned back in her seat with a sigh as she looked at the clock, then over at Agate, who was watching her.

"If you'll excuse me. I'm going to curl up in a tiny ball under my desk for a bit."

"Hiding?" Agate teased. "Mind if I join you?"

Marsee chuckled. "I'm not sure both of us would fit under there, but I need a nap, or I'll fall asleep during the meeting."

"No worries, if you start to nod off, I'll make sure you wake up," Agate teased.

Marsee glared as Agate unintentionally mimicked Rip's actions in the canyon by letting out a tiny spark on her wiggling fingers, but Marsee quickly covered up her reaction with humor and waved her paw. "Poof. Apprentice. Now get out of here before I make you sweep the warehouse."

Agate's skin bubbled with humor, but she left. "Sweet dreams, Translator."

"Aris, I don't want to be interrupted for the next half hour unless there's an impending supernova. Scratch that. Don't bother me for that either."

"Yes, ma'am," Aris replied and hit the switch to shut the door.

She set a backup alarm, leaned up against her net, closed her eyes, and fell instantly asleep.

Half an hour later, she jolted awake as her alarm blared, threw her tablet across the room to turn it off, and closed her eyes again. She heard the door slide open but didn't bother checking as her nose told her who it was.

"I heard you had a busy night," Avery said and swam her tablet back over.

She snorted, then rubbed at her eyes. "Nothing escapes you, does it?"

"Sadly, far too much for my liking, but Kendra was quite impressed with you, according to the report I had from her this morning."

She snorted again, then frowned. "Where's Aris?"

"I ordered her to get some rest," he replied.

She grunted and climbed out of her net. She was about to swim out, but he held up a hand to stop her.

"I owe you an apology for the way I treated you last night. You were right to insist I get treatment for my injuries. I was far more injured than I thought I was, and I allowed my bruised ego to get the best of me. I promise to do better in the future."

She nodded. "Apology accepted. I'm just glad you're okay. I've grown rather fond of your bruised ego these past few weeks."

"You know, I'm honestly not sure if that's a compliment or not."

She grinned as she swam past him but didn't clarify. He followed, silently as ever, as she met up with Agate, and they swam over to the meeting together.

Little Flower waited for her outside of the chamber, but they didn't have time to talk. It was far too public of a venue to discuss what had happened anyway. After a quick hug, they swam inside and off to their respective booths.

She nodded to the councilor next to her and had only just taken her seat when the Seniors entered. Their faces were the same blank masks as the day before, but their bodies told a different story. They all looked as exhausted and weary as she felt.

Clear Seas took his seat. "This council is now in session. Before we start the planned agenda, there's a recent change. Guild Master Chenzira provided the Senior Council with updated reports following her investigation into the reports that *Former* Senior Staffer Irukandji had accessed or modified. Those updated reports are attached to the docket item. Guild Master Chenzira, if you would be so kind, please provide the Council with a summary of the changes."

She stood and took a deep breath to control her nerves. "I'll put it bluntly. The Council Platform warehouse is missing approximately ten percent of its inventory based on an audit that concluded about an hour ago, and initial reports coming in from other warehouses across the Consortium are showing similar levels of discrepancies, although those audits are not complete. We've adjusted the reports to account for expected shipments and..."

One of Saber's councilors slammed his button and stood, not waiting for Clear Seas to give permission to speak. "You've adjusted several districts by far more than ten percent, including mine."

She nodded. "Ten percent is the average for Council Platform. Your district, Councilor Withrope, provides a significant portion of the high-tech medical equipment used by the Consortium, which, unfortunately, was one of the areas we found gutted. Most of that tech was listed as critical and expected to ship out to local districts once the funding was approved by the Council today and will need to be replaced to meet the current requests. I don't know what happened to it as of yet, and I'm hopeful we'll find it miscategorized in another warehouse or that it's at least been put to good use if shipped to the wrong location. Until a full inventory can be completed, I felt it was best that we prepare for the worst, which would be if we had to replace everything."

Winthrope nodded and sat down.

Several other people hit their lights.

Clear Seas called on the first one.

"How did so much inventory go missing? I thought there were automated systems to prevent that."

"We've determined that many of the items were marked as damaged on arrival. That was one of the reasons Ellie and I came here early, as a higher than average number of items being shipped here were arriving damaged."

"So you believe there's a shipping issue?" the next person asked.

"I don't know," she lied. "We're looking into that, too."

"A number of the missing items you have listed were scheduled for delivery to the new shipyard. Do you believe Rip was involved in this, too?"

"That is a distinct possibility and is still under investigation," Clear Seas answered for her. "Our offer from yesterday stands. If anyone knows anything about the missing inventory, we request that you come forward within the allotted week."

There were murmurs throughout the chamber, but no one else requested to speak.

Clear Seas turned to her. "Thank you, Guild Master. We'll now move on to the first item. Councilor Garaptk, I believe this is your request. The floor is yours."

The rest of the meeting was reasonably uneventful, although there were several rather heated arguments as Councilors pushed her hard to see what they could get away with. She expected it and had come prepared. Still, she was honestly glad she didn't have any fur, as her tail would have been fully poofed — and not because of the negotiations. She was prepared for those. What gave her pause a time or two was the looks from members of her own council. She was too far away to sniff them out during the meeting, but unlike Councilor Goodwin the night before, those she passed during the breaks were decidedly uncomfortable being around her.

After Clear Seas called the meeting to an end for the day, she started to make her way over to her sister's booth but was stopped halfway by none other than Councilor Parner. He had once been her family's biggest thorn, but he'd survived the culling of the previous day and was still listed as her uncle's Acting Senior. She was honestly relieved. He'd become a close family friend during the month leading up to her sister's trial, and he was one of the only ones who had visited New Hope before the Hallowed Eve Festival. They certainly didn't agree on policy, but he'd been the first to admit he'd been wrong about her sister and her sister's people, and she respected him for that.

"Councilor," she nodded, sniffing deeply to try and get a sense of why he was approaching. He had the same hint of grief that everyone in the Council had, but she sensed no signs of malice or fear from him, which put her at ease.

He grinned at her. "I'm honestly not sure what title to use with you these days. Do you prefer Guild Master, Translator, or Leviathan Slayer?"

She snorted. "Good question. I'll let you know when I figure that out. Then again, wait a few days, and it might change."

A hint of a frown crossed Paxton's face. "I hope that isn't in reference to your mentor. Is everything okay with her?"

She plastered a fake grin on her face. "As far as I know, she's fine. I was referring more to the fact that Ellie likes to change my rank on a daily basis. It's a running joke between us."

"Ahh. Rumor has it she's not the only one. Is it true you demoted her?"

She chuckled. "I did, all the way back down to Apprentice. She was surprisingly happy about it, too. Granted, she got even by making me take point on the requisition meeting the next day. Needless to say, I reinstated her rank and seriously considered quitting the Guild after that."

Paxton's tail spiraled with humor. "I don't blame you. That being said, you seem to be doing an admirable job in her place. I was quite impressed today."

She flicked her ears back in surprise.

"I'm serious," he replied, and she could tell he was. "They were pushing you hard, and you were both well-prepared and far more stubborn than I think they were expecting."

"After the past two weeks, what's a few grumpy councilors?" she asked.

He snorted and then frowned. "Speaking of that. How *are* you doing?" She only sniffed concern from him.

"About as well as everyone else, I suppose. I'm recovering, but I imagine it'll be a long time before I'll feel safe again." She glanced around at the half-empty room and sighed, noticing that several were watching her conversation. "Thankfully, I have my guards to keep watch while I recover."

He gave a slight tilt of his head in acknowledgment. "I hear you're training with them?"

It was her turn to snort. "Word gets around fast."

"Your uncle mentioned it the other day," he replied.

She wondered just what else her uncle had mentioned and decided to keep her answer vague. "It's been a good outlet as I've worked through my trauma and honestly far more enjoyable than swimming laps in the Trauma Center."

He nodded again. "I'm glad. Are you planning to join permanently?"

"Oh gods, no. The last thing I want to do is spend my days standing outside a door and staring at a wall. I'd honestly rather attend requisition meetings."

"Somehow, I find that hard to believe. Staring at a wall sounds lovely right now."

She grinned.

"Well, I should probably be going. I have a committee meeting in a few minutes to deal with the fallout from your updated reports."

"Sorry about that," she replied.

"Don't be. I'd rather have accurate information now than deal with the consequences when the books don't line up later. I'm honestly impressed you managed to pull it all together in one night."

"I had a lot of help and haven't gone to bed yet. Thankfully, the days are shorter here because I have a feeling it's going to be another long night."

"Indeed," he replied, nodded, and swam off.

She watched him swim out of the chamber, still not sure why he'd sought her out. Then, with a shrug, she turned to find her sister.

WIND RIDER: SOURED OATH AND PRANKSTER GODS

ind Rider was so tired by the end of that day's meeting that she didn't even bother sticking around for the discussion that usually happened after and swam right out the other door.

The press was waiting outside, a respectful distance from the entrance, but they swarmed her the moment she swam out. "Not tonight," she said and kept swimming. They followed. "I'll give a statement in the morning, but right now, I have nothing to say."

To her surprise, they actually backed off. She wondered if that had anything to do with Little Flower stunning them the day before.

Maybe we should shoot them more often, she mused as she swam out the back door and straight up to the surface.

The sky was dark and turbulent, as were the waves that tossed her the moment she broke free, but she had grown up on the sea, and she had more than earned her name. As the largest female of her species, there were few storms that could ground her. Grinning at the challenge, she launched herself into the air and veered sharply as the wind fought her for control, pulling her away from the platform.

All thoughts of fatigue left her as she focused on the currents. Static electricity made her wings and scales tingle like the effects of bosa berry, and lightning flickered in the clouds above her, but she wasn't particularly concerned. Her entire body acted like a lightning rod, designed to redirect electricity away from her vital organs. If she were struck, it would hurt, but it wouldn't kill her. Rip hadn't realized that when he'd first tried to shock Petra.

If only she had screamed, she might not have had her wings broken. She chided herself for that unkind thought, as it wasn't her daughter's fault that she had been tortured by a monster.

She had to wait for her turn to enter the shield that protected the top of the platform and the ships that were docked there, but she didn't mind. She needed to stretch her wings. Taking advantage of the delay, she dove and spun, following one of the more interesting currents. She wasn't the only one out, she saw, as two other members of her council broke free of the ocean to do the same.

She had absolutely no desire to speak to anyone, but that didn't stop them from launching into the air and flying straight towards her rather than the platform.

"Unless it's an emergency, it can wait until morning," she called out, but they didn't respond or stop. The wind was whipping, so she couldn't be sure they heard her.

She flew hard to avoid them, but when she glanced back, they were still following. Sighing, she shifted her wings so they could catch up. "What is so important that it can't wait until morning?" she asked when they were next to her.

"Stopping you from exterminating our species," a male voice said above her. She had been so focused on the two that she hadn't seen the third person drop down from the clouds above her.

Claws raked her back as he slammed into her, but she spun and flung him off her, then dove to avoid the two females that lashed at her.

They dove after and started gaining on her. The ocean's surface was quickly approaching, but she didn't slow. Instead, she waited until the last second to open her wings.

Her muscles screamed as she banked hard into the wind, using it to increase her speed. She grinned when behind her, there was a sound of a splash. She risked a glance back and growled with annoyance to see that only one of the Nest Mothers had crashed, and the other was quickly catching up to her.

She didn't see the male, but she knew he would have had to pull up long before she did, and there was no way he could keep up with them. He was far too small.

Wind Rider slowed her pace slightly, allowing the female to catch up, then flared her wings and flipped around, landing neatly on the back of the other Nest Mother. With a screech of rage, Wind Rider snapped both of the Nest Mother's wings, then before the female could even cry out in pain, Wind Rider bit down hard on her foe's neck, let go of her wings, and rolled off.

The combined weight of her body and the g-forces of her roll snapped the female's neck. She let go the moment she was sure the female was dead, letting the body drop into the ocean below, then banked hard again, looking for the other two.

The female that had crashed into the water earlier hadn't taken flight again, and based on the sharp angle of one of her wings, she couldn't, but Wind Rider found no sign of the male.

As she scanned the clouds looking for him, she heard the sounds of wingbeats behind her and spun to see a pair of her guards flying hard in her direction. One pointed up and behind her, and she spun around again, catching a glimpse of the male, far off in the distance. He was making a run for it.

"Arrest her," she ordered. "I'll take care of him."

Not waiting for them to reply, she took off after the male, who had disappeared into the clouds again.

Two can play at this, she thought as she climbed into the clouds after him. There was no way he could outrun her, but he could hide in the clouds if he was smart, just as she could.

He was not smart.

Feather-brained weryling, she thought, when she caught a glimpse of him again, flying hard in the direction of the islands. *How could he have possibly thought he could get away?* Her target in sight, she flew hard, but only a minute later, a squad of ships flew past her, containing three

Sea Patrol ships and one Honor Guard ship, based on their colors. She expected them to try to force the male to land, but the Honor Guard ship fired, catching the male squarely in the back. She hovered and watched as the male fell.

Deciding the patrol had the situation well under control, she turned and flew back towards the Platform. With the immediate threat over, her back began to throb. Assuming the male was still alive, his interrogation and execution could wait until morning.

More Honor Guard ships flew out of the ocean and proceeded to help clean up her mess. She didn't stop. Not even waiting for authorization, she ducked through the shield that protected the landing platform and landed neatly next to her ship.

Only one guard remained on duty outside of her ship.

"Thank you for staying and protecting Petra," she said to him as she snaked her neck around to look at her injuries.

"Of course. You're hurt?"

"Not badly," she replied and palmed open the door.

Sun Chaser hissed and lunged towards her but skidded to a stop as soon as he recognized her.

She stopped the guard that turned to protect her. "It's alright. Where's Petra?" she asked.

"Locked in her room," Sun Chaser replied, then frowned. "You're hurt!"

"Not badly," she repeated. "I'll meet you in the med bay, but I want to check on Petra first," she said, then trotted down to her daughter's room. Once there, she knocked loudly. "Petra. It's me. I'm okay!"

The door slid open, and Petra practically ran into her, wrapping her neck around hers in a hug. "The guards said you were under attack before they ran out."

She nodded. "Councilors Hearth Fire, Dewdrop, and Pummace. Hearth is dead. I'm not sure about Pummace. He took a ship's stunner at point-blank range before falling into the sea, and I'm fairly certain Dewdrop has a broken wing. Either way, both will die tomorrow."

"Two more Nest Mothers?!" Petra exclaimed, then spun back into her room, kicking at a pillow on the floor. "I'm never going to be able to leave Flyer again, am I?"

"I know it's scary now, but I refuse to allow them to win. I will do everything in my power to make it safe for you."

To her surprise, Petra hissed at her. "Safe?! It will never be safe for me. Rip should have just killed me."

She frowned with worry. "You will get better. Please give it time."

"And then what?" Petra asked. "Spend the rest of my life in forced servitude and rape, trapped on Flyer unless I decide to join the Council and make myself a target again?"

"No, of course not," Wind Rider replied with a worried frown. "Where is this all coming from? I told you I changed the law after what Marsee told me. You are free to do whatever you want with your life."

"Thirty-six Nest Mothers will be dead by tomorrow. Do you honestly think anyone will let me get away with not doing my *duty*? What happens when our population plummets?"

Wind Rider walked into the room and up to her daughter. "I don't care what anyone else thinks. I am not and will *never* force you to mate. I will not force you to remain on Flyer or live a life you don't want. I will do everything within my power to see that you are able to live the life you dream, happy, healthy, and free, even if that means I clutch non-stop for the rest of my life."

"You would put my happiness before the extinction of our people? What about your oath?"

"I gave an oath to protect the rights of this Consortium, and I will always honor *that* oath. If we cannot exist without slavery and rape, then we do not deserve to exist."

Petra stared at her, slack-jawed in disbelief and amazement. "You're serious?"

She flicked her wings back in surprise that her daughter would even ask that question. "Of course I am! I knew what I was risking with my decision. But I also knew that if we had any chance of saving our society, I had to fight for the society I want for my people, for you. It doesn't matter to me what path you choose in life. It doesn't matter to me if no one else on our planet would choose your path. What matters is that you're happy, and I will fight to my last breath to protect your right to choose the future that is right for you. Just as I did today."

Petra swallowed hard with realization. "That's why they went after you?"

She nodded. "So Pumace claimed right before he attacked. It's not surprising, honestly. My queue is overflowing with requests for leniency for their Nest Mothers, including from other members of our Council, but even if I could, I wouldn't. It would put a handful of people above the law simply because of their biology."

Her daughter slumped and tucked her head under a wing in a sign of distress.

"What is it?" she asked.

"How am I going to face the people of Sea Cove and tell them no?" Petra asked from under her wing. "I asked for that station. They're going to be so disappointed."

"You asked under duress. It's no more valid than what Rip forced you to do. You tell them the truth, or I'll tell them for you. Perhaps it's time we spread our wings and find new nesting grounds, ones where our females can be anything their heart desires, and perhaps you're the one brave enough to take us there."

Petra came out from under her wing. "You mean that?"

"I do, and if that's truly what you want, then you need to put some effort into your physical therapy, Master Pilot. Only the fittest of pilots can handle the rigors of deep space exploration, and if I'm going to sponsor an expedition, then I want to ensure success."

"An expedition!"

She nodded, and Petra practically flung herself on her with another hug.

"Thank you, Mama! Thank you!"

She leaned against her daughter until Petra pulled away again, but instead of smiling, she was frowning.

"You're bleeding!" Petra exclaimed.

"It's nothing," Wind Rider replied. "I'll get it treated in a minute. How are you doing? You appear to be moving better today."

Petra shrugged and extended her wings a bit. The room was too small for full extension, but the grafts didn't look nearly as tight or raw as they had the other day. "Sun Chaser and I came to an understanding last night. I wouldn't bite his head off if he let me sleep for a full six hours."

She chuckled. "Six hours?! I'm honestly jealous. I can't remember the last time I've had a full six hours of uninterrupted sleep."

Petra nodded, then shrugged. "I think so. Then again, I wouldn't have put it past him to have changed the clocks while I slept."

She grinned at the reminder of the prank she'd played on Petra as a child. "Now, who would do something like that?"

Petra rolled her eyes and changed the subject. "I'm assuming you haven't eaten, either?"

Wind Rider shook her head. "No, I left as soon as the meeting was over."

"Well, you're in for a treat. Opal sent up another meal this morning, and there's still quite a bit left. Go get that wound treated, and I'll get it ready. We can talk about that expedition while we eat."

Wind Rider nodded and hugged her daughter again before watching Petra practically prance down the hall. It was good seeing her daughter excited again. Sighing with relief, she turned in the other direction.

Sun Chaser was waiting for her in the med bay and motioned her to the sensor plate in front of the monitor. "You lost a few scales, and you have a minor strain in your left wing, but nanos and a scale patch or six should take care of it." A few minutes later, the patches were applied, and nano cream rubbed into the muscle that she hadn't even noticed. She thanked Sun Chaser, then returned to the main room, where Petra had laid out several dishes.

She had just sat down in front of hers when a call came in from Clear Seas. She contemplated ignoring it but, with a heavy sigh, placed it up on the main window, deciding he wouldn't call without reason. The other Seniors were still with him in the Conference room.

"Word has it that you had an exciting flight this evening," Clear Seas said.

"You could say that," she replied. "I'm fine. Just a couple of missing scales."

"I'm relieved to hear it. I figured you'd want to know that Hearth Fire and Pummace are dead. Dewdrop has a broken wing, and my son found a ship and half a squad of your guards waiting for them on the islands. Pummace was leading you into a trap. Everyone is in custody."

She raised a brow. "Would I happen to know any of those guards?"

"Probably not. They're all Junior Guards from Hearth Fire's district."

She grunted with disappointment, hoping that they'd found their mystery Senior Guard. "Well, they can cool their wings until morning unless you feel the urge to ruffle them a bit before then. I'm going to have dinner with my daughter and then go to bed. I haven't slept in four days, and if I went back down now, I have a feeling I would kill them first and then try to ask questions."

"Pay up," she heard Sammianna say.

Clear Seas chuckled. "She figured as much when you didn't stick around after the meeting. Pleasant dreams, Councilor," Clear Seas replied and disconnected.

She yawned and grabbed a piece of food from the plate closest to her. She had no idea what any of it was, but their meal at Fire Sticks had been phenomenal. She popped it in her mouth and chewed. A moment later, her face contorted and puckered as a burst of sour flooded her taste buds.

"Do you like it?" Petra asked. "Opal said Little Flower ordered it, especially for you. Apparently, it's one of her favorites."

"Hue-mans," Wind Rider snorted, then shook her head. "I suppose I deserved it after yesterday's verdict."

"Why *did* you allow Damon and Snapper to go free and not the others?"

"I didn't initially. Before Tabor spoke up, we were nearly unanimous in our planned decision."

"*Nearly?*! Who was on their side?"

"Jeran."

"You're joking!" Petra exclaimed and grabbed a bite of her own meal.

"No. He had come to the same conclusion that Tabor had but didn't know what to do with either of them. He insisted their cases be brought before the Full Council, and Marcus seconded it. Even still, he and Marcus ultimately voted for their deaths, but their Advocates won over the rest of us."

Petra snorted, then fluttered her wings in a shrug. "Well, hopefully, they live up to the chance they've been given."

She nodded and grabbed another piece of the sour food.

"You're eating more of it? How? It's revolting!"

"No more so than anything we gave Little Flower to eat at the Agency. Besides, I recognize a punishment when I see it, even if it is disguised as a gift." She chewed slowly. "You know it's honestly not that bad once you get past the initial shock. Better than three-day-old stinky fish anyway."

Petra snorted. "Well, that's a matter of opinion. I'd rather have the fish. It's all yours."

"That it is," she replied and yawned again. "Every last sour bite. Now, about this expedition. Any idea where you'd like to go?"

Petra grinned and grabbed another bite of food before answering. "Earth first, then Sirius," she replied.

"Sirius? I've never heard of it. Is that a Hue-man word?"

Petra nodded and brought up a star map on her tablet. "That's their current name for it, but it was once known as Loki's Torch."

"Loki? The Hue-man's god of mischief?"

Petra nodded. "The one and the same. Can you think of a better place for a Flyer to visit than the home of the Prankster God?"

"No, I suppose not," Wind Rider replied. "Tell me more."

As tired as she was, she stayed up for another several hours as Petra told her everything she knew about the star and the Hue-man's

Trickster God. She didn't stop until Petra realized she was fighting to stay awake.

"I'm sorry, Mama. You need your rest."

"Don't ever be sorry for sharing your passion with me," Wind Rider replied. "I want to know everything, but if I don't go to sleep soon, you're going to have to carry me into my room."

Petra snorted. "The best I could manage right now would be to drag you by your tail. Happy dreams, Mama."

"You, too," Wind Rider replied, then hugged her daughter before practically crawling to her room. She was asleep before her head hit her pillow, but her dreams were anything but happy.

2 8

MARSEE: NIGHT WALK

Even though Marsee kept her meeting with Agate short that evening, By the time Marsee returned to the suite, her tail was dragging on the floor, and she didn't even bother trying to walk on two feet, even though her shoulder and paw hurt. She was pretty sure she'd strained something when she'd missed a jump on the obstacle course that evening and landed hard, but she was far too tired to bother with getting it checked out.

Hope was already asleep when she arrived, but Little Flower lay sprawled across the bed on her stomach, working on her homework for Ammond, tablet, and scanner in front of her.

She didn't bother taking her gear off as she crawled into the room and flopped across the foot of the bed, right in front of her sister.

"Watch it, Chenzie Butt!" Little Flower growled as she yanked her tablet and scanner from under her.

"I hurt. Will you check my shoulder and paw?" Marsee asked.

"Why didn't you stop at the Trauma Center on the way back?"

Marsee shrugged. "I didn't really notice until we entered the platform when I put weight on it. I didn't feel like turning around. I'm too tired."

Little Flower picked up her scanner. "So what happened last night?"

"I figured out what was going on. Iruki was involved in a major smuggling operation, not just theft."

"Huh," Little Flower snorted, her attention focused on the scanner. "I don't think you broke anything, but you might have torn something. I've sent the scans off to Ammond. Until I have permission to slather you in nano cream, take your stuff off, and I'll massage your shoulder while you tell me everything."

Marsee groaned her way up into a sitting position long enough to toss her stuff aside and flopped back down with another groan. She was halfway through telling her sister what happened when she yawned and fell asleep.

Only a few hours later, she jerked awake from a night terror. Disoriented from her unusual sleeping position, she rolled over and promptly fell off the bed with a thud. Instantly awake, she yelped and swore, having landed hard on her already sore shoulder. When she sat up, Little Flower was still asleep.

Rubbing at her now throbbing shoulder, she considered waking her sister to scan it, but deciding she didn't care if she had permission or not, she walked over and scooped out a large glob from the jar of nano cream that sat on the counter, and sighed with relief as it kicked in.

She looked back at the bed and then the clock. It wasn't even midnight yet. She was exhausted but didn't want to go back to sleep and risk another night terror and potentially hurt her sister in the process. Grabbing her tablet, she crawled onto a pillow and pulled up a book to read, but she couldn't focus on any of the words as the images of her night terror, fueled by the stresses of the past few days, played over and over again in her mind.

Sighing, she set her tablet aside and decided maybe a walk would help. Movement had always helped to calm her anxiety in the past.

Neither Aris or Thatcher seemed surprised to see her, and she guessed they'd heard her walking around inside and probably heard her fall off the bed, too. Thankfully, they didn't tease her about it.

Aris followed her without prompting, and they wandered the plat-form for some time until they came to a quiet, hidden alcove with a few cushy chairs and pillows.

"Do you want to talk about whatever's bothering you?" Aris asked.

"I can't get my brain to even form a coherent thought," Marsee muttered as she flopped down in the nearest chair, wincing as the motion aggravated her shoulder. "I'm exhausted, but I can't sleep. I had another night terror, and my shoulder and paw hurt, even after a large dose of nano cream."

"I'm not surprised on either account," Aris said as she began examining her injuries. "The last few days have been rather eventful, and you did land wrong tonight. We should work on that. What was your night terror about? Iruki's attack?"

"You'd think it would be, but it was the Ice Giant's this time." She winced as Aris poked and prodded at her shoulder.

"Well, that makes sense, too."

Marsee snorted. "None of them put up a fight and likely knew nothing about what was in the containers they were transporting. I didn't sniff any lying or threat from the Ship Master. Did you?"

"No, but Ice Giants are the hardest to read. Regardless, he could have been a threat. You knew that was a possibility, or you wouldn't have asked for backup. Several Ice Giants were waiting to kill your sister, and far too many on their council and guard intended you and your family harm. Not to mention what they did to your neighbors."

She sighed, then winced again. "I never noticed how big the males were before."

"Why would you? They weren't a threat before."

She stared off into the distance for a long time, trying to get her thoughts to solidify, but then stood and paced as her anxiety bloomed again. Eventually, she walked over to the window, leaned her head up against it, and watched the fish swim about in the lit-up perimeter around the base of the platform.

Aris walked over and wrapped a tail around her. "What's really bothering you?"

"Everything!" She started pacing again but then turned and faced

Aris. "I feel...I feel like an imposter, and at any moment, everyone's going to find out. I felt so tiny and insubstantial on that platform, staring up at that Giant. I don't know what I'm doing one minute to the next. Agate should be the one in front of the Council, but she's treating me like I'm already the Senior Guild Master. The plan on the way here was that I would sit back and observe, but from the moment we landed, everyone has been treating me like I outrank the Senior Council and expecting *me* to lead. I don't know how to do that! Translator Chenzira? Who *is* that? That's not me. I'm a shy, introverted cub who likes to read books and craft things. I want to spend time with my family. Yet here I am, giving reports in front of the Full Council, arguing with Councilors over the details, training with the Honor Guard, and uncovering smuggling operations in my spare time. I don't know who I am anymore."

She turned and faced the window again, but her reflection stared back at her this time. The white lines of her scars were bright against the dark sea beyond, and she growled with frustration.

"Who *is* this? This isn't even my reflection! Clear Seas looked at me in horror yesterday. I still don't know why. It wasn't just an act for the Council or the people watching. He's seen my scars several times now, but it was like it was the first time he'd seen them. Yet when I walked into Senior's room this morning, all I sniffed was awe. From all of them, even Sammianna. Why? Why should they be in awe of me? I hadn't even spoken yet. Uncle Marcus called me cub as a joke, and Clear Seas nearly took his head off for the insult. It was even worse after. It was like I had performed magic or something. All I did was get a hunch that something was up with that shipment and decided to check it out."

"No," Aris said. "You did far more than that. You put the entire puzzle together, or at least a big part of it."

She shrugged.

"Marsee, look at me."

She rolled her eyes but turned and faced Aris again.

"You've been thrown into this position far faster than most people, so it's no surprise that you're struggling with your current rank and authority. But whether you feel you've earned it or not, you *have* earned it. Ellie wouldn't have promoted you if she didn't believe you were up to the task."

"*Why*, though? What have I done to deserve it? Really deserve it, besides giving up a bunch of credit? That doesn't make me a leader."

"Well, for one, you agreed to run the research division. That alone is worth your rank as a Guild Master, but you were never destined for that position. Whether it happens next week, next month, or in a few decades, you *will* be the Senior Guild Master, and right now, you're Acting Senior Guild Master because you chose to step up. You could have let Agate handle the meeting and focus on your new duties as head of the research division, but you took charge and didn't even question your right to that position."

"Nardal is Ellie's Acting Senior," Marsee replied, confused.

Aris snorted. "Nardal isn't the one standing before the Senior Council making decisions on behalf of the Guild. You are. Ellie left Agate in charge in front of the entire Senior Council, not Nardal, and Agate handed that power over to you in front of the Full Council. And rightly so. Agate's good at what she does, but she's not a leader, not like you are."

Marsee rolled her eyes at Aris. "No, I'm not. I'm nothing but a cub."

Aris's expression changed, and without warning, she hit her on the side of her head hard enough to knock her to the ground.

Marsee scrambled back with a growl. "Explain yourself, guard!" she hissed, preparing to fight back.

She didn't have her tablet or stunner on her, but she'd seen other guards about on her walk, and she knew they were close enough to hear if she yelled for help.

Aris's expression changed immediately, and she chuckled. "I'm trying to make you see what everyone else sees in you. Listen to yourself. You didn't run or cower. You prepared to counter, and you demanded an explanation as if you were my senior. When it matters, when you don't think about it, you take charge and do what needs to be done, rank be damned. That's who you are. Just like you took charge in the canyon, like you took charge of the Guild, and again during the investigation last night."

Marsee rubbed at her sore head as she considered. "I wasn't in charge last night, Stinger..."

"Stinger had the authority to arrest, but it was *your* investigation from the beginning. You called in the Guard. Kendra followed your lead on how you wanted to approach the situation and led you to the ship. You weren't following her. It might not seem like much of a distinction, but it's a big one. Kendra had to call in for authority to arrest, but that was just protocol in a non-violent situation. Stinger came to add his authority. You stepped forward as he approached, and he addressed you, not Kendra, to find out what was going on. You let them handle the interrogations while you focused on what only you could have pulled together. The only point where you hesitated was when you asked about protocol in informing the Seniors, but you wouldn't have even asked if you didn't believe you had the same rank and authority as both of them. And frankly, after what happened yesterday, they were right. You have far more. The Senior Council doesn't trust anyone in the Guard, much less the Senior Honor Guards. It doesn't take much to sniff that out if you even bothered to try."

She flopped back down in the chair with a groan, burying her head in her paws as her anxiety and fear grew again.

Aris sat down in front of her. "What's really scaring you?"

Marsee couldn't even say it. When Iruki had attacked, she'd frozen again, just like she had in the canyon when Rip had snuck up on her, only this time, she hadn't had her instinct to snap her out of it. How could she protect her family when she kept freezing in the face of danger? Her breath turned ragged, but she didn't look up until she realized her paws were shaking.

"There it is," Aris said softly.

"What?" Marsee managed to gasp out as she stared at her paws, wondering what was going on. Had she been hurt when Aris hit her?

"The reaction we've all been waiting for," Aris said, then pulled her in for a hug and started purring. "Deep breaths. Let it happen. You're safe. I trust Kendra with my life. She's saved mine on more than one occasion, and I trust everyone on our squad. We'll protect you and your family with our lives."

"You...shouldn't...have to," Marsee replied through gasping breaths.

"No, but we will anyway. I will. I give you my oath. For as long as you want or need me, I will protect you from monsters and villains and the occasional platform wall."

A brief snort of laughter escaped at the last bit, but it quickly turned to hiccuping sobs. "But what if I'm the monster?"

Aris snorted. "You?! What makes you think you're a monster?"

She pulled herself together to explain. "I have to go back to Saber. If Ellie's..." She couldn't complete that thought. "I *want* to be with her, but everyone back home is going to see me as a monster. The Council certainly does. They're all waiting for me to lose control. I can see the way they look at me. The ones who dare talk to me are all trying to find out how close I am to losing control, and the rest look like I already have."

"You're no more of a monster than I am," Aris said. "But I don't envy you the next six months. It will be hard, downright impossible at times, but you'll prove yourself. You already are. You didn't lose control yesterday when Iruki attacked, but nearly half of those arrested did before your uncle got to them, many right there in the chamber. We've been watching and listening to everyone else. They don't fear you. They don't think you're a monster. They just don't understand you. They don't understand how you survived. They'll soon learn how fierce you are and come to respect you for that."

"I didn't remain in control. I froze. Again," Marsee spat. "If Agate hadn't been there, I'd be dead. I just let her drag me off and did nothing."

"Ahh. That's what's really bothering you. Isn't it?"

She nodded. "I keep freezing. I froze in the cave and again in the canyon when Rip attacked. But then, I had my instinct to snap me out of it. How am I going to protect anyone if I keep freezing when something happens?"

"With training," Aris replied. "You didn't freeze a moment ago.

You're not the first guard to freeze, and you won't be the last. The Ancient Gods know I've frozen a time or two myself. If you want terrifying, try going up against a Heela Monster. They make Rip look like a cub. We'll work on it in training, and now that we know, we can be your instinct. For what it's worth, you did the right thing in the chamber yesterday. Your aim is not nearly good enough to hit a moving target like Iruki, especially when being tossed around at the same time. You could have easily shot and hurt someone else. If you noticed, we weren't firing either. None of us could get a clear shot. I'm still not sure how your sister managed it."

She sighed and leaned against Aris, praying her guard was right about everything. It took her a long time to recover as all the pent-up fear from the past few weeks boiled over, but Aris held her tightly the entire time. When she finally pulled away, she was surprised to see Avery sitting not too far away from them.

"When did you get here?" she asked.

"I've been around the corner the whole time. Thatcher notified me the moment you left. We've been expecting it."

Marsee sighed but then glared at Avery. "So why didn't you do anything when she hit me?"

"Because it's exactly what you needed, and you had everything under control," Avery replied. "However, I think we should have you checked over before we head back. I don't like the way that lump on the side of your head looks, and I know just how hard Aris can hit. Plus, your shoulder should be feeling better by now, based on how much nano cream you slathered on it, but you're still favoring it."

She snorted but didn't argue and climbed out of her seat with another groan. Half an hour later, she was treated for her 'training injuries' and back in the suite.

Little Flower was awake and waiting for her. "Where did you go?"

"I had a night terror and went for a walk to think," Marsee replied as she curled protectively around her sister. "I didn't want to wake you."

"Ahh," her sister replied and snuggled in. "Do you want to talk about it?"

"Nah, I'm good now. Aris knocked some sense into me. In case you're wondering, she hits harder than Ellie."

Little Flower chuckled. "Well, if you have a headache, you'd better have the trauma center check you out. We haven't gone over concussions yet."

"Already treated," Marsee replied.

Her sister shifted to look up at her and then snorted. "Good thing you have a hard head, Chenzie Butt."

"One of us has to, Fish Breath."

Chuckling, her sister soon fell back to sleep, but she lay there for a long time thinking about everything Aris had said.

Her last thought as she drifted off to sleep was to wonder if she would ever feel like the person everyone else seemed to think she was or if they, too, would come to see her as a monster.

29

MATING CLINIC

Quinn walked the grounds outside of the mating clinic. There were guards permanently stationed there, as fights occasionally happened, but he wasn't leaving the Senior Guild Master's safety up to them or the half squad that was hidden on Ellie's ship, even if he didn't have direct orders from his Mentor.

His dreams that night had been full of passion that had ended with such horror that he'd woken fully poofed, and he had nearly activated every guard before he realized it had only been a dream.

The guards here were all older, female, and semi-retired, with injuries that made patrol difficult. If someone planned to target Ellie, they would be hard-pressed to defend her or contain the males at the clinic.

A full contingent was on alert nearby, hidden and out of nose reach. They didn't know the reason they'd been activated, although he imagined most had already guessed.

The clinic guards were surprised to see him, but he didn't bother explaining. There was no need. It didn't take them long to put the pieces together, either. Ellie's continued absence at the council meeting was all over the news, even with the culling that had occurred. No one had been able to identify any particular family emergency, as Marsee had indicated, and all anyone had learned so far was that her ship had left the platform.

Most were under the assumption that the Seniors, expecting an attack at the Council Meeting, had purposely fabricated an excuse to get her off the planet, just as they had kept Petra and Temperate from attending. Those in the Guard who didn't know what was going on were speculating that she was suffering from the early stages of psychosis brought on by her trauma, and he'd overheard many others of his species speculating the same.

But he knew Ellie far too well, although they rarely interacted. She had dealt with her fair share of trauma over the years, including controlling situations when members of her Guild lost control before the Guard could arrive, and she had never once so much as wavered. Her ferocious tenacity matched the Senior's calm mask blow for blow in every council meeting and was likely what kept her fighting to stay alive until help could arrive.

Due to her high-profile status, he often led the watches that followed those incidents, and he had grown to respect her over the years. In recent years, he'd taken to attending council meetings whenever she was in attendance simply to watch her deft maneuvering of the Council — to feel a part of her life, even if he was destined to always remain in the shadows.

I wonder if she ever thinks of me.

He sighed at what he knew could never happen, then chided himself to focus on the task at hand. He had responsibilities for the people of Saber and Little Earth. Now would not be a good time for him to get distracted by pheromones and a relationship that could never happen, as much as he wished it could.

The yard was already full of people waiting, mostly young males, but that wasn't uncommon even when someone wasn't inbound. The lingering smell alone was often more than many could resist, and people of both sexes would make use of their reaction, even if not chosen, which was why the clinic was on the outskirts of the city, hidden from view behind a large flowering and fragrant hedge wall.

He smelled desire and mating pheromones everywhere, but not a hint of malice. The pheromones didn't bother him. He'd long since learned to control his desire around females in heat. He'd endured his growth spurt longer than most, insisting, knowing his bigger size would make him a better guard, as most males in the Guard did, even if the risk were higher due to injuries they'd sustained during training. He was strong, fast, and the highest-rated fighter, and surprisingly still Second in Command. He was confident in his abilities, secure in his power and authority, and all of that, wrapped up in a pretty bow, was everything their mating instincts desired, and he knew it.

The males in the yard knew it, too, and they watched him warily as he passed. Walking the grounds was a risk. His presence could cause the other males to react violently if they felt their chances with an incoming mate were threatened, but they were all younger, smaller, and afraid of him and the badge on his harness.

He made a point of visibly leaving the grounds, not that he actually was. He wasn't leaving until Ellie was safely inside the mating clinic. Not surprisingly, speculation and excitement bloomed the moment they thought he was out of earshot. They might not know him personally, but his rank was fully visible.

After observing their speculation for a bit to see if anyone's attitude changed, he circled back around to the hidden guard station on the edge of the yard to wait. The Squad Senior was there waiting for him.

"I take it we're getting a high-profile guest today," she said as he sat down next to her to peer out the hidden window, where she'd been watching.

He checked the time. "Just about as high as it gets. She should be here in a few minutes."

"I wonder who won that bet?" she mused.

He chuckled. More than a few had tried to get information out of him already.

"I'm assuming her implant was damaged after what Rip did to her?"

"Not damaged, missing."

"Missing?! Why would he do that?"

"Not a moons' forsaken clue unless he meant for her to go into heat at the meeting. Could you imagine that scandal?"

She snorted. "I'd rather that than what we've all been through this past week. I wonder who she'd have picked. The Seniors?"

He shrugged. "I have no idea. She is friends with Jer and Marcus, so that's a possibility, but I think if she wanted to go that route, she would have remained on the Water World."

He dropped the conversation as his tablet dinged with the alert indicating Ellie's ship had exited jump. A few minutes later, he could hear the sounds of her ship approaching, and he left the guard station for a better view of her ship and the two escort ships that flanked it, watching for incoming traffic or other signs of threats, but there were none.

ELLIE SQUIRMED IN HER SEAT, nearly out of control with the need for a proper mate by the time they approached. She'd long since lost the ability to speak in anything but sign language as her mating instinct took full control, but even Myra's attention no longer helped. Her instinct wanted nothing to do with Myra anymore. It was all she could do to keep from snapping at her friend.

Her claws dug deep into the armrest of her seat as she focused on her breathing. She didn't want to appear out of control. She wanted to take her time and enjoy the selection.

Yes, make them prove themselves worthy of us, her instinct purred.

She felt the slight bump of the ship as it landed and fumbled with the clips on the safety harness, struggling to remember how to use it. Myra reached over and unclipped her, and the moment she was free, she ran for the door.

Kneading with anticipation, she barely regained control of herself as the door slid open and the ramp extended.

Potential mates waited for her. She surveyed the crowd, seeing if any caught her eye. Her instinct purred with the knowledge that they were all there for her. They needed a mate, and there were so many to choose from! All thoughts vanished as she reveled in the worship of her suitors.

She took a deep breath as their intoxicating scents reached her. One in particular caught her instinct's attention, and her mouth watered and opened wide to explore the texture better.

Yes. That one will do nicely.

Her purr grew to a roar as she announced both her need and dominance. The males reacted to her instantly, roaring back, the sound making her insides squirm with desire.

Slowly, deliberately, she made her way down out of the ship. She knew her worth and had no intentions of settling. This was her last chance for cubs, and if it didn't go well, she intended to make her last days glorious. Only the very best would do for her. She rubbed her way along the first of her suitors, tail up and squirting with need, as they growled and purred their own excitement. She dismissed several immediately. They smelled wrong and were entirely too puny, and there were so many others to choose from.

One had the audacity to push his luck, but she snapped at him with a ferocious snarl, and he quickly backed off at her show of strength.

Puny! she huffed with disgust and continued working her way through the crowd, reveling in the feel of their attention, but frustration grew in her when potential mate after mate was not acceptable. They were *all* too puny, not worthy of her attention or notice, and not what she was looking for at all, not the one she'd scented earlier.

Where is he? Has he been chosen by another already? That thought made them angry. There was no female higher ranked than them, and they deserved the very best.

When the last of her suitors had been deemed unworthy, she roared her frustration, calling for him, for someone better, someone worthy of her. She sniffed deeply, ready to start hunting him down and fight for him if that's what it took.

QUINN GASPED as the door slid open, and Ellie appeared, tail up and paws kneading. Her short fur accentuated her strong muscles and glistened in the morning sunlight. She surveyed the crowd as she waited for the ramp to extend, standing tall and confident in her worth and her power, on display but letting every male know *she* was the one in control.

She was divine femininity, a gift from the gods, very life itself.

The sight burned in Quinn's soul. He couldn't pry his eyes off her as she roared her challenge and began a slow sauntering walk down out of the ship, showing no sign of weakness or her past injuries.

He shook his head hard to clear it and grit his teeth to avoid responding to her challenge along with the other males. A wave of desire crashed over him, but he squashed it down hard, too. He was here on duty, not pleasure. He had given an oath to protect her. His own desires and feelings didn't matter, but he still couldn't take his eyes off her as she strode through the first of the males, rubbing against them, sniffing, and ultimately dismissing them.

One male tried to mount anyway, but she spun and snapped at him with a snarl. Quinn took a step forward, both jealous and worried about a fight, but the male backed off.

Ellie snorted and turned back to the rest of her suitors, flicking her tail in disgust at the other male's audacity for thinking he was good enough for her.

None of them are good enough for her. She deserves so much better.

"Focus, Quinn," he muttered to himself as he pulled his attention back to his duties and checked the surroundings for threats.

He managed for a bit, but then the wind shifted and brought her scent to him. His legs nearly buckled out from under him by the strength of it. He'd never smelled anything like it. It wrapped around him in thick chains and tugged.

"You're on duty!" he hissed at himself. He tried to force himself to leave, to return to the guard station, to get away before he broke his oath, but his legs wouldn't move.

Their mating instinct was the one thing unaffected by the Transition. It was fighting him for control, nearly as strong as it had been the day he transitioned, and he was sorely tempted to give in.

He watched as she rubbed up against every male, sniffing, testing, and finding them wanting, jealous of even the brief moments they had with her. He was breathing hard, struggling with his control, and nearly drawing blood with his own claws to contain it.

Ancient gods! he prayed, not sure what he was praying for, willpower or the complete loss of it.

"We'll protect her. Go," the Squad Senior said quietly behind him.

He growled but didn't move. Every fiber of his being wanted to go, wanted her, the way he'd never wanted anyone before, but he was on duty. He was supposed to be protecting her, not lusting over her like an untrained junior guard. He was Second in Command. He didn't lose control. He *never* lost control. Oh, gods, but I did *want* to lose control.

Ellie snapped at another male and roared her challenge again, her scent changing to fury and disgust at their inadequacy.

"You'll be able to protect her better from inside," the Squad Senior said. "She won't pick any of them. She's already turned down the more dominant males, and if she doesn't find what she needs soon, she's going to leave the grounds. She's been hurt badly and needs a guard to protect her and her cubs. More than likely, she's already picked up on your scent and is looking for you. Go before someone gets hurt, before she gets hurt."

* * *

Ellie sniffed hard, looking for that scent she'd first picked up on, and roared with frustration and need when she couldn't find it. Another one of the puny males took his chances, and she snarled and swiped at him, furious that he would even dare. There were others far better than him, not that she would choose any of them. They were all unworthy. They didn't care about her or her future cubs. All they wanted was the status of mating with her.

An answering roar came from behind her, deep and powerful.

She turned and saw him. His powerful muscles flexed and bunched as he ran. He was bigger by far than all the rest, strong, fast, and oh-so yummy. She started purring immediately, intoxicated by his strength and beauty, then roared as his scent reached her, full of his own desires — a desire to protect her, a desire to care for her and her cubs, a desire for her to love him as much as he loved her.

Love? she thought, momentarily surprised out of her haze.

Yes! He will be good for us. This is who we were looking for, her instinct thought, pleased, and took control again.

He roared his virility, followed by chuffing so deep that it made her squirm with need, but she lifted her head and waited for him to approach, haughty, demanding that he prove his worth to her.

Her eyes remained fixed as he slowed to a walk and made his way through the crowd of other males vying for her attention. They backed off, sensing a more dominant male.

She examined every inch of him, pleased by his confidence, and then recognized why as she saw his badge. *Honor Guard*, she thought with relief. *Someone who really could protect her and her cubs from harm!* He looked familiar, but she couldn't place him through the haze of her heat, but it didn't matter. Her instinct did, and it trusted him implicitly.

He was a guard. He had protected those she cared about before, had risked his life for them, and would do so for her and her cubs. That's what they needed, wanted, and desired. It was why they had returned, why they had waited so long. They had waited for him.

She rubbed up against him as he approached. He smelled divine, and she wanted to taste every last part of him to see if he tasted as good as he smelled. Making her way to his backside, he lifted his tail aside, and she gave into that desire. *Perfect!* she thought, as waves crashed over her, and she made a sound she didn't even know she could make.

That was all the approval he needed. He spun and grabbed her by the scruff with his teeth and pinned her to the ground, mounting her.

Her instinct reacted immediately, and she roared with desire and feeling as he pumped several times. Waves of pleasure rolled through her by his overpowering act of dominance, yet at the same time, he was so very gentle with her. His bite was only strong enough to hold her in place but not enough to hurt or break the skin, and every warm exhale felt like a caress.

Far too soon for her, he stopped, but before she could object, he lifted and flung her over his shoulders as if she weighed nothing and carried her into the clinic.

He's even stronger than he looks. He will make an excellent mate, her instinct purred as the hands holding her in place began to explore, sending wave after wave of pleasure through her body.

She had to agree.

The healers led them into a suite and scanned them as they passed, but she didn't notice them. All she could see from her position, slung over his shoulders as she was, was his beautiful and muscular behind. She began kneading it with her paws, fascinated by its perfection, and he groaned, letting off waves of his own desire, his tail flexing and shuddering with her touch.

She ran one hand along the length of his silky smooth tail, which was softer than anything she'd ever felt before.

His legs nearly buckled, and he let out a tortured whimper before setting her down gently on the bed and rubbing up against her face.

"You smell like a gift from the gods," he growled before flipping her over and pinning her to the bed with another strong bite to her scruff.

She roared her approval, shifted her back feet under her to raise her haunches up, and held her tail to the side, giving him access.

He nipped his way down her spine and then licked her, causing her to orgasm almost instantly. It made what Myra had done to keep her sane through the trip seem pitiful in comparison. He groaned with his own orgasm but didn't stop his attention on her and proceeded to find every spot that ached and throbbed in her until she lost all sense of who she was.

It was almost as if he could read her mind or her body. He seemed to know what she needed before she could barely recognize it herself. She tried to return the favor, but he wouldn't let her up. Every time she tried, he pinned her again and didn't let go until she gave in, not that she tried to fight back. Her instinct gloried at how strong their cubs would be.

When they both came up for air hours later, he continued to lavish her with attention, handing her a drink and feeding her so she didn't even need to move. While they no longer hunted as a species, their instincts wanted a mate that could provide as well as protect, but it wasn't long before she forgot all about the food, wanting to taste him again instead.

He finally let her return the favor, and she made sure he knew who was in charge as she pinned him and made him squirm and then roar with need. His scent alone did things to her that she'd never experienced before, and his taste even more so.

Finally, beyond exhausted, sleep began to overpower her need to mate, and he curled around her protectively.

"Sleep. You're safe. I will protect you," he murmured.

It was exactly what she needed to hear, and, with a contented purr, she drifted off to the feel of his strong embrace.

She woke sometime later as his paws gently stroked her fur. At first, she purred with pleasure, enjoying the sensation, but then frowned as she realized he was tracing the scars under her fur.

He stopped instantly, and she rolled over to look up at him. His expression was one of both sadness and awe, and perhaps a hint of embarrassment.

She raised a brow in a wordless question.

He opened his mouth to answer, but words wouldn't form, so he switched to sign language. "I have seen so many succumb to injuries far less than what you endured. To survive as long as you did shows such incredible tenacity and strength. It may be wrong of me, but I'm beyond thankful it occurred so that I could have this opportunity with you. I don't know what I did to deserve the gift the gods have given me, but I will thank them for the rest of my life, and I fully intend to worship your body until the only thoughts you have about these scars are memories of me."

She smiled at him, purring with the desire and love she saw in his expression, and groaned with pleasure as he began fulfilling his promise — until there was nothing left to her but bliss.

30

MARSEE: MEETING'S END

The next six local days passed with uneventful, if exhausting, routine for Marsee: council meetings, training, and prep for the next day. Little Flower grabbed lessons with Ammond when she could, either early morning before the meeting or when Marsee went back to the Guild to prepare for the next day, and Tamarin started sticking around after her shift was over to help Little Flower care for Hope.

To her surprise, Little Flower never said anything else about Damon's release, but she did catch her sister practicing her throw one evening when she returned from the Guild, as she bounced one of Hope's toys off the wall while lying on the bed. Marsee said nothing as she curled around her sister protectively, knowing Little Flower would tell her what was bothering her when she was ready.

She didn't see her father or the rest of the Seniors outside of official business. She wasn't even sure where her father was sleeping. He never returned to the suite, or at least if he did, she never heard him. She was pulled in a few times for discussion after a meeting or during deliberations if they had questions, but nothing else was mentioned about what she'd found, and nothing further was brought up during the meeting. Per the orders from the Seniors, guild punishment would have to wait until after the full standard week was up and any other convictions were announced. By then, she prayed, Ellie would be the one to manage that.

She avoided watching the news if she could. She really didn't want to know what people were thinking of her, and while the press kept sending her requests for an interview, which she purposely ignored, they surprisingly hadn't bothered trying to corner her for one yet, but then she supposed her sister shooting them might have had something to do with it. That or the fact that her guards suddenly got very menacing any time someone approached, and the reporters suddenly found they had somewhere else they needed to be. She was seriously considering keeping the guards around permanently for that benefit alone.

Both she and her sister were getting stronger every day. She significantly cut her time on the obstacles, and her sister managed an entire lap without falling or needing to drop down to a walk. They both trained hard in the shooting gallery. She could now hit the targets reliably through several levels of the simulator. Her sister's shot at the meeting impressed everyone, and several guards had since challenged her to a shoot-off, to her sister's highly amused and profitable benefit.

Marsee stifled a yawn. The latest council meeting was nearly over, and they had been discussing an item that didn't directly affect the Guild for over an hour. In an attempt to stay awake, she was spending the time reviewing the next day's planned agenda, all of which had been marked as provisional, in the hopes that she could call it an early evening. She rubbed at her face and was about to turn her tablet off when a message came in from her mother.

We've landed safely, and she's attracted a very
large, exceptionally strong, and yummy-
smelling honor guard. I was quite impressed.
He actually picked her up and carried her into
the clinic like she weighed nothing.
Everything's going well so far, and I'm
reasonably optimistic we'll have a viable
embryo.

She sighed with relief and nudged Agate. Agate peered over. Marsee could smell her amusement and relief, but nothing showed on her skin.

She really wanted to ask her mother who it was, but she knew her mother wouldn't say — patient confidentiality and all that. She was bending the rules by letting her know as much as she did as it was, even if Ellie was her Mentor.

She looked up as Clear Seas called out for a vote on the current item. A few moments later, the votes were in, and it passed with a wide majority.

"As the remaining items on the docket are provisional, the Senior Council has decided unanimously to end the session rather than bring anything in, as most of the items that were to be presented were being championed by districts that no longer have representation, unless someone wants to champion those items or believes they cannot wait until the next meeting," Clear Sea's stated. "If so, please indicate now."

Only one councilor hit their light.

"Councilor Parner, you have the floor."

"Thank you, Senior Councilor. I would like to request that we review docket item S43. The trauma center being proposed has been pushed off for several sessions now, and while that district no longer has a councilor, it would be located in a community near the southern border of my district. While neither area has a large enough population to automatically qualify for the center being proposed, the nearest clinic for the people who live there is over an hour away by ground crawler, and neither of our districts have a level four trauma center, which is why it has been proposed."

Several lights flickered on, and Clear Seas called out the first person.

"Why isn't there a clinic or trauma center there now?" the person asked.

"There was a clinic until two years ago when the healer stationed there died. Convincing healers to station themselves in a remote desert community is...difficult, which is why we proposed making this a training facility. The community where it would be built is nearing town size and is prepared to support the expected increase in population if approved."

The other councilors turned off their lights, apparently having the same question.

Clear Seas put it to a vote, and it, too, passed with a majority approval.

When no other items were brought forward, Clear Seas ended the meeting and swam out, not even waiting for the other Seniors.

"Well, that just freed up my schedule a bit," Marsee said to Agate after the Seniors had left. "I'm thinking about taking the night off. Shall I meet you in the morning to review that trauma center?"

"That works for me," Agate replied. "Nice and early, say noon?"

Marsee chuckled and agreed. She nodded to Agate and swam down to Little Flower, who was talking with GrandFather and Henry.

Just as she approached, every one of the Hue-man councilor's tablets dinged or buzzed.

"Looks like we're scheduled to fly out first thing tomorrow morning," GrandFather replied. "Unless you'd like us to stick around until you're cleared to jump home."

"There will be more than enough room on my ship if you want to stay," Marsee replied, "but it's going to be several weeks before I'm cleared to jump, and I was thinking about bouncing around and hitting up the other guild halls while I'm here as part of the research fund."

"You should head home," Little Flower said. "If for no other reason than because Buster is waiting for his reward. Besides, both of you have your own training to attend."

"Didn't you hear?" GrandFather asked. "Nazari's on maternity leave. Councilor Harding gave up custody to Nazari right before we flew out. She's taking a month or two off to spend time with him."

"No, I hadn't. I'm so happy for her," Little Flower replied and looked around the other milling councilors. "I don't remember seeing Councilor Harding here. Did she attend?"

"No, and I think she's planning to step down from the Council, too," GrandFather replied.

"Why?" Little Flower asked.

"I'm not at liberty to say," he replied.

"Well, I, for one, never liked that decision," Marsee stated. "I'm glad she finally gained custody."

GrandFather pursed his lips and took a deep breath. "There were a number of reasons it made sense at the time, but what matters is that the child is cared for and loved. I'll admit part of the reason I didn't vote for Nazari was because of my own trauma. She was my healer at the Agency, but I've gotten to know and respect her since, and I think she'll make an excellent parent. From my observations, the child appears to have significant learning disabilities as he's well past the age where one of our children should be able to speak or sign, but he seems happy and content with her. Anyway, shall we hit up Fire Sticks tonight? Marsee's paying."

Marsee snorted, and her tail curled at his audacity, but she would never turn down a trip to Fire Sticks. She texted her father to see if he wanted to attend, too, but she got a response back that he would be working late and would meet them all in the morning before flying out.

The next morning came far too early. Within minutes of waking, Little Flower bolted across the hall to her grandfather's with Hope. Her sister didn't say anything, but Marsee had a feeling she needed some alone time with him. They hadn't spent much time with them since arriving, and it would be weeks before they returned. That was a long time for the Hue-mans, as she understood far too well now.

She was digging through her messages when there was a knock on her door from her father's room. "Come in," she replied.

"Morning, Kitten," he said.

"Morning, Papa. I wasn't sure if you were still staying there. I haven't heard you in a while."

"I've been staying with Marcus. Neither of us wanted to be alone after..."

She nodded her understanding. "How are you two doing?"

He shrugged. "As well as could be expected. I'm honestly looking forward to the flight back and intend to sleep through most of it.

Although, if I can't, your uncle has, for some strange reason, developed a fascination with the lifecycle of the blubber fish and has raided Clear Sea's archives of every book he could find for the return trip. I'm sure he'd let me borrow one as long as I don't drool on it."

She chuckled and wondered what was so interesting about a blubber fish besides the name. "You're flying back together then?"

He nodded. "My ship is still on Saber. How are you doing?"

"As well as could be expected," she replied, repeating his words and causing him to chuckle.

"I hope you know I'm very proud of you. You've really stepped up these past few days. I think you even managed to impress Sammianna."

"Well, I'm sure it wasn't with my impeccable math skills," she replied, rolling her eyes.

He laughed. "I wouldn't be so sure about that. She's referenced your saying several times now."

She frowned at him, wondering what he was talking about.

"Two plus two equalling six," he clarified. "She seems to find it very amusing."

Marsee rolled her eyes again. "Great. Watch that be the thing that gets carved onto my tombstone."

"Well, it could be worse. At least it's done with respect, although by the end of all of this, 'I found another six' might just turn into a swear used by all of us.

"I wouldn't blame you if it did," Marsee replied. "I might have to use that myself. It is rather catchy."

"Are you going to be okay here by yourself?" he asked, changing the subject, his face shifting to worry.

She nodded. "I'm not alone. I have the universe's best sharpshooter for a partner and a squad of impudent and hard-hitting guards to protect us. Oh, and in case you're wondering, Little Flower is still furious with you. It's probably a good thing we'll be a universe apart for a few weeks. She *might* calm down by the time we return home."

Aris, who was still on duty in the hallway, chuckled. Moments later, she heard Aris and Thatcher making bets on it.

It was all she could do to keep from laughing at their exchange.

Her father sighed and shook his head. "You're probably not wrong there. Wind Rider and Sammianna have a bet on how long it'll take her to shoot me."

"I know. I heard as I left the conference room that first day."

He rolled his eyes again, but his mood shifted, and he was silent for a moment, collecting his thoughts. "Kitten, I know I've said this before, but I am sorry I hurt you, and I'm sorry you've been hurt because of me. You need to be careful. You're more of a target now than you ever were before, but not because of me, but because you stepped up, and if Ellie doesn't survive, I fully expect there will be another attack or attempt to make you step down before the vote."

"I know, and it terrifies me, but the last thing I'm going to do is let them destroy Ellie's legacy, too."

He smiled sadly at her and shook his head. "I can't believe how much you've changed this past year. What happened to the cub who hid from the press only a few months ago?"

"She's still hiding," Marsee replied. "They've asked daily for interviews, which I'm currently ignoring. Thankfully, they haven't gathered the courage to make it past my growling shadows or Little Flower's stunner."

"We were wondering about that. Wind Rider and Sammianna have bet on when they finally manage to corner you, too."

"So do the guards, but if I have my way, never."

"Sorry, Kitten. It comes with the job."

She glared at him. "You can leave now."

"Yes, ma'am," he replied and stood, his eyes twinkling with humor.

She rolled her eyes at him again.

"Where's your sister?" he asked.

"Across the hall with GrandFather."

He nodded and left after giving her a long hug.

She gave them a few minutes before deciding to head over. She was lost in thought about what her father had said as she hit the door switch, then yelped with fear and scrambled back as her uncle appeared in front of her as it slid open, arm up and raised to strike.

He slowly lowered his arm. "I'm sorry. I didn't mean to startle you. I was only knocking."

She relaxed slightly but didn't approach. Aris and Thatcher were watching, but they hadn't restrained him. As far as she could tell, he was telling the truth.

"Everyone else is across the hall. I was just about to head over," she said eventually.

"I know. I was just there. I want to talk to you for a minute, alone. I assure you, I mean you no harm."

She raised a brow but nodded to let him in. "What is it *this* time, Uncle Sun?"

His eyes twinkled at the obvious reference to his teasing earlier in the week and her purposeful mistranslation of his name sign, but otherwise, his expression never changed. He stepped in and stopped, keeping the distance between them. "You looked relieved right before the end of the meeting. Do you know what's going on with Ellie? I know her ship arrived on Saber yesterday, but no one has seen her, and Quinn Bluestone, the Acting Senior Honor Guard, hasn't responded to any of my messages."

"Oh, ho! So that's who she caught!" Marsee grinned. "Good for her!"

Marcus looked at her with confusion.

"Papa didn't tell you?"

He glared at her. "*Obviously*, or I wouldn't be here questioning you. What do you mean by caught?"

"Rip removed her implant. She went into heat."

She'd seen a lot of expressions on her uncle's face over the years, but never this one, and it made her tail curl. He was absolutely flabbergasted and at a complete loss for words.

"Mama texted me, stating that Ellie'd caught a very strong and yummy-smelling honor guard who picked Ellie up and carried her into the clinic. She didn't say who it was, but it doesn't take strong math skills to see two plus two equals Quinn."

He still didn't say anything.

"The message Ellie got at dinner that night was from me, warning her. And you should probably know, if you don't already, it's her third heat."

Her uncle's expression changed instantly to horror, then slammed behind his mask again.

"You know something, don't you?" Marsee asked.

"No one can know he took the implant," he ordered. "If you have to say something, say it was damaged."

"Why? What did Rip intend to do with it?"

"I'm honestly not sure." He pulled out his tablet and, a moment later, handed it over to her. "Does any of this tech mean anything to you?"

She flipped through the images attached to the ticket. "Yeah, sure. This is all pretty standard medical tech. Mama had a lot of this in her clinic, although nowhere near as nice. This is top grade, the kind of stuff you'd only find in a level three trauma center or higher. Mama would have drooled over even one of these devices for her clinic. I don't even think what we have in New Hope is as nice."

"What could you do with it?" he asked.

"Research, print body parts, medicines, and other tech, like nano's and braces. Every device should have an inventory model and number on it, which would bring up a catalog of detailed capabilities. Although I'm guessing what he had wasn't obtained legally, more damaged goods, I'm assuming?"

He nodded. "It's a small fraction of what you're missing, but we're assuming some of it is."

She told him what she knew about each device and showed him how to do a reverse image lookup for the items she didn't recognize.

He shook his head. "It looks like I'm going to have to add tech classes to council training. Your help has been invaluable in our investigation."

"You're more than welcome to ask me any time you have a question on tech or anything related to the Guild. If I don't know the answer, I know how to find out."

"I fully intend to take you up on that offer. I'm sending you a number of cases we're still looking into. Anything you can add will be greatly appreciated, even hunches, as your hunches seem to be quite reliable. What I send you, you share with no one, not even your sister, Ellie, or any of the guards. Is that understood?"

"Yes, sir," she replied.

Moments later, her tablet dinged with a number of messages. She opened the first one and clicked on the link provided.

"Names have been redacted from each of the tickets. Only the Seniors have that information. If you find something critical or life-threatening while we're still in jump, inform Clear Seas and let him handle it. I'm sure I don't have to remind you how dangerous things are right now."

"But you just did," she replied. "And so did Papa a few minutes ago. Is there anything else you need? I want to say goodbye to GrandFather and Henry."

"Just one last thing," he replied. "I'm sorry. I'm sorry I didn't trust you and that I wasn't there for you when you needed me the most. I know this past year has been difficult, if not downright impossible. Know that you can talk to me about anything, and I promise to listen and be your uncle, not your Senior Councilor, unless that's what you want or need. How are you doing? Really doing?"

She smiled up at him but then turned away and sat down on the edge of her bed. She'd been expecting this conversation and was surprised it hadn't happened already. "It's been downright impossible," she replied, using his words. "I'm recovering. I'm stronger every day, but that hollow feeling is still there. It's not as bad now. Little Flower and Hope help to fill it in, but I feel..."

She struggled, trying to find the right word, and looked up at him as he sat in front of her, still out of arms reach. His mask was completely dropped, and her loving uncle looked at her with compassion. It had been years, a decade, really, since she'd seen this side of him.

"I feel like a completely different person. My senses are back, and they're overwhelming at times, like my hearing was before, but I'm learning to manage them. I'm far more of a klutz because it makes me dizzy. I'm surprisingly better at math, or at least I can focus on it now.

I think it bored my instinct before, but then what does an instinct need of math? Mostly, I'm scared. I'm worried about who else Rip told about my illness, and I'm worried about going home. It doesn't take much to sniff out how much the members of our species fear me right now. The looks from most of our council are..."

She sighed. "Will I ever be free of this?"

He nodded. "You will. Your performance this week has gone a long way towards convincing people that it's possible to survive psychosis, but it will take time, just as it did with me. What you survived would have put any of us over the edge, even if there hadn't been issues. I've seen it too many times. We all have. I honestly don't think I would have survived. If your father or the guards haven't told you, I've changed our policy around psychosis because of what you've shown me is possible. I've ordered that people be brought into the guard at the first sign of an issue and taught sign language if they don't already know it. We're doing everything we can to teach our children sign language as early as possible, and I've ordered that pain be treated before requiring people to turn off their instincts. Clear Seas was right. That we forced you to do so was both cruel and unnecessary, and I'm sorry I didn't recognize how badly you were injured. We should have listened to what you needed and given you the time you needed to recover. The next six months will be hard, but if you've shown me anything this past week, it's that you're up to that challenge. You've been through far worse and survived. I have no doubt you'll survive this and be respected more because of it."

Everything he said smelled true, although she still smelled hints of unease and worry from him. She smiled sadly at him. "Thanks, Uncle."

He nodded. "What can I do to make it easier for you?"

She shrugged. "If I knew that, I'd be a god." She shook her head. "Your apology is enough. If I think of anything, I'll let you know."

She stood and, after a moment of hesitation, held her arms out, offering a hug, even though she was still scared.

He honestly seemed as surprised by her offer as Clear Seas had been but gently returned the hug.

She allowed herself to pretend he wasn't a threat anymore, that he was just her uncle, but she couldn't keep up that facade for long. He let go the moment she pulled away and said nothing as she left the room and made her way across the hall.

Her father's expression didn't change when she entered GrandFather's suite, but he smelled of relief.

She made eye contact with him for a moment, letting him know she understood, then ignored it, focusing on GrandFather and Henry.

A few minutes later, they all trudged to the top of the platform where the council transport ships were waiting. The wind was whipping harder than it had the last time she'd been up here, but no one stopped to stare at them, as there was a long line of others making their way across the platform to the ship.

Ammond was waiting for them outside and scanned both her and her sister. "I'm not sure I feel comfortable leaving the two of you here alone. You seem to find far too many ways to get into trouble," he grumbled.

"That may be, but there are patients back home who need you far more than we do right now," Marsee replied. "Thank you for coming all this way for me."

He nodded, crushing her in a hug, before turning to Little Flower. "I expect your homework to be done on time, and I've spoken to the Senior Healer. She's agreed to put up with you while you're still here and expects you at the Trauma Center promptly at seven each morning."

"Well, there goes my vacation," Little Flower replied with a heavy sigh.

"Apprentices," Ammond muttered, rolling his eyes, but picked Little Flower up and enveloped her in a hug. Then he took Hope from Marsee's carry sack. "You make sure you give your Mama and Papa lots of attitude for your Uncle Ammy."

"Kay," Hope replied.

"You would take his side," Little Flower muttered but took Hope back from him after he was done showering her with affection.

After they hugged GrandFather goodbye, they waited until everyone loaded on the ship and then backed off to the viewing area to wait until it left. Once clear, they made their way back down to the terminal where her uncle's ship was now docked and wished her father and uncle goodbye.

Her uncle entered the ship with little more than a nod to both of them, but her father hugged them both tightly, then glared at Avery for a long moment before boarding the ship.

"Papa's still mad at you, I see," Marsee said.

Avery grunted but didn't reply.

A few moments later, they watched as the plank was retracted and her uncle's ship flew away.

"Now what?" Little Flower asked.

"Well, I have a meeting with Agate, and it sounds like you have lessons with the Senior Healer," Marsee replied.

"Not until tomorrow. There's a whole planet to explore. Why don't you cancel that meeting and we'll go do something fun, like visit the Habitat. We've both been stuck in meetings for days, and when I do see you, you're being chased around the arena by Avery, and I haven't seen anything but the market yet."

Marsee frowned, feeling conflicted as she had information for her uncle to look up and other work to do, but she looked down at Hope. She'd barely spent any time with her child, and she could use a break, too. Her uncle wouldn't be able to review the information she found until they landed on Saber anyway.

So, on the spur of the moment, she rescheduled the meeting for the next day and almost immediately received an 'Oh, good. I was hoping you would. I'm going back to bed,' message in reply.

Laughing, she shared the message with Little Flower, and they made their way down to requisition a shuttle as her new ship hadn't arrived yet.

It ended up being one of the best days of her life. When they finally returned to their suite, exhausted, well after midnight, Marsee curled around her partner and happily purred them both to sleep.

31

STORMY: HEIR TO THE THRONE

Stormy floated outside his primary school, holding a small, misshapen basket and trying to find the nerve to swim in. Swimming into the Council had been easy by comparison, but now he had to face his peers, many of whom were now grieving the loss of a parent or family member, and we wondered how his new status would change things with his peers.

His father had said nothing about his interview with the press or the fact that he'd taken his place among the Council Staffers, but then he'd barely seen his father. Nor had his father picked a new Senior Staffer or officially promoted him. Not that it mattered. Everyone was treating him as if he was his father's chosen heir, anyway.

"You've faced down Leviathans. What's a few primary school students?" he muttered to himself in Hue-man.

Squaring his shoulders, he swam in, followed by the guard his father had insisted he keep.

As he expected, the hall was packed with students. They all stopped what they were doing and turned to face him when he appeared.

One Sprite swam forward out of the pack, flickering red around the edges. "Oh look, if it isn't our future king, coming down from on high to mingle with the commoners. All hail, his royal highness, Prince Stormy." Nettle gave an elaborate bow that was anything but respectful.

The words were dripping with sarcasm, and most of the others flashed outrage or shock, but there were a few who laughed.

He raised a hand, and everyone calmed their skin. "I know you have reason to hate me, Nettle, but I didn't commit the crimes that got your mother killed. Your mother did. It's my father's responsibility to see that justice is served. Your mother was involved with Rip, knew he had the Translator, and did nothing to save her."

"Justice?" Nettle spat. "If there was any *justice* in the universe, my mother would have been able to plead her case before the Full Council, but no, she was dragged off to be executed. She would never have done what they accused her of. We thought you were family. *I* thought you were family, but you betrayed us. You had her killed and then took her spot. You claim they were staging a coup, but I think you and your father were the real ones staging a coup. You got rid of everyone who didn't agree with you in one fell swoop, didn't you?"

"We have footage of Rip handing her the boxes that contained the Translator's claws, yet she told my father that it was delivered through the mail," Stormy replied. "Perhaps she was being blackmailed, too, but she did not take my father's offer or even demand a trial. Nor did I take her spot. I purposely left it vacant, just as the Senior Council left the Council seats vacant. It will be up to the Guilds and people to fill those positions. You might not believe me, but I grieve for your mother's loss, just as I am burned by her betrayal."

Nettle snorted. "Those are nothing but colorful words meant to impress the masses, but it doesn't impress me. Know that I will *never* vote for you. In fact, I intend to do everything I can to ensure that no one in your family ever takes your father's place, and I will prove my mother's innocence if it's the last thing I ever do." With that, she turned and swam away.

The guard behind him started to swim after her, but Stormy stopped him. "Let her go."

"You're going to let her threaten you like that?" the guard asked.

"She's grieving, and I won't stop her from defending her mother. If she should find proof that the Senior Council was wrong, I will be the first to champion her mother's case. That being said, I have seen the evidence to prove her guilt, and I doubt she will ever find that proof."

The guard didn't look convinced but didn't swim off either and then glanced down.

Stormy followed his gaze and sighed when he realized he'd crushed the basket he was carrying. He'd spent hours trying to wrangle the reeds into place before the meeting and had even missed out on dinner with the Translator and Little Flower because of it.

After tossing it into the nearby waste recycler, he swam off to his first class, doing his best to ignore everyone who watched him swim past.

When he reached his class, his guard insisted on checking it over before letting him in. He frowned at what he saw inside but took up position beside the door without comment.

Stormy swam in and found the room empty, save for Carrie, who sat in what had become her usual seat in the back. He wondered what she thought of his interview. Had she been hurt thinking there was more to their relationship?

She smiled at him. "I was wondering if you were coming today."

"My father says I need to finish primary school, and I suppose he's right. How are you doing?"

She shrugged. "It's been awkward, but thankfully, most people just ignore me now."

"I meant with your father?"

She shrugged again. "Even more awkward. We talked for several hours after he was released, *with* the guard present. They insisted, but I suppose it was for the best. I honestly don't know how I feel anymore. One minute, I want to claw his eyes out, and the next, I want to curl up in his arms and forget it all happened. I've granted him supervised visits for now. One hour every evening after he gets home from work."

"You don't trust him?"

She snorted. "I don't think he'll hurt me. It's me I don't trust."

"That's fair," Stormy replied. "Although you have every right to shock him."

She shrugged, then tilted her head. "He says your brother has allowed him on his squad and has even spoken up for him a time or two."

"That's my brother for you. I'm still in disbelief, but your father has to go somewhere, and I suppose it's easier to keep an eye on him this way. He says your father has been behaving. Granted, the guards my father put on him are rather intimidating."

"So I saw," Carrie replied, then looked up as another student swam in.

That student glared at him and then took the seat furthest away.

Right behind them was his friend Bramble Weed. Bramble saw him and bolted over and bowed. "Good morning, Your Highness. Might I have the pleasure and honor of sitting next to you today?"

Unlike Nettle, Bramble was teasing him and having a hard time keeping the laughter off his skin.

"I will shock you," Stormy replied with mock seriousness, "if you refer to me as 'Your Highness' ever again. Consider this your only warning."

"After having seen the torment you put that poor basket through, I thank you for the warning…Prince Stormy," Bramble bolted out of the way as Stormy lunged for him, but a moment later, he flopped into the seat next to him, laughing.

Stormy rolled his eyes at his friend but was honestly happy to see their relationship hadn't changed.

The same couldn't be said for the rest of his class.

By the time the class started, the lines had been drawn as clearly as if they were opposing forces on a battlefield, as people shifted their desks from one side to the other. Those who hated him were fewer, thankfully, and were honestly easier to handle, as he'd expected it. He understood their reasons and respected them for owning them.

Of the rest, some were simply making a political statement, but others were so obviously maneuvering for a relationship with their future Senior Councilor that it made him sick to his stomach.

He expected it from those who were in line for a Council rank themselves, but what he hadn't counted on were those trying to woo him. He might be a legal adult, but he didn't know how to handle the flirting, fawning, and sly looks from the female members of his class, so he ignored them.

That didn't go over well either, and several snubbed individuals pointedly shifted allegiances, earning boos from his followers and cheers from the others.

He had never been more grateful for his teacher to swim in or a class to begin than he was that day, even if the first thing his teacher announced was a pop quiz on material he'd missed while the Council was in session.

3 2

MARSEE: FAILED HEAT

*M*orning came far too early for Marsee the next day, and she groaned when her sister's alarm went off, but Little Flower woke angry, snarled out three different swears in Saber, and threw her tablet across the room with a growl to shut it off before storming into the waste room to shower.

Marsee blinked in surprise at the outburst before sliding off the bed with a yawn to make sure the tablet wasn't broken.

Thankfully, the Hue-mans' newly invented protective cases for their tablets seemed to have worked. She'd seen Little Flower angry on many occasions, but her sister only threw things when she was really upset.

"You don't have to keep training in Healers if you don't want to," Marsee said as she set the tablet down on the table. "We have more than enough to live on."

"I want to," her sister replied.

"So what's bothering you?"

"Nothing," her sister growled, then stormed her way over to her wetsuit and started yanking it on, muttering under her breath the entire time.

Marsee walked over and sat down in front of her. "It's not nothing. You don't get angry like this unless there's something wrong."

"There's *nothing* wrong. I just woke up on the wrong side of the bed."

"You woke up in the same place you always do," Marsee replied, honestly confused. "What does that have to do with anything?"

Her sister rolled her eyes. "It's a Hue-man expression. It means I woke up grumpy."

"You *always* wake up grumpy," Marsee countered. "But you only throw things when you're upset. *Please.* Tell me what's bothering you."

"It doesn't matter," her sister replied.

"If it's bothering you enough to throw your tablet, it matters. Have I done something wrong?"

"No," her sister replied.

"Then what is it?"

Her sister let out a heavy sigh. "It's my birthday."

Marsee frowned, even more confused, as all the Hue-man birthdays had been set to the date of the Cataclysm, and it wasn't her sister's Name Day either.

"My *Hue-man* birthday," Little Flower clarified. "I would have been turning twenty-one today on Earth. It was a big day for us, like your Name Day. GrandFather didn't remember before he left, and no one else is alive that knew, and I know it doesn't matter because I'm already an adult, but I'm missing my family and…and…"

Little Flower growled and swore again as she struggled into the top of the wet suit, but when her head appeared through the top, her face was streaked with tears.

Marsee's ears drooped, and she pulled her sister in for a hug. "Of course, it matters. Merry Birthday, Fish Breath."

"Happy Birthday," her sister replied with a sob that broke free.

"Happy Birthday," Marsee corrected. "So what do you do on your birthday to celebrate?"

"Party, go out with friends to the club to dance and get drunk," her sister replied through the tears and sobs that shook her.

"Drunk? There's a ritual drink? Is this part of your religion?"

Little Flower snorted. "I guess you could call it that. We drank alcohol and lots of it. We weren't legally allowed to until then, at least in my district. I dreamt that my mother had made me one of her famous death-by-chocolate molten cheesecakes. The same thing she made me every year. Everyone was there, and we set off the smoke detector with all the candles on the cake. I can almost taste it. Susie was there helping me pick out an outfit for the club, only that *stupid* alarm went off and..."

She held her sister, purring, until her sister shoved away and walked over to the table, wiping the tears off her face.

Little Flower grabbed her tablet and mask. "I need to go, or I'll be late." Without another word, she snagged her flippers in an angry huff and left, not even bothering with breakfast and leaving Marsee to watch Hope.

Marsee let out a heavy sigh. *Some partner I am. I didn't even know it was her birthday.*

After marking it down in her calendar, she turned to Hope, who was currently trying to climb her way out of her crib. "Well, Hope. What shall we do for your Mama's birthday?"

"Poop," Hope replied.

Marsee snorted. "I don't think that will help, Little Monkey." Still, Marsee scooped her daughter up before she could hurt herself and carried her over to the waste room.

Hope was just as cranky as her mother that morning, refusing to wear anything, and by the time Marsee left for the Guild, she was decidedly frazzled, but she stopped short when she walked out and found both Avery and Tamarin on duty.

"Who's watching Little Flower?" she demanded.

"Honor Guard Tanner and her son Red Fin," Avery replied. "They offered, and it will be easier for them to guard Little Flower in the Trauma Center than one of us. They'll be more inconspicuous. Clear Seas sent the last of our guards home last night with the Council. Except for a pair of guards who are on special assignment, only my half-squad remains, and while our only responsibility is guarding you, we'll still need assistance, and out of any of them, I trust them the most. If you want different guards…"

Marsee shook her head. "I trust them. I had Little Flower look into both their records after meeting Red Fin. I wanted to know what happened with his father, and after what we found, I have no doubt that Rip captured and tortured Red Fin on purpose, and *not* just to pressure Petra into confessing."

Avery raised a brow. "What makes you say that? I read the official report after Aris said Red Fin told you his father was killed. I didn't see any connection to Rip."

"It took some digging into the Archives and Little Flower's access to figure it all out. It's a tragic love story full of jealousy, unrequited love, and *murder*," Marsee said, pinning her ears and barring her fangs for emphasis. "I might have to turn it into a book." She paused as she considered the idea, then shrugged. "Perhaps someday I'll tell you, but today is not that day."

The look of astonishment on both guards was entertaining, to say the least.

Tail curled, she trotted away, and they followed, completely ignoring their duties.

"If you know something, you need to tell," Avery insisted. "Hiding evidence is a crime."

"The Seniors already know," Marsee replied.

Both guards reeked of frustration, but she felt they thoroughly deserved it since they still refused to tell her about Kendra and Rowena.

"Fine," Tamarin huffed. "I'll tell you, but you tell us what you know first."

She grinned with her victory. "The long and short of it: Rip's childhood sweetheart, Coralline, was in love with Red Fin's father and tried to get Tanner out of the way by staging and accusing Tanner of theft, but…"

"You're pulling our tails," Tamarin said. "Rip actually loved someone besides himself?"

She shrugged. "So it would appear."

"How did you determine that?" Avery asked.

"Nothing ever gets deleted on the servers, even if Rip thought it did. We found several examples of rather atrocious poetry that Rip sent to Coralline when he was still in primary school, professing his undying love."

"Poetry?!" Tamarin snorted.

"The seas hold nothing so fine as the eyes of my sweet Coralline," Marsee quoted.

Both guards snorted.

"I've heard worse," Tamarin said a moment later.

"That was honestly the best we found," Marsee countered. "Anyway, Red Fin's father claimed he was responsible for the theft to save his partner and the love of his life. When Red Fin finally proved his father's innocence, Coralline was executed, and Clear Seas gave Red Fin the right to perform it. I'm assuming that's why Rip hated Clear Seas so much, and likely his father, seeing as Rip killed his father only a few months later."

Avery reached out a paw and stopped her. "You're telling me all of this happened because Clear Seas executed Rip's girlfriend?"

"It would appear that way, although girlfriend is a bit of a stretch. Coralline loathed Rip. She only tolerated him because they were both in line for the Council. We found several texts that she shared with one of her friends trolling Rip and his poetry. I'm sure if we found it, Rip did, too. Although, it's possible that Rip planted the whole thing out of jealousy. I suppose we'll never know. Now tell me about Rowena and your tail."

"Not here," Tamarin replied. "I'll tell you tonight when we go to train. I imagine your sister will want to hear it too, and I'm not telling it twice."

Marsee nodded, accepting the delay, recognizing that they were out in public and that Tamarin might not want anyone else to hear, even if no one was around.

The moment they exited the lift, her guards resumed their menacing persona as her shadows, and nothing more was said as she grabbed a drone and took off.

They were in the middle of Market Square when she had an idea and veered suddenly to backtrack and duck down the side street where Fire Sticks was located, hoping that Opal was there that early in the morning. She was and swam over almost as soon as Marsee entered.

"Translator, will it be just you this morning?" Opal asked.

"I'm not here for breakfast. I'm hoping you can help me solve a little problem," Marsee replied and proceeded to explain.

Opal frowned in consideration. "I have no idea what that food might be, but I will see what I can do to find out and reproduce it if I can. Either way, I will gladly make something worthy of this special day."

"Thank you," Marsee replied and swam out.

When they arrived at the Guild, Marsee swam into the warehouse, hoping for inspiration. She growled in frustration after making her way through several sections, not finding what she was looking for.

"What *are* you looking for?" Tamarin eventually asked as they wandered the lighting section.

"Candles," Marsee replied.

Avery snorted. "You're not going to find that on this planet, and even if you did, you'd have platform operations and the fire brigade breaking down your door if you lit one."

"I know that," Marsee replied. "but I was hoping to find something similar that I could use."

"I have an idea," Tamarin said and swam off. Marsee followed her to the toy section, of all places, and she did her best to ignore her embarrassment when they swam past the very large section of Crawley Man toys.

Tamarin slowed and scanned the shelves. "Ah, here it is. My cubs used to love these." Tamarin turned and handed her a box.

Marsee grinned as she saw what it was. "That's perfect!"

She quickly purchased it and then made her way to the art section, where she grabbed more of the special paper that her sister was using these days and an even larger assortment of pens. She knew her sister would like it, but it didn't seem like nearly enough for such a special occasion. After grabbing a random assortment of other items, she was hit with a burst of inspiration and took off again. Fifteen minutes and a dozen wrong turns later, she tracked down the person she was looking for and explained what she wanted.

"Easily Translator. I'll bring it up to your office when I'm done."

She thanked them profusely and swam off as she was already late for her meeting with Agate.

"Sorry I'm late," she said as she swam in.

Avery took up guard outside, but Tamarin swam in with her to watch Hope so that Marsee could focus on her work.

Agate swam over as Hope started doing somersaults and giggling in the water. "She moves surprisingly well for a creature not designed for the water."

"They're far more adapted than we are for it, even with our webbed feet. It's difficult getting the cubs out of the pool back in New Hope. They spend most of their free time there. Little Flower is a far better swimmer than I am, even with her injuries and without the fins."

Agate spent a moment checking out the pair of tiny fins that Hope was wearing.

Hope was picking up on how to use them surprisingly fast, but it was challenging to get them on her and even harder to keep them on.

"They're quite clever," Agate decided.

"I wonder if they would work for the other species," Marsee mused and stretched out her legs, trying to approximate the motion Little Flower used. Even though she could walk on two legs, she wasn't fully bi-pedal the way the Hue-mans were. "Perhaps...but that motion is awkward. Maybe for the Ice Giants. They have similar body mechanics."

Their planned meeting devolved into a design session and a trip down to the floor to use one of the printers. Several prototypes later, Marsee had functional fins that worked for her species, nearly tripling their speed in the water. They still weren't as fast as the Sprites, but with a little practice, they were as good, if not better, than using the drones because she could move in different directions far quicker.

Remembering her thoughts on the adjustments she wanted to make to her sisters, she went back to work. Several more prototypes later, she ended up with what looked like nothing more than gloves she could wear all the time but, with a hard flick of her paws, would extend out into long fins that would expand and collapse with their normal swimming motion, yet still left her fingers and claws free.

She had dozens of ideas on how to improve them later and gave the techs she'd wrangled into helping a budget out of her research fund to work on those ideas, but for now, it would work.

Avery understood the benefits immediately. He printed out a set for himself and the rest of his squad, and she felt some of her anxiety ease.

When they swam back up to Agate's office to focus on the meeting at hand, Agate looked at her curiously. "I'm quite used to Ellie going off on a tangent whenever an idea strikes, but you seemed far more focused on this project than just a whim, and it's not like you to drop your responsibilities to go craft."

Marsee nodded, her face serious. "I wasn't fast enough."

Agate sighed her understanding but dropped the subject, and they went back to work.

She was in the middle of eating her lunch when her order for Little Flower arrived. She examined it with delight. It was even better than she had hoped, and she gave the crafter a substantial bonus.

Shortly after the crafter left, Avery got a call stating that Little Flower was heading back earlier than expected, so Tamarin took off to guard her as the Sprites couldn't do so easily in the platform and took Hope with her as Hope was getting cranky again.

A few hours later, she had a call from Opal.

"I've had a reply from one of the Hue-mans back in New Hope, and they sent me instructions, but I have no way of creating it as it requires several food sources I don't have, along with one of the heating units the Hue-mans use. However, I've done my best to come up with what I hope is an adequate substitute."

"Thank you, Opal. I appreciate the effort, regardless. I'll be right over."

She packed up, wished Agate a good night, and made her way over to Fire Sticks, where Opal immediately led her back into the kitchen. The other Sprites crowded around to see her reaction. Marsee had seen and tried most of the Hue-man foods, but what Opal showed her looked nothing like anything she'd ever seen before. It was a work of art. Bright red and orange flowers and intricate designs covered it and made it look like a stream of molten lava cascading down the side of a cliff, with flowers decorating the rest of it.

"It looks almost too beautiful to eat," Marsee replied.

Opal beamed and held up a plate and sticks to try it with. "Everything is edible and safe for both you and Little Flower, but before you try, you should know that it's made with animal products. It was necessary to get it to hold its shape. I know your species does not eat meat, but this was the closest I could come."

Marsee took the plate. "I've tried a number of the Hue-man foods out of curiosity and find them quite enjoyable, although I would rather others not know that. It's a bit of a taboo for our species."

"Your secret is safe with us," Opal promised.

She sniffed deeply, took a careful bite, and groaned with happiness. It was like fire sticks and chocolate chip cookies rolled up in one, and whatever the texture was, it melted in her mouth. "I don't know if Little Flower will like it, but *I* love it! What is it?"

Opal listed off the ingredients, most of which she'd never heard of before. "I'm thinking of calling it sweet lava in our language. Honor Guard, would you like to try some, too?"

Avery nodded. "I don't have my species aversion to meat either. As part of our training, we sample and learn all of the species' foods in the event of an emergency, what's safe for us anyway. I will admit, I'm not partial to the few foods that are safe for us to eat on Digger."

"I don't blame you," Opal replied, laughter flickering across her skin. "I'm not a fan either. It doesn't seem right to eat food that's still alive, even if it is a crawley."

Avery sighed with contentment as he tried his piece. "I must admit, the Translator's association with you is by far the biggest benefit of our assignment."

Marsee laughed as Opal lit up bright blue with the compliment. "And here I thought chasing me around the arena was the highlight of your day."

"That's a close second," he replied.

Laughing, Opal packed up her order along with a large order of brenna berry sticks for their evening meal, in the event Little Flower didn't like the cake, and they returned to the suite, although Opal insisted on carrying the cake as far as the platform for them. She took it carefully from Opal with her thanks and promised to let her know what Little Flower thought of it.

Her sister was asleep, curled up under a blanket on the bed when Marsee entered. Hope had climbed out of her crib and was quietly playing with her toys on the floor, so she set everything down on the table and made her way over to wake her sister up, nearly bouncing with excitement with her surprise, but as she approached the bed, her nose picked up the smell of blood — a lot of it. Running over to her sister, she pulled back the blanket and froze with horror. Her sister was face down, and there was blood everywhere on both her sister and the bedding.

Ancient Gods, not again!

Panicking, she shook her sister hard. "Little Flower, wake up!" she cried. "Tamarin, help!"

"Huh? What's wrong?" her sister asked, waking up and rolling over as Avery and Tamarin bolted into the room. There was even more blood under her.

"You're covered in blood!" Marsee exclaimed in near panic as she tried to find the wound.

"I am?" her sister asked weakly as Tamarin shoved Marsee aside.

"No one's been in the room, and she's been snoring for the last hour," Tamarin said, frowning at all the blood.

Avery bolted for the attached suite, checking for signs of an intruder before returning and checking the waste room.

"I can't find a wound," Tamarin said and forcibly rolled her sister over to check her back.

Little Flower squawked at the unexpected motion, then yelped and scampered away when Tamarin touched Little Flower's leg near her groin.

"Don't touch me there!" Little Flower hissed in Saber, surprising all three of them, then looked down at the blood and let out a heavy sigh. "I'm fine. I'm not injured," she signed. "I've started my period. Ugh, what a mess. Well, at least that explains why I've been so grumpy all day." She rolled off the other side of the bed, leaving a trail of blood behind her, and shoved her way past Avery to start digging through the drawers where her clothes were stored.

"Tamarin, do something!" Marsee ordered.

"She ordered me not to touch her," Tamarin replied. "I can't."

"I'm fine," Little Flower growled.

There's so much blood. How is she not in agony? Marsee wondered. She knew her sister had a high tolerance for pain, but her sister was acting like she wasn't even hurt. "This can't be right. You need to see a healer. Please let Tamarin examine you."

"I'm fine, Marsee," Little Flower called back. "I don't need treatment. This is normal. The universe does have a sick sense of humor, though. I would get my period on my birthday."

"Normal?! How can this be normal? You're covered in blood!" Marsee exclaimed.

"It's been years since I've had a period. I suppose it's not surprising it would be heavy."

Little Flower stripped off her soiled clothing and tossed them in the cleaner, not even caring about the two guards still in the room and watching.

Marsee flattened her ears in horror, as her sister never undressed in front of anyone outside of her or her mother. She sniffed again, focusing hard, and noticed the lower portion of her sister's stomach was bright red, even where there wasn't blood. The rest of her skin was nearly as pale as when Hope had first been born.

Blood continued to run down her sister's legs as she jumped in the sonic shower and cleaned herself up. When she was done, she unwrapped a new pair of the underclothing she wore and put them on. "These are supposed to be absorbent and catch it, so we'll see how well they work. Can you strip the bed and throw it in the cleaner?"

"Blood is pouring down your legs, and you're worried about the bedding?!" Marsee exclaimed.

"I'm fine," Little Flower replied, but then grunted and rubbed at her stomach.

She must be delirious from blood loss, Marsee decided. She ran over, scooped her sister up, and started to carry her out of the room. Tamarin might not have the authority to treat Little Flower after having refused, but she knew the Senior Healer could override it, especially if she felt the patient was unable to make a rational decision.

"What are you doing? Put me down!" her sister yelled.

"No, you're delirious. You need a healer," Marsee said, grabbing her sister's mask and forcing it on.

"Marsee, I promise you I'm fine," her sister complained as she struggled to stop her. "Put me down!"

"You. Are. Not. Fine. You're seeing a healer, and I'm not taking no for an answer. Tamarin, watch Hope," she ordered and bolted out of the room.

Avery followed right behind her.

She felt her sister wince and smelled more blood moments later. She ran for all she was worth. She was not going to be too late a second time.

"Marsee, it's okay. It's just a cramp."

She growled and activated their masks moments before she dove through the shield into the ocean.

"Grab my harness," Avery ordered, stopping her from grabbing her own drone. "It'll be faster than you'll be able to manage holding on to her."

She did, and Avery punched his drone as fast as it would go while she used her back fins to make them go faster.

Her sister sighed in defeat and stopped struggling, but that scared Marsee even more.

She let go of Avery the moment they arrived and swam as hard as she could. Bursting through the door of the Trauma Center, she swam over to the triage healer. "I found her covered in blood. It was all over her clothes and our bed. She washed herself off in the sonic shower, but it just kept running down her legs. She must be bleeding internally," Marsee said, praying the healer understood Saber.

"Marsee, I'm telling you, I'm fine. Healer, I've just started my menstrual cycle. This is normal, but since I'm here, I could use something for the pain," her sister said in sign at the same time.

Marsee shook her head. "She's not fine. She was rubbing at her lower stomach and wincing in pain. She's very pale, and I can smell more blood. She's not acting normally, either. She changed her clothes in front of the guards, and she *never* does that. It's a cultural taboo."

The healer hit a switch on her desk, took Little Flower from her, and bolted back to the trauma bay, not even bothering to examine her.

Marsee and Avery followed right behind. Her sister huffed in annoyance but didn't fight the healer.

Moments after the healer set her down on a bed, the Senior Healer appeared, and the other one left back to her station after giving the information Marsee had provided in rapid-fire Water Sprite. It was so fast that Marsee only caught a few words.

The monitor sprang to life, and the Senior Healer examined them for several moments. "You are both correct. Marsee, this is her menstrual cycle. My information states that this level of bleeding is normal for her species, as are pain and mood swings. However, Little Flower, you're also dehydrated and anemic. Not enough to require a transfusion, but I'm going to give you fluids, an iron supplement, and vitamins to help with the anemia. How would you describe your pain?"

"Annoying and covered in fuzz," her sister said, pointedly glaring at her.

The Senior Healer bubbled with amusement.

Marsee was not the least bit amused and lashed her tail.

The Healer's skin immediately cleared, and Little Flower sighed. "It's a dull cramping ache, normal for me, maybe a four out of ten. I've had far worse."

"I'll get you something for the pain," the Healer signed and left, returning a few minutes later with supplies. The Healer gave her two shots and then hooked up the I.V. "This may make you a little drowsy." A few moments later, her sister relaxed as the pain meds kicked in, and only then did Marsee start to calm.

"Do you think maybe you can believe me next time?" Little Flower asked with a glare.

"No. The last time you were covered in that much blood, you ended up in a coma, and you clearly needed medical treatment," Marsee glared right back. "I wasn't fast enough before, and I almost lost you." She wasn't the least bit sorry for dragging her sister over.

"I'm sorry I scared you, Chenzie Butt," Little Flower replied and closed her eyes with a yawn. Her eyes didn't reopen.

Marsee frowned at how quickly her sister had fallen asleep, but she knew enough to read the vitals on the monitor, and they were steady and strong. She floated there, not sure what to do, until the Senior Healer returned a few minutes later.

"Okay, very drowsy," the Senior Healer flashed with further hints of amusement. "I'll make note of that. We've only used that particular pain medicine once with her species, but sleep would be good for her right now. While we're waiting for her treatment to finish, how are you doing?"

"Physically, quite a bit better," Marsee replied. "I'm probably in better shape than I was before everything happened. My hand still bothers me, though. It's either numb or aches, but then I'm using it a lot."

The healer gave her a scan, and while she was professional enough to keep it off her skin, Marsee sniffed out surprise. "I may have to take a trip over to the arena to see what you're doing for physical therapy. You're far more recovered than I expected. How far can you run?"

Marsee shrugged. She had no idea how long the laps were. "I usually do five laps at the beginning and end of each session. Sometimes more."

"Her current max for a single run without a break is five and a half leagues," Avery called out from the hall.

This time, the healer wasn't able to keep her surprise off her skin. "Well, if you can manage that, then you should have no problems with a jump."

"I'm not leaving until she's done her cycle," Marsee replied.

"That's probably safest for both of you," the healer said as she began unhooking her sister from the I.V.

Her sister didn't wake up.

The healer left and returned half an hour later, examined the scans again, and handed Marsee a bag. "Her vitals are much better. Instructions are in the bag. Your sister is trained to use all of these, but if you have questions, call or ask Tamarin. Take her home and let her sleep it off."

"Leave?!" Marsee asked with wide-eyed astonishment. "But she's still bleeding!"

"She will for days, maybe as much as half a standard week. There's nothing I can do to speed it up; only treat her symptoms, and it'll be safer and more comfortable for her in your suite."

"Safer?!" She could tell the Healer was serious, but she couldn't believe it. There had been so much blood!

"Gravity will help clean out the shedding lining, and before you ask, none of our dry rooms are equipped for her species. I can't justify taking a trauma bed for this. It's not life-threatening. She's honestly at far more risk of infection by staying here."

Her nose flared with the smell of blood, and she frowned and looked back at her sister. This went against everything she'd ever been taught about healing. Her mother had certainly never let a patient leave when they were still bleeding.

"I know you're worried, but I assure you, this is normal for her species, and from what your mother told me, the Hue-mans prefer privacy and the comfort of their own suites during this time. The pain meds I gave her should wear off in about eight hours. If she hasn't woken up by then, or if you notice any trouble breathing or a rash, bring her back."

She handed the bag to Avery before swimming over and gently

scooping up her sister. Little Flower's eyes fluttered open briefly and then closed again as she snuggled in against her side.

She pinned her ears at the healer. "If you're wrong…"

"I am well aware of the consequences, Leviathan Slayer," The Senior Healer interrupted. "I promise you, she'll be fine, and she'll be far happier in your suite."

She glared at the Senior Healer for a moment longer before swimming out.

Avery clearly wasn't happy about it either, but he said nothing as she swam past. He dragged them back over to the Platform as quickly as they'd arrived. Her sister didn't so much as shift in her arms the entire way.

When they made it back to the room, the bed had been changed, and Tamarin was curled up on one of the cushions around Hope, who had fallen asleep, using the honor guard's arm for a pillow and her overly fluffy tail for a blanket.

"Stay, please," Marsee said as Tamarin started to get up. "I'd prefer the company right now, and she looks comfortable."

Tamarin nodded and settled back down as Marsee carefully laid her sister on the bed and curled just as protectively around her to wait, praying to every ancient god in the universe that the Healer was right and that her sister would wake up.

LITTLE FLOWER: MERRY BIRTHDAY

*L*ittle Flower stretched with a groan and blinked in surprise, then rubbed at her eyes. "When did I get back here?"

"About three hours ago," Marsee replied. "How are you feeling?"

"Sleepy," she replied, then rolled over as she needed to use the hole of muck.

She snorted with laughter as she caught sight of Tamarin and Hope. Hope was sprawled across Tamarin's arms with one foot planted squarely between the guard's eyes. "I don't know how she sleeps like that, but don't move. I want to draw that after I use the hole of muck. Where's my tablet?"

Tamarin let out a heavy sigh.

"Poor abused Honor Guard," Marsee snickered and leaned over to grab her tablet for her.

"Well, at least *she* doesn't snore," Tamarin replied.

Little Flower snapped several pictures, then stood up and almost immediately fell as the world spun on her.

Her sister caught her before she could. "Are you alright?" Marsee asked, ears drooping with worry.

She was used to the world spinning, but for some reason, it made her giggle rather than feel sick.

"I don't know what was in that pain medicine, but it certainly is fun," she replied. Then, holding onto random pieces of furniture, she stumbled her way over to grab a change of clothing, with Marsee right behind her, ready to catch her if she fell again. "I'm fine, Marsee. You don't need to hover."

Marsee ignored her reassurances and didn't leave her side until she was safely sitting on the hole of muck.

Little Flower examined the absorbent underwear with curiosity. She was rather impressed at how well it had done its job, but she stepped out of them so she could change into a fresh pair.

Marsee was still in the way and hovering as if afraid she was going to fall off the toilet. To be fair, she had, twice, during her convalescence.

"If you're going to hover, toss these in the sanitizer," Little Flower said, holding up the soiled underwear.

She expected Marsee to be disgusted and bolt for the door, but her sister took them from her without complaint, although her ears drooped further.

"There's so much blood. How do you manage this every couple of weeks?"

She shrugged. "We just do. I don't know how you manage not to trip over your own tail, so I suppose we're even."

Marsee didn't even chuckle at the joke as she placed the soiled garments in the sanitizer.

"Marsee, I assure you, I'm fine. I promise to let you know if I need anything. Right now, I'd really like a little privacy."

Marsee didn't look convinced, but she nodded and left the room. The door slid shut behind her.

She breathed a sigh of relief, then winced and doubled over as a cramp hit her. She breathed through it, then decided to take another shower before putting on her clean clothing. The nice thing about the showers on the Water World was that there was no shortage of water. They had installed an actual shower in addition to the static ones she'd gotten used to back on Saber, and thankfully, as she was still a little dizzy, they had even included a seat.

As she let the hot water pour over her, she absently wondered if they had provided the rest of her council with similar facilities or just her, owing to her disabilities. It was one of the nicest bathrooms she'd ever seen and perfectly suited for her.

She leaned against the wall and let the hot water pour over her until her cramps faded, and she was about ready to fall asleep again, even though the water was so hot it nearly scaled her. She could almost hear her mother yelling at her for wasting the hot water. With a depressed sigh, she pushed off the wall and finished her shower.

A few minutes later, cleaned and changed and feeling somewhat better, she made her way back out into the common room but stopped and gasped as the door slid open. She rubbed at her eyes, sure she was dreaming or hallucinating from the drugs.

There, in front of her, was her family. Her parents, her cousins, her grandfather Ben, and even Susie. They were all smiling and waving at her.

"Happy Birthday, Jessica," her mother said.

Tears started streaming uncontrolled down her face. "How... How did you do this?"

"I took your drawings to one of the local techs and had them generate holo-vids based on your drawings and scans of you and the other Hue-mans. If something's not right, we can have them tweaked."

"They're perfect," she replied, then hiccuped as a sob escaped. "Oh god, Marsee. I miss them so much!"

Marsee ran over and hugged her until she managed to bring her emotions back under control. When she could finally see through her tears, she walked over and examined them closer, marveling at the details. They were so lifelike. She put her hand up and felt resistance. It wasn't quite like touching a person, in the same way that the walls at the Agency had felt off, but so close that she had to wipe more tears from her eyes.

"It's based on static shield technology, so you can interact with them. They can be programmed with different movements and voices.

If we had a recording of their voices, the AI could use that, but since we don't, I had them take your voice and adjust based on your species' gender differences and age changes. If it's not right, I can show you how to change it until we can find something that matches."

"This is by far the best birthday present I have ever been given. Thank you, Chenzie Butt."

"You're welcome, but that's not all I got you," Marsee said, waving her over the table. Marsee lifted a cover to reveal. Well, she wasn't quite sure what she was looking at. 'Cake' was too plain of a word for whatever this masterpiece was, but it had 'Happy 21st Birthday' written on the top in slightly skewed English.

"Opal tried to make you a cake, but she didn't have the right ingredients or one of the heating units, so she invented this instead. Candles proved to be far trickier. If I even tried to light one, the fire brigade would be at our door within seconds, but Tamarin came up with a solution."

Marsee hit the lights, plunging the room into darkness, save for the light of the holo-vids of her family. Moments later, colored lights began dancing around the room.

"Flicker Flyers?" Little Flower asked with surprised laughter.

"Toy versions," Marsee replied and turned the lights back up, but not all the way.

"They're perfect, too. Thank you. There's only one problem. Without candles, I can't blow them out and make a wish."

"That's what you wanted the candles for?" Marsee asked.

"It's tradition. One candle for each year. If you can blow them all out, your wish will come true. You also sing an absolutely horrible song as badly off-key as possible. Why or how that became a tradition, I have no idea. Thankfully, my family never went along with the birthday spanking tradition, although I suppose the lack of a pinch might account for why I'm so short."

Both Marsee and Tamarin looked at her with a mix of confusion and horror. They didn't have a sign for spanking, so she'd invented 'butt slap' instead.

"You were hit on your birthday?" Tamarin asked.

"What does pinching you have to do with your height?" Marsee asked before she could answer the first question.

She shrugged in response to Marsee's question. "The tradition there was one spanking per year of your life, never hard, and a pinch to grow an inch. Although a spanking," she signed and said the word, "was a common form of punishment for children, usually just with the open palm."

"Usually?" Tamarin asked with a frown.

She shrugged. "Some people used belts, wooden spoons, or other objects. My mother preferred the bottom of her slippers." She glanced at Marsee briefly, slightly embarrassed as a thought occurred. "And it could be sexual in nature, too, or so I've been told. That's nothing I have any interest in, but to each their own, I suppose, as long as it's consensual."

"Your parents abused you?" Tamarin asked again with a frown. "Has GrandFather ever spanked you?"

She raised her hands to reply, trying to figure out how to explain when the conversation had gone so badly off the rails, and scratched her head instead.

This made both Tamarin and Marsee frown.

"Little Flower, is your grandfather hurting you?" Tamarin insisted, going full guard.

"No!" she replied immediately. "Nor has he ever spanked, hit, or otherwise hurt me. My birth father was another story, but I suppose I deserved it both times. The first time was for sneaking out with Buster in the middle of the night to go for a moonlit ride. I thought it would be fun, but I didn't realize how hard it would be to see the footing. Buster was hurt badly enough that my grandfather had to stitch him up, and they couldn't use him for farming for a couple of weeks while he healed. The second time, I was sloppy with handling a weapon and pointed it at my father by accident. I never made that mistake a second time."

She shuddered at that memory. It was the one time her father had really scared her. He'd changed. She hadn't understood then, but she did now, and she was terrified that she would hurt her daughter unintentionally during one of her panic attacks the way he had hurt her.

Tamarin's eyes narrowed. "You're scared. Why?" she demanded. "Who's hurting you?"

"No one," she replied and looked over at the holo-vid of her father. The eyes weren't quite right. There was no soul behind them, but it reminded her of the look that she had seen that day, the soldier.

"My father suffered from the trauma of being in a war. I knew from a young age never to sneak up on him, but I forgot. We were out hunting for deer. They're kind of like your doba. Usually, we would just sit and wait for them, but it was a beautiful day, and my father was trying to teach me how to track them. Eventually, we found a spot to take a break and wait. After a while, he stood and stretched and then walked away. I packed up the remains of my lunch and followed a minute or two later. When I caught up to him, he was hunched down, peering through some bushes and waiting. I figured he'd seen something, so I got my weapon ready and tried to approach as quietly as possible. I didn't realize he was having a flashback at the time. I stepped on a stick just behind him, and he spun. A second later, I was face down on the ground with a knife at my throat and a broken arm. My father wasn't my father anymore, and he didn't see me. All he saw was an enemy with a weapon aimed at him. I was lucky that the only thing that happened was a broken arm. It was the last time we ever went hunting together. That was about a year before the cataclysm. I don't know if he ever told my mother what really happened. I told everyone I had tripped on a root and landed wrong."

Tamarin seemed to accept her story, but Marsee just stared at her. "Why didn't you ever tell me?"

She shrugged. "It was in the past, and I wanted to remember the good moments I had with him instead." She decided to lighten things up, "As for my mother, she usually used her slipper in much the same way Ellie does her tail with Marsee, but she did throw it at me a time or two, but then I had a bit of an attitude when I was younger, and my mouth got me into a lot of trouble."

Marsee snorted, and Tamarin relaxed. Tamarin said something to

Marsee, and Marsee snorted again. Marsee didn't translate, but she had a feeling it was along the lines of "Some things never change."

"Mostly, though, they just took privileges away," she continued. "They learned pretty quickly that taking my art supplies worked far better as a consequence."

"Well, thankfully, you don't have to worry about that today either," Marsee said. "I also picked up more art supplies for you. Mostly, the paper you've been using, along with every color of pen I could find."

She nearly dropped the massive bag Marsee handed her as it was far heavier than she expected and grinned at what she saw inside. "Did you leave anything in the warehouse?"

"Some," Marsee replied with a grin. "But not much. So what's this horrible song we're supposed to sing."

She grinned, and both sang and signed it for them.

Marsee's ears pinned, and she cringed from how offkey it was, but a moment later, the holo-vids of her family started singing, and Marsee and Tamarin joined in. Tamarin couldn't form half the words, but somehow, that just added to the effect. It was so loud and obnoxious that it woke Hope.

Both laughing and crying, Little Flower wiped the tears away. "That was the best worst song I have ever heard. Thank you."

Marsee beamed a smile.

"Why do you sing it off-key?" Tamarin asked.

She shrugged. "I don't know, just to be silly, I suppose. There were variations, too, depending on who was singing it and how annoying they wanted to be." She signed a few of them as Marsee grabbed dishes from the kitchen. Tamarin snorted.

While Marsee dished them all up slices of the cake, she dragged Aris and Thatcher, who were now on guard outside, in for their slices. There was no way she could eat it all.

Whatever it was, it smelled delicious, although it was more gelatinous than cake-like. She grabbed a spoon, and as she liked everything Opal had ever given her to try, she didn't hesitate to take a large mouthful.

It. Was. A. Mistake.

Pain exploded in her mouth. She started coughing and gasping for air. Tears streamed down her face as she ran for the fridge to find something to put the fire in her mouth out. She grabbed the pitcher of juice and drank straight from it, but that only spread the fire. Setting it aside, she pawed through the leftovers, then sent up a prayer of thanks when she found a package from the night before. She ripped it open and shoved the leftover jelly eggs in her mouth, then sighed with relief when it finally cut the pain to a somewhat manageable level.

"What in the blazing inferno is in that thing?" Little Flower signed as she was still gasping too hard to speak.

Marsee's tail spiraled tightly in response.

She scowled at her sister. "Did GrandFather put you up to this?"

Marsee's tail drooped slightly, and she tilted her head with confusion at the question. "No. It's what you asked for this morning."

"What I asked for?" she asked.

Marsee nodded. "We weren't sure exactly what you dreamed about, but Opal said GrandFather told her that you used to have something called a death pepper. We figured that must be what it was. She used the hottest thing she could find that was safe for your species. I hope you like it. I happen to think it's delicious."

It took her a moment to put the pieces together, and she burst out laughing at the horrible mistranslation. "It's called a ghost pepper, not a death pepper, and the molten part meant there was a layer of melted chocolate inside and right out of the oven hot, not spicy hot, but it's perfect anyway." She smiled with an innocent expression. "And I'm sure Grandfather will be just as amused on *his* birthday."

Marsee grinned with relief, but then her ears drooped again. "I'm sorry I didn't understand about the candles and that you won't get your wish."

She wiped the tears that were still streaming from her eyes and hugged Marsee. "Don't be. There's nothing I could wish for that you haven't already given me. Thank you for making this a birthday I'll always remember."

Marsee purred and leaned against her for a second but then, a moment later, reached around and pinched her butt — hard!

"Ow!" she yelped and scrambled away. "What was that for?"

Marsee plastered on an innocent expression that was in no way innocent. "I didn't want you to miss out on *any* of your traditions. So, twenty-one butt slaps, is it?" Marsee raised her paw, and her expression changed to one of mischief.

"Try it, and I'll shoot you with my stunner," she replied. "That's one tradition I have absolutely no intentions of keeping."

"Spoilsport," Marsee replied with an exaggerated sigh, and all three guards burst out laughing.

She snorted at her sister. "You are such a Chenzie Butt."

Marsee grinned. "I know, and I love you, too. Fish Breath."

3 4

ELLIE: MATING PSYCHOSIS

Over the next several days, the instinctive need to mate drove Ellie to pinnacles so high that she thought she could never exceed them, only to blow past them moments later. They barely ate or drank and would go until they crashed with exhaustion, only to wake a few hours later and begin again.

This state of bliss continued until she felt a sharp pain in her side.

The unexpectedness and intensity of it made her cry out, and she snapped and growled at her mate, furious at him for hurting her.

How dare he! They hissed.

He backed away quickly before she could maul him but only looked confused by her actions. "What's wrong?" he signed.

She paused, confused by his concern. *If he didn't hurt us, why are we in so much pain?* She looked back at her side, expecting to see blood from how much she hurt, but there was nothing.

There was a sound of swoosh, and she looked back just as two strangers bolted into the room and grabbed her mate. He snarled and writhed to defend himself but wobbled and collapsed to the floor, unmoving a moment later.

Terrified for her mate and deciding they were somehow the cause of her pain, she launched herself at them with a vicious snarl.

Leave him! He's ours!

They growled at her but backed away from her mate. She rushed to his side and stood protectively over him, growling until they backed up further. She continued to glare and growl at them as she sniffed at her mate and nudged him with her head, but he didn't move. He was still alive and breathing, though.

Not sure what they had done to him, she carefully grabbed him by the scruff with her teeth and dragged him to the far side of the room where she could protect him better.

They hissed and growled at her but didn't approach.

When he was as far away from them as she could get, she nudged at him again and whimpered.

Get up!

As she did, a third person entered the room, looking familiar, but she couldn't remember who they were. They stopped by the door when she roared her fury.

"It's me, Myra," they signed. "I'm your friend. I'm not going to hurt you, and neither are they."

Friend? How could they be friends? They attacked our mate!

"Sniff me," Myra signed. "Remember me. I'm family. I'm here to help you, not hurt you. I'm on your side."

Ellie sniffed deeply.

Yes! Family. Sister, her instinct determined, and they were immediately comforted by the familiar scent, even if they didn't recognize the other people in the room. The familiarity of the scene and her sister's scent triggered another memory.

This happened before, she reminded her instinct. *With...with...what was his name? Why can't I remember?*

Another wave of pain made her wince and growl again.

"You're in pain," Myra signed. "I only want to help. You're safe. I promise I won't let anything happen to you. I need you to trust me. Turn off your instinct and let me approach. No one is going to hurt you. I just want to stop your pain."

Her instinct trusted Myra but not the other two and refused to let her turn it off. She pinned her ears and growled at the strangers.

"Would you like them to leave?" Myra asked.

She rolled her eyes and huffed at the ridiculous question. Of course, she wanted them to leave.

Myra growled at the strangers. They growled back, but her sister merely scowled at them, and they bolted out of the room.

Ellie snorted at their weak behavior but didn't stop growling until they were gone.

"There. It's just us. Can I approach?"

Ellie huffed and flicked her whiskers forward in agreement, then looked down at her mate, who still hadn't moved. She whimpered with fear and worry as she licked his face, then shoved her head hard against him, trying to wake him up.

Myra slowly walked over.

Ellie looked up at her sister and whimpered again, asking for help. Somehow, she knew her sister could fix him. She was special.

"He's alright. He's just sleeping. Would you like me to wake him up?"

Before she could answer, another wave of pain struck her side, and she whimpered again, this time in fear. Wondering what the others had done to her.

"Can you turn your instinct off? I'll be able to help you better if you can tell me where you hurt."

Oh yeah, I can talk, Ellie suddenly remembered and flicked her instinct off to do so, but her pain flared the moment she did, and it dropped her to her knees.

"It hurts," Ellie groaned and grabbed her side.

Myra pulled out her scanner. "I know. It's alright. It's just your eggs releasing. You'll be fine. I promise."

Ellie looked up and swallowed hard at the look in her friend's eyes.

Myra's mask was on tightly, but it didn't hide her fear at all.

She winced as another wave of pain hit her. "Whatever happens, thank you for trying, Myra. I love you."

"I love you too, Ellie," Myra replied, then pressed a sedative to her arm.

ELLIE: AGAINST THE ODDS

*E*llie woke slowly from the sedative to find Myra sitting beside her, waiting for her to wake up. "Did it work?"

Myra nodded. "So far. We ended up with six viable embryos. Now, it's a matter of waiting to see if they successfully implant. We'll know in a few hours."

Six chances, Ellie thought. *And I only need one. Please! Give me one beautiful, healthy cub. That's all I'm asking for. Just one!*

"Your guard said to contact him if you're interested in pursuing a relationship. I believe I heard 'gift from the gods' as he walked out."

Ellie smiled and leaned back into her pillow. "If I survive, I might just consider it. That was…hmm… Let's just say if I die, I will die extremely satisfied. *Mee-oww.*"

Myra chuckled. "He certainly is yummy to look at, although that's usually the furthest thing from my mind when he's around."

"Look at, touch, bite, lick…" She sighed with happy memories of the past few days. "Peter was an amateur, and I'm sorry, Myra, but he beat you paws down."

"I should hope so," Myra replied.

Ellie frowned at her. "He looked familiar. Who was he, and when did you meet him?"

"You really were out of it," Myra replied with a grin. "That was none other than Quinn Bluestone."

"Kendra's second!" Ellie squeaked and lay back with a groan of embarrassment. "Please tell me that's not all over the news? Ancient Gods, they're going to think I'm taking over the Guard now, too."

"No one knows where you are, patient confidentiality and all that, and believe me, the Press is not happy about it. Neither is Marcus. I had at least a dozen messages from him demanding to know where you were until they suddenly stopped. I'm guessing it's because he's in jump, or he finally cornered Jer or Marsee about it. In case you're wondering, the healers were quite interested in our little experiment. You produced far more eggs than last time and two more viable embryos. They're going to see if that helps improve the odds for high-risk patients."

"Isn't that a risk for the other females, though? I was far more out of it than last time, and you weren't exactly supposed to be using your instinct. I can't believe I attacked you. I didn't even recognize you at first."

"You wouldn't be the first, but it's far safer now than it ever was before. There are guards stationed here for a reason, and you responded quicker than any of us expected, especially after what happened to you. There was a whole squad waiting outside, just in case."

Ellie's eyes widened as she realized what Myra was implying. "How often does that happen?"

"Far more often than I like. Just as with using our instinct, the risk increases with each heat. It's the real reason we don't allow a third heat. The odds of dying from Mating Psychosis is actually far greater than a miscarriage and nearly as high as hunting, but we don't tell people that, or we'd never have any cubs. It's the whole reason I wouldn't let you try a third time. You were far too close with your first two heats, and if it weren't for sign language today, I don't think you would have survived. You didn't understand the others, did you?"

She swallowed hard and shook her head. "No, but I understood you and Quinn. What about you? How are you doing? Any issues after our little experiment?"

"I'm fine. I've been tested three times since we arrived, including once by Quinn a few minutes ago. I spoke to him at length about our little experiment before he left. From his experience, as long as you're in full agreement with your instinct, there's never a problem. So, as long as the partners are willing and know sign language, it should be an enjoyable experience for everyone. I know it was far better for me than anything Jer and I have tried since Marsee was born, and if I weren't being watched, I'd seriously consider trying that with him when he gets back. It was a good distraction and one I think I needed. I feel a lot calmer than I did before."

"Well, thank you for taking the risk anyway. I would have been in agony if you weren't there. It was hard enough even with you there."

"Of course," Myra said.

Ellie squinted at her. "Wait, what happened between you and Quinn? You're not referring to the Trial, are you?"

Myra looked away, looking like a naughty child. "I may or may not have gotten a little upset when I found out what Jer did to Marsee. Quinn followed to make sure I wasn't out of control, along with what looked like two full squads of guards."

Ellie snorted. "I bet you did. I nearly bit Marcus's head off when I found out the full extent. I was so mad, I even yelled at Avery."

"You knew?"

"Marsee told me some of it the day Jer came to my house to get her, but I promised not to tell anyone. It was the only way to get her to tell me what was going on. Kendra spoke to me after, as she heard the whole conversation through an open window. I didn't even know she was there, but I'm glad she was. Marsee has your attitude when she's mad, and I'm not sure I could have stopped her if she'd gone after her father."

Myra frowned. "You should have told me."

"I keep my promises, but I did what I could to protect her. That's one of the main reasons I moved my office to New Hope. I'm sorry I didn't do a better job on the Water World. I should have gone to the

Arboretum with her, but I thought she'd be safe with the guards watching her."

"That wasn't your fault," Myra replied. "And you've more than made up for it, but if you hear of Jer laying so much as a whisker on her again, you let me know."

"There won't be anything left of him if he does. Marsee will see to that. Any word on the Council Meeting?" Ellie asked, changing the subject.

"Oh yeah. You missed a doozy. Nearly a quarter of the Council was executed, and another quarter voted out or stepped down, along with a good forty or fifty others across all the guilds. A Sprite by the name of Irukanji attacked Marsee, along with several others. One nearly killed Avery, but Little Flower stunned them all before the guard could react."

"Iruki?!" Ellie exclaimed. "I don't believe it."

Myra nodded. "According to the information the Seniors released, she was stealing from the Guild and working with Rip to bring down Clear Seas. It's how Rip found out about Snapper Fish, along with dozens of others he was blackmailing. Rip intended to make her Senior Guild Master, or so he promised."

Ellie frowned. "She's a Staffer. She wouldn't qualify."

Myra shrugged. "I doubt that would have stopped him. There's more. Henry Curtis, Stormy Seas, and Deep Current were all awarded the Consortium Medal of Honor, and Buster and the other horses were granted protected status. Marsee was awarded the Leviathan Cloak by the Council, not just as a gift, and Clear Seas publicly apologized for voting with precedent at Little Flower's Trial and nearly taking Marsee's future cubs away from her. You really need to watch that part. Marsee was...well, your protege. Then Tabor surprised everyone by showing up and advocating for Damon and Snapper."

"What?!" Ellie exclaimed. "Tabor?!"

"Yup, Not only did she successfully reduce their death sentences down to community service and garnished wages, she convinced the Senior Council that the Hue-man Council was biased against the males, and they changed the Consortium Charter such that anyone earning Journeyman rank in *any* guild would qualify for adulthood. The Council also dropped the adulthood requirements for joining the other guilds as well as the adulthood requirement for living independently for the Hue-mans."

"How under the three moons did she manage that?"

Instead of answering, Myra handed her her tablet so she could watch the meeting herself.

Ellie flicked her ears back in ever-growing astonishment and horror as scene after scene played out. She had to stop it after the culling, as she was shaking too hard to continue.

Myra held her while she tried to contain her emotions that swung wildly from grief to rage. She had considered them all her friends and colleagues, and to know that so many of them had plotted against her and were now dead was too much. She couldn't cry, couldn't yell. She just felt numb.

Eventually, though, she calmed enough to continue with the meeting and was sad she'd missed the vote in time to make a difference, not that it mattered. Still, she switched over to her messages and voted for Marcus anyway, knowing he would appreciate it. She might still be furious with him, but she trusted him more than anyone else. She wasn't a resident of the South District, but as a resident of Council City, her district shifted to whoever was the current Senior Councilor.

Her jaw dropped as she watched the scene with Marsee and Clear Seas. She replayed it a second time, pausing several times to take screenshots. Assuming she survived, she wanted them printed out and hung in her office.

She fast-forwarded through the votes and stopped to watch again when the prisoners were brought out.

"She offered to *adopt* Damon?!"

"And the Council awarded it, too," Myra said.

"The others must be furious," Ellie replied.

"Little Flower is, or was anyway. I had a message from Kendra that she nearly broke their shooting range after the Council Meeting. Keep watching."

Ellie looked up at Myra with concern after the Senior Council left for deliberation, astonished. "How do you feel about all this?"

"Honestly?"

"Honesty is usually best."

Myra snorted. "You've been hanging around Marcus too long. Honestly, I came to the same conclusion after listening to Damon give his testimony and had a long conversation with Jennette before we flew out. I knew what she was planning to do and gave my approval."

Ellie stared at Myra in shock. "You're pulling my tail. After what he did to your family?"

"I'm not. He's a child who was abused by his own father, disowned by his people, and manipulated by someone he should have been able to trust. We failed him. I failed him. I was so focused on taking care of Little Flower that I stopped caring for the people of New Hope. I'm the one who removed his skin drawings. I knew he had lost a partner and a child, yet never once bothered to see how he was doing."

"You believe him?"

She nodded. "You can't fake the grief that comes from the loss of a child, and he was suffering from isolation sickness as much, if not more so than the others were at the Agency. There, they were simply isolated, but here, he was deliberately excluded. I saw the same thing happen with Marsee after her friend died as a cub. She retreated into her books and crafts, but she, at least, had us, her siblings, and the instructors you sent to the Guild. Damon had no one but people who took advantage of him. He was forgotten. Her family will be good for him."

"But what about what Little Flower said? The whole point of the delay was to give the Hue-man males time to prove they could be trusted before gaining a spot on their council. At least four of them have proven they couldn't be trusted. Those odds are worse than my odds of survival."

"And how many of our Council proved they couldn't be trusted, either?"

Ellie had to give her the point. "Well, if anyone can keep Damon in line, it's Tabor. I just hope she's not involved with this mess. Are you sure it isn't retaliation?"

Myra frowned, then shook her head. "No. If it were retaliation, she wouldn't have spoken to me, and there's been no sign of animosity towards our family since she arrived. She's taking quite the risk, not just to herself but to her cubs, in adopting him, and if he does anything, she'll pay for it."

Ellie nodded that point, too. "So, how did the rest of the Council go?"

"If you're asking about Marsee, she took over from Agate as if she'd been running the Guild for years, even growled down a councilor or six. They ended the meeting early, but I've had messages from all of the Senior Councilors indicating how impressed they were with her. Well, five of the six, anyway. I'm not entirely sure how to take Sammianna's message. I can't tell if it's sarcasm or praise."

This piqued Ellie's interest because the Diggers were not known for sarcasm, as it usually bounced off their shells, although Sammie was one of the more emotionally aware Diggers she knew. Myra pulled up the message, and it left Ellie scratching her whiskers, too.

"A Digger praised Marsee for her math skills?" Ellie asked after the first paragraph. "Marsee?!"

"But then she goes on to say that Marsee is the only one she knows capable of making two plus two equal six," Myra replied.

Ellie kept reading and shrugged as she handed the tablet back. "I think it's praise. I've never known Sammie to be sarcastic or to use clichés. She writes exactly what she means, although I have absolutely no idea what she meant." She looked at her friend hard. "I know you. Something else happened. What is it?"

Myra sighed. "Apparently, my parent's shuttle accident wasn't an accident."

"Oh, Myra! I'm so sorry! Why would anyone have hurt your parents?"

"They were going after Jer," Myra replied. "We didn't think anything of it at the time because it was such a horrible storm."

"But that happened decades ago. What does that have to do with Rip or any of the others involved?"

Myra sighed again. "They didn't say anything in the meeting, but it didn't take much to figure out. The press is surprisingly quiet about it, though. If I found it, I'm sure they have, too. Brandon, the tech who sabotaged Temperate's shuttle, had a daughter with psychosis. Brandon's father covered it up. He was the Councilor of the South District before Jer. I'm pretty sure that's the reason he stepped down mid-term, too, as it was only a few months before."

"How horrible."

Myra shrugged. "What's done is done. I'm sure Jer's terrified that I'm going to tear him a new one when he gets back, but I understand Brandon's grief. I did attack Marcus when I thought he was trying to kill Marsee for her psychosis, after all."

"You did what?!" Ellie exclaimed.

"Pinned him to the ground. I'm honestly surprised he didn't arrest me," Myra replied as her tail curled.

"Oh, I wish I could have seen that. Care to give a repeat performance?"

Myra chuckled. "I'm sure that *would* get me arrested. Now, get some rest if you can. I'll be back in a few hours to see how you're progressing. No food or drink until we know, just in case we have to bring you in for surgery."

Ellie nodded her understanding and used the time to start catching up on messages. She smiled as she read through the messages the Seniors had sent her. Marsee had done exceptionally well and really had risen to the challenge. The response from her Guild Masters was equally good, and she sighed with relief. If everything went downhill, she had no doubt Marsee would be voted in as the next Senior, and her Guild would be well cared for.

She chuckled as Marcus's messages became far more urgent, going from expressing concerns about her family, to demanding that she inform him where she was, to the not-so-subtle reminders that she was on a watch. She was honestly surprised that he hadn't figured out where she was and wondered why he hadn't tracked down her ship or tablet, although Tamarin had stated that they'd hidden her trail. She'd have to find out what they had done.

She hit reply and tapped her claws for a moment before she began typing.

> *My Dearest Marcus,*
>
> *I appreciate your concern for my safety and well-being. That being said, if I wanted you to know where I was, I would have told you. I'm honestly disappointed you haven't figured it out yet. Do I need to sign you up for remedial tech classes?*
>
> *As for your not-so-subtle threats about my watch, I assure you, I have been in the presence of a guard since the moment I left the restaurant, so you can take those threats and shove them where the moons don't shine.*
>
> *All the best, Ellie.*

Chuckling at his imagined reaction, she filtered her inbox for messages from Marsee but surprisingly didn't find anything.

"Myra," she called out.

Myra appeared at the door a moment later.

"Have you heard from Marsee? I don't have a single message from her since we left."

Myra nodded. "She's sent a few pictures of Hope. You won't get a message from her until she knows you're going to survive. It's a trauma response. When her friend died as a cub, she found out before we could figure out how to tell her. She tried to send her friend an apology for getting her in trouble and got an automated response from the system. She wouldn't text any of us for months after for fear of getting the same reply."

"Oh, how horrible," Ellie said, ears drooping.

"Marcus found her out under a scrub tree in the middle of a sandstorm, just waiting to die. She felt guilty about her friend's death as she was the one who suggested they practice. She still doesn't know that Marcus put her friend down. She believes her friend pounced on a Sand Spinner. We came so close to losing her then. She was practically non-verbal with grief for months. I honestly don't think she would have survived without your intervention, then or now."

Ellie sighed. "I'm honestly still surprised Tabor and Kendra allowed her to transfer to the Guild. I've tried several times since with others, but for one reason or another, they were all denied."

"You and me both," Myra said, then shrugged. "Well. That's ancient history, and you need to rest."

Ellied nodded, and Myra left again.

She sent Marsee a message stating how impressed she was with her performance this past week, along with her love. She thought about giving an update on her status, but it would be hours before she would know anything worth sharing. She didn't want to get Marsee's hopes up, only for them to be dashed later.

After that, she pulled up a book and began to read. Her affairs were all in order, and messages were ready to be sent out in the event of her death. Marsee and Agate were handling the affairs of the Guild, and for the first time in nearly a hundred years, she had nothing she needed to do.

When she'd read the same paragraph half a dozen times without comprehending it, she sighed and gave up. She couldn't focus on it. Her brain was stuck repeating the same prayer over and over.

Please! Just one. One will be enough. Six will be better, but I'm not greedy. One will be enough. Please?

She dozed off as she waited but woke as Myra returned several hours later, her healer's mask firmly in place, and began scanning her. She watched her friend closely for any sign of a reaction. *Please, just one. That's all I need.*

After an eternity, Myra looked over at her and then broke into a wide grin. "Congratulations, Ellie. You're pregnant!"

Ellie closed her eyes and shook with relief. *"Thank you! Thank you! Thank you!"* she whispered, then opened her eyes to look at Myra, barely daring to ask. "How many?"

"All six."

Ellie's heart exploded with joy. "Six!"

It was unheard of for a second or third pregnancy. She hugged Myra tightly, but when Myra pulled back, there was a frown on her face.

"We may have passed the first hurdle, but the next few months are going to be just as dangerous, if not more so. Six cubs with a second or third pregnancy is unprecedented. Your body may not be able to handle the strain because of your injuries. You didn't manage four before, and this will be even harder. Don't get your hopes up. If we manage to bring one to term, it'll be a miracle. You're officially on bed rest. I'll bring you something to eat and drink, and then we'll head back to New Hope. Do you need anything from your home before we leave?"

"No, I have everything I need right here," Ellie said, holding her belly, where six incredible chances were developing.

ELLIE: ANOTHER SIX

After a large meal and being evaluated by a guard stationed at the clinic, they boarded her ship and took off for New Hope, but they weren't alone. Two Honor Guard ships flanked them the entire way back, and she grinned, recognizing both the ship and the pilot in one of them.

He was still protecting her, although he hadn't attempted to talk to her. That was standard protocol. He'd left his contact information, which signaled his desire to further their relationship, but it would be up to her to reach out first.

She hadn't sent him a message yet, and she wasn't sure if she was going to. If it had been another guard, she wouldn't have thought twice about it, but the way things were right now, she knew it would only make her family more of a target.

She wanted to, though. She wanted his protection, and she'd spent many a dull meeting daydreaming about him instead of paying attention to whatever was being discussed, especially in recent months. She had always respected him, but that respect had grown at Little Flower's trial when he'd protected Little Flower from the Seniors. She sighed and gazed out the window at his ship, wishing he was still running his paws all over her body and not the controls of his ship.

"Are you going to contact him?" Myra asked with a knowing grin.

"I don't know," Ellie replied. "Maybe later, if things work out. I doubt he'll want to move to New Hope."

"Well, Jer says he'll be there for at least a month until the Guard Station is built. It might give you enough time to convince him to trade one district for another. Personally, the way he was grinning, I don't think it'll take all that much convincing."

She purred at that lovely idea, and Myra chuckled.

It wasn't long before they landed in New Hope, but when they exited the shuttle bay, there was no sign of Quinn or either of their ships.

Myra grinned at her but said nothing as they walked across the compound to the Tower.

Before she let Myra drag her into the room where she'd be spending the next two months, she insisted on seeing what the Guild had done to restore Marsee's room.

Myra was curious, too, so it wasn't all that difficult to convince her. Myra gasped with astonishment as they entered, and Ellie grinned.

They will be pleased, Ellie thought as they wandered the room. She had ordered her best crafters to repair and enhance the room and to spare no expense in materials and quality, and they'd gone above and beyond. She'd charged it all to Marsee's account, of course, but Marsee hadn't even missed it as the gifts kept arriving.

"Little Flower's painting?" Myra asked. "Were you able to save it?"

"It'll be here before they return," she replied. "They're finishing the repairs now. Thankfully, Damon only cut the canvas. We lost a few of her other drawings, but most of them were salvageable. Sadly, none of Marsee's furniture or other crafts were repairable."

"I'm not surprised. Damon shattered everything, but I know for a fact that Marsee's given away most of her crafts, at least the ones she was really proud of."

After they finished exploring, Myra led her back down to the room below, which had also been transformed. All of Little Flower's and Hope's belongings had been removed, and the swinging bed had been replaced with an adjustable trauma center bed. The rocking chair remained, and she grinned at the sight. The spot where Hope's crib had once been now housed a crafting desk, and where the playpen had been, there was now a small refrigeration unit.

Ellie pointed to the desk, which she hadn't ordered. "I thought I was on bed rest."

"You are. As long as you take it easy and remain within range of the monitors, which is anywhere within the tower, it's fine, at least for the first month or so. After that, we'll see how you're doing. Some movement and exercise will be good for you. We'll go for walks so you can have a change of scenery. The important part will be to avoid mental and physical stress, and I know you far too well. Two days in that bed, and you'll be pacing without something to do. Now, let's get you hooked up."

Myra injected her with the sub-dermal sensor that connected to the monitor in the room, scanned her to confirm it was working appropriately, and then brought an image up on the screen. "Right now, there's not much to see. But there they are."

Myra pointed out six tiny dots.

Please let them be healthy! Let them survive! I'll do anything!

Myra took a screen capture and sent it to her. Ellie stared at that beautiful image for a long time, and then, taking a risk, she sent it along to her guard.

She would need help if all six survived, and while she would never admit it to anyone, Rip Current's attack had shaken her to her very core. Having an Honor Guard around to protect her felt like a very good idea, and Myra had been right. He was *very* yummy. Purring at the memory, she curled protectively around her growing embryos and continued to pray.

Myra sat at her desk, working, but her tablet dinged a few moments later. "Looks like Jer and Marcus just exited jump. They'll be here in a few minutes. I'm sure Marcus will want to make sure you're alive in person. Do you want to walk back over the shuttle bay and watch Jer squirm for a bit?"

Ellie's tail spiraled, and she leapt off the bed. "Do I *ever?!* Are you sure I can't convince you to pounce on Marcus, too? It would make me very happy, and I'm sure that would do *wonders* for my stress levels."

Laughing, they made their way out.

By the time the ship appeared overhead, Myra had pulled her Healer's mask firmly in place. Her arms were crossed, and the tip of her tail thwapped as she leaned against the wall of the shuttle bay while they waited for the ship to land.

It was all Ellie could do to keep a straight face at Myra's act as the ship landed, but the door didn't open. She wondered who would break first.

Apparently Myra.

"Jeran Frederick Chenzira, hiding on that ship won't help your case any."

The door slid open, but neither Jer or Marcus exited.

Snorting, Myra pushed off the wall she was still leaning against and entered the ship. Ellie followed behind, tail curled tightly in anticipation.

Both Councilors were still strapped into their jump seats. Neither looked at them as they entered, but both looked like cubs being scolded by their mother.

"Shut the door," Marcus said. "We need to talk."

"Yes, we do," Myra replied, glaring at Jer.

Ellie hit the switch and grabbed a seat across from the two, where she could get the best view of the show.

"Ellie, It's a relief to see you healthy, but I would have really appreciated you letting me know what was going on," Marcus said. "When neither you or Myra responded to my messages, and Quinn disappeared, I got a little worried."

Ellie scratched the back of her neck. "Well, we were a little busy."

Jer snorted.

"So I've heard," Marcus replied. "You could have told me. I would have kept your secret."

"I figured you'd track me down, or Jer would eventually tell you," Ellie replied with a shrug.

"You asked me not to tell the others," Jer stated, raising a brow.

"Marcus isn't others. He's my protege's uncle, which makes him family, as fur-brained as he can be sometimes," she replied. "But I thank you for keeping my secret. So who did tell you, if not Jer?"

"Marsee," Marcus replied. "I cornered her in her suite and ordered her to tell me what was going on. I knew she had sent you the message to leave the restaurant."

"I'm surprised you didn't keep reading."

Marcus frowned. "I checked several times for an update, and as far as your most recent message, believe me, not only have I been looking for you, but so has Lowell. I came very close to issuing a search for you when your ship went dark, but Kendra insisted you were safe and that your location had been hidden to protect you, but she refused to tell me where you were, stating that doing so could put your safety at risk."

"Huh," Ellie said. "My apologies then. I clearly need to talk to Tamarin to see what the Guard did to cover my trail. While I appreciate the privacy it gave me, you should still have had access. I'll make sure that little flaw is taken care of personally."

He nodded. "Much appreciated on both accounts, although I will admit, I was quite amused by your message."

She grinned. "I'm sure you were, Senior Councilor."

Myra, however, was not amused by the conversation and continued to glare. "Why didn't you tell me about my parents?"

Jer swallowed hard and sighed. "I'm sorry, Myra."

"That's all you've got to say for yourself?" Myra replied.

He shrugged. "What else can I say? My actions have hurt this family, and nothing I can do will ever bring your parents back. Tell me truthfully, if you'd known, would you have been able to stop yourself from going after him? I couldn't risk losing you, too."

"My instinct is perfectly under control," Myra replied. "If I can bring Damon in unscathed, I can certainly wait to punish someone for a crime twenty years old. And if you need proof, I've been tested three times in the past several days. Once by Quinn himself."

Marcus glared at Myra. "Why? Did something happen when you found out?"

Myra snorted. "No, but like you, everyone assumed I would. Let's just say I did a little medical experiment on the trip back that was...*very* informative. It worked. Ellie is pregnant with an unprecedented six embryos, and the Healer's Guild is now looking into it as a possible means to save those with high-risk heats."

This stunned both of them as they realized what Myra meant, but she was the one now squirming with embarrassment. "Myra, did you have to tell them that?"

"Yes. I gave my oath to tell Marcus any time I used my instinct, and he would have found out anyway."

"Why?" Ellie scowled, not liking this change in the conversation. "My medical record should be private."

"Normally, yes," Myra replied. "But you are on a watch, and you did attack two guards at the mating clinic."

Ellie groaned and leaned back into her seat. "Those were guards?"

Myra nodded at her, and both Jer and Marcus frowned.

"As I feared after her last heat, Ellie had a severe case of Mating Psychosis triggered by the pain of her eggs releasing and the length of her heat. Once she realized she wasn't being attacked, she recovered. As far as I could tell, she had no problems understanding sign language, and she was tested before we left."

Marcus leaned forward with interest. "Did you? Understand, that is?"

She stared at Myra for a moment, then turned her head to face Marcus, wondering if she was going to sign her own death warrant with this conversation, but maybe her experiences would help Marsee. Taking a deep breath, she nodded. "Sign, yes. Speech, no," she replied. "I lost the ability to speak about a day into our flight. I'm honestly not sure when I lost the ability to sign, but I never had any problems understanding it."

"We were about six hours out when that happened," Myra said. "She wouldn't let me near her at that point either. She was able to follow instructions but couldn't figure out how to use any of the tech, including her jump seat or the door switches."

"I knew what they were, but I couldn't remember how to make them work," Ellie said. "It was the strangest thing. All we knew was that we were getting close to the mating clinic, and we were *very* impatient."

"We?" Marcus asked.

Ellie nodded. "I don't know how to explain it. I was both me and we, and my instinct was both it and we."

"Did you hear your instinct?" Jer asked.

She shrugged and tilted her head as she considered. "Maybe? I honestly couldn't tell you if it was my thoughts or my instinct's. They just were. They were more…more primal. More feelings than actual words."

"I want to know immediately if you hear a voice," Marcus demanded.

She nodded but glared at Jer and then Marcus. "Don't even think of doing what you did to Marsee to me. Because believe me, if you so much as raise a paw to me, it won't be my instinct responding, and you will never raise a paw to another person again. If there's even a hint of an issue, I'll go to Kendra and deal with it."

Marcus leaned back in his seat with a scowl. "You know I could arrest you for that threat."

"It's not a threat. It's a promise. But by all means, go ahead and arrest me."

He matched her glare for a long time before speaking. "What happened when your eggs released? Why did you attack the guards?"

"I thought Quinn had hurt me at first, but he backed off, confused as to why I was snapping at him. When the guards entered and sedated him, I decided they had somehow caused the pain, and I was furious at them for hurting my mate. I made them back off and pulled Quinn back to where I could protect him. I didn't know what was wrong with him. I didn't understand that he'd been sedated, and I didn't even recognize Myra at first, not until I got a good sniff of her. I couldn't turn my instinct off until the other two were out of the room, either. It didn't trust them, but it trusted her. She was our sister."

She smiled at Myra, and Myra smiled back.

"I couldn't remember what a healer was, but I knew Myra was special and that she could help. Once the others were out of the room and Myra reminded me that I could speak, I had no problems turning it off. I feel perfectly normal now and didn't have the slightest issue when the guards at the clinic tested me. If anything, I feel calmer than I did after being attacked."

"Incredible," Jer said.

"Indeed," Marcus replied. "As far as I know, you're the first to survive Mating Psychosis. This will go a long way towards helping Marsee's case and proving sign language's effectiveness."

It was her turn to be stunned, and she looked at Myra and then back at Marcus. "What are you talking about? I thought it was like that for everyone. I mean, I know attacking the guards was different, but I was just beaten by Rip, so it's not surprising that my instinct's first thought was that we were being attacked."

Myra shook her head. "Most people will only lose the ability to speak while they're actively mating and for a short time after, much like how you were when we first left the Water World. They don't lose the ability to understand speech until about the fourth day, which is why we will medically intervene with pheromone blockers if a heat lasts more than three days. We tried to do that with you in your first heat, but it didn't work. Only the fact that you were still able to understand us is what gave us the time to figure out what was wrong with you and fix it. With your second heat, I couldn't tell if you could understand me or not, but you let me approach and sedate you, and you were fine when you woke up."

She frowned, trying to remember, but it had been such a long ago that she couldn't. "Why didn't you tell me?"

"Guild Secret. I gave an oath not to."

"I mean, I understand not telling me before, but why didn't you tell me when you found out about my missing implant? If I knew the length of the trip was going to be a problem, I would have stayed on the Water World."

Myra sighed. "I didn't want anyone to see you in that state, and I hoped that I would be able to save you, either via sign language or transitioning like Marsee. Plus, you were still at risk for hemorrhaging if the implantation failed."

"I suppose that's fair. Still, it worked." She grinned with happiness and held her stomach but then frowned. "I just wish I knew why he took my implant in the first place."

"That's one of the things we need to talk about," Marcus said. "Rip had an entire lab full of medical equipment in his home. Based on what Marsee identified for me and a notebook we found, we believe he was running experiments specifically related to our heats. Myra, I need you to review that information and tell me what you think he was trying to do. Ellie, when you inevitably have to announce what's going on, I think it would be prudent not to release that your implant was taken. Say it was damaged."

"That was my intention all along," Ellie replied.

Myra nodded her agreement as well. "I'll take a look, of course, but on one condition."

Marcus raised a brow. Refusing a direct order by the Senior Council came with serious consequences, bribery even more so.

"You tell me what two plus two equalling six means."

Both Jer and Marcus burst out laughing, but it was Marcus who managed to speak first.

"How did you hear about that?" he asked.

"Sammianna set me a letter praising Marsee," Myra replied. "At least I think it was praise."

Marcus shook his head. "Your daughter uncovered a major smuggling operation and dragged several squads of guards up to the platform, including not one, but two Senior Honor Guards, and arrested the crew of the ship involved."

Ellie let out a low growl, but before she could say anything, Marcus continued.

"I can't tell you any more than that until after the week's grace period is up, so don't ask, and for your own safety, don't go digging. When she informed us of what she found, I questioned her on how she figured it out, as her math skills, or complete lack of them, is quite notorious. She replied that she kept adding up two plus two and getting six. It's Sammie's new favorite saying, although it's turning into a bit of a swear at this point, and I'm personally getting very tired of hearing 'I've found another six.'"

Myra turned to look at her with astonishment. "You've managed to teach her math, too?! What are you, a magician?"

"Don't look at me. I've been trying, but we honestly haven't made all that much progress," Ellie replied and then leaned back as she considered. "Now that I think about it, though, she was understanding the reports far better the day I left and didn't seem to have any problem understanding the terms of the contracts we sent. Maybe it has something to do with her instinct or lack thereof. She does appear to be far more focused than before, but then the events of the past few weeks could account for that, too."

"I was wondering if that was the case," Marcus replied. "She seems to think so, but I haven't had a chance to talk to Kendra about it yet. I'll let you know if she has any insights into it."

Ellie looked at the two Senior Councilors and squinted at them with a glare. "You said *one* of the things. What else is going on?"

They both sighed, and Jer's expression was one she couldn't remember ever seeing on his face, or at least one he'd always tried to hide before. He was flat-out terrified.

"Another six," Jer began after taking a deep breath and bringing his emotions back under control. "When we rescued the survivors from the cave, we found a letter that included a ticket number for the Guard's system. That ticket was Kendra's investigation into Marsee's medical flag and included Marsee's personal journal, which very clearly documented everything she was going through with her psychosis and my test of her. According to Marsee, Rip was trying to make her lose control and attack me, which she probably would have if the Senior Healer hadn't restrained and sedated her. Since we made the arrests, several of Clear Sea's councilors have stated they thought

Rip was going to bring that information before the Council and insisted that the information against them was fabricated, like with Clear Seas."

He paused, but it was Marcus who finished.

"All evidence is now showing that to be the case, or enough anyway, to put the rest in doubt, and they've demanded a Full Council trial. We're not sure what to do to protect Marsee or Saber, and we have no idea who else knows."

MARSEE: THREAT OF EXPOSURE

The next six local days passed with excruciating slowness as Marsee waited for word on Ellie, yet it never seemed like there were enough hours in the day.

Tamarin was on official cub-sitting duty while Marsee spent every moment from dawn to dusk at the Guild doing her best to manage with Agate's and Nardal's help. The press continued to hound her about giving an interview, but she continued to ignore them. In the evenings, they trained. When she felt good enough, Little Flower went for walks around the platform with Tamarin and Thatcher while she was chased around the Arena by Avery or Aris, sometimes both.

To Marsee's relief, Little Flower survived her failed heat, although she was grumpy and in pain the entire time as she refused to take any more of the pain meds, and the nanos did nothing to touch it. She didn't blame her sister for her grumpiness. She was honestly horrified by what her sister was going through, even if it was normal for her species, and it made her even more terrified for Ellie.

The morning Little Flower stated she thought she was done bleeding and decided to head back to work, they escorted her over, but Marsee insisted that she be checked over by the Senior Healer.

"She might have a little spotting, but I believe she's mostly recovered. Based on what I know of the Hue-man's cycle, I expect she may go into heat again in another five or six local days. Unfortunately, the implant your mother ordered won't be here for another standard half week."

Marsee nodded her understanding. "Unless something happens with Ellie, we'll ship out right before," she decided. There was no disagreement from her sister.

She was just about to leave when her tablet dinged with a message from Ellie. She fumbled pulling her tablet off her harness, and would have dropped it if they hadn't been in the water.

"Bad news?" Little Flower asked, seeing her expression.

"There's no update, just a quick message saying she's proud of me for stepping up. Why isn't she saying anything?" Marsee stared down at the tablet. "She's dying. Isn't she?" She started shaking as her grief nearly threatened to overwhelm her.

"She probably doesn't know yet," the Senior Healer replied. "If she just woke up from the procedure. It will take four or five standard hours before they'll know if the embryos are implanting."

"I hope you're right," Marsee said.

Please let her be right, she prayed.

The hours passed slowly. By the evening meal, they still hadn't heard, and Aris and Thatcher ran her into the ground to distract her. She was halfway through the training course when she heard her tablet ding with Ellie's sound again and nearly missed the jump she was making. She scrambled down and ran with everything she had for her tablet.

Little Flower and the others stopped what they were doing and waited.

Marsee read the message and cheered. "Six embryos implanted," Marsee called out before making her way back down.

"Six!" Aris replied, stunned. "That's incredible for a second heat, much less a third."

Her sister frowned. "She's probably not going to be able to keep all of them. She didn't have room the last time, according to what Mama told me, and her injuries will make it even harder this time."

Marsee shrugged. "If anyone can save them, it's Mama. Ellie's through the most dangerous part now, which is what matters." She took off with a much lighter heart as she completed her training.

Exhausted, they made their way back to the suite, and she passed out sound asleep almost immediately. The short days and shorter nights were leaving her chronically fatigued. She barely woke as Little Flower climbed into bed sometime later and purred herself back to sleep, for the first time in weeks feeling hopeful.

She should have known it was too good to last.

Several hours later, she was startled awake by the blare of an urgent call from Clear Seas. It was all she could do to keep from crying before she answered it. She just knew something was horribly wrong. He wouldn't call if there wasn't.

"Translator, I know it's very late, but can you come down to my office? There's something I need to talk to you about."

"Is my family alright?" Marsee asked.

"As far as I know," he replied. "I would prefer to talk about this in person."

"Of course, I'll be right there," she said, and he disconnected.

After explaining what the call was about, she hugged her sister and made her way out. Aris followed her.

When they arrived, Clear Seas' door was open, and he was floating by the window looking out. In the reflection of the window, she could see hints of sadness and worry on his face and skin, but when she knocked and he turned to face her, it had vanished.

"Thank you for coming so quickly," he said.

"Of course," she replied and went to shut the door, but he stopped her.

"Your guard should probably hear this, too," he said and motioned Aris in.

Aris swam in and shut the door, and Clear Seas hit a switch on his desk, which she assumed was for a privacy screen, although she couldn't hear it.

"Something *is* wrong with my family?"

"No, not that I know of. It's you I'm worried about," Clear Seas replied.

Marsee flicked her ears back, and then her face hardened. "Something's planned?" It was more of a statement than a question.

"No, something was planned." He paused, and hints of indecision flickered across his skin.

She waited, concerned that he even showed it.

"Several members of my council claim that the charges against them were fabricated. They also claim that Rip planned to come forward at the meeting to accuse your father of abuse and Marcus and Kendra of hiding it. Our investigation shows that there's a strong probability they're telling the truth. They know about your illness. We don't know if they know the full extent of it or not, but we have to assume they do. They're demanding a trial before the Full Council. Which is their right."

Marsee swam over to the nearest net and sat down with a groan, grabbing at the short fur on the back of her neck.

"We, your father, uncle, and I, have decided to let you decide how you want to handle this. We can bring this before the Council, let them go, or execute them so no one finds out."

Marsee looked up at him in surprise. "You would execute someone who didn't commit a crime?"

"To protect an entire species, yes," he replied, "and you should know that. You yourself informed me of the risks of others finding out about your illness, as did Marcus, and after what I witnessed, I believe you're both right."

Marsee nodded the point and sighed. "How confident are you that they're telling the truth?"

He didn't answer, but his scent told her everything.

"How many are there?"

"Seven."

Seven! Her mind was in turmoil as she tried to figure out the possible repercussions.

Aris was silent, her face a blank mask, but her scent told Marsee that she was scared, and that downright terrified her.

It can't go before the Council. To do so would expose everything, and no one would ever trust me again, no matter what I did. Papa and Uncle Marcus's reputation would be ruined along with all of Saber. If they are innocent, then perhaps I can tell them just enough to make them understand, but if not... It would be so easy to have them executed and remove the threat, but if I do that, would I be any better than Rip?

No one said anything, as she thought.

"If it was just me..." Her voice trailed off, unsure of what she would do if it *was* just her, and that thought horrified her. "Can I speak with them?"

"Of course," he replied. "I expected as much. Would you like to speak to them individually or as a group?"

"A group. I don't want to have this conversation more than once," she replied.

Clear Seas nodded and hit another button on his desk. "Stinger, have them all brought to interrogation room B."

"Yes, sir," came the immediate reply.

"I take it he knows?"

"He knows about your flag and witnessed you throwing your father out of your room. He knows what the seven told us, as he was with me at the time, but what else he knows, I don't know," Clear Seas replied.

"Do you trust him?"

Clear Seas snorted and looked astonished that she would even ask. "I don't particularly trust any of the guards at the moment, except perhaps yours, but we've removed those we had evidence against."

She pursed her lips at the implied warning. There were others involved, and they didn't know who. She looked over at Aris.

Aris was silent for a moment. "I have never found reason to mistrust Stinger in the past, but far too many of those under his direct command were involved. Many in the Guard believe all of the Senior Guards should have been removed from their positions, if not executed, and were honestly surprised that didn't happen."

"We seriously considered it, but in Stinger's case, we found evidence that Rip intended to put someone else in charge of the

Guard, so we decided that the enemy of our enemy was, if not our friend, better than putting someone who could be our enemy in power."

She couldn't fault that reasoning as it was pretty much the entire reason she'd voted her uncle back in, even knowing he might still kill her someday.

"Show me what you've got on them," she said.

They spent the next hour reviewing all of the evidence, and Marsee spent some additional time digging, using Clear Sea's authorization to verify a few items before Clear Seas led them down to the hall where the guard's offices were located.

Two guards floated outside of one door, but a third, Stinger, floated outside of the one next to it. Stinger hit the switch as they approached, and Marsee swam in, only to find herself in a room split by a large window. There was a desk with nets on either side of the widow, but the one on her side had a large control panel embedded in it.

Seven people, cuffed and collared, floated in the other room, surrounded by guards. Only one was one that she knew personally, a councilor by the name of Snapping Turtle, one of the ones who had met her the day they arrived. It was the same one that had affected Clear Seas so much at the meeting. She wondered again at their relationship but didn't ask. She wasn't sure she wanted to know.

None of them reacted to their presence. She frowned at the sight of the window and the fact that it would hide their scent from her. She was hoping to have that to help her decide if she could trust them.

"They can't see or hear us until we drop the privacy screen," Stinger explained before she could even ask.

She turned to face Stinger, deciding to start with him first. "What do you know of what happened between my father and I?"

"Nothing but what they claim," he replied. "I, of course, went to investigate the moment you threw your father out of your room, but your medical record has been locked, as is the ticket associated with it."

His scent didn't change.

"And my illness?" she asked.

"I've researched the illness itself, honestly finding little about it, simply that it was a brain defect that ultimately proved fatal." His skin flashed with worry and a hint of sadness. "How long do you have?"

She didn't answer and looked over at Aris.

Aris said nothing, but she was worried.

"Thank you. Please leave."

"Ma'am, if your father is abusing you..." he started, his skin flashing with concern.

Marsee glared at him. "If my father was abusing me, he'd be dead right now. Leave."

Stinger's eyes flashed to Clear Seas.

"Do as she says," Clear Seas demanded.

"Yes, sir," Stinger replied, clearly not happy with his orders, but he turned and swam out anyway.

"I'm assuming there are cameras. Can they be deactivated? I don't want anyone getting a record of this conversation."

Aris swam over and hit a switch.

"Do you know how to run this panel?" she asked Clear Seas.

"I do," he replied.

"Good. Aris, go replace those guards. I want as few people involved as possible."

Marsee smelled relief from her guard, and she quickly swam out. Once the guards were swapped out, Marsee had Clear Seas lower the privacy screen.

She said nothing as she watched to see how they reacted. Most seemed surprised to see her, although a few appeared relieved. Perhaps realizing that they hadn't been dragged out of their cells to be executed.

"My understanding is that you were informed that my father was abusing me. What were you told?" She already had their prior statements, but she was curious if they would slip up or change what they'd said before.

"Rip shared with me your medical flag," one Councilor stated. "It very clearly showed claw and teeth marks. I was in the guard for a while, so I know what that looks like."

The others all nodded their agreement.

"That doesn't mean that he was behind those injuries. What made you believe my father was the one to make them? I could have been attacked by a wild animal outside of New Hope. There are plenty of creatures that could make the same injuries."

"You hid the injuries from your mother but not your father, which would indicate that he already knew about it," another person stated. "And the size of the bite wound is consistent with the males of your species."

"Circumstantial. My father has access to every medical record, whether I hid it or not. You must have had more evidence than that to go along with Rip. What was it?"

"Ma'am, it wasn't just abuse," Snapping Turtle stated. "Rip showed me evidence that indicated that your father and uncle were...executing children without evidence of a crime."

"It wasn't just them, though," another added. "All of the councilors from your planet are involved, assuming what he showed us was true. And your Guard."

"Rip showed me evidence that you had the same illness that was listed on many of the executions," a third stated.

"What evidence was that?"

"He showed a statement that he believed you had written, submitted by your father to the Senior Council, along with the comments your father made with his vote at your sister's trial where he claimed you had this illness."

She pursed her lips and mentally swore at her father and uncle. "Do you have proof of the rest of your claims?"

"I do," one of the others stated, "or I think I do. The number on top of one of the cases Rip showed me was 7389CC132-P. If I remember correctly."

She turned to Clear Seas, who opened his tablet, pulled up the case number, read through it, and then showed her. She let out a heavy sigh.

"Did you have any knowledge of what Rip planned to do with me?" she asked next.

They all shook their heads. "No, ma'am."

Aris frowned.

She glared at them. "You're lying. What did he tell you he was going to do?"

None of them spoke.

"Councilors, if you value your life, you'd better speak now."

Snapping Turtle sighed. "He told me he wanted to get you away from everyone else to try and convince you to tell him what was going on and press charges against your father if he was abusing you. I swear I had no idea he was going to hurt you."

"But you knew he was going to kidnap me?"

"No, I expected him to call you to his office or invite you to his home or something."

"Why didn't you come forward when I went missing?"

"Because I didn't think he was behind it. He was heavily involved in your search, and the ransom note implicated the protesters. I'm sorry. I should have brought it up as a possibility. I just couldn't believe he would do something like that."

Aris flicked her whiskers forward in a yes.

Marsee gave a single tilted nod of her head, acknowledging his statement. "I've reviewed all the evidence the Council has against each of you and the investigation that has since been done to try to prove your claimed innocence. The Seniors have given me the choice about what to do with you, and...I believe you're telling the truth."

Waves of relief flashed across all of their skins.

"However, if I inform you of what really happened, or if you brought this before the Full Council, you could harm not just myself but all of Saber in the process, and I'm not sure I can put my people at that kind of risk."

Fear now flickered on their skin as they tried and failed to hide it.

"Would my word that I was not abused and that my father and uncle were justified in those other deaths be enough for you?"

They were all still and silent. Most couldn't look at her.

"Ma'am, at risk to my own life, I can't take you at your word," Snapping Turtle finally replied. "The tickets I reviewed showed no evidence of a crime occurring or reason why a child should have been executed by the Council or Guard. I gave an oath to investigate accusations like this, and as your family is involved, you could be trying to protect them or being threatened to keep your mouth shut. Even if this was a case of assisted suicide for a fatal illness, there are procedures and protocols that need to be observed that were not included in any of the cases I reviewed."

She was honestly surprised he didn't take her offer.

"If I tell you what's really going on, do you promise not to tell anyone, under penalty of death, if you do?"

"As long as no crime has been committed," he replied.

"On my word that no crime has been committed," she added.

They all nodded their agreement, so she had each of them give their oath individually. Aris twitched her whiskers forward with each.

She was silent for several long moments as she considered exactly what she was going to say and decided to focus on the illness itself, hoping that would be enough.

"Rip was partially correct. I do have psychosis."

All seven flickered with the dark blues of sympathy and grief.

"Until recently, it was fatal for our species. It's a...fairly rare defect in our hunter's instinct. As you saw at my sister's trial, our cubs pounce on anything and everything that moves. By the age of three, most of us learn to control that urge, but with a few, it gets worse. With this illness, we eventually lose all sense of who we are and revert back to the wild state of our ancestors. We can't speak or understand anyone around us, and we'll hunt anything we perceive as prey. Without a cure, the Council and Guard had no choice but to put those afflicted down before someone else got hurt. I'm told it often manifests in single cubs around the age of adulthood, as it did with me, and yes, I did write that statement to the Senior Council, at severe risk to myself, hoping that my experiences would help others inflicted with this illness. As far as I know, I'm the first person to ever recover from that state, but I came very close to killing my sister before that happened. It's through her bravery that we learned about the effectiveness of sign language and what ultimately allowed me to learn to control it. I have been working with my father under the observation of the Guard since then to ensure I have control and have been sharing my experiences in the hope that it will help others."

"How does sign language help a brain defect?" one of the Councilors asked.

"They're still trying to figure that out. In my case, I could understand sign language, but I couldn't understand speech. Master Healer Rowena told me that she believes that there's a...a sort of mini brain that controls our instinct that gets stuck and that sign language allows us enough access to the thinking parts of our brain to remember how to flip the switch back, so to speak."

She saw recognition of Rowena's name along with confusion at her explanation. She scratched at her ears. "The best way I can explain it would be to imagine that you were scared by someone sneaking up on you, and you shocked them accidentally. Most people would be able to recover quickly and stop once they realized they were safe. In my case, I couldn't. The first time it happened to me was the day my sister came to live with us — when I scared her with the knife. I was triggered by the sight of her leash as she ran out the door, and I pounced on it before I even knew what I was doing. When I caught sight of her at the end of the leash, everything changed, and I started hunting her. I was aware of what was happening, but I couldn't make my body stop. Thankfully, I was able to regain control before she was hurt, but I was so scared I didn't tell anyone what really happened. It wasn't until I had an episode in front of everyone, including my father and uncle, that they realized what was going on. I was able to remove myself from the room before anyone got hurt, but I was non-verbal several times that day in front of my father, unable to speak or understand him, and while I didn't know it at the time, my uncle planned to call in Tabor and the guards the next day. That evening, I admitted to Little Flower what was going on, and she actually suggested I try to practice my control by hunting her. We figured out a reasonably safe way for that to occur under both my father's and uncle's observation.

That time, I had no knowledge of who I was, and they came very close to putting me down before Little Flower signed, and I remembered who I was. It took me several hours that evening to learn how to control it, but I did, enough for my uncle to call off Tabor, although I still remained on a watch for the next six months to ensure I was safe to be around."

"Marsee has been very forthcoming with her experiences," Aris added, and they all spun to look at her. "And her observations have been invaluable in saving others. Senior Councilor Surellis has recently changed the policy around this illness to require those with the early signs of the illness to be brought in and taught sign language if they don't already know it. The early results have been very promising."

Snapping Turtle turned back around to face her. "And what of the flag on your medical record? I heard you threw your father out of your room and accused him of attacking you. Is that what happened, or did he stop you from hurting someone?"

She sighed, wondering just how many people knew about that. "I was exhausted and overwhelmed by my sister's illness and caring for a new cub and went out for a run and ran straight into my father. I didn't want to talk to anyone, much less him, and ran from him. I didn't stop when he ordered me to, not realizing it was an order from a Senior Councilor and not my father."

"You ran while on a watch?" Sea Turtle asked, flashing his horror. "That's an immediate death sentence."

She nodded. "I didn't even know I was on a watch. They were keeping it informal to protect my reputation, and everyone assumed that everyone else had informed me of my restrictions." She rolled her eyes and shook her head in annoyance. "And before you ask, I'm not pressing charges over what was an unintentional mistake."

"So that's how you were hurt?" Sea Turtle asked.

She considered lying, but Aris frowned slightly.

"No."

Surprise flickered on all their skins, and Aris frowned again. Clearly, she'd misunderstood what Aris had been trying to tell her.

"He pinned me but backed off once he realized I was in control, but that only made things harder to control. I gave him a piece of my mind and took off again. He followed and observed me for some time before deciding that he needed to know for sure if I could remain in control if pushed hard. He told me that what he did was similar to the test you're given as a Junior Councilor. I passed, but not before landing wrong and breaking my shoulder."

"So why throw your father out of your room if it was only a test?"

"Rip did everything he could to twist my feelings, thoughts, and memories of that test so that I would lose control and attack my father, including using my father's term of endearment every time he shocked me. I was distraught over just learning about an injury that wasn't released to the public. At the time, we thought that injury would be fatal. My father slipped up while trying to comfort me, and all of my rage that was really meant for Rip got redirected at him."

"Was this another episode of psychosis?" another councilor asked.

"No. Just trauma brought on by the psychological abuse I endured. If I had lost control, I wouldn't have been able to speak to order the guards to throw him out, and I'd be dead now. If not by my uncle's hands, then by the guard's."

"What was this injury?" Sea Turtle asked.

"I temporarily lost my sense of pain. Without it, I wouldn't have survived my growth spurt and likely would have been seriously injured before then without knowing about it."

"There were others, older, who were listed with this illness, and records indicate that they were on a watch without suspicion of criminal activity backing it, too," Snapping Turtle asked next. "My understanding is that your mother and Healer Jabri are both on a watch following your sister's rescue. I don't understand why."

She nodded, but again, it was Aris who answered. "Hunting can be a major trigger for psychosis. It's the whole reason hunting is illegal for our species. The watch is merely a precaution, as both healers used their instinct to track Damon down, and that's close enough to a hunt to be concerning, even if Damon was brought in unharmed. Both healers have gone through extensive training to be licensed to work with prey species to ensure they're not at risk for this illness, so I am not particularly concerned, but it is standard protocol. We take the safety of our people very seriously and would much rather work with people at the first signs of an issue than have to put them down when it's too late. None of us like having to kill children. It's by far the worst part of my job."

This seemed to convince that councilor as he nodded.

"Are you still suffering from this illness?" Snapping Turtle asked Marsee next. "If hunting is a trigger, I imagine killing Rip would be even more so."

She shrugged. "I don't believe so, but only time will tell. I did struggle after killing Rip, but I don't know if that was due to psychosis or my injuries. I didn't go non-verbal, but I was very confused."

Clear Seas spoke next. "Councilors, I'm sure you're all aware of the neurological damage that can occur from a shock, even at a lower level and duration. Not only did Marsee's mask fail, but by my observation, she was given a fatal shock on at least two occasions, possibly three."

The Sprites flashed both disbelief and confusion.

He reached down and lifted her paw, turning it so her palm and wrist were showing. "This mark here only occurs above a certain amperage, which in our species is fatal. Marsee has this same mark on all four limbs, both sides, and the back of her neck. I don't know if it's a species difference, the effect of her mask, or her own willpower, but she's lucky to be alive and recovering as well as she is. It was enough to require four replacement organs, at the very least. I witnessed her confusion, but as she stated, she was fully verbal and didn't hurt anyone. It's both my belief and the belief of our Senior Healer that what I witnessed was a result of her injuries, not psychosis."

Marsee turned her wrist to look at the mark and swallowed hard before returning her focus to the group. They all had a mix of emotions on their skin, but horror, fear, and awe were the predominant colors.

"We've seen no signs of issues either," Aris added. "And we're with her all the time. She's shown all the normal reactions of someone dealing with severe trauma but not psychosis.

"How prevalent is this illness?" Snapping Turtle asked Aris.

"On average, we have to put down a few dozen people every year. Since we learned about sign language, we've only lost one child. She didn't know sign language and was gone before we arrived."

Marsee waited a few moments to see if they had any other questions. "Councilors," she said, gaining their attention again. "Whatever your feelings or beliefs are about my family, my father and uncle are two of the most honorable people I know. They wouldn't kill without just cause. If you were to share this information with the wrong people or bring it before the Full Council, people would start fearing us, and innocent people would get hurt. I'm taking an immense risk with my people's lives and my own reputation by telling you all this. I hope you recognize that."

They nodded.

She considered for a moment and nodded back herself, decision made. "Aris remove their restraints."

Aris responded immediately.

"Before I release you," Clear Seas stated. "I need you to take your oath again. The people may very well vote you out immediately, but that's out of my hands. Marsee's illness and any statements regarding it will be redacted before being released to the public to protect her and Saber."

They all nodded their understanding and gave their oath.

Aris gave a slight nod after each, and she sighed with relief. For the moment, at least, they were telling the truth.

Clear Seas left the room briefly to inform Stinger, who was still waiting outside with the other guards. Clear Seas returned a few minutes later and stared at her from the open doorway, but she didn't notice right away. She was staring at the marks on her wrists.

"I am so very sorry for the harm you've endured," Clear Seas said softly, "but I am honestly surprised at your leniency."

"The evidence says they were innocent, and even if they weren't, what can they do to me that hasn't already been done?"

He said nothing as she left her seat and swam out of the room.

38

MARSEE: LEVIATHAN

Even though it was late, Marsee didn't return to the suite. Her anxiety was at an all-time high, and she knew she needed to run it off, even though she was still exhausted from her workout earlier. She'd always been fairly sedentary, focusing more on her crafts or books than physical activity, but she'd often run around the compound when she'd start to feel twitchy, what she'd now learned as her instinct demanding to run to become a better hunter, but even then she'd rarely pushed herself.

Only occasionally would she run until she dropped, and usually only when the world completely overwhelmed her, as it was now. She'd been attacked multiple times now. Both her father and uncle had warned her that it was not over with, and she may have just added fuel to the fire by letting the others go.

She ran until she stumbled from exhaustion and brought herself down to a walk.

Aris trotted up when she stopped running. "Feeling better?"

"Not really," Marsee replied. "I don't even know how to explain it. I feel...I feel like a Leviathan is about to swallow me whole, and there's nothing I can do to stop it. My father and uncle knew something else was going on, but they couldn't tell me. Of that, I'm sure. I know you all know my uncle sent me stuff to look into, which I can't discuss, but I can't help trying to fit that information into the puzzle. Only none of the pieces fit."

"Maybe they go to a different puzzle," Aris replied.

Marsee nodded the point and stopped, turning to face Aris. "Did I do the right thing tonight?"

Aris sighed. "I don't know. You sided with the evidence over your own safety and reputation. You recognized the risks to your people and did your best to mitigate them. You did the honorable thing, and seven people have their lives back because of it. What they do now is out of your control."

That didn't help her anxiety any, and she kept walking.

"If it helps, I'm proud of you. You didn't take the easy way out."

Marsee pinned her ears back in surprise. "Killing people is the easy way out?"

"For some, yes. It would have been the safest, for sure. Rip would have killed them in a heartbeat."

"I considered it," Marsee admitted.

"I know you did, and it horrified you. That's why I like you so much. That and the fact that you feed us so well."

Marsee chuckled.

"So, what are your plans when you return home? Do you plan to continue training with the Guard?" Aris asked, changing the subject.

Marsee recognized her guard's attempt to distract her. "I'll probably be continuing to cover for Ellie, so it depends. I think my sister wants to, but Ellie's going to be in New Hope for the next several months at least, which means that's where I'll be, for the most part anyway, and New Hope doesn't have a Guard."

"It will. Kendra has been speaking with your father. After what happened to your family, and considering how quickly New Hope is growing, we're building a Guard Station. Our squad will be moving there permanently once it's complete."

"Really? What about your families?"

"Our children are all adults now, and we don't tend to partner outside of the Guard anyway. The Guard is our family, and we take care of our own. Most people outside the Guard wouldn't understand why we're never home. We never know when we're going to find ourselves strapped to a makeshift seat on an experimental ship and spend a month on another planet, for example."

"Thank you for that," Marsee said.

"Of course. It's what we do," Aris replied. "So, are you ever going to tell Avery the trick to the maze?"

Marsee laughed. "He hasn't figured it out yet?"

"No, and he's thoroughly annoyed about it. I'm honestly surprised he's not still here trying to figure it out. He's been here every night, as far as I know."

"Is that a subtle attempt at figuring out how to do it yourself?"

"Nah, I figured it out a long time ago. We have a wager going among the guards on how long it will take him."

"I'm surprised he didn't just sniff out the answer," Marsee replied.

"He's too honorable for that. He would consider that cheating."

"Ahh. That makes more sense. So what's your guess?" she asked.

"Right before we ship out," Aris replied.

"What's his current time?"

"Last I knew, fifteen minutes and twelve seconds."

"What's the bet?"

"Five credits with the pool going to whoever has the closest time."

"Put me down for seven the morning we ship out," Marsee said. "If he hasn't figured it out by then, I expect he'll spend all night here."

Aris squinted at her. "You're not going to give it away, are you?"

"I'm far too honorable for that, and besides, I wouldn't dare spoil everyone's fun," Marsee replied and stopped for a drink.

Her anxiety bloomed the moment she looked at the exit.

Aris frowned at her reaction and hit her comms unit. "Command, can I have an escort back to the Platform?"

"On their way," came their immediate reply.

"Thank you," Marsee said.

Tanner was waiting for them outside the arena when they left. It was a dark night and hard to see, even with Tanner helping to light up the way. The drone had lights, but they didn't travel far in the water either.

She'd realized early on that Aris was purposely taking her back a different route every time they returned to the platform. This time, they were heading away from the training halls in the direction of the market. She couldn't see very far, and it put her even more on edge. Nervous, she brought her senses to the foreground, but it was much harder using her echolocation skills out in the open as smaller fish and creatures swam about.

They were just about to the intersection of First and Market when she froze as something massive appeared in the street ahead of them.

Tanner went dark, and Aris shut down her drone. Marsee did the same with hers. The world bloomed around her as Aris began slowly clicking her tongue next to her, far slower than she would have liked. Her vision bloomed and darkened in slowly pulsing clarity.

Whatever was in front of them was massive. It must have spotted them as it turned and started swimming towards them.

Suddenly she felt Tanner shoving her hard in Aris's direction.

"Get her out of here! I'll distract it!" Tanner yelled.

Before either of them could move, a screech so incredibly loud that it made her ears ring and her bones vibrate with the impact, stunned her. Her brain translated the noise into a white light so bright that it blinded her.

Her vision cleared just in time to see the massive creature lunge towards them, mouth open wide to show hundreds of razor-sharp teeth. It was big enough to swallow all three of them whole with ease.

Aris grabbed her and fumbled with the drone to start it up again, but it didn't start. Dropping the drone, Aris swam hard with everything she had.

The beast was nearly on them, and Marsee screamed in terror.

Tanner grabbed both of them and flung them to the side, then bolted straight up. Reaching out with one of her tentacles, she shocked the creature as she swam over its head, then flashed hard to get its attention. Tanner was close to thirty feet long but looked ridiculously tiny next to this thing.

The creature swam up to follow Tanner, snapping hard at the Water Sprite, nearly catching one of her tentacles. The backlash from the creature's change in direction, sent both of them tumbling, but Aris kept swimming.

Tanner must have shocked it, as it screeched again, once again blinding Marsee.

She rubbed at her eyes to try and clear her vision as Aris shoved her hard against the wall of a building, then let go to peer back around the side.

Marsee peered over her shoulder just in time to see the beast as it snapped at Tanner again, this time catching one of her tentacles along with both of their drones.

Tanner screamed with pain and shocked the creature again, but it didn't let go.

The creature yanked, and Marsee watched in horror as her tentacle was pulled right off her.

Tanner's scream changed in pitch, to a tone Marsee had only ever heard once, when she was killing Rip. Yet as horrible as the wound was, it didn't stop Tanner as she swam as fast as she could to get away with blood streaming behind her.

"Get your stunner out," Aris hissed at her and fired her weapon at the beast to give Tanner time to escape.

The creature screeched again and turned in their direction, letting Tanner go.

"Marsee! Snap out of it! Get your stunner out!"

She fumbled to unclip her stunner, brought it forward, aimed, and fired, as Aris fired several more shots, but their shots only angered the creature and it screamed again.

"Get her out of here and call for backup," Tanner yelled. "The stunners won't work! She's too big!"

The stunners might not work, but Tanner used the distraction. Rather than swimming away, she charged the beast that was nearly on top of them and flashed hard to catch its attention again. Blood clouded the water from Tanner's missing limb, and she wondered how Tanner was still able to swim with such a horrifying wound.

The creature turned again, deciding that Tanner was the easier target, and exploded off after her.

Tanner ducked and weaved, delivering shocks and flashing as she led the creature further away.

Suddenly, Tanner went dark.

It was all Marsee could do to keep from screaming and going after her, but Aris grabbed her hard and wrapped a paw over Marsee's mouth.

"Stay quiet," Aris whispered.

Marsee nodded, and Aris let go.

Moments later, Tanner lit up again, flashing brightly off to the side some distance away, and she sighed with relief.

The creature screeched again and changed direction to follow, knocking into a small building as it did.

She heard screams as the side of the building collapsed. This time, she didn't hesitate. She flicked her fins out and swam for all she was worth towards the building.

"Marsee, stop!" Aris called, but Marsee kept going and made it to the building moments later with Aris right beside her. Thankfully, the creature, whatever it was, continued to chase after Tanner and hadn't noticed them.

"That was stupid," Aris hissed at her but quickly called in an alert and then started digging through the rubble with her until they found a small, badly injured Sprite.

"Get her to the Trauma Center," Marsee whispered. "I'll keep digging."

Aris hesitated, clearly not wanting to leave her alone.

"Now!" she hissed. "That's an order!"

Aris turned and bolted off, swimming as fast as her flippered feet could go.

CLEAR SEAS: ALERT LEVEL FIVE

Clear Seas watched Marsee swim down the hall, followed by her shadow. A shift in the current caught his attention just as the pair swam up the shaft at the end. He turned to find Stinger floating behind him, mask fully in place. "Do you need something?" Clear Seas asked.

"Yes," Stinger replied. "I need to know what's really going on. It's illegal to turn off the cameras during an interrogation, and you know it."

He stared at Stinger for a moment, trying to decide how best to respond. "This wasn't an interrogation. Marsee was sharing private medical information with members of the Council prior to their release. It is her right to keep that information private, which is why I allowed the cameras to be turned off and why their statements regarding her illness *will* be stripped from the record. I assure you, whatever your concerns, the Senior Council has already thoroughly investigated them."

Stinger's eyes narrowed slightly, and he had a feeling his Senior Honor Guard didn't believe him, but he understood. It was exceedingly rare for a Senior Honor Guard to be denied access to a person's record. "So…she does have psychosis?" he asked instead.

He snorted at Stinger. "If she wanted you to know that information, she would have told you. The only thing you need to know is that her medical record and account were manipulated and used against her and her family. Because of that, her account is locked and will remain locked to everyone outside of the Senior Council unless she personally grants them access."

Stinger started to argue the point, but he raised a paw to stop him. "That decision was unanimous and final, and this conversation is over."

He swam off, deciding he'd had enough for one night. He'd already sent out the prepared press release and redacted evidence, so it was no surprise that several members of the press were waiting for him by the exit, but he waived them off. "Everything you need to know is in the press release. If there are questions, I'll answer them in the morning."

They, of course, didn't back off, but he kept swimming and ducked onto his ship, which he kept parked outside, rather than swimming home. He knew the press was tenacious enough to follow him the entire way home. They had done so on more than one occasion. The pilots dropped him off outside his home a minute or two later. Thankfully, no one was waiting outside, save for the two guards who were now permanently stationed there. He hated that need, but until things calmed down, he was not taking any chances. His Council Ship was too big to fit in his shuttle bay, even when Temperate wasn't home, or even land in the space out front, so his pilots hovered until he swam off, then flew away the moment he was clear, as was their normal procedure.

Temperate was still up and sprawled in a net in the family room. He hadn't told his son what he had planned for that evening, nor had he given any update on the investigation, and Temperate, to his credit, hadn't asked. His son flashed a greeting and then returned his attention to whatever he was reading on his tablet.

"Son," he said, getting Temperate's attention. "Snapping Turtle has been cleared of charges and was released a few minutes ago, along with six others."

A massive sigh of relief crossed his son's skin. "Thank the bountiful seas!"

"You're still interested in a relationship, I take it?"

"I don't know, but I am thankful for Melody's sake. We haven't spoken since I informed her you agreed to look into his case further, and our relationship was strained before. She wasn't happy about me returning to the pilot's net. I imagine it's going to be even worse now."

"You're probably not wrong there. If you are still interested, it might be good to wait to announce anything until after things settle down a bit. Even if we have cleared them, I have no idea how the people are going to react. They may react favorably or decide that I've released Snapping Turtle because of your relationship with his daughter. There have already been reports of violence against the families and Juniors of those who were involved or voted out."

"I know. That's a major reason I've kept my distance."

He nodded his head and changed the topic. "Where are the others?"

"Mama went to bed early, and the last I knew, Stormy was in your workshop making a mess and swearing up a storm."

"Is he still having problems with that basket?"

Temperate's skin flashed with humor. "No. Thankfully, his latest monstrosity actually made it all the way to school in one piece, and his instructor decided to take pity on him and let him move on to a different craft. From the sounds of things, I'm not sure it's going any better."

He chuckled and flashed a good night to Temperate before swimming off to see what was left of his workshop. He found Stormy slumped in defeat, with a pile of rubble in front of him. "Problem, son?"

Stormy let out a heavy sigh but didn't turn around to face him.

He swam over, picked up the biggest piece of rubble, and examined it for a moment before setting it back down. "Do you want to talk about what's bothering you?"

"I'm thinking of dropping out of school," Stormy flashed. "Or, at the very least, finishing up my education remotely."

"Why? Did something happen?"

"I don't know how to explain. I knew it would be different once people knew I was a Staffer, but I didn't realize how different."

"I know. Within five minutes of my father announcing I was his heir, I had no less than five hundred invites to dinner, most from people I had never even met."

"How did you reconcile that?"

"I didn't, and I still don't. It's even worse now. I acknowledge it for what it is and look for those people who don't treat me like royalty. Your mother is a prime example. She's the first person who ever swore at me. It was a lecture for the record books, but to be fair, I deserved it. I'm pretty sure I fell in love with her that day."

"What did you do?" Stormy asked.

"I had the utter audacity to cut in line in the market. It was a few years into my term, and by that point, I had gotten so used to everyone swimming out of my way and letting me cut that I didn't even question my right to do so anymore. She lectured me for a good ten minutes before shoving me aside and making her purchase. I honestly didn't know what to say. I just floated there like a slack-jawed scooper fish and watched her swim away. It took me months to find out who she was. Everyone was so convinced I was going to arrest her for her insults that they wouldn't tell me, but she was entirely correct, and I just wanted to apologize."

"How did you find her?"

"I swam into her, quite literally, while she was moving an ancient sculpture that she had just spent months restoring, which I broke. She swore at me again, then informed me that she expected me to make up those hours I'd wasted or she would press charges for the destruction of public property. I, of course, tried to pay her, but she demanded I work it off, then made me fix the sculpture, under her supervision of course. If you're wondering, it's the one she keeps front and center in the lobby. The next time you're there, check out the plaque."

"The one she calls The Folly of Pride?" Stormy asked.

He nodded.

"I always wondered why she never changed up that display. It's rather ugly."

He chuckled. "And made even worse by my horrible attempts to repair it. Thankfully, I got a little better at it over the years."

Stormy glanced at the pile of rubble on the table. "I doubt even your skills could fix this."

"Oh, I don't know about that. The breaks look fairly clean, and with the right materials, I think we could salvage it. I'd be glad to show you how. Did you know that one of the Hue-man cultures has an art form entirely dedicated to this process? They repair broken pottery with gold to make it more beautiful. Councilor Ito displayed several of her pieces at the Hallowed Eve Festival, and I spoke with her at length about her process. I think we can do the same here."

His son picked up several pieces and examined them before nodding. "While I would prefer not to break everything I touch, I suppose I should know how to fix it if I do."

He chuckled. "I believe those were your mother's exact words. Granted, they were laced with a few more colorful expletives at the time." He swam over to his cabinet to gather the supplies and had just set them down on the table when there was a loud knock on the front door. He frowned at the late hour and swam off to check, with Stormy following behind. When he arrived, he put a hand up to stop Stormy and shifted back into the shadows to give Temperate the semblance of privacy.

Melody was there, and they were hugging tightly. His son was bright blue with happiness.

When Melody pulled away, she caught sight of him. "Thank you," she flashed.

"Don't thank me. Thank the Translator. She's the one who found the last bit of evidence we needed to clear him and the others, and it's because of her honor that he's free."

Surprise and confusion flickered across her skin. "How would her honor be involved?"

He paused for a moment before answering. "Rip fed your father misinformation that, if released, would hurt both her reputation and her people's. She chose to take your father at his word that he could be trusted. You should know that I purposely kept your messages hidden from her because I didn't want your relationship with Temperate to influence her decision, and I have no proof, one way or another, that he shared any of what you sent to him with Rip. What I do know is that your father's account was compromised. If you're going to be a part of this family, you'll need to be more careful with secure information and who you share it with. Consider every act of communication a possible threat if it gets in the wrong hands."

Melody nodded. "I am so very sorry if that information was used to hurt your family, and I promise it won't happen again. I was worried Papa was involved after the accident, but I couldn't believe he'd do something like that. It's the whole reason I tried to pressure Temperate into moving to Command. I figured it would be safer for him there."

He flashed his understanding. "It will take time for all of us to heal and regain our trust."

Temperate was about to say something when all of their tablets went off with an emergency alert. Before he could even look, the comms unit on Temperate's harness blared louder. "All available units, Alert Level Five. Leviathan Attack. This is not a drill. I repeat. All available units, Alert Level Five..."

Temperate hugged Melody briefly as the alert continued to blare with the locations of the latest sightings and reports of casualties. "We'll talk more later," he said and bolted for the shuttle bay, narrowly missing his mother, who was swimming down the hall.

Clear Seas turned back to Melody. "You should stay here until it's safe to go out. Jewel, take them and the guards outside to the safe room."

"Aren't you coming?" Jewel asked with a flicker of worry. "The Leviathan is only a block or two away from here. You should wait until it passes."

"No. My people need me." He ordered the guards in to protect his family and swam hard, not towards the Council Building, but in the direction the Leviathan had last been seen, staying as dark as he could and praying to the gods of deep to protect his people and that his charge was fully recovered.

TEMPERATE: WAVES

Temperate powered up his ship, overriding the pre-flight checks, and strapped into his safety harness. A moment later, he was taking off.

"Command, this is Temperate Seas. Reporting for Duty."

"Copy. Sending you the coordinates now."

He punched his ship the moment the coordinates arrived and swallowed hard as it was over a highly populated residential area not far from his own home, but only a heartbeat later, he swerved hard as the great beast launched out of the darkness towards him with a furious screech and took after him.

He swore. "I have visuals. She's in pursuit." His display split to show the beast right behind him.

"Copy. Backup is on the way. ETA thirty seconds. See what you can do to lead her out of the city."

"Bait," he muttered and shifted his flight path to a less dense area of the city, but the beast stopped following almost immediately and took off after another target. He flipped his ship around, groaning at the g-forces that pressed him against his net, and fired as he realized the Leviathan was after an easier target. "Command, she's after someone, and they appear to be injured."

"Copy. Trauma ships are standing by."

The Leviathan screeched but didn't chase after him. He fired several more shots as another ship arrived and took aim, but the beast didn't turn, intent on its victim.

"Cover me!" he replied, slamming his shields to full charge and diving to cut in front of the beast as he continued firing.

The Leviathan took the bait and snapped at his ship instead, catching the very tip of the wing. The shields delivered a powerful shock, protecting the ship, and the creature let out another ear-piercing screech and flung his ship away. He spiraled and managed to regain control moments before colliding with a building.

"Bank right!" someone yelled out, and he did, swerving around two other buildings, but the Leviathan swam right through them, angry and in hot pursuit of him now.

Two other ships flew past him in the other direction, taking aim and giving him a moment to gain some distance as it lost interest in him and went after the other ships. His display lit up, showing that it was members of his squad, Rolling Waves and Snapper Fish.

He flipped back around to give chase. "We need to get her above the buildings," he called out. "Force her up."

"Yes, sir," Rolling Waves called out and dove to get under her. The Leviathan noticed and roared her fury.

"Waves, look out for her tail!" he yelled, but it was too late. His Second's ship was hit hard by the Leviathan's tail and sent careening towards a building, one wing badly crumpled. "Eject! Eject!"

A moment later, the ship slammed into the building, followed by a shockwave as the ship exploded. "Waves! Gods. Waves! Answer me!"

There was no answer. He swore. "Command! Ship…"

"Temperate! To your left!" Snapper Fish yelled, and he shifted his attention back to the Leviathan and saw it heading right towards him.

He punched his ship to move out of the way as proximity sensors lit up around him and swore when his ship didn't move.

MARSEE: RUBBLE

Marsee grunted with the effort to move a large block of rubble aside, and then another, until she had an opening big enough to wiggle through into what was left of the building. With her nose and hearing turned up to the max, she followed the scent of blood to the next victim and started uncovering them. She finally found them and used her scent to determine that nothing was broken, but the female Sprite was bleeding badly. Marsee fumbled for her first aid kit and slapped the two emergency bandages she had over the worst of the wounds, but blood continued to cloud the water.

The Sprite woke as Marsee treated her, recognized her, and weakly flashed the purple and silver, even as she began writhing in agony.

"None of that. Are there others in your home," she both signed and said, not sure if the Sprite could see her in the dark or understand Saber.

"My daughter," the Sprite flashed, barely bright enough to see.

"We've already found your daughter. She's alive and on the way to the Trauma Center. Do you think you can swim?"

"I don't know…" she flashed as her eyes closed again, and the words faded.

Marsee checked for a pulse, found one, and then glanced around, trying to figure out how to get the injured Sprite out of the rubble and through the tiny hole she had cleared. She knew moving the Sprite was a risk, but the house was crumbling around them, and it was far more dangerous to wait for help.

Frowning as only one solution presented itself, she carefully grabbed the Sprite's shoulder with her teeth and started crawling backwards to drag her through. Blood from the Sprite's injuries welled in her mouth, but unlike with Rip, it made her feel sick to her stomach.

She had only just managed to get the Sprite clear of the tunnel when the rest of the house collapsed. She half-swam, half-scrabbled away as fast as she could from the falling rubble, and only stopped when they were a safe distance away.

Panting hard to control her panic, she checked on the Sprite again and frowned at the puncture wound left behind by her teeth when she'd scrambled back away from the falling building. From what she could tell, it was minor compared to the rest of her injuries, and since she was out of bandages, there was little she could do about it.

She debated waiting for healers, but when the Sprite's breathing changed, she decided she couldn't wait any longer and carefully placed the Sprite over her shoulder and turned to swim toward the Trauma Center. She didn't get very far before Aris reappeared with several healers in tow. Moments later, a dozen Sea Patrol ships zoomed past, and she heard the creature scream again somewhere off in the distance.

Handing the injured Sprite off to the healers, she informed them the building was clear. They thanked her and bolted off.

"Have you heard from Tanner?" Marsee asked Aris.

"No," Aris replied with a frown. "We'll guard the healers back and wait for her there."

Marsee grabbed tightly to Aris's harness as her guard directed her new drone after the healers. The moment they arrived back at the Trauma Center, Marsee dragged Aris onto a trauma ship that was in the process of loading with other healers. She wasn't waiting around when there were others who needed help.

There weren't seats for everyone, so she wrapped her arms through mesh netting along one wall and held on, as Aris was doing. A few minutes later, they landed and bolted out of the ship. A row of homes had been flattened on the way out of the city, only a block from Clear Seas home.

She and Aris took different piles of rubble, guiding the rescuers to the injured. They had their scanners out, but they could only cover a small distance. Her nose was far more accurate.

Several more ships arrived, and she looked up at one point to see Clear Seas helping to remove the rubble from one of the homes — her pile of rubble cleared, she swam over to his. "Over here," she told him. "There are two Sprites on this side of the home. No one is where you are."

He didn't even hesitate to question how she could tell and just started digging with her.

"What are you doing out here?" he asked as they lifted a large beam and flung it away.

She quickly explained, and he flashed a hint of worry when she mentioned that Tanner was injured.

A guard swam up to them. "Sir, we have word from the Patrol. The Leviathan's not leaving. Three shuttles have already been knocked out of commission, and we have another row of homes that have been damaged."

"If it won't leave, we have no choice. Order the Patrol to kill it," Clear Seas said. "Do we have rescue teams on the other homes?"

"Yes, sir, on both accounts."

"Good. Inform me the moment it's been taken care of."

"Yes, sir!" The guard swam off, calling in orders as he left.

Clear Seas watched the guard leave and sighed. "So much damage. It's been centuries since a Leviathan has attacked a village, much less a major city."

"Do you think it's the same one that was in the Trench with

Stormy?" Marsee asked as they turned back to digging through the rubble.

"Most likely," he said with a sigh. "They don't tend to share territory. Old Bessie has been reasonably docile, for all her size, for the last several decades, so we've left her alone. She goes near the travel lanes and outer communities occasionally but never the main part of the city. I wonder what changed."

"Rip Current, probably," Marsee said as she lifted a large piece of rubble and tossed it aside.

Clear Seas stopped digging and looked hard at her. "What do you mean?" His normally melodic voice was harsh and demanding of an immediate reply.

"He said the other victims were in the Trench," she said with a frown at his sudden change in demeanor. "He's probably been feeding it to get rid of his evidence and keep people from finding the cave. He's no longer dumping bodies, so it probably got hungry and came hunting."

Clear Seas sighed and nodded. "You're probably right. Even dead, he still continues to harm my people."

They uncovered another victim. Clear Seas flashed over healers, and they moved on to the next location.

Marsee sniffed the rubble and frowned. "There's someone here, but I think they're already dead. It smells...wrong. Unpleasant." Marsee continued examining the rubble. "Start over here. This person is still alive."

"I had no idea your noses were so sensitive," he said as he lifted a large boulder out of the way.

"I didn't either until just recently," she said, not sure how much Clear Seas had been told about her recovery.

He looked around and saw that they were alone. "Your father said your loss of pain and other senses were tied to your instinct. Is it recovering?" he asked quietly.

"No. I still can't use my instincts the way I could before, and according to Rowena, I probably won't ever be able to. That mini brain I spoke of is completely fried. The rest of my brain is recovering, but my senses are all mixed up now, and everything is too bright or too loud, or in this case, stinky."

He frowned at her as he tossed a boulder aside, and she wondered if he was worried she was lying. "I am sorry you are still suffering from your injuries, but I am quite relieved your nose is working again. You've been invaluable in helping to find the victims, and a lot of people are going to survive that might not have if we'd had to dig through everything."

Her nose told her he was telling the truth. "Well, perhaps my injury will help us find a cure in the future."

He tossed another boulder aside. "Why didn't you tell the others about it?"

"Because I didn't think they'd believe me. My own uncle didn't even believe me, even with the scans."

"That fact still bothers me," he replied. "Although he *claims* he no longer considers you a risk."

She shrugged, recognizing that Clear Seas wasn't any more convinced her uncle could be trusted than she was, and then tossed another rock aside. There wasn't anything she could really say or do to change it, and at the moment, it didn't matter.

"I received notice that you're going home in a few days?"

She nodded. "We are. I know it's still a risk, but hopefully less so now."

Their conversation stopped as he lifted off another big rock to reveal an arm. He reached down and checked for a pulse and then flashed over healers to be ready once the rest of the debris was off enough to pull the victim out.

That was the last home on this street, so they switched over to pull out the body. Then Clear Seas checked with the Patrol, and they all swam over to another street, where they were still looking for survivors.

Massive lights had been set up to aid in the search efforts, and in addition to destroyed homes, they found the crumpled remains of a shuttle with trauma healers and guards trying to cut the injured pilot out.

Clear Seas bolted straight for the shuttle, and they followed. She didn't recognize the pilot, and since there was no reaction from Clear Seas, neither did he.

They were helping to pull the metal back when a loud screech made them all jump and turn to see the great beast swimming straight at them.

Marsee froze in absolute terror at the size of the creature she could now clearly see. It was so big it made the massive public transport ships look small. Dozens of shuttles were attempting to turn the Leviathan away from them with little success, their shots deflected by the hide of the beast and doing nothing more than annoying it. They looked like Flicker Flyers in comparison.

Suddenly, one of the ships flew right into the side of the Leviathan, causing the ship to explode. The Leviathan screeched and turned away, a gaping wound now visible on its side from the impact.

The remains of the ship spiraled off and landed several blocks over as the Leviathan swam away, chased by the other shuttles, who now focused their shots on that wound.

Clear Seas ordered several of those helping to extract the current pilot off to see if there was anything left to the pilot from the other ship, a look of worry on his face, but then he went back to helping to extract the current pilot.

When that pilot was free and the rest of the injured cleared from the nearby rubble, they boarded the ship back to the Trauma Center and helped unload the victims.

They'd just finished when the Senior Healer floated up to them and began scanning them both.

Their hands were both raw and bleeding from digging through the rubble. She hadn't even noticed.

Hyacinth led them to a station where several healers were treating the rescuers for similar injuries. She made quick work of cleaning and bandaging their wounds, although Clear Seas insisted she be treated first.

"Do we have a count?" Clear Seas asked while Hyacinth worked.

"Three dead, twenty-four with severe or critical injuries, and another eighteen with minor injuries so far, not including those sustained from digging through the rubble, like you," the Senior Healer replied. "The worst have been placed in stasis while we treat the others. I still have a ship out trying to clear the Sea Patrol pilots from several other damaged ships, and no, I haven't had an update on who they are or their condition yet."

Clear Seas nodded, and she could tell he was worried.

"Temperate was on duty tonight, wasn't he?" she asked.

"No, but he went anyway when the call came in."

"Do you know if Honor Guard Tanner was brought in?" Marsee asked as Hyacnth started treating Clear Seas.

The Healer flashed the dark blue and black of mourning. "She was. She didn't make it."

Marsee closed her eyes and swallowed hard to keep from crying out in her grief. She didn't know the guard well, but she'd given her life to protect them. When she opened her eyes again, the Senior Healer had already swum off to treat another patient.

Before she could say anything, a Water Sprite guard swam up. "Sir, I've just been informed that the Leviathan has finally been killed out by the ledges. They want to know what you want done with the body."

"Have there been any other injuries among the Patrol?" he asked instead.

"Yes, sir, we lost at least a dozen ships. I don't have word on injuries or fatalities yet."

"I want the names of everyone who was injured or killed," Clear Seas replied. "As for the body of the Leviathan, guard it from predators."

"Yes, sir," the guard stated and swam off.

Clear Seas turned to her. "Translator, will you…?"

"It would be my honor," she replied. "Send me final numbers on the displaced and where they're being housed as well. The Guild will provide supplies and whatever you need to rebuild."

Clear Seas gave a single nod and swam off.

With a heavy sigh, she tracked down Aris, who had drifted off to help a healer with another patient and left for the Guild the moment she was free.

ELLIE: BREAKING NEWS

llie walked back to the tower with Myra, deep in thought, while Jer left for his office and Marcus flew off to Council City to deal with the mess that awaited him there.

Myra scanned her, confirmed everything was still progressing normally, and sat down in a chair with a heavy sigh.

"It's Marsee's life to live," Ellie said softly. "It's only right that she decides what to tell those councilors. If they're telling the truth, which appears to be the case, they'll protect her and Saber. If not, then most likely, it won't matter anyway. We have no idea who else Rip told."

Myra nodded. "I know. That doesn't make this any easier or my anger with Jer any less."

Ellie stared at her friend. "No, it's not Jer you're angry with. You're angry at yourself for not realizing what was going on with your daughter."

Myra let out a heavy sigh. "There's that too. I was so focused on saving Little Flower that I neglected Marsee when she needed me, and now there's absolutely nothing I can do to protect her." Myra stood and left without another word.

Ellie watched the door for several moments and then sighed herself, worried about the mess she'd left Marsee to deal with. *Well, for the time being, I can start picking up some of the slack. Your vacation is over, and you have work to do, Senior Guild Master.*

Grabbing a snack, she set it down on the table beside the bed and climbed in with her tablet, fiddled with the settings on the bed until she was comfortable, and threw the news up on Myra's medical grade monitor. The quality of the image was stunning, and Ellie drooled over it for a bit. It was far better than the current one she had installed in her office at the Guild. *Time for an upgrade,* she thought, but dismissed it since it would be months before she was back full-time if all went well.

She only half paid attention as she worked through the thousands of messages waiting for her. Several hours later, she stopped for a break and grabbed another drink on her way back to the bed.

"We interrupt our normal broadcast with breaking news. We have just received word that there's an ongoing Leviathan attack on the city of Council Platform on the Water World. There are reports of dozens of casualties at this time."

The glass fell out of her paw and shattered. "MYRA!" She screamed in panic. "MYRAAAAAA!"

Myra burst through the door at a full run, scanner in hand. "What's wrong?"

Ellie just pointed to the monitor as the news broadcast continued.

"Dark moons!" Myra whispered, and then unhooked her tablet and called Jer. "Turn on the news!" she ordered the moment he picked up.

Ellie heard Jer swear.

"Where are you? he asked.

"Ellie's room," Myra replied.

"I'll be right there," he said and hung up.

A few minutes later, the three of them watched and waited as events, nearly two hours old, started making their way across the universe to their world.

A few minutes after that, GrandFather showed up. "I just saw. Have you heard anything from them yet?"

"No," Ellie replied, although they all checked to make sure they hadn't missed anything.

Footage played of casualties being unloaded from trauma ships, followed by the first images of the damage. Whole streets were completely leveled, and rescuers were digging through the rubble by hand. It was hard to tell where they were, though. She thought she recognized the crumbled remains of one home just down from the Guild. They waited for more information, scouring the footage for anyone they knew.

While the broadcasters waited for more information to arrive, they started displaying information about the Leviathan. When they compared its scale to an adult Saber, everyone in the room swallowed hard.

She had briefly seen the Leviathan as it jumped out of the ocean towards her ship, but she hadn't realized the true scale of the beast until now, and she wondered how Stormy had ever managed to face off against it, not once but twice, to save Marsee.

From the news reports, it was quite clear that this was the same beast, and the reporters even switched to comparing it to Stormy's size. The creature's teeth were bigger than Stormy, and there were hundreds of them.

"We've been informed that Senior Councilor Clear Seas will give a press briefing in a few minutes," the news broadcaster informed them, and then began playing new images that were coming in of more casualties being unloaded and other damaged homes and buildings.

"There! That's Little Flower! She's at the Trauma Center helping out," Ellie cried out as she saw the brief flash of a tiny human swim by carrying supplies. It wasn't close enough to see her clearly, but as she was the *only* adult Hue-man on the Water World, it had to be her.

They all sighed with relief.

"We are switching to a press briefing coming to you live as it arrives from the Water World."

Clear Seas swam into view and faced the camera. "At approximately 10:45 last night, a call came in from the Honor Guard reporting a Leviathan on First Street heading towards Market Square. I have since learned that Translator Chenzira and Honor Guards Aris

Zatara and Tanner were making their way up First Street when the beast attacked."

They all gasped, and even a few of the reporters flickered with worry.

"Honor Guard Tanner attempted to lure the beast away and towards a less populated area of the city. When the Sea Patrol caught up to Tanner, they found her badly injured, and she ultimately died of her wounds. Translator Chenzira and Honor Guard Aris were not injured."

Ellie gasped. She'd come to know Tanner well during their time at the Trauma Center but then sighed with relief to hear Marsee was unhurt.

"As of right now, we have three confirmed dead, twenty-four with severe or critical injuries, and another eighteen with minor injuries. We also have reports of over a dozen downed Sea Patrol shuttles, but no word on casualties there. A few minutes ago, I was informed that the Leviathan, which refused to back off, was finally killed, so the risk of further attack has been neutralized. The Patrol is currently running a sweep of the city and outlying communities to determine if more homes were damaged. We do know of at least one other damaged street, and crews have just arrived to begin digging out the casualties. Are there any questions?"

Several flashed their request to speak. Clear Seas indicated one.

"Do we have a list of casualties?"

"It's being gathered now. We should have that shortly." He pointed to another reporter.

"Which communities have been damaged?"

"Right now, the entire street of Jelly Lane is rubble, one home just down from the Council Building, on the corner of First and Honor, a dozen homes on Cliff View Heights, and fourteen homes along the intersections Fourth Street and Drummer's Way."

"Where will the casualties be housed?"

"We're setting up an emergency shelter in the Full Council Chamber while more permanent housing can be arranged."

At that moment, an honor guard swam up. Hints of grief flickered on the guard's skin. She wondered who the Guard had lost. "The casualty report you requested, sir."

Clear Seas took the tablet, looked down to begin reading out the names, and froze.

The look on his face said someone he knew well was on that list, and she held her breath.

"I'm sorry, sir," the guard flashed.

Clear Seas closed his eyes and took several deep breaths, but his grief leaked through his control anyway.

"I have just learned that...that my... my son, Master Pilot Temperate Seas..." Clear Seas' hands shook as he signed the words, "has been killed. Forgive me." He turned around to bring his emotions under control. The press and broadcast remained silent out of respect.

"No!" Ellie whimpered as Jer gasped beside her. They'd both known Temperate since he was born.

A few moments later, Clear Seas turned around, his grief firmly locked down, and began reading off the rest of the dead and injured.

They all gasped, even the Press, when Snapper Fish's name was read off.

"Will there be a state funeral for the dead?" a member of the Press called out.

"Yes, with all honors," Clear Seas stated and swam off.

Ellie couldn't take the news anymore and turned off the monitor. They sat there in silence, each lost in their grief and thoughts.

"What's the custom for when someone dies on the Water World," GrandFather asked after a while. "Should we send a formal message from the Council, donations, food, flowers? We should at least do something for that one Honor Guard that died saving Marsee."

Jer nodded and thought for a moment about what would be most appreciated. "Clear Seas indicated they'll be given honor pay for their sacrifice, which means the families themselves will be well cared for and will not suffer financially for the loss of a partner or parent. The damage that was done to the city will be expensive to repair, although the Council will rebuild those homes or move people elsewhere. Those families likely lost everything, though. I think in this situation, a donation to the Leviathan Fund in their names would be appropriate. Ellie, I'm assuming you'll agree to a payout from the fund to help the victims?"

"Of course," Ellie replied. "Are you donating personally or as a Council?"

"Personally, at the very least, but I'll call an emergency meeting and propose it to my Council. I'll send a message off to Marsee, as well, but I'm sure she'll agree."

Jer and GrandFather left, and she leaned back in the bed and closed her eyes, trying hard to keep the tears from falling. She hated crying in front of people, even those she considered family.

"Are you okay?" Myra asked.

"Physically, yes, mentally, no. I'm heartbroken. I've barely begun to process what happened at the Council Meeting, and now this? I've known Temperate since he was born. He wasn't much bigger than Hope when she was born. It was expected he would be the next Senior Councilor when his father died, but he never really wanted it. His heart was always in the Sea Patrol, even as a child. He loved to fly and was one of the best pilots I've ever seen. He had a wonderful sense of humor and the most incredible love of life. I can't believe he's gone. I just saw him a few days ago. He and Stormy came by every day to help cheer up Marsee, and he told us he was hoping to partner with a Sprite named Melody."

Myra squeezed her paw and then reached her arms out to see if Ellie wanted a hug. Ellie leaned into her arms and let herself be held.

When she finally pulled away, Myra pulled out her scanner. "You should rest. Your cortisol levels are too high from all the stress."

Ellie nodded, and Myra left. She checked her tablet for messages but, not finding anything, she fiddled with the controls until the bed was flat and curled up into a ball to try and sleep away her grief.

Silent tears began streaming down her face, and now alone and unobserved, she let them run unchecked as she grieved for everyone she had lost, not just Temperate, and she wondered how many more friends she would lose before the week was over.

43

MARSEE: THE SONG OF LIFE

*L*ights flickered on as Marsee swam down into the depths of the Guild, taking several wrong turns, even with a map and Aris's help, until they finally found Trench's office again. She knocked hard on the door and kept knocking.

"Hold your tentacles. I'm coming!" a grumpy voice yelled back in Saber, followed by a muttered swear and the sounds of him bumping into something, but a minute later, the door opened, and Trench appeared. His skin shifted from a tinge of annoyance, presumably at being woken up at such a late hour, to a flash of surprise at the sight of them.

"Translator?! What are you doing here this late?"

"There was a Leviathan attack…" she started, but she didn't even get a chance to finish.

"I understand. How many cloaks do we need, and where's the body?"

"I don't have the numbers yet, but I know of at least one death, Honor Guard Tanner."

Aris gasped and turned away to regain her composure.

"I'm sorry," Marsee said. "I thought you heard the Senior Healer."

Aris didn't reply, but a moment or two later, she turned back around, full mask in place.

"Honor Guard Tanner personally saved our lives and the lives of many others by leading it away from the city," Marsee explained. "There are at least a dozen other downed ships, but I don't know their status. I'm told the Leviathan's body is out by the ledges."

Trench flashed the silver and purple in Tanner's memory. "I'll have the cloaks for you by the end of the day tomorrow." He frowned, noticing her bandaged hands. "You're injured? From the Leviathan?"

"No. It's from digging people out of the rubble," she replied. "I'm fine."

He frowned again. "Please. It's late. Go home and get some rest. I'll take care of everything."

She didn't bother to argue with him, but she did not go home. After navigating their way back up to Ellie's office, she called Agate, praying the Sprite didn't live in one of the affected neighborhoods. Marsee sighed with relief when Agate answered, yawning and half-asleep.

"I'll alert the others and meet you there in twenty minutes," Agate replied, snapping awake at the news and hung up.

Marsee sighed at the blank screen and then tapped a claw. "Now, what?" she muttered to herself, trying to figure out what was most important to do next.

"Activate the emergency plans if they aren't already," Aris replied. "You should have access to them with your current rank. If not, focus on shelter and basic necessities for the displaced until Agate arrives. The Council should keep some supplies on hand, but they won't have enough based on what I saw today."

It didn't take her long to locate the emergency plans, find the one that best fit their current situation, and activate it. She pinned her ears as her tablet blared and flashed an alert to inform her that the emergency plans were activated and that all other priorities were to be suspended until the emergency was lifted. She acknowledged the notice, and an entirely new dashboard appeared, organized into channels based on what was needed.

Swallowing hard at the level of responsibility she was taking on, she updated the various channels based on what little information she had. People notified by the alert started logging on, claiming tasks that needed to be done, and coordinating the response for their departments.

When that was done, she decided to make her way down to the warehouse to start gathering the supplies for the displaced. By the time she arrived, that effort was already well underway by the night crew. They could swim far faster than she could, so she pitched in with those helping to pack them.

Trench appeared carrying a large bag to gather the supplies he needed, saw her helping out, smiled, and then pulled the largest of Sprites off the line to go with him, which she supposed made sense. They only had a small window of time to retrieve the hide before the site attracted other predators. Even with the Sea Patrol there, it would be dangerous.

Agate showed up a few minutes later and grabbed several others to prepare a space for processing the hide with the hasty instructions Trench had sent her.

By the time the kits were complete and sent off, the Master Builders had finished examining the first of the destroyed homes and appeared to gather their own supplies. She redirected her helpers to gather whatever they needed while she and Agate reviewed the latest flagged tickets that needed their attention.

Trench returned about an hour later, with the hide cut into relatively smaller and slightly more manageable pieces — each rolled up and carried back by nearly two dozen Sprites.

While she had seen the beast, she still had a hard time grasping the size of it.

"What are you going to do with all of that hide?" She asked Trench. "There's enough there for thousands of cloaks."

"We'll store it until needed. Your cloak was the last made of actual Leviathan hide, but it was not the last cloak to be made. A fabric cloak is typically given to those who die with honor now, but we'll use this until it's gone."

She nodded. "What about the rest of the creature?"

"It was far enough away from the travel lanes that they decided to leave it where it was. It'll take months for the beast to be consumed, and an entire ecosystem will form around its remains, bringing new life and habitat to a succession of creatures for decades to come."

That thought brought her a tiny piece of joy. "You don't eat it yourself, like other fish?"

"No. It...just feels wrong for some reason. We never hunt the Leviathan, even in its safer juvenile form. They can live for thousands of years, and I don't know. There just seems to be something intelligent behind those massive eyes."

"Have you ever tried to communicate with it?"

He chuckled. "No. How would we? It doesn't have our color-changing skin, and the only sounds we've ever heard are its hunting screech."

"Perhaps it's out of your hearing range like the Hue-mans are for us."

"Perhaps, but as it clearly sees us as food, I doubt anyone will ever attempt to find out."

She watched momentarily as the other Sprites cut the bloody hide down into more workable pieces. She was thankful she no longer had an instinct to deal with, as she'd have had a hard time with the blood if she had. As it was, she still felt uncomfortable with how good it smelled, and she wondered why it and Rip's body had smelled so good, yet the bodies of those she'd rescued, both dead and alive, had not.

"Do we have a list of those to honor yet?" Trench asked after a moment.

She pulled out her tablet and found a message from Clear Seas, opened it up, and let out an anguished whimper as she struggled to contain her grief at the first name she saw.

"No...Oh Gods. Not him."

When she looked up from the tablet, Trench was watching her with a mix of compassion and concern. She handed him the tablet, unable to speak it, and watched as his body slumped and turned solid black with grief.

After taking a deep breath, he turned and called out for everyone's attention, not that he needed to, as everyone was watching. Many were already flashing matching colors of worry and grief, but their skins all shifted to dark blue or black as he announced Temperate's death.

Overall, there were six dead and fourteen injured among the Patrol and Guard. Among the civilians, there were currently sixteen dead, twenty-eight with severe or critical injuries, and forty-two with minor injuries so far. Another long row of damaged houses had been found as the Patrol began a sweep of the city, and they were still clearing those out.

That grief didn't last long as they quickly shifted to surprise at Snapper Fish's name. If they knew the others in the patrol that had been killed, it wasn't obvious, but as Trench began reading out the names of the victims, several Sprites began wailing their grief while others tried to console them, their own grief fully visible on their skin.

The sounds of the Water Sprites' cries were something she knew she'd never forget. Almost everything she'd heard from the Sprites, except from Rip Current, the occasional warning call, and the scream of pain from Stormy and Tanner, had been melodic. Even Clear Seas' harsh demands were melodic in their own way. She'd never heard them sing before, and she'd always been told their songs were only for mating purposes, but even when speaking one of the other languages, they always spoke with the same hauntingly beautiful tones.

This, however, was bone-jarringly dissonant, and it made her ears pin flat. Yet gradually, that dissonance changed with a single inter-twining counter melody that everyone, even the most grief-stricken, eventually harmonized with, and as they did, their skin shifted from the dark blues and blacks of mourning to the bright blue of joy.

She floated in wonder, unable to do anything but allow herself to experience the song. If she hadn't been underwater, tears would have been streaming down her face, and what little fur she had would have been standing on end. Eventually, the song faded away, and they floated there in silence for several moments before going back to work.

"Come on. Mourning can wait. We have work to do." Trench handed her tablet back and then, quite literally, grabbed her arm and dragged her towards one of the smaller hides. She didn't argue or fight the unexpected contact as she trusted him, but Aris apparently felt otherwise.

Aris snarled and shoved her way in between them. "Let her go!" she demanded, claws out, teeth barred, and stunner raised.

"I mean her no harm, Honor Guard," Trench said as he immediately backed away.

"It's alright, Aris," she told her shadow, seeing the truth of Trench's words.

Marsee fully expected a lecture based on the look Aris gave her, but her shadow backed off after giving Trench another low warning growl.

"My apologies, Translator. I meant you no disrespect or to scare your guard. When you're as old as I am, time loses meaning, and it feels like I've known you forever, even if we've only met a few times."

"None taken," she replied. "These past few weeks have lasted a lifetime. Now, what do I need to do?"

Trench handed her a strange tool and explained what needed to be done, although it wasn't the first time she'd worked a hide, even if the texture and tools were different.

The repetitive motion calmed and centered her. It had the same prayer-like feeling as when she'd carved the frame for her sister's painting. That fact surprised her as this creature had killed two of her friends and so many others. Her thoughts drifted to her prior confusion about the way her body reacted to the smell of its blood.

"What's bothering you?" Trench asked, picking up on her mood. "If you find it too uncomfortable to work the hide, I understand. You've already done enough."

She shook her head. "That's not it at all. What you're doing is not much different from the skills I learned from Councilor Kai." She used Kai's name sign, which she knew Trench was more likely to know."

"I didn't realize you've done this before. I thought your species didn't work with hides."

"We don't, but it's an important part of her culture, and I wanted to learn. It made translating her stories and diagrams easier."

"Ah. I've watched many of her recordings," Trench replied. "I had hoped to talk with her about them during the meeting, but she didn't attend."

"No. She's on maternity leave. I heard she gave birth to a daughter last week. Her name is Hózhó. I don't know if she's given the child a name sign yet, but it means..." She paused to consider. "It means walking in balance at peace with the world around you."

"That's a beautiful name," Trench replied.

"Her whole language is beautiful, and it's much easier for me to pronounce than my sister's."

"They have more than one language?"

She nodded. "Of the five hundred people rescued, there were native speakers of forty-two different languages. Most speak my sister's language, but not everyone. Sign is the only language everyone speaks, but we're working to preserve all of the languages. I don't know them all well enough to be considered fluent, but I do know the basics and have made a point to focus first on those languages where there's only a single speaker. Navajo was the first language that I learned after my sister's."

"Forty-two languages? How did they possibly communicate?"

"Badly. From what I understand, there were hundreds of distinct languages and thousands of regional dialects. That's been the hardest part of learning their languages, even their most common ones, as the same word can have multiple meanings, and their language is constantly evolving. If they don't have a word for something, they'll just make it up on the spot, and everyone somehow just understands. You should hear my father complain about it. He's passable in their written and spoken language now, but I get messages daily from him to help translate. Granted, the Hue-mans have a bit of a Flyer streak in them, and they're purposely making it difficult for him, but don't you dare tell him."

"So that rumor *is* true?" Humor bubbled on his skin but then shifted to curiosity. "So, if it's not treating the hide that's bothering you, what is?"

She sighed. "I'm not sure I can explain. My heart grieves for my lost friends, but there's no anger towards this creature, not like I feel towards Rip. If anything, I'm sad that it had to die, too."

Trench flashed his understanding. "It is not this creature's fault that it needed the meat of others to survive. Nor is it at fault for fighting back to protect itself. It was a predator, but not a monster. It lived in balance with the world around it, as nature intended. It ate others, and others will eat it in return. Part of the reason we make the cloak is to honor the Leviathan. A lasting reminder of the majestic creature it once was. Rip, however, was an aberration, a true monster. What he did was not for survival, but because he wanted to make people suffer."

She stopped her work and rubbed at her injured hands. They were aching from the work, but that wasn't what was bothering her."

"You're having a hard time dealing with the fact that you killed him, aren't you?"

She sighed and nodded. "Very much so. I enjoyed every second I made him suffer, but I don't like who I became in that moment, even though I would do it again in a heartbeat if I had to."

Trench flashed blue-green with happiness.

She frowned at him. "I don't understand your reaction."

A bubble of humor crossed his skin before he spoke. "Because even after everything that happened to you, you still live your life with honor." He reached out and gently took her hands, turning them over to show the bandage putty. "Rip wouldn't have risked his life, much less dirty his hands, to dig strangers out of the rubble unless it benefited him in some way. I have a feeling you didn't even stop to think about the risk to you."

"She *never* thinks about the risk to herself," Aris muttered from behind her. "It makes our job downright impossible. Chasing after

Leviathans, crawling into crumbling buildings, walking into platform walls, ordering her protection away, letting Sprites drag her off without even *trying* to resist…"

Marsee rolled her eyes in Aris's general direction as her guard continued listing off all her failings.

"And there's the lecture I've been expecting," Marsee muttered.

"Come on," Trench replied, bubbling with laughter. "We should probably get back to work before we cause any more problems for your guard."

Grinning, she returned to cleaning the hide but spent the remaining time thinking about what he'd said.

After the cleaned hide had been placed in a solution to cure, Marsee followed Agate back to her office to deal with other urgent demands.

Agate slumped into her net with a heavy sigh and let the grief she'd been hiding slip free.

Marsee said nothing for several moments. "May I ask you a question?"

"You just did," Agate replied, humor now bubbling on her skin. "But you may ask another."

Marsee rolled her eyes. "You've been hanging around with Ellie too long."

Agate grinned. "Technically, she got that from me. What is it you want to know?"

"The song earlier. I…I know you sing our songs, but I didn't know your people sang outside of mating."

Agate didn't answer for a long time.

"If you don't want to answer, it's okay."

Agate sighed. "Your curiosity is justified, and I half expected you to ask, but I'm not sure how you'll take the answer."

"I promise to be open-minded," Marsee said.

Agate nodded but paused again before answering. "We do not sing as the other species do, or necessarily for the same reasons, although we love all forms of music. Our own songs are a very private affair, although it was not always that way, and it's one of the reasons people are unhappy with our membership in the Consortium."

Marsee raised a brow in surprise but didn't interrupt.

"There are no words to our song, only feelings, and every song is different. What you heard today is something that I doubt any off-worlder has ever heard before and one that will not be sung at the state funeral, even if someone does cry out their grief, because of how public it will be. There are two parts to our song of life. One is our song of pain, and the other is our song of joy, or what your people call our mating song. Without one, the other cannot exist. You heard both today."

"That was your mating song?" Marsee asked with ears-back astonishment and slight consternation.

Agate must have picked up on her unease and continued. "As with any species, when we're in pain, we cry. As a small fry, we can make a few sounds, and I know you're familiar with the few spoken words of our language."

Marsee nodded.

"Contrary to popular belief, we don't suddenly learn to sing when we become adults, although our range and ability to vocalize and control that sound increases dramatically at that time. Our children must learn how to sing in harmony to be successful at mating. We start at birth, singing through the pain of their delivery. There is no greater joy that comes from pain than that of childbirth. When our children are injured or upset, we take their song of pain and turn it into the song of joy, just as you heard today. It takes years for our children to learn both the skill to harmonize and the control necessary to elicit a biological reaction, and we practice with them often."

Her ears flattened at what Agate was implying, but she immediately corrected herself. She had promised to listen and be open-minded.

Agate frowned at her reaction. "This is why I hesitated to answer your question. I doubt any off-worlder has ever been told before, as the Charter explicitly forbids mating with children, and for good reason. We are not mating, but we worry it would appear as if we were to an outsider. This training is necessary for our species' survival. If we can't sing, we can't reproduce."

Marsee nodded the point. That had been her first thought, too.

"Funerals are the only time we collectively sing anymore. Since we joined the Consortium and learned your ways, we've kept this private for fear that people wouldn't understand. For us, it's a way to symbolize that life goes on even after the greatest of tragedies."

Marsee nodded her understanding and swam over to the window, looking out as she collected her thoughts.

"Forgive me if I've made you uncomfortable with this information," Agate said behind her.

Marsee didn't turn around but looked at Agate through the reflection in the window. "No. On the contrary, I'm honored that you trusted me enough to share and that everyone felt comfortable enough to sing out their grief around me. I can't even begin to explain how either song made me feel. Your song of grief cut me to my very soul, and your song of joy is perhaps the most beautiful song I have ever heard. I promise I won't tell anyone what you told me."

"So, what *is* bothering you?"

"I'm…I'm trying to reconcile all of this with what happened to me in the cave."

Agate swam over, hesitantly wrapped an arm across her shoulder, and hugged her gently when she didn't flinch or pull away. "My apologies. I should have realized this would be a trigger for you. Do you want to talk about what happened to you?"

"I honestly never want to think about it again," she replied, leaning into Agate's hug.

Agate nodded but continued to hold her as she stared out the window for a long time, trying to make sense of her feelings.

"What I heard in the cave was nothing like what I heard today," she finally said. "But if that's something normally taught by someone's parents, it makes me wonder if he was abused or neglected as a child."

Agate spun her around to face her. "Don't you dare give that monster a free pass! What he did to you was inexcusable!"

"I'm not. He deserved to die for what he did. I'm more concerned about other children. Would a lack of being able to harmonize signify potential neglect, especially if you no longer sing in public?"

Agate flashed surprise at the question. "That thought has honestly never crossed my mind. I suppose it could very well be. We do have *special* singing classes to help our youth if they need or want it, both to help them learn the skills necessary to mate and to control their natural reaction to music. That knowledge is also kept from off-worlders."

Marsee nodded her understanding. "It seems to me that the laws of the Consortium should account for different cultures and biological needs. At the very least, you shouldn't have to hide parts of your life cycle because they differ from ours."

"I don't disagree with you there, but how do you explain to another species that something they consider taboo is biologically necessary without it turning into a scandal or worse? We could be kicked out of the Consortium."

She snorted. "I would give anything to know that answer."

Agate frowned at her. "Somehow, I feel you're not talking about our song anymore."

"No, I'm not." She glanced in the direction of the hall where Aris floated and sighed.

Agate nodded her understanding and didn't press.

"It seems to me that hiding information does more harm than good," Marsee said instead. "Everything about mating and raising children is hidden from us until we go through our growth spurt. Because of that, I was terrified of ever having children, and I had no idea how to care for Hope when she was born. What's worse, though, is that I didn't even understand what I was seeing when I watched the video of my sister's rape, and not understanding your mating practices meant I didn't know what Rip was really doing to me. When Little Flower went into heat, and I reacted to it, I didn't realize it or even know that I could react without being in heat, and we both had to figure it out on our own. I wonder how many of our children have been sexually assaulted and never knew it. How do you report a crime when you don't know it's a crime? If someone had made me feel the way Little Flower did when I was a cub, I wouldn't have known it was wrong. I would have thought it was normal. I couldn't even tell my father what happened to me in the cave because I didn't have the words to do so. I couldn't help my sister through her trauma because everything about abuse is considered protected information. *Council's eyes only.* Clear Seas had to share council training material with me before I could even begin to process what I'd been through."

Agate hugged her again. "I am truly sorry for what happened to you."

Marsee's tablet took that moment to ding with the sound she'd added for Clear Seas, not wanting to miss another message from him. Praying it wasn't more bad news, she read through the short message. "Clear Seas sent the final number of damaged dwellings and displaced people. Looks like they need a few more emergency kits. I'll take care of those if you want to handle the rest."

Agate flashed her agreement, so Marsee left to wrangle a few Sprites in the warehouse to help her deliver the kits.

4 4

KENDRA: RANDO TAT

Kendra set her tablet down and stood to pace in her office, trying to decide what to do or if there was anything she could do. She'd only been back for an hour, returning with the Council's ships, and she was waiting in her office for Marcus to show up to finish the interrogations, but Clear Sea's press release on the seven councilors had just arrived, followed almost immediately by Aris's report on the situation, along with the fact that Marsee was currently running herself into the ground in the arena. Aris was justifiably concerned, and so was she.

After several minutes of pacing, she left and made her way to Marcus's office. His door was open, and he was talking with his Senior Advocate when she arrived.

Marcus took one look at her and ordered Samantha out.

Kendra shut the door and turned on the privacy screen.

"What is it?" he asked.

"Marsee let them go," Kendra replied.

Marcus flicked an ear back dismissively. "I never expected her to do otherwise. I had word from Clear Seas about it a few minutes ago. I'm assuming her guards told you?"

"Yes, and I saw the press release," she replied but then frowned. "Why did you let her decide?"

"Because they would never have believed us. It had to come from her. In any event, Clear Seas is quite impressed at how thoroughly she investigated the evidence before making her decision. She found several additional pieces of evidence that corroborated their story and as far I can tell, didn't give away any of what we can do with our instincts. According to him, she made it out to be much like any other brain defect that could cause similar issues. Hopefully, they'll think this is nothing more than another fatal illness and drop it."

Kendra pursed her lips, wondering just how much Marsee had shared with her family about what they could really do. Then again, Marsee didn't even know what they could really do, even if she was already showing the early signs of many of those abilities.

"The risk to her is far greater now and to Saber," she said.

He shook his head. "The risk was always there. We have no idea who else Rip told, or how much for that matter."

She sighed. "This isn't going to go away."

Before he could reply, there was a knock on the door. He turned off the privacy screen, and Samantha entered, a look of worry on her face. "Sir, you need to turn on the news."

Marcus raised a brow but did as requested. They both stared in horror at what they were seeing, but there was little either of them could do. Digger would be the one to respond if necessary, as they were the closest to the Water World.

Marcus sighed with worry and refocused on her. "Well, since you're here, we might as well get this over with. Waiting won't make it any easier."

She nodded and followed him down to the holding cells, locking everything behind her mask. She loathed this part of her job, but she'd reviewed all of the evidence against her guards, and so far, none had claimed innocence like the others. They knew the consequences of their infractions long before they were ever put on duty. Their abilities to sniff out the truth usually kept her guards honest, but it wasn't the first time she'd had to put one of her guards down for committing a crime, even those she cared about, and there were many she cared about.

Marcus was thorough with his investigation or tried to be, but they all refused to speak.

She sensed anger, resentment, and determination from them. They had felt justified in their actions and accepted the consequences. She supposed, in many ways, she'd been no different when she'd stood up to Tabor, but they'd gone about it the wrong way, and innocent people had been hurt and killed. Still, for all their crimes, Marcus made their punishments quick and painless. For that, she was grateful, even if she would have been far less kind in his place.

Her respect for Marcus had grown over the past week. He hadn't wavered in his duty, even when it had broken his heart. She only sensed regret and frustration from him now — emotions she fully understood. Every act of silence was another act of treason, one that likely meant they were protecting others.

The only two he didn't execute were the two who had been involved in Lyrik's death, as that investigation was still open. She was certain they were lying about forgetting to turn on their cameras, but there was nothing she could use as proof, and she doubted Marcus would believe her if she tried to press the issue.

Marcus watched as the last body was carried away, rubbing at his palms and lost in thought.

She watched him silently from the shadows to give him time to process before testing him. She didn't need to, but he expected it. She could already tell he was in control. There was no reason for him not to be. He had no attachment to these people, and they had plotted against him and his family. His instinct was in full agreement that they should die, but he was a kind soul and felt every one of their deaths.

His emotions shifted to regret and sadness as he realized he was rubbing at his hands and, with a heavy sigh, dropped them.

She respected that about him, too. That he still cared. She'd long since become numb to the act herself and had lost count of the lives she'd taken long ago. As she waited, she wondered how many more lives she would take before someone managed to kill her. She prayed fervently that they'd avoided the war, but two centuries of training told her otherwise. This was just the opening volley. She had no doubt Rip, and the others would become martyrs to those who remained. It was already starting. The people were far more divided than she'd ever seen them, and it was getting worse by the day.

"Do you have more names for me?" she asked quietly.

He shook his head and stood. "No. No one has come forward yet, but I can still hope."

She ignored the lie and watched as he left the cell without waiting for her to test him. He made no attempts to hide his emotions behind his normally calm mask, enough that several others in the hall stopped to watch as he walked past them. He was weary and worried, ears drooped, and tail dragging behind him, every step heavy with the weight of responsibility.

She let him leave but wondered just how long he would last as a Senior Councilor. He was intelligent and good at what he did, confident in his abilities and power, but he had changed over the past few weeks. He had the steel of an Honor Guard, and he'd done what needed to be done, but he was bending under the pressure. She'd seen it far too often and wondered what would ultimately cause him to break or if that steel would become tempered and hardened as it had with her and was happening with his niece.

She returned to her office to sign off on the executions but stopped to watch the news. Grief was palpable in the outer office, but based on everyone's hurry to return to their duties at her appearance, it had nothing to do with those she'd just executed. She sighed as she read the list of casualties. She'd worked with Tanner often over the years, and she'd been relieved that the Sprite hadn't been on the list of those brought in. Tanner had been one of the best, but her reputation had been tarnished when her son went missing. There was no questioning her honor now, and for that, she was grateful.

It wasn't until late that evening when the report from Aris on what had happened with the Leviathan finally came in, and it shook her even more than the first message had.

"You look like you've seen a ghost," Quinn said from her door.

She motioned him in, had him shut the door, and refocused her attention on him with a smirk. "I was wondering when you were going to report in. I see you took your orders quite literally."

He chuckled. "That certainly wasn't my plan, but where better to guard her from? So why are you so scared? I haven't sniffed that from you in years."

Rather than replying, she slid the tablet over to him and let him read through Aris's past two messages.

"It could just be a coincidence," he said, handing it back.

She snorted and dropped her voice down. "Five minutes before being attacked by a Leviathan, she's nearly out of control with anxiety and tells Aris she feels like a Leviathan is about to swallow her whole. No, that's no coincidence, and you know it. I'm not surprised in the least. She was showing signs of accessing the Knowing before she even transitioned, and this is at least the fourth incident since her transition."

"You really believe Marsee can tap into the Knowing?" he asked. "I know everyone is talking about her dream, but…"

"I don't know why you find that hard to believe," she replied. "So can you."

He scoffed. She'd told him that before, but like most in the Guard, he didn't really believe it and brushed it off as a coincidence or the result of decades of training.

"I'm serious," she replied. "How many times have you been anxious and found yourself exactly where you needed to be or drawn to something seemingly unimportant that played a crucial part later? Do you really think you just happened upon the Ice Giants in the middle of the Wilds?"

He pursed his lips.

"Quinn, you're my second for a reason. You need to pay attention to your feelings, now more than ever."

"Why do I have a *feeling* I'm not going to be your second for very long?"

She chuckled. "The way Marsee's progressing, I have a feeling we're both going to be demoted soon, but that does bring up another thing I wanted to talk to you about."

She switched back to a normal voice. "Jeran has finally agreed to a permanent guard presence in New Hope, although out of respect for his people, he wants them hidden as much as possible."

"Understandable. You want me to take over there?" he asked.

"No. Believe it or not, Jeran picked Avery as his Senior, but I want you there, too. He doesn't have the experience you do, and New Hope is still far too vulnerable."

She wondered if he would react negatively, thinking he was being promoted, only to find out he would be taking the lead from Avery, who was fifty years his junior, but there was no sign of jealousy. If anything, he seemed both relieved and happy about the assignment.

He gave a single nod. "Yes, ma'am."

"Until they return, you'll remain as Acting Senior. Oversee the build and prepare for possible retaliation after the Seniors announce their next set of people."

"Have they identified anyone?"

"Not yet, but Marsee uncovered a smuggling operation and an entire shipload of contraband on an Ice Giant Ship. So, I know at least several dozen high-ranking people involved and possibly a few in the Council. The evidence there was circumstantial at best, but I don't know what else the Seniors might have on them. It's not a capital offense, but people will be demoted or kicked out of the Guild at the very least."

"Ice Giants..." he muttered.

"Indeed," she replied. "I'm sure you've noticed the backlash against the Council and Saber growing on their planet. They weren't happy with us to begin with and are most certainly not happy with Marsee's sudden promotion, regardless of the actions that prompted it. Rip was very popular on that planet, as was Breydihk."

He shook his head slightly. "I honestly don't know how they're going to react to Marsee's release of the seven or the next round of arrests."

"Hopefully, nothing, but we should expect the worst," she replied.

He nodded in agreement and then pursed his lips as if not sure how to broach the next topic.

She waited him out.

"I'm worried about Myra," he finally said. "She informed me that she used her instinct fairly heavily to... 'help' on the trip back. She was in full control, but the waiver I saw before was still there. No worse, but no better, either. The healers at the clinic were very interested in what happened, as Ellie produced six viable embryos for a third heat."

"Six!" she exclaimed. "That's unheard of."

He nodded. "They're interested in doing a trial to see how effective a treatment it might be for high-risk heats. I suggested that they start with volunteers from the Guard or their families first. Ellie...struggled at the end of her heat. I was sedated for most of it, but she attacked two of the guards before recovering. To be fair, I did, too, but I didn't know who grabbed me. She didn't have any trouble understanding sign, but she couldn't understand the guard's speech. Her record has been locked, but I thought you should know."

"After what happened to her, I'm honestly not surprised. Did you test her?"

"Liv did. I didn't want to make things awkward, but I watched from a distance. There wasn't the slightest issue."

"Good. I didn't see anything when I tested her. Issues after what she went through are expected, but if she could understand sign and recover, that's very promising, especially if Myra managed to stay in control, too. I'll talk with Nerissa and test Myra myself going forward."

He nodded, but frowned and dropped down to subvocalize again. "Is there a particular reason why you wanted me to bring Myra into the Guard? Did something happen?"

She nodded. "One minor incident, but...Myra informed me that she's always heard her instinct."

He stared at her in shock. "Always? How is that possible?"

"I honestly don't know. For now, we'll wait and watch. I'm worried her instinct will be too strong to Transition, but as long as she's still in control, I have no grounds to bring her in. Nothing Marcus or Jer would accept anyway."

He nodded and left.

Six! she thought in amazement as her mind drifted over the conversation.

A part of her wanted to be a part of that trial, to have a family again. She'd been through both of her heats. She'd only had one cub with her first litter, and she'd miscarried with the second early on in her pregnancy. She sighed at the memory of her daughter and shook her head. *No. I can't go through that again. Not now.*

Full of her own growing anxiety, she left her office and made her way to the Arena. It was dark when she entered, and the lights flickered on. No one was there training as she'd ordered extra patrols of the city. She took a deep breath, allowing the calm she always felt when she entered this space to soothe her anxiety, and took off, pushing herself hard through the course several times. She was nearing the end of her third run when she heard the sounds of someone entering. She stopped and looked back, raising her brow.

"I figured you'd be here."

Kendra snorted, jumped down from the obstacle she was on, grabbed a drink, and then leapt up to the balcony where Oscar waited for her. "What brings you to my domain this late at night, Commander?"

"Where else am I going to see you?" Oscar replied, rubbing against her side and twining his tail around hers.

She purred but untangled her tail and made for the exit. "You could have come by anytime today."

He snorted and followed after. "And give those harbingers something to squawk about? No, I think not."

"Are you referring to my guards or the press?" she asked with a chuckle.

"Oh, I'm sure your guards already know or have guessed by now," he replied. "For that matter, I imagine half the Guard has bets placed on when we're going to move in together."

She chuckled but didn't reply as they walked the rest of the way back to her suite in the Guard complex in companionable silence. It was a beautiful night, and she was thankful to have this quiet moment of peace before the coming storm.

She considered her growing relationship with the Senior Commander of the Ship's Guild. They'd been friends since they were cubs in primary school but had only become more than that in the past few years. She'd never officially ended her partnership, but after her daughter had died, he'd left, unable to deal with the grief or knowledge of what she'd been forced to do. Although, as far as anyone outside the Guard and a few close friends knew, they were still together.

Oscar had never partnered but had become the guardian of his nephlings when his sister died suddenly from spotted fur. They were all grown up and moved out now.

Their lives were chaotic, and their time together limited, but he never pressured her for more. He was happy to spend a few hours losing a game of Rando-Tat to her. Part of her wanted to make their relationship something more, but she didn't know if she could go through that again, especially now when everything was so unsettled.

They didn't say anything until they arrived at her suite. She unlocked it and shut the door behind them, which automatically turned on her privacy screen. When her nose told her no one had been in the suite in her absence, she finally allowed herself to relax. Tossing her carry harness over the back of a chair, she grabbed drinks for them and collapsed into her favorite chair with a groan.

He sat down across from her in his usual chair, the Rando-Tat board already set up and waiting between them. "I see you impounded one of my ships the other day," he said after taking a drink.

She sighed, having hoped they'd avoid talking about work, but then decided that was rather wishful thinking. "You know I can't go into details."

He snorted. "And you should know, I've already watched the footage of the whole thing. I must admit the sight of Marsee standing off against the pilot was rather entertaining, even if my pilots were involved."

"They were released. We found no evidence they knew what was in those shipments," Kendra replied.

His humor turned to worry, and he shook his head. "That may be, but I am under no allusion that others from my guild won't be added to the pile of bodies we've been transporting lately. Smuggling on top of what Ellie's pilots did?" He shook his head. "I'm surprised the Seniors haven't called for my head, too."

"Do they have reason to?" she asked. He didn't have the same oath she did, and she honestly had no idea how high up the smuggling operation went.

"Not that I know of, but if Rip was planting evidence against others, who knows what he might have put in place against me? Granted, I'm honestly more surprised they let you live."

She breathed a sigh of relief, not having sensed any deception from him, then snorted. "That makes two of us. Thankfully, I already admitted to all of my crimes."

He raised a brow. "You committed a crime? Seriously?"

"That depends on who you ask, I suppose. Thankfully, the Seniors found in my favor."

"What did you do?"

"Treason," she replied and chuckled as he nearly spit out his drink in surprise.

"I wasn't sure if the Council could be trusted during Little Flower's trial, so I put measures in place to ensure they couldn't do anything to hurt them and watched and recorded the Senior's deliberation so I'd have both warning and proof."

He chuckled. "Well, that seems more like the Kendra I know. Still, I'm glad the Seniors found in your favor, if for no other reason than it gives me one more chance to beat you at Rando-Tat."

"*That* is never going to happen, Commander, but if by some chance you did win, you'd better call a Trauma Ship."

"Is that a threat, Senior Honor Guard?" he asked with a glare, although she could tell he wasn't serious.

"No. The ship will be for me. The only way you'll win will be if something is seriously wrong with me."

He snorted, grabbed the deck, and began shuffling. "I suppose that could be arranged, but luckily for you, I'd much rather lose to you than lose you."

She smiled at him. "Good, because I am far too ship-lagged to deal with all the paperwork necessary if I had to drag you in by your scruff."

He grinned wickedly. "Now that's music to my ears. I might just have a chance of winning after all."

"I may be tired, Commander, but you're still not going to win."

"Care to place a bet on it?"

She grinned with a nearly feral expression at him. "Gladly. Same bet as last time? As much as I love my current ship, it's getting a little slow, and the way things are right now, I have a feeling I'm going to need something far more capable."

He was so surprised that the cards actually went flying. It had been decades since he'd last convinced her to go along with a bet. Her smile deepened at his consternation, but he recovered quickly and bent to pick up the cards, then began shuffling again.

"Seven moves, was it?" he asked as he started dealing the cards.

She nodded and picked up the first card, pleased at what he'd dealt her, but by the time the cards were handed out, her happiness had turned to worry, not because she'd been dealt bad cards, but because she'd been dealt a perfect hand. The odds were one in a trillion. The fur on her scruff stood straight up before she could control it.

Oscar grinned, seeing her reaction. "That bad?" he asked. "You really did like my decorating job the last time, didn't you? I'll be sure to copy it. I want you to be happy."

She smoothed her fur. "It's revolting, ostentatious, and downright gaudy, but you're still not going to win. I'll even let you go first and pick the dice we use." She had a rather large collection, mostly gifts from people who knew her love of the game. It was the one avarice that she allowed herself.

He scowled at her, whether for her insult, which was as much a part of the game, or because of her quick recovery, she wasn't sure, but he took her offer and walked over to the display case where she kept most of her dice. But she gasped a moment later as he picked the one set she'd never allowed him to use. It was the set she'd given to her daughter on her name day with her own custom board, only a week before she'd died.

He turned back to her with a raised brow at her audible reaction. "What is it about this set?"

She'd never told him, and he'd never pressed before. "They belonged to Arianna."

He softened with understanding and went to put them back, but she stopped him. "No. I said any set, and that's the one you picked."

"Are you sure?"

She nodded and motioned to the table. "I wouldn't want you to accuse me of cheating."

He scowled at her again. "Are you cheating?"

"I would never," she replied. "Under the display is a certificate of authenticity from the crafter who made them. You're welcome to check."

To her surprise, he did, although she only sensed curiosity from him, that is, until he read the certificate. "Master Odsworth made these?"

"They're the last set he ever crafted, I believe. I paid a small fortune for that set. It was her name-day gift. As far as I know, they've only been used once." She swallowed hard as grief hit her at the memory of that game. It was the only game she'd ever lost. Her daughter had used her instinct to win, to sniff her out, and she'd gotten angry and yelled at her for cheating. There'd been a waiver, but she hadn't wanted to believe it, and she'd allowed her daughter to leave, deciding it was only anger, not the first signs of a loss of control.

If only I had stopped her. She shoved that thought aside hard. All the what-ifs in the universe wouldn't bring her daughter back.

Oscar watched her closely but said nothing as she shoved her emotions behind her mask and motioned to the board. "Are we playing or not?"

He squinted slightly, suspicious of her sudden calm, but sat and rolled the dice.

Five moves later, she had him pinned.

"Impossible," he whispered. "It's not possible to win in five moves. Even the Masters can't do that."

"I've seen a dozen impossible things this week," she replied, outwardly calm, but inside, she was shaking. The dice had rolled in her favor every time. "What's one more. Now, as for my ship..."

His expression shifted from disbelief to astonishment and then consternation as she told him what she wanted.

"What game are you really playing at?" he finally asked her.

"I am not playing, Oscar. I'm deadly serious. The rules of the game have changed, and we need to adapt, and adapt quickly before it's too late. They've already tried to take over the Council and burn New Hope to the ground. The guards we executed today were hiding something or someone. They all refused to speak. Something's coming. I'm sure of it, and people will die if we're not prepared."

"That may be, but what you're asking for is..."

"Nothing I've asked for is illegal," she replied. "I wouldn't do that to you."

"That's only because it's never been done before. Do you really want to go down this route? Look what happened to Little Flower and her people. This seems...dishonorable somehow."

"Honor will get us nowhere if we're dead. If you need approval from Marcus, do so, but not where it can be recorded. Our accounts are compromised."

Oscar leaned back in his seat for a long time before nodding. "I don't like it, but I'll do it. On one condition."

She raised a brow.

He leaned forward and picked up the dice, slowly, deliberately, one at a time. "These are mine. If you use what I provide you without provocation, I will make you watch as I destroy them and then destroy Arianna's memorial."

She nodded, accepting those conditions. "I, Kendra Arianna Hunt, give you my word that I will only use those weapons in self-defense or the defense of others, and I pray I never have to use them at all."

45

MARSEE: SHADES OF PERIWINKLE

The Sprites, of course, refused to let Marsee carry anything, but rather than argue, she simply went with them.

Several hundred hanging nets were scattered around the perimeter, hanging from hooks on the walls that she hadn't known were there. Booths, seating, and tables took up the majority of the center. People waited in line for food, medical care, housing, and supplies. Grief and fear were palpable in the room, but curiosity and surprise replaced them as she swam in with the others and over to the supply booth.

"Translator, thank you!" The Staffer working the booth signed.

"You're very welcome. Do you need anything else?"

"Nothing right now. Thank you," he replied.

"Let me know if you do," she said, then turned to swim out but found herself staring at the crowd watching her, all except for one tiny Sprite curled up in a net that was far too big for them, slightly away from the others. She could barely see the child through the wall of fear that surrounded them, even though the child's skin was pure white.

She thanked her helpers, sent them back to the Guild, and swam over. As far as Marsee could tell, the child didn't even notice her approach. Small shivers of fear sent ripples in the water. A bandage wrapped around one tentacle and the side of her face, and she wondered if the child was in pain.

"Hello. Are you alright?" she asked in Saber.

The Sprite opened her eyes and blinked up at her with a tiny gasp, but to Marsee's consternation, the Sprite's fear only increased.

"It's alright. I'm not going to hurt you," Marsee said in sign. "Why are you scared of me?"

"I'm not," the child flashed. "I'm scared you have more bad news."

"Oh," Marsee said, drooping with understanding. "Did you lose someone?"

"My mama," she replied before her skin shifted to black. "Papa's hurt really bad, too. He's in stasis."

Her heart broke for the child. "I am so sorry. Would a hug help?" Marsee held out her hands, and the tiny Sprite bolted into them. She purred deeply to comfort the child until they pulled away. "What's your name?"

"Periwinkle," she replied.

"What a beautiful name. That's one of my favorite colors. Do you have any other family?"

"My older sister, Sienna. She was here with me, but her head hurt really bad, and she threw up. The Healers took her back to the Trauma Center. I wanted to go with her, but they told me to wait. They said she wouldn't be long, but that was *hours* ago."

Marsee frowned and looked back to the Healer's station, motioning one of the healers over. They swam over immediately. "Do you have an update on Periwinkle's Papa and sister?"

"I don't, Translator, but I can find out."

"Please."

After asking their names, the Healer dug up the information. "Your sister has been treated, and she's in recovery right now. They've decided to admit her for a day to watch to make sure there aren't further issues from her concussion," the Healer replied in sign.

"What's a concussion?" Peri asked.

"The bump to her head," the healer replied in Sprite. "As for your

Papa, it looks like he just came out of surgery. Based on his injuries, he'll spend a few days in the Trauma Center and need some physical therapy after, but I expect he'll make a full recovery."

Periwinkle flashed a brilliant blue of happiness and smelled of relief.

"Thank you," she told the Healer, who nodded and swam back to her station.

"Do you have anyone you can stay with while your family recovers?"

"I don't know. Sienna sent a message to Grammy to let her know about Mama, but she's at a conference on Digger. The last message Sienna got before she got sick was that the soonest she could get a return flight was tomorrow night."

"Tomorrow?! Well, we can't have that," Marsee said. "Do you know where your grandmother is on Digger?"

Peri shook her head.

"I can find out," Aris said. "I'm assuming you want to arrange transport?"

She smiled at her guard. "Yes, and have them send me the bill."

Peri flashed her thanks and gave her another hug. While she was hugging Peri, she felt a tap on her arm and looked over to see another young Sprite, perhaps as old as Stormy.

"Forgive me for interrupting, Translator," he replied. "Is there any way you could get me a new tablet? Mine was destroyed, and I keep having to ask to borrow others to check on my family. I'd get one myself, but they won't let me leave without an adult."

"Of course," she replied and turned to the crowd that was watching her, as she realized that tablets weren't in the packet of emergency supplies, but likely everyone had lost theirs. "Does anyone else need a tablet or anything else that I might be able to help with?"

Hands raised all around the room, so she motioned people over and started putting in orders for what they needed. Tablets were the biggest need, but like Peri, many needed information on loved ones or help with transportation.

By the time they finally left the Council Building, morning had arrived, and her stomach grumbled nearly as loudly as her sister did in the morning. She called Agate to see if anyone had ordered breakfast for the crafters.

Agate wasn't aware of anyone doing so, so Marsee made her way down to the Market and bought out several vendors' worth of food. She sent one to the Guild and the others to make their way around to the various cleanup sites.

After grabbing a quick bite for herself from another vendor, she started making her way back to the Guild again but stopped when she saw the Sprite she'd rescued floating outside of the rubble that had once been her home. A large bandage wrapped around her side and over her shoulder. Builders were shoring up what little remained of her house to keep it safe for the others who were helping to dig out her belongings. She was honestly surprised to see the Sprite had recovered enough to leave the Trauma Center.

"How's your daughter?" Marse asked.

The Sprite flashed the silver and purple and bowed stiffly before switching to rough sign language as the bandage made it difficult for her to speak. "She still in Trauma Center, but they say she be okay. Few more minute, she might not. If not you help, we both be dead."

Marsee sighed. "You might not have been injured if it wasn't for me. Honor Guard Tanner was trying to lead it away from me. Save your respects for her. She gave her life to save mine and the rest of the city. I'm sorry you were hurt and your home destroyed in the process."

The Sprite shook her head. "If not us, someone else. I see damage to city. A Leviathan here! I still can't believe. No, I think more dead if you not here to chase away."

Marsee tilted her head, not willing to argue the point. "Do you have somewhere to stay?"

"Yes. My sister. Thank you."

"I'm glad to hear it. Stop by the Council. Emergency supplies are available for everyone displaced, but if you need anything else, please let me know. I hope you and your daughter recover quickly."

"Thank you, Translator."

Marsee nodded and continued on her way. When she returned, the

Guild was a flurry of activity. The food she'd purchased was being distributed to the workers, who only stopped long enough to eat and then returned to work.

She checked on the orders she'd submitted and found them mostly complete, but then, in a burst of inspiration, she grabbed several Sprites and raided the toy department. The emergency kits and requested supplies had all been essential items, but the children would have lost everything, and she remembered how much the stuffy her niece had sent to the Agency had meant to Little Flower.

Word of what she was doing spread, and a moment later, others arrived with large bags and began filling them with their own donations, not just for those seeking shelter but for all of the displaced children. Some of whom, like Peri's sister, were still in the Trauma Center.

When the bags were full, she and a group of her helpers returned to the Council Chamber with the toys and the other requested items.

Any shyness they'd had before completely vanished. The moment she started handing out the toys, she was swarmed with tiny Sprites, not waiting for their names to be called out.

"Do you know any other Crawley Man stories?" Peri asked as Marsee handed over the bag she'd picked herself for the child. Included were several Crawley Man toys and a coloring book based on her drawings, along with a selection of markers.

"I don't, but I just finished the translation of a story about another one of the Hue-man gods called the Night Flyer. Would you like to hear it?"

Flashes of agreement and excitement spread through the crowd, and not just from the children. Once everything was distributed, she swam over to sit on the edge of the Senior's podium so everyone could see and used her authority to connect her tablet to one of the monitors in the chamber so she could show the drawings along with her story.

Then, once everyone was situated around her, she began. "Not all of the Super Heros the Hue-man's call their gods are actually gods, and neither are their villains. This story is about one such pair, both starting out life in the same way, as orphans when their parents were killed by criminals. I'll let you decide which is the real villain and which is the hero. I once thought I knew, but now, I'm not so sure."

Her audience was appreciative, and she did her best to ignore the press drone that appeared the moment she took her seat. She'd gotten used to it during the Council Meetings, and like then, the press thankfully remained in their booth.

When she finished, the children all flashed their happiness and thanks, but she noticed the adults were far more unsettled by the story. It wasn't lost on her the parallels of the past month. The villain in this story could have easily been Snapper Fish, or so many of the others caught up in Rip's scheming, trying to save their families at the cost of others, and the hero had made his own mistakes that made everything worse. He could have helped the villain long before it got to the point that the villain acted out of desperation and grief, but he hadn't.

Avery was waiting for her just outside the Chamber when she left. "Little Flower is over at the Trauma Center helping out, with Thatcher watching her, and Tamarin is watching Hope," he told her as Aris swam off to get some sleep.

She nodded and took off in the other direction, heading for the Trauma Center, not to see Little Flower, but to deliver the remaining toys for the children, but moments after entering, she passed Little Flower in the hall. They hugged briefly before Little Flower took off on whatever task the Senior Healer had set her to. She watched for a moment before continuing on her way, first through the Trauma Ward, stopping in briefly to talk with the victims, if they were able to talk, and their families, and then made her way over to the children's ward for those with less life-threatening injuries.

By the time she returned to the Guild, the hide had finished curing. While she'd made clothing, she didn't consider herself an expert by any means, but Trench once again recruited her for the task, only this time he shooed everyone else away.

"A cloak personally made by the Translator will have far more meaning to the families of the dead," he explained and showed her what to do. It was actually a fairly simple pattern. The thickness of the hide was the challenging bit, but they had tools for that, and by that evening, the cloaks for the dead were finished.

Avery called in the Honor Guard to transport the cloaks to the Council. A squad of Water Sprites appeared a few minutes later, including Senior Honor Guard Stinger, lined up by rank in a semi-circle around her. Avery had given her a hasty tutorial on what would happen, so she was somewhat prepared.

After a lengthy pause, Senior Honor Guard Stinger swam forward. He was halfway to her when Aris came zooming into the room at full speed with her drone. The watching Sprites bolted out of the way. At the edge of the semi-circle, she tossed her drone aside and swam forward until she was directly in front of and facing Stinger.

The Sprites watching flashed their surprise, as did a few of the guards, before getting their reaction under control.

Marsee had no idea what was going on, and apparently, neither did Stinger.

"What is the meaning of this disrespect, Honor Guard?" Stinger demanded, in Water Sprite, laced with flickers of anger.

"Sir, I mean no disrespect," Aris signed in reply. "Honor Guard Tanner died saving my life. I will never be able to repay that debt, and I know I do not have the rank or even the right to ask you, but I beg that you allow me the privilege to honor your protege by carrying her cloak."

Stinger took a deep breath and calmed his skin. He didn't answer for several long moments but then nodded, turned, and swam back to his place in line.

Aris turned sharply and bowed deeply to her. When she straight-ened, Marsee handed her a cloak, which she carefully laid over one arm, turned, and swam back about halfway before turning to face her again.

She expected Stinger to come back for the next cloak, but a different Sprite swam forward.

"Leviathan Slayer, I beg that you allow me the privilege to carry the cloak for Master Pilot Blue Grass. He was my cousin and a good friend."

Marsee nodded and handed him the cloak. He swam back to float next to Aris.

She did the same for the next two cloaks to different guards, but when only Temperate and Snapper Fish's cloaks remained, there was a slightly longer hesitation before Stinger swam forward again.

"Leviathan Slayer, I beg that you allow me the privilege to carry the cloak for Master Pilot Temperate Seas. I have known him since he was a child and cared for him deeply."

Marsee could tell he was telling the truth, but she shook her head, which caused others to murmur or flash their surprise. "No. I mean you no disrespect, but I will carry his cloak. He was my friend." Her arms shook with emotion as she wondered how many more friends would die because of her. She had nearly lost everyone she considered a friend these past few weeks, and now Temperate and Tanner and four others had died as an unintended consequence of her actions. "He was *my* friend."

Stinger nodded and started to swim back again, but she raised a hand to stop him. "There is another cloak that I imagine no one will swim forward to claim. Will you do him that honor?"

The silence that followed spoke volumes, as did his inability to meet her gaze.

"I will," a voice rang out from behind the crowd. The crowd split, and for a moment, it reminded her of her mentorship ceremony, as she was just as surprised to see Red Fin as she had been Ellie.

Avery had informed her that he wouldn't be here as he would be the one receiving the cloak in his mother's honor. Snapper had tarnished Red Fin's honor by implicating Red Fin in her kidnapping. She couldn't understand why he would be here now, and clearly, neither did anyone else.

Red Fin swam forward, and Stinger backed off. "Leviathan Slayer, I ask that you allow me the right to restore Red Fin's honor and carry his cloak."

"Why would you want to do that?" she asked. "He tarnished your own honor and the honor of your mother by his actions."

He shook his head. "No. My dishonor is my own. I failed to protect you and this community by not seeing the threat he and Rip posed, but whatever Snapper Fish's actions were before, he tried to make up for them. Who knows how many future lives he saved by routing out the corruption in our Council, but countless lives were saved by his actions last night alone, and as far as I'm concerned, he paid the ultimate price, and his honor is no longer in question."

She smiled at Red Fin and handed him the cloak, then grabbed the last remaining cloak and swam out. She didn't have a clue what she was doing, but she didn't particularly care. The guards followed her lead.

They kept to her pace, which she purposely kept slow so she would be able to swim the entire way back without getting tired. Everyone shifted to give them room to pass and bowed low, flashing the purple and silver.

Word must have reached Clear Seas as he waited for them at the entrance. He didn't even bother to hide his grief as they passed. They made their way down the hall and past the people still set up in the chamber, although nearly half appeared to have been moved to more permanent housing.

All conversation ceased as they appeared and made their way to the front. The desks on the Senior's platform had all been removed, and the poles that normally held the flags of the Consortium were lowered. Large plaques with the names and images of the dead were hung there instead. Each of the guards, including herself, lined up in front of the appropriate plaque, and, in one solemn motion, they hung the cloaks on the hook below each of them. Then, as one, they bowed while the Sprites also flashed the silver and purple.

It was all she could do to keep from crying as she placed the cloak she was carrying on Temperate's hook. Images and short videos of his life played on the plaque, but when one of Temperate and Stormy playing with Stormy's Crawly Man figurines displayed, she could no longer hold the tears back.

She closed her eyes and took several deep breaths to contain her emotions. No one moved, waiting for her. When she turned around, two honor guards took their place on either end of the podium while the rest of them filed out after her.

As they left the chamber, additional guards took up positions on either side of the door or made their way around to the other entrances to guard them as well.

"Translator, a moment, please," Clear Seas called out before she could swim off.

Marsee stopped and turned to face him, struggling hard to control and contain her grief. He'd pulled himself together and looked as calm as always, but it did nothing to hide his grief from her nose.

Her voice broke with emotion when she spoke. "My condolences, Senior Councilor."

She caught a brief flicker of grief before he clamped down on it again.

"Thank you, Translator. I wanted to let you know that the state funeral will be held the day after tomorrow at noon. I was hoping that you would give the speech. I...I am not sure that I'll be able to."

Marsee smiled at him with both compassion and understanding. "It would be my honor," she replied and bowed to him.

He bowed back, turned, and swam away before his grief could overwhelm him again.

Marsee watched him leave, her heart heavy with the weight of his request and torn with her own grief.

46

MARSEE: STAGE FRIGHT

Marsee looked down at the floor outside Ellie's office and the organized chaos left behind. Agate had sent everyone home while she'd delivered the cloaks and had told her to go home, too. Most everyone had been up for two days straight, but she was used to the longer days and had work to do.

Sighing, she swam back into Ellie's office and hit the privacy screen. The moment it was turned on, she roared as loud as she could, letting the past few days of terror and grief out.

"Ancient Gods! What was I thinking?" She grabbed the back of her scruff and twisted hard as she began to shake. *Me?! Give a speech?! Oh, I think I'm going to be sick.*

Breathing hard, she managed to somehow pull herself together, thankfully without throwing up, turned off the privacy screen, and started the arduous process of writing said speech. She'd barely made any progress several hours later when her sister arrived with food she'd picked up from Fire Sticks.

"Eat," her sister said, setting the package down in front of her.

With a sigh, Marsee set her tablet aside and opened the package to see a large order of fire sticks and brenna berry sticks. She grabbed one and groaned as her hunger and exhaustion kicked in. She called the guards in and shoved the package towards them. They each grabbed several sticks and made their way back out to their guard position. After eating two of each, Marsee leaned back in her seat and sighed again.

"What are you working on?" her sister asked.

"Clear Seas asked me to give the speech for the funeral," she told her sister. "Everything I write feels…unworthy and trite."

"Whatever you say will be perfect because it's coming from you. Your very presence will be enough," her sister said. "Just speak from your heart like you did the other day."

"I've tried. How do I write about people I barely know?"

"You know them better than you think you do. They're honor guards and sea patrol. They knew the risks and knew every day there was a chance they wouldn't come home. Think about everything the guards and patrol have done for you, for us, but first, you need sleep. You've been up for two days straight. You'll be able to think clearer after a good night's sleep, and we should probably have your paws checked to make sure they're healing on the way back."

Marsee looked down at her paws. She'd forgotten all about her injuries. She sighed and reached for the last stick, barely feeling the bloom of heat from the fire fruit, as it was nothing compared to the ache in her heart. After tossing the remains in the recycler, they left and eventually made their way back to the suite, where they found Tamarin lying on the floor, entertaining Hope.

"Thank you for watching her. I know it's well past your shift change," Little Flower said.

"The Guard takes care of its own," she said before patting Hope on the head and climbing to her feet. To Marsee's surprise, Tamarin gave her a hug before leaving.

Marsee stared at the closed door after Tamarin left for several long moments. After a quick trip to the waste room and giving a hug of her own to Hope and Little Flower, she climbed onto the bed and was asleep within moments. She didn't even wake as her sister climbed in beside her.

Her dreams were turbulent as her brain tried to process the events of the past two days, and she woke with a start early the next morning, long before her alarm went off.

Climbing carefully out of bed, she grabbed her tablet, curled up on one of the pillows, and began writing. She was still writing when her alarm went off, and her sister woke up.

"How long have you been up?" her sister asked.

"A few hours," Marsee replied as she switched over to read her messages. After responding to the ones that needed an immediate reply, she stretched and began preparing breakfast.

There was a knock at the door. Little Flower walked over to open it.

"Marsee, it's for you," Little Flower said a moment later.

Marsee set down the knife she was using to chop up breakfast, walked over to the door, and blinked in surprise when she saw a Sprite in one of their transport carts, which allowed them access to the dry areas.

The young Sprite, who looked familiar to Marsee, although she couldn't place her, bowed low and flashed the purple and silver.

"May I help you?" Marsee asked.

"Translator, my name is Carrie. My father was Snapper Fish," the Sprite flashed.

The guards immediately stiffened, although there was little the young sprite could do in the cart.

"While going through my father's personal belongings last night, I found this." The Sprite held out a sealed envelope through the static shield of the cart.

Avery took it from her and opened it to confirm there was nothing dangerous inside before handing it over.

"I am sorry for the harm he caused because of me." She looked away briefly before taking a deep breath and facing her again. "Rip did everything he could to make me mistrust my father, to hate him, and for a time, I did. But he's my father, and even after everything, I still loved him. I don't know how to reconcile that, and I don't know if I ever will. One minute, I love him. The next, all I feel is rage."

"Rip did the same to me with my father," Marsee said. "So I understand. It took me a long time to forgive him, too."

"How did you?"

She paused, considering. "I guess, in the end, I decided whose words and actions I trusted more."

A ripple of a sigh crossed Carrie's skin, and then, without another word, she turned and drove her cart away.

Marsee watched her leave until she was out of sight before shutting the door, then sat on the edge of the bed to read the letter. She stared at the envelope for a long time before she opened it and pulled out the slip of paper inside.

> *Honorable Translator,*
>
> *If you're reading this, then it means I've passed away. I pray that it was in the line of duty. I know I can never make up for what I did to you. I swear I didn't know what Rip intended, although I know that's no excuse. I knew what he was doing was wrong, and I should have gone to someone, anyone, when Rip first threatened me, but by the time I'd gained the courage, my daughter was missing. I went along with what he wanted, hoping that I could find where he was keeping her, but I never did.*
>
> *When I joined the Sea Patrol, I took an oath to serve the people of my community before myself and my family. I broke that oath, and you and so many others suffered for it. I know you won't believe me, but I am truly sorry for what I did.*
>
> *The Gods of the Deep somehow answered my prayers, and my daughter was found safe, although I still cannot fathom why they allowed me to live. I can only assume it was to allow me the opportunity to make amends. I can never thank you enough for finding my daughter and ridding the world of that monster. My last wish is that someday, somehow, you will find*

it in your heart to forgive me, and that in my death, I will have made both you and my daughter proud.
Your humble and undeserving servant, Snapper Fish

Marsee sighed and stared at the letter, not really seeing it, until motion caught her attention. She looked up, and Little Flower handed her a plate of food. She took it and set the letter aside.

Little Flower picked up the letter but frowned when she realized it was written in Water Sprite. "What does it say?"

"It's an apology," she replied but didn't translate it, and her sister didn't push. Marsee set the plate of food aside, untouched. She wasn't hungry anymore. Instead, she threw on her carry harness, cloak, and mask, hugged her sister, and left without another word.

It was still very early, so rather than heading straight for the Guild, she made her way to the arena and trained for an hour. The arena was empty now that the other guards had returned to their planets following the end of the Council Meeting. Only Avery and her two regular night guards were there, as she'd left Tamarin behind to guard her sister and Hope.

Little was said as they trained, each lost in their own thoughts and grief.

Feeling like she'd worked hard, but not enough to make the day a slog, she finally made her way over to the Guild. The place was already packed, but Agate had everything firmly under control, so she went back to the Trauma Center and made another round of visits with those who still remained.

Before she left, the Senior Healer flagged her down. "I want to thank you for your visits these past two days. The morale boost you've given them has helped a great deal, especially those who have lost loved ones. You've made our job far easier."

"It's the least I could do to make up for having to put up with my grumpy face for so long," she replied.

The Healer flashed her humor. "Well, you should know, your

grumpy face is welcome here any time, as long as you're here to visit and not stay."

"I'll keep that in mind," she smiled back.

A ding sounded. "If you'll excuse me?" the Senior Healer asked.

"Of course," Marsee replied, and the Senior Healer swam off.

On the way out, she saw Little Flower swim by with her arms full of supplies. She saw no sign of Tamarin. "Who's watching her?" she asked Avery

"Red Fin," Avery replied, pointing to an alcove down the hall. It took her a moment to spot him as his skin matched the color of the wall.

"Thank you," she signed to Red Fin.

Red Fin nodded back, then swam off to follow Little Flower.

Marsee turned to Avery after Red Fin was out of sight. "He's not on bereavement?"

"Of course not," Avery replied, seemingly surprised by her question.

"*Of course not?!*" she exclaimed. "Are you telling me you don't get bereavement in the Guard?"

"We do if it's requested," he answered, then paused and frowned, seeing that she wasn't the least bit happy with that answer. "The Council may have found Red Fin innocent, but he still believes that he has a debt to pay to you. He turned down his promotion and personally requested this assignment, knowing we needed him. He didn't have to do that. He's trying to make up for the harm he caused you by protecting your sister. If you turn him away, even under the guise of allowing him to grieve, it would further dishonor him."

Avery stopped her before she could get a protest out.

"I know that's not your intent. Our oath is to the people. Even in normal circumstances, we rarely take bereavement. We honor those lost and move on. We don't stop to grieve, not when others need us. This is who we are."

She nodded and swam off to the council chamber but found it empty, save for the guards. The guard stationed outside the main door informed her that the last of the displaced had been moved to temporary housing that morning, so she returned to the Guild to continue working on her speech.

Struggling to figure out what to say, she dug into their public records, trying to find out more about each person, their families, hobbies, news articles — anything that might tell her who they were. When that failed, she dragged Avery into her office and asked him if he could dig into their records for her.

"What is it you're looking for?" he asked.

"Something to tell me who they are. The only person I knew was Temperate, and I barely knew him. Everything I write feels so impersonal, and then there's Snapper Fish…"

"You know everything about them that's important," Avery replied. "They died with honor."

"Honor. What does that word even mean?" she sighed with frustration. "What would you have me say if I spoke at your funeral?"

He shrugged but leaned back in his seat to consider her question. "I honestly wouldn't care what you said about me. In the grand scheme of things, my life doesn't matter. I'm just a guard. What really matters is who or what I died to protect. A funeral is for the living, not the dead. I would want my family to be comforted with the knowledge that my death had meaning and purpose. I'd want them to remember me with pride for my sacrifice rather than grief at my loss."

She sighed, not sure how to do that.

"May I make a suggestion?"

"Of course."

"Watch the footage, all of it, not just what's been released to the public."

She swallowed hard, not sure if she could do that, but nodded. They'd died to protect her. The least she could do was observe their sacrifice.

Avery logged into his account and pulled up the first of the recordings. When he was done, she buried her head in her paws and shook, knowing that their screams and last words would haunt her dreams for the rest of her life. It was so much worse than she could have even imagined.

"Are you alright?" he asked quietly.

"No." She took several deep breaths and looked up. He was perfectly calm. "How many people have you seen die that you can sit there and not react?"

"I deal with death every day. My squad specialized in containment. I've lost count of the number of people I've killed, the tests I've observed, the family and friends I've lost. Moons, I've witnessed the death of a planet and breathed the last breath of burning air ever taken on it, but I've also witnessed the miracle of birth and experienced the joy of reuniting a lost child with their families. I consider it an honor and privilege to spend every day of my life fighting the evils of this universe so that others may live their lives with peace and happiness, and if the gods bless me, I will die as quickly and with as much honor as these six."

She nodded, seeing the truth of his words, and he returned to his station.

Hours later, when she finally felt like she had something worth saying, she checked in with Agate, who still had nothing for her to do and ordered her to go home and get some rest, but there was no way she was going to sleep. Her nerves about actually giving the speech she'd written had kicked in now that she had nothing to do to occupy her brain, so she swam to the Arena instead and found the others there. Aris and Thatcher were working with Little Flower while Tamarin attempted and failed to corral Hope.

She didn't even wait for Avery to give her instructions. After hanging up her cloak and carry harness, she trotted down into the arena and started running. She ran with everything she had until she couldn't run anymore, rested, and then started running again. She didn't stop until Avery physically dragged her to a stop.

"You're going to hurt yourself if you keep going like this. What's bothering you? Are you trying to outrun your grief?"

"Honestly? I'm afraid I'll mess up the speech, and they deserve better than that. The one time I had to give a speech in school, I threw up all over my teacher about five minutes before, and it was about all I could do not to pass out."

Avery snorted, surprised by her response. "Are you telling me that the mighty Translator, Honor Guard, Guild Master, and Leviathan Slayer…is afraid of giving speeches?"

"Yes," she replied. "Terrified."

Avery snorted again, tail spiraling in humor. "You had no problems at the council meeting or reading to the children yesterday. What's different now?"

"Everything," Marsee replied, unable to explain the difference.

"Well, there's only one way to get over that. Practice." Avery whistled and motioned the others in, then flopped down on the sand. "Go on, give us your speech. We promise to tell you if it's horrible."

Marsee stood there, mouth open, unable to form a single word.

"You're off to a horrible start," Tamarin teased. "Speeches tend to have words to them."

Marsee snorted and turned to retrieve her tablet.

"Running away already?" Avery called out after her.

"No, I'm getting my tablet," she growled back with an annoyed lash of her tail.

A minute later, she returned and began reading it out loud. When she was done, she looked up and found all five of them lying on the dirt, pretending to be sound asleep. Only Hope was awake, and she threw sand at her.

"Boring," Avery said, still sprawled in the dirt.

Marsee slumped. She'd worked so hard at her speech.

"The speech itself was fine. Your delivery was awful. Think about how the Seniors give their speeches. They aren't reading off of their tablets, not unless there are specifics they need to make sure not to miss. Their heads are up, they're looking at their audience, and they project confidence and authority. They use…*dramatic*…pauses…to emphasize…their words. Again. This time without the tablet."

"I can't do that!" Marsee squeaked.

"Of course, you can," Aris said. "You did it the other day without any preparation. You can do it now."

"Just pretend you're Little Flower chewing out Councilor Tabor," Tamarin suggested.

Her sister snorted. "I'm not sure that's the kind of speech they need."

"If the public boards are any indication, half the people that will be there tomorrow could all use a…what was it you called it…butt slap? To knock some sense into them."

Her sister snorted again.

Marsee ignored them and read through the speech, trying to commit it to memory, then tried again. She had to look down at her tablet several times to remember what to say.

"Try to remember the main point of each section, not every individual word," Thatcher suggested. "It doesn't have to be exactly as you wrote it. Let it flow."

Marsee tried again and managed not to look at her tablet, but she hesitated often.

"Better," Avery said. "Now make those pauses bigger. It'll give you more time to remember what you want to say. Slow it down. There's no rush."

Marsee tried again, and again, and again, until the speech finally started to flow, and she wasn't hesitating quite so much.

"Good, now go deliver it from the balcony," Avery ordered.

Marsee shrugged and trotted up to the balcony, but when she turned around, the others had moved and were now sitting propped up against the wall of the maze or about as far away from her as they could get. Taking a deep breath, she started giving her speech again.

"We can't hear you!" Avery called out. She had no problems hearing him.

Marsee tried yelling.

"Don't yell. Project. From your belly," he ordered.

It took her a dozen or more tries before Avery let her get past the first sentence.

"That's better, but you're forgetting one *very* important thing," Avery called out.

"What's that?" she asked, confused.

"They're all going to be Water Sprites. You need to sign, not speak in Saber," he replied.

Marsee groaned and slapped herself in the head. *Idiot!* "See, I told you I'd mess it up!" she signed back and began her speech again, only this time silently.

"More emotion!" Little Flower signed back. "Bigger arm movements. I can't see it well from here."

Marsee tried bigger, but that just felt odd.

Avery stood and walked up so he could speak privately to her. "Marsee, I just lost someone I've known for decades. Tanner gave her life to save yours. Clear Seas lost his oldest son. They protected you and were your friends. Channel that emotion. Let them see you grieve with them. Let them see what I saw this afternoon and what I saw last night. This is not a time for masks."

Marsee closed her eyes, summoning everything that had happened to her over these past few weeks, and focused entirely on Avery.

When she was done, Avery swallowed hard, and his voice cracked with emotion. "*That* was a speech worthy of their sacrifice."

"Thank the moons," Marsee sighed with relief. "And thank you for the help."

Avery nodded. "Of course. Now, come on. We have work to do."

"We do?" Marsee asked with surprise. She was hungry and exhausted. The only thing she wanted to do was hide under her pillow.

"Yes. You're leading the funeral procession. I want to make sure you know exactly where you're going and what you're going to do every step of the way. Delivering the cloaks was one thing. We just followed your lead, but a state funeral has protocol that needs to be observed."

"I'm what?!" Marsee squeaked as her tail shot straight out in fear, along with every tiny little hair on her body.

"You're the Translator, the only *living* Leviathan Slayer, and you're an Honor Guard. No other Honor Guard will stand before you tomorrow. Not here on this planet. *You* will lead the procession. *You* will give your speech. And *you* will present the cloaks to their next of kin. Presentation of the cloaks is normally Clear Seas' responsibility, but he can't, not when his son is being honored. He needs to be allowed to grieve, too, and he should be with his family."

Marsee gulped but nodded. Avery was right.

Avery dragged her over to the Water Sprite arena and had to wait for them to gain approval to enter. Several squads were inside training, but they all stopped what they were doing at her appearance and swam forward. She recognized a few of the guards but didn't know any of them particularly well.

A massive guard with jet-black ear fins swam forward out of the group. She recognized him as one of the guards who had been stationed outside the Council Chamber on the first day of the meeting, but she frowned when she noticed his rank — District Senior for Council Platform. He had been promoted to replace Tanner.

"How can we help you, Translator?"

Avery answered for her. "We're here so the Translator can practice for her part in tomorrow's ceremony."

"Ah, good. Stinger thought you might be by and asked us to wait. My name is Obsidian, Translator. Has Avery explained what you need to do tomorrow at all?"

She shook her head. "Not really. I've seen them a few times but never really paid much attention. Certainly not enough to lead one."

He nodded. "By the time we're done tonight, I promise you'll be well prepared for tomorrow."

They practiced for hours until she felt confident about her role, but she was still terrified.

Avery chuckled at her emotions as they escorted her back to the suite.

"I don't see what's so funny," Marsee growled at him.

"I just find it amusing that after everything you've been through, giving a speech is what terrifies you."

She stopped and glared at him, ears pinned with a fury that was fueled by her exhaustion and anxiety.

"Yes, I'm nervous about giving a speech," she spat at him. "I have always hated public speaking, but it's far more than that, and you should know it!"

His expression told her she'd caught him off guard, but she didn't back down.

"I've barely been able to go a day since I landed on this planet without something or someone trying to kill me. People hate the power and authority that my family has, that *I* have, and now I'm going to be floating for hours *unarmed*, in the middle of Market Square, taking the lead in a state ceremony, in the place of a member of the Senior Council, on a planet where perceived hierarchy means everything. If someone is going to do something, it'll be tomorrow, and more than likely, I or the other members of my family will be their primary target. My life hangs in your hands right now, and *you* can't even make it around a simple maze in the dark. So yes, I'm terrified, and I don't find it the least bit amusing."

With that, she turned and stormed off, tail lashing hard behind her.

47

MARSEE: HONOR GUARD

*W*ell before dawn, Marsee put her cloak on and stared at herself in the mirror for a moment before taking a deep breath and walking out of her suite. All four of her guards were there, dressed in their finery, even though Tamarin and Thatcher would be on duty guarding her family and wouldn't be in the procession.

She raised a brow at their gear but didn't stop to talk. Her squad wore their carry harnesses as usual, but they'd been swapped out for more decorative ones provided by the local guard to match their outfits. Each harness was silver with iridescent purple buckles, and they were wearing a cloak much like hers, but it was all silver with just a trim of purple and made out of some sort of shimmering fabric, not Leviathan hide. The center of the cloak contained the stylized Honor Guard logo, also done in purple, and it clipped to their harnesses rather than wrapping around their shoulders as hers did, clearly designed to ensure their hands remained free. There was no hood either.

She had nothing on but her Leviathan Cloak and fins. She needed nothing else to signify who she was or her rank. It was a risk not carrying a weapon, and they'd debated it for a long time, but ultimately, they decided she wouldn't. This needed to be a moment of peace. The fins, they'd determined, were necessary for her to keep up with the Sprites during parts of the ceremony and, if necessary, allow her to escape quickly, as she wouldn't have a drone.

Avery led her around to the Senior's entrance, where Stinger waited for them. The normally open doors of the main entrance had been closed, and Stinger was the only one with authorization outside of the Seniors to enter. He followed after them, shutting the door behind him. Everyone else was already there, lined up by rank inside the council chamber.

She had never seen so many Honor Guards in one procession, but there was at least a full contingent of District Seniors in line based on their badges, if not two, followed by those of lower ranks from Council Platform. She briefly wondered if all the District Seniors were there as she took her place and what message they were trying to make. Were they honoring the dead or simply trying to fix their reputation?

She was in the lead, followed by the Water Sprites and then the visiting members of the other guards from the planets close enough to be able to attend. Councilor Sammianna and Wind Rider were not in attendance, but they had sent two squads of guards along with resources to help with the rebuild. Most of their guards were being used to help secure the ceremony, but a pair of each filled out the half-squad that included Avery and Aris, who represented both Saber and the Hue-mans. The only guards not in attendance were the Ice Giants, but Senior Councilor Apkana and her Council were still in transit on their way home and likely didn't even know what had happened yet.

Directly behind her was Stinger and Obsidian. She would have felt better having her guards behind her, but it was customary for the guards to be lined up by species, then rank. Both guards had their masks on tightly, and she couldn't sniff anything from either of them. She just prayed that if they were involved, they wouldn't try anything when the public was watching.

When everyone was in position, she waited, watching the clock until the exact moment when she would step out. She gave the command, and the two guards who would remain and guard the entrance swung the doors slowly open. She was told others were hidden from view, but only those two would be visible, at least to start.

They made their way out of the council chamber at the pace she set, slow for the Sprites but faster than she would have been able to manage without the fins. She led them across the center path of Council Square and down the street to Market Square, which had been cleared of booths the previous evening.

Members of the Sea Patrol lined the entire way in their ceremonial outfits. They had the same ceremonial carry harness but didn't have the cloak of the Honor Guard, their rank and guild, designated only by the badges on their harnesses.

At the entrance to Market Square, they stopped. Marsee gave a command, and all but Stinger, his second, and twenty-four of the Water Sprite guards peeled off and made their way to spread out around the perimeter of Market Square. The remaining guards floated behind her, and they all waited until exactly dawn, when the first rays of sunlight glittered on the surface above them, broken moments later, when a ship carrying the caskets of the deceased flew in.

Motionless, save for their cloaks, which fluttered in the ship's wake, they watched as the ship approached and hovered for a moment. Marsee stared at the Water Sprite Pilot, who was nearly black with grief. She had never met the Sprite, but Avery had told her that it would be flown by the Senior Commander of the Sea Patrol, who was also Temperate's mentor.

It took everything she had not to react to the Sprite's grief. She'd never been good at hiding her emotions behind a mask like her parents, but as a member of the honor guard, she was supposed to remain both motionless and emotionless throughout the watch.

The ship slowly pivoted and landed, and a moment later, the cargo hatch lowered.

Marsee gave the next command, and as one, they swam forward.

Stinger and Obsidion peeled off and took up guard on either side of the ramp while the others followed her inside.

She stopped at the head of the first casket, which was draped in a massive bouquet of purple and silver flowers, and waited until the rest of the guards took up positions around all six caskets, four on each.

Each casket was clear and placed on an ornate platform, with what appeared to be the bodies visible inside. She knew from her guards that it was a holo-vid, like the ones she'd given to her sister, as the injuries had been too severe to show the actual bodies. But they were inside, locked in a stasis container below the platform, hidden by what appeared to be nothing more than the weighted stand.

Even knowing it was a holo-vid, she still had to take several deep breaths at the sight of Temperate laying peacefully inside before she felt safe calling out the next command. She watched as the guards pivoted, unlocked the restraints that kept the platforms and caskets in place during transport, and slowly lifted them.

When everyone was ready, she pivoted, counted to ten slowly in her head, and as one, they moved out. Unable to see behind her, she had to rely on Stinger to inform her when everyone was out and sufficiently far enough away from the ship. Based on her practice, she knew approximately how many paces there would be, but it didn't account for variations in the current that could affect their pace.

About when she expected, Stinger called out that they were clear and she responded, calling the guards to a stop.

A few moments later, she heard the sounds of the ramp being raised. The ship departed slowly, leaving their capes once again fluttering in the wake. There, they would remain, unmoving, until an hour before noon, when they would begin an even slower procession back to the council chamber.

For the next several hours, the families and friends of the deceased approached, spent the time they needed, and made their way down the path guarded by the Sea Patrol.

It was one of the hardest things she had ever done. Not only was maintaining her place in the moving current difficult, requiring far more physical effort than she'd expected, but it was also emotionally draining and exhausting to keep her focus and mask in place as family members wailed out their grief.

As Agate expected, there was no answering song of life, and somehow, the sounds of their cries dying off unanswered broke her heart even more. She tried to ignore it and keep her focus on the peak of the Archives directly ahead of her, where the Sprite's equivalent to a clock showed the current time. Every second seemed to tick slower than the one before.

When Clear Seas and his family finally arrived, it was all she could do to keep still and her head facing forward. Temperate's mother wailed out her grief.

It was too much for Marsee to bear. It broke her heart and her mask. Her eyes watered, and her jaw shook as she struggled to control her emotions. She knew she could never reproduce or match their song, and she wouldn't do it the dishonor of even trying, but she just couldn't let Jewel's cries go unanswered.

So, even though she had once said she would never sing in public, she began singing one of her older sibling's songs. Her voice cracked with emotion, but she didn't stop.

It was her mother's favorite. She hadn't realized until this past year that it was about her littermate. It spoke of the love a mother had for their child and the grief of their loss, but also the joy of their memory. She poured every bit of emotion she could into that song while also signing for those who didn't know Saber.

The crowd around her stilled and quieted, and Jewel stopped her crying to listen.

Marsee kept her face focused forward even as Clear Seas and his family moved in front to watch. By the time she finished the first verse and chorus, Jewel had regained her composure. When she sang the chorus the second time, Jewel joined in, harmonizing, the colors of mourning on her skin changing, brightening. On the third verse, the rest of the honor guard joined in, and on the fourth, the entire crowd.

It wasn't their song, but it was the closest translation of their song of life she could give them, and it allowed them to keep their secret until they were ready.

When the song was done, the crowd quieted and stilled.

"Thank you, Translator," Jewel flashed. "That was exactly what I needed."

Marsee gave a slight nod in acknowledgment and watched them as they swam away. It took her several long moments to bring her emotions back under control and regain the calm mask expected of her.

Clear Seas and his family had been the last to approach, timed such that they'd have to wait the least. So it was only a few minutes later that they took a single pace forward and stopped. There was no command, purposely. She was told it added to the mystique. After every motion forward, they would pause for a beat and take another step. Out of everything, learning the skill to appear effortless as they moved forward and stopped had taken her the most amount of time. It was anything but effortless.

As they marched, the ceremony in the council chamber would start. While it was a state funeral, they still honored the religions of the people who died. For the Water Sprites, it was a ritualized ceremony where they beseeched the Gods of the Deep to welcome the deceased into the afterlife, and in doing so, spoke of their life and accomplishments and informed the gods why they deserved such a place of honor.

Her own people didn't have any religious beliefs about where they went when they died, and she'd never really thought much about it. They were buried, and their bodies would provide nutrients for other creatures, so in that way, they would live on forever. As she marched, her mind drifted in thought, wondering where their souls went and what even was a soul. What had happened to the voice in her head when her instinct died? She wondered if it was better to believe they just died or to believe in an afterlife. Did one bring more comfort than another or make for better people?

When they made it to the end of Market Square, the other Honor Guards flowed in behind the caskets and followed. As they passed, the crowd flashed their respects in purple and silver and the deep blues and blacks of mourning.

The turn onto Council Square required a sharp pivot, which she hoped she executed correctly. Thankfully, she didn't have to manage the complex maneuver the guards with the caskets had to do. Large monitors on the outside of the Council Building showed both her and the ceremony occurring inside the chamber.

She ignored them. Clear Seas now floated at the entrance of the Council Building, his body still and face a mask, as he waited for them to approach. She kept her gaze firmly fixed on his. At the end of the path, she stopped. The guards behind her stopped as well, again without a command.

"Senior Councilor Clear Seas, it is with our deepest condolences that we return your son, Master Pilot Temperate Seas, to you, along with five others, District Senior Guard Tanner Fin, Master Pilot Blue Grass, Master Pilot Snapper Fish, Junior Pilot Rolling Waves, and Junior Pilot Sea Foam. Know that they gave their lives as they lived, with the greatest of honor." Marsee signed the ritual words, hating the need for every one of them.

"Thank you, Honor Guard, for seeing them home," Clear Seas replied, then turned and led them into the building. She was surprised that he managed to keep the emotion off his skin, but then he had a century of practice. As they made their way into the council chamber, those inside rose and flashed their respects as well.

An aisle ran down the middle of the chamber to the platform in front. People sat in both the council seats and in seats that now filled the chamber. When Clear Seas reached the front of the chamber, he stepped aside.

Marsee continued to swim forward until she reached the platform and stopped. The guards stopped behind her. She called out a command, and the guards brought each casket up to line up in front of the hook with that person's cloak on it.

She waited until they were all in place, called out another command, and they all pivoted to face the crowd. Stinger and his second were now in the lead, back by the entrance.

With another command, the guards moved off and pivoted to make their way around the chamber, with each guard in the lead pivoting off when they reached their place. She waited unmoving until the last guard was in place, doing her best to control her breathing and not let her panic show.

"Please be seated," she signed.

The speech she'd written and practiced so hard at now seemed wrong, although she wasn't sure why or what to say instead.

Channel their emotions and speak from your heart, she reminded herself.

Her eyes drifted around the room, finally landing on Clear Seas, who now sat almost directly in front of her.

How different he looks to me now. I would recognize him anywhere.

She smiled at the thought and, inspired, directed her speech towards him. "When I left my home only a few short weeks ago, I was nothing more than a young and naive Journeyman on my first real adventure with my new mentor. I knew next to nothing of your customs and culture. I'd never even been off-world before and had only ever spoken to a few members of your species. I was fortunate enough to have a mentor who *tried* to knock some sense into me, hoping I wouldn't accidentally insult the first person I met. And I'm pretty sure I failed."

Clear Seas looked back at her in confusion. "Thankfully, Senior Councilor Clear Seas was a gracious host, even though I had absolutely no idea who he was. I had so little exposure to your people that you all looked the same to me, and my overwhelmed and stupid brain decided that he must be one of the guild masters I was supposed to meet."

Humor bubbled across Clear Sea's skin. She looked out at the crowd, wondering if anyone took that as an insult, but she saw only the same humor.

"So you can all probably imagine my surprise when he addressed me first and not with my guild rank, but as Translator, and suddenly afforded me with more respect than my mentor. On the tour he gave, I was hoping that at least *one* vendor in Market Square would address him or the others in the delegation, but they never did. In fact, they completely ignored everyone but me. I heard 'Translator! What an honor to meet you,' from everyone. I had absolutely no idea why. It didn't make any sense to me. What did I do to earn such respect?"

She scratched at the back of her neck, pretending to be confused, and waves of humor rippled across the crowd.

"When my highly amused mentor tried to explain it to me later that evening, I still didn't understand. Sure, I had done the hard work of filling in the sign language guide and spent days translating for my sister, but I hadn't invented sign. Sina Greyfoot did. I didn't know then that my translations were popular here, but I don't consider that to be my work any more than I consider the words I translate to be my own. When I found out there were *toys* based on my drawings, I wanted to go find a cave to hide in."

More laughter, but it stilled as her face turned serious, and people remembered that she'd been held in a cave.

"In case you're wondering, I don't recommend it. When Master Trench gave me his brother's cloak, I still didn't understand. I hadn't killed a Leviathan, literally or figuratively, at least not then. All I had done was survive. If anyone deserved this cloak, it was that young Sprite sitting in front of me."

She smiled down at Stormy. "Stormy braved a Leviathan twice to save my life. Master Trench told me it would help protect my family, to help prove their honor through me. So I wore it. But even as he tried to explain, I still didn't fully understand, and I was embarrassed with every flash of silver and purple. Master Trench told me it would make Rip seethe to see me wear it, and he was right. It did. One of the last things Rip ever said was that I didn't deserve it, and at the time, I agreed with him."

A mix of surprise and anger crossed the room.

She shook her head at them. "You see, the problem was, I had the wrong definition of honor, and so did Rip. I may have given you the signs to speak for yourself, but signs are only half the story. Without a shared understanding, they're meaningless. If you'd asked me a few months ago what honor meant, I probably would have told you it was the respect you gave to someone of higher rank."

"The day after I arrived here, I met with Deep Current to better understand why he was protesting. One of the things he said to me that day was, 'There is no greater honor than to give your life to save another.' I misunderstood and thought he was only trying to earn recognition for his mother's deeds. I didn't realize that he was trying to explain a fundamental tenet of your society. Because I didn't realize that honor was also a code of conduct to live by, one that placed integrity and sacrifice above all others. Little did I know that only a few days later, he would show me the true meaning of that word."

Stormy flashed his grief at the memory of Deep Current's loss.

"Just like bravery can't exist if you're not scared, honor can't exist if you're not tested."

She shifted her gaze back to Clear Seas. "How can you know if you're honorable until you're forced to make a difficult decision? When doing the honorable thing means risking the lives of others, whose life do you value more? Who is to say what the right decision is when every choice you make could hurt someone?"

He tilted his head, acknowledging that fact.

She turned her focus towards Snapper Fish's daughter. "None of us are perfect, and we all make mistakes. What matters is what we do after. Do we try our best to make amends and learn from our mistakes, or do we hide from them?"

She refocused on the crowd. "Do we live each day trying to be our best selves by lifting others up, or do we try to lift ourselves up by tearing others down? The people lying here before you all knew what it meant to be honorable and tried their very best to always live by that code of conduct. They took an oath to protect others before themselves and their families. They risked their lives to protect ours, knowing that one day, they might not come home. They never knew when the call might come in. Yet no matter where they were or what they were doing, they would drop everything and go."

She paused and looked around the room for several moments before continuing, her expression hardening again. "When we act without honor, we not only harm ourselves but those around us. It spreads like a disease and infects everyone it touches. One person acted without honor, and it was enough to dishonor the Council, the Sea Patrol, and even the Honor Guard. It spread across all of the planets and species like a plague, killing and hurting people, tearing families apart, and ripping out the very foundation of our society."

Her gaze locked on Stinger's. "Who do you turn to when you can't trust the people who are supposed to protect you? How do you restore honor and trust when it's been lost, and the world is nothing but darkness, fear, and greed?"

Ripples of shame flashed across his skin.

"It's not easy. Trust, once lost, is almost impossible to regain, but it can be done. You do it by acting with so much honor and integrity that nothing and no one can tarnish it. When you act with honor, you radiate a light so bright that it burns away the darkness. It's by loving and caring for others before yourself that you can conquer hate and fear, and it's by sacrifice that we become wealthy, not with credit or power, but with friendship, trust, and a life that's worth dying for."

He nodded, and his back straightened with purpose.

She motioned towards the caskets. "None of those you see before you were on duty that night. Yet they didn't hesitate for a moment when the call came in. They gave their lives to save ours and to protect this community. There is no greater honor than to be able to give someone their life back, to give them a chance at a bright and happy future. It's up to us now to honor them back by living our lives by that same code of conduct, to put others before ourselves, to be willing to make the ultimate sacrifice to save someone else, to choose compassion over greed, to live our lives with integrity, courage, and love, to make every moment for the rest of our lives matter, and ones that are worthy of the honor of their sacrifice. Add your light to theirs until there is nothing left of the darkness, nowhere for it to hide, and no way for it to infect you or anyone else ever again."

At those words, Stormy floated up and flashed his skin as bright as he could — not the white of fear but softer, warmer, and laced with a rainbow of brilliant colors representing joy, happiness, and love. It reminded her of the pendant Trench had hung from the display case.

She watched as others in the room followed suit. It spread out through the chamber and out into the crowd beyond until it was so bright it hurt to look at.

Blinking hard, Marsee smiled and nodded to Stormy. He floated back down and dimmed his skin. The others followed his lead, but the guards around the chamber kept their skin lit bright.

Deciding that was as good of an ending as any, she paused for a count of ten and then called out a command.

Six honor guards made their way up to float in front of the caskets and bowed low, changing from the brilliant white light they still shone to the silver and purple. As they did, it too spread across the crowd in a wave. As one, the guards swam up to stand in front of the cloaks, paused for a count of ten, removed the cloaks from the hooks, and pivoted back around to face the crowd. After another count of ten, they moved forward, cloaks now slung carefully over their arms to stand in front of each of the families.

She made her slow way down, pivoted, and swam across to the casket on her far left, pivoted again to face the guard with the cloak, bowed low, straightened back up, and carefully removed the cloak from the guard's hands.

When she had it, he bowed low in return.

She pivoted to face the family and gave a single nod.

One member of the family swam forward.

"It is with the greatest of sympathy and respect that I present this cloak to you on behalf of your honorable son, who made the ultimate sacrifice. May his honor and legacy be remembered for eternity."

Marsee flung the cloak around the pilot's mother, clasped it in place, took one step back, and bowed. As she did, the entire room bowed and flashed another wave of silver and purple.

After she straightened, she took a moment to say a few personal words to the pilot's mother about some of the things she'd learned about him, and then turned and made her way down to the next family and did the same.

The third person she presented to was Tanner's son, Red Fin. He was the only Honor Guard not in the procession or on duty, as he was Tanner's next of kin. She wrapped the cloak around his shoulders but dropped the ritual words.

"I was with your mother when the Leviathan attacked. Had she not been there, Honor Guard Zatara and I would have surely died. Even though badly injured, she never stopped trying to protect us and led the beast away from us and out of the city. She's personally guarded me and my family on many occasions, but the first time I met her, she apologized on your behalf for what happened to me. She said that she would do everything in her power to make up for the fact that I was hurt while being guarded by you. That debt is paid in full, and then some, because there was nothing for her to apologize for. You did not fail me that day. You were as much a victim as I was, and you very nearly paid the same price, not just to protect me but to protect the entire Consortium. You allowed yourself to be tortured rather than let Rip force Petra into making a false confession, and you now carry the same scars I do. Honor Guard Red Fin, it is my personal honor to present you this cloak, not just to honor your mother's sacrifice but to recognize and honor your own. Wear it proudly. You've earned it."

She didn't know if she legally had the right to do that, but she didn't particularly care and doubted anyone would stop her.

Red Fin struggled hard to keep his emotions in check, and they flickered on his skin. "Thank you, Translator," he signed back. "Your forgiveness means more to me than I can ever begin to express."

She nodded once, gave him a fierce hug, and then stepped back and bowed before moving on to Clear Seas and his family.

She had to pause for several seconds to bring her grief under control before turning back around with the cloak, but when Stormy swam forward, she very nearly lost it. She'd been expecting Clear Seas to accept the cloak as he'd been listed on the information she'd been sent, but he remained seated and made no attempt to control his emotions as a mix of grief and pride for his youngest son radiated off his skin.

Stormy, however, was trying hard to keep his grief in check, but it was leaking around the edges.

"It is with the greatest of sympathy and respect that I present this cloak to you on behalf of your honorable brother, who made the ultimate sacrifice. May his honor and legacy be remembered for eternity."

Marsee flung the cloak over him, and the sight of it nearly made her cry. It was far too big for him and hung well below his tentacles. It would be a very long time before it would fit him, but Stormy floated proudly before her and stretched out as tall as he could, although flickers of his grief continued to seep through his skin.

She bowed low and then smiled at him.

"This cloak is also for you, braving not one but two Leviathans. Thank you for saving my life. Keep shining your light, my tiny super-hero, because I have a feeling that by the time you grow big enough to fit this cloak, your light will be so bright that the darkness won't know where to hide."

When she realized he was going to lose control of his emotions completely, she crushed him in a hug. She could feel his body shake with grief, and she held him until he regained his composure and pulled back from her. She looked over at the rest of Temperate's family and made eye contact with Clear Seas.

He swallowed hard and nodded to her.

She stepped back and bowed to Clear Seas before moving off to present to the next pilot.

The final pilot was Snapper Fish, and the only one there for him was his daughter, Carrie. When she'd finished the ritual words, she paused for a moment to collect her thoughts.

"In the letter you brought me, your father said that he hoped his death would be in the line of duty and that he would make us both proud of the way he died. I want you to know that he did. In his death, your father fully restored his honor by making the ultimate sacrifice, and in doing so, saved the lives of many people that night, including my own. I didn't know it was him at the time, but I watched as he purposely crashed his shuttle into the Leviathan to turn it away from us when the weapons on the shuttles were not working to stop it or even turn it away. That action ultimately proved to be the killing blow. He saved us all. He fought back against the darkness that nearly swallowed him whole, and his honor shone so brightly it lit the dark seas for all of us to see. With his last breath, he called your name and begged for your forgiveness. I want you to know that I personally forgive him for what he did to me, and I want to personally thank you for what you did for the others. My friend Petra, along with thirty-six others, are alive today because of your kindness, sacrifice, and honor. I can see that your father taught you well."

Carrie's skin was solid black with grief as Marsee hugged her.

She held the child until Carrie let go, then bowed low and returned to the center.

"Go forth now and spread their light to the world, and take comfort knowing they died the way they lived, with the greatest of honor."

Before she could give the command to move out, Stormy bolted up to his brother's casket, his oversized cape flowing behind him. He touched his brother's casket with his palm and then slowly lit up his skin as if it was traveling up his arm until it spread over his entire body. He turned around and swam to his father and held out his hand.

Clear Seas smiled at his son, grasped the hand firmly in his own, and did the same. He then turned and did the same to his partner's hand and then his daughter's, and it continued until everyone in the room was lit, and it spread out into the crowd like wildfire.

Stormy turned back around to face her, and she smiled at him with pride before calling out the next expected command. The twenty-four guards returned to the caskets and picked them up again, and she led them out. Behind the caskets, the immediate family followed, and behind them, the rest of the Honor Guard.

Their return procession was faster but not rushed as they returned to Market Square, where a larger transport ship was waiting for them. Marsee led the procession to the foot of the ramp, pivoted, and took up position to the side, then directed the twenty-four guards to load and secure the caskets.

The rest of the guard peeled off to circle the square again, all except for Stinger and his second. Obsidion followed behind the family members as they boarded the passenger entrance and took their seats. When the last of the family was in, he swam in behind them and closed the door.

When the last of the caskets were in and secured, she boarded behind them and pivoted to float in the center of the open doorway as Stinger flashed the purple and silver, followed by the crowd.

She kept her gaze locked on him. Outwardly, his body showed his respect, but his scent radiated an inner turmoil. He should have been the one escorting the bodies to the burial site. Tanner had been his second for decades. He wasn't jealous or angry or radiating his grief at the loss of a friend and protege. He was ashamed.

She waited until he bowed his head, unable to meet her gaze. Only then did she reach up and hit the switch to close the door.

48

MARSEE: GUARD OF THEIR HONOR

Marsee had only been told they would be flying out to the burial site, located out by the Trench. She expected nothing more than the rocky ledges she'd seen before, but what awaited her as the doors slid open again was a protected oasis teaming with life and color. Small to medium-sized creatures swam everywhere. She'd never seen anything so beautiful or full of life before. Several religious leaders bedecked in capes of flowers waited in front of a massive natural archway that felt ancient, in much the same way the Archives did. On the other side of the archway was a path that led to what looked like a large hole, although it was hard to tell as it was surrounded by more flowering plants.

She waited while the families exited the ship and lined up on either side of the ramp. When they were in place, Marsee gave the command, and they escorted the caskets through the small crowd and lined them up in front of the religious leaders before backing off to give the families the space and time they needed to grieve and say goodbye.

The religious leaders once again begged the Gods of the Deep to find their souls worthy enough to return home.

She managed to hold her tears in check until one of the leaders swam forward to Temperate's casket, deactivated the holo-vid, and opened the lid to reveal the real body contained inside.

A mix of horror and grief flashed across Clear Seas' skin at the sight of his son and the damage to his body. Screams of pain and grief broke free from Jewel. Moments later, the rest of Temperate's family joined in.

Clear Seas reached in and gently lifted his son's body out, cradling it tightly to him as he wailed out his own grief and swam through the archway, followed by the rest of his family. They each said goodbye, then almost unwillingly, Clear Seas let go of his son and watched as Temperate's mangled and burnt body sank and disappeared from view.

Jewel wailed again and swam away quickly, unable to watch. The others soon followed, all except for Clear Seas, who just stared at the hole, his skin so black she could barely see him against the dark sea beyond. The religious leaders began praising the Gods of the Deep, thanking them for finding Temperate worthy enough to find a place of honor in the afterlife, then began singing the song of life. The others soon joined in with the celebration. It was a long time before Clear Seas was able to join in and swim away.

Red Fin went next. He sighed as they opened his mother's casket, but no cries of grief escaped. He caressed his mother's face, radiating love, respect, and pride for her rather than grief, and then lifted her body and swam her through the arches and over to the hole and let her go. He didn't wait for the religious leaders to start singing before he closed his eyes and started singing a beautiful melody, which the others joined in before he turned away and disappeared into the garden rather than returning to the group.

One by one, the others sang their goodbyes until only Snapper Fish and Carrie remained. Carrie tried to pick up her father, but she was far too small to move his body.

No one moved forward to help her, even as she wailed out her grief and struggled to lift him. Even though Snapper Fish had been given state honors, one by one, she watched as the guards turned their backs, and so too did the rest of the group until only she, Stormy, and

Clear Seas remained watching. Then, to her disappointment, Clear Seas glanced at her before turning his back, too.

The religious leaders continued to beg the gods but did nothing to help.

She could see Stormy was trying to figure out what was going on. His gaze kept going between her and his father and back to Carrie, with flashes of confusion and disbelief on his own skin.

With a snort of disgust at all of them, she swam over to Carrie.

Waves of relief flashed over Carrie's skin, followed by a thank you.

She nodded and looked down at Snapper Fish's body. Her stomach roiled at the smell of burnt skin, death, and decay, but she clamped down hard on it and reached in to lift him out. He was far larger than the Sprite she'd rescued the other day, and without the buoyancy their bodies had in life, it was heavy, far heavier than she'd expected.

As part of her training, the guards had taught her how to lift and carry someone larger than her, and she was thankful for that training now. Even still, she barely had the strength to lift him out either, but somehow she managed. His weight pinned her to the ground, as her mask wasn't compensating for the weight of the body as it did with other objects. She realized that it must be programmed to keep a barrier between her and the Sprites, which made sense. If they were brought inside the shield, they couldn't breathe.

She turned and started walking towards the archway but nearly fell with the first step, unused to how different it was to walk underwater. She needed both hands to hold the body so she couldn't use them for balance to steady herself and stumbled forward, struggling hard to catch herself.

Suddenly, Stormy was at her side and grabbed her arm to steady her. It wasn't much, but it was what she needed. Carrie saw and immediately did the same with her other side. Then, together, they made their way through the archway, one slow, stumbling step at a time. They were about halfway to the hole when Red Fin reappeared, took one look at what was going on, and quickly swam over.

"Let me take him, Translator," he said.

She shook her head. "I've got him," she replied. "But the hand of a friend is always appreciated."

He nodded and held out a hand to Carrie with a compassionate smile.

Carrie flashed her surprise but took his hand and smiled through her grief, and together, they made their way over to the hole.

When they finally arrived, she looked down to see vibrant flowering plants that appeared to be growing out of the darkness below. There was no sign of the bodies that had gone before or any indication of how deep it was.

She waited on the edge while Carrie said goodbye to her father. Then, when Carrie indicated she was ready, Red Fin helped her out over the center of the hole, and Marsee let go. She watched with the others until the body disappeared out of sight and wrapped her tail around Carrie as she wailed out her grief.

Stormy didn't wait for the religious leaders to make their proclamation. Like Red Fin before him, he began singing almost immediately. His counter melody was simple but pure and full of life.

Marsee smiled a him with pride, but he frowned back at her.

"Sing," he signed.

So she did. She wasn't sure if she did it justice, but Carrie's skin lit up a vibrant blue the moment she started to sing, and her song changed to one of equally sweet melody. Together, they swam out as the religious leaders and Red Fin joined in the song and flashed their thanks to the Gods of the Deep for finding Snapper Fish worthy enough to find a place of honor in the afterlife, although no one else did.

After a closing prayer, people dispersed throughout the oasis in small groups or with their families to grieve in private. Separate shuttles were available to bring them home when they were ready. Her part in the ceremony was over now that the bodies were laid to rest. The religious leaders collected the caskets and swam off with them, leaving no sign of what had occurred.

When the families were all out of sight, she turned and glared at the guards who were waiting for her command to disperse. Full of fury, she swam over to Obsidian and yanked the badge off his harness.

Shock radiated off of him, but he didn't stop her.

She moved on to the next and did the same. Then continued on down the line before turning back to face them. "I am absolutely disgusted with each and every one of you. Regardless of your feelings towards Snapper Fish, what you did to Carrie is inexcusable. You should all be ashamed of yourselves."

Surprise and further shock rippled across their skin.

"Ma'am, it's one thing to get a state funeral, but he didn't deserve a place of honor in the afterlife," Obsidian countered. There were nods of agreement from all of them.

"And you do?" she hissed. "What kind of Honor Guard treats a grieving child like you just did? You're no better than Rip."

Flashes of astonishment and confusion now radiated off their skin.

"Rip showed one face in public, pretending to live a life of honor, but he turned his back on all of us. To treat someone with honor in front of the public and turn your back on them the moment you're in private is no different. You lied to the people. You lied to Carrie, and if I hadn't been here, you would have added to her pain and grief. It's not her fault she's too small to carry her father or that she doesn't have any other living relatives. She wasn't at fault for what happened. She was a victim, held captive longer than any of those rescued, and she was alone with her grief. If you couldn't honor him, you should have at least pretended and honored her. She kept one of your guards alive along with thirty-five others, even though those thirty-five turned their backs on her, too. Her father made mistakes, but in the end, he saved my life, along with Clear Seas, the healers that were there, and members of the guard. And you still had the gall to turn your backs on him?!"

They all stared at her in shock, but none of them seemed ashamed of what they had done. They believed they'd done the right thing.

"Get out of my sight," she growled.

They bolted.

She watched them swim off and then looked down at the badges in her hand with a snort at her own audacity, wondering just how she was going to explain kicking twenty-four of the highest-ranking members out of a guild that she wasn't even officially part of. She turned around to look back at the burial site and stopped. Clear Seas was watching, his face and body a mask.

She glared at him, too.

He was the first to look away, but he didn't swim off, so she waited, curious what he would say or do.

It was at that moment that Carrie swam back into view with Stormy by her side, flashing in an animated conversation. She stopped short, taking in the tension of the scene, and sighed, realizing it was about her.

Marsee raised a single brow at Clear Seas and tilted her head in Carrie's direction.

Clear Seas turned and saw the two of them, closed his eyes, and took a deep breath before opening them again and swimming over.

"Carrie, I'm sorry. It seems the Translator has once again shown me the error of my ways. It was wrong of me to turn my back on you in your time of need."

She flashed her surprise. "I understand. My father did a lot of bad things that hurt you."

"No, I don't think you do," he replied. "The dishonor wasn't his. It was mine, and I let myself forget that. I executed people that he brought in on Rip's command, which he had no choice but to follow. I was burnt out and tired, and I let other people do my job. I took Rip at his word and signed off on the executions without performing my due diligence. I should have stepped down, but I wasn't going to force my children into that position like I was."

"So why didn't you let someone else take over, Papa?" Stormy asked.

"Because I didn't trust anyone else enough to take over. When you work with people for a hundred years, you learn their character. They can't keep their masks up all the time. I certainly didn't expect what Rip did, but I ignored his behavior, his and the others. I knew about many of the smaller crimes that my council was committing, but I chose not to investigate. I let them slide as my father and grandfather did because it takes time for people and a culture to change."

He shifted his gaze back to Carrie. "I didn't know about the major crimes or what Rip was doing to you and the others. I swear. I wasn't as honorable and as responsible as I should have been, and you and others were hurt. You were held for months, and I didn't even know you were missing. I turned my back, not because he was without honor, but because I didn't have the right to decide if he deserved that place of honor when I don't. I promise you this, though. I will do everything in my power to live my life with honor going forward, to prove that my life is one worth him dying for."

Carrie took a deep breath and nodded. "I accept your apology and forgive you."

"Thank you," Clear Seas replied. "Now, the Translator also reminded me that you don't have any living relatives. Where are you staying?"

"I have my own place near the school," she replied.

"Alone?!" he asked, surprise rippling across his skin.

She nodded.

"Why weren't you assigned a guardian?"

"No one came forward at the request, and it's okay. I don't need one. I emancipated myself. I've been caring for myself for the last six months, and this is far easier."

"Emancipated?!" he flashed, once again surprised.

"You didn't know?" she asked.

"No, and once again, I'm sorry. I should have made sure you were properly cared for. You shouldn't be alone with your grief and trauma. If you'd like to, you're welcome to come and stay with us."

"Thank you, but that's not necessary."

Marsee could tell Carrie didn't believe the offer was genuine.

"Please, come," Stormy said and held out his hand. "I could really use a friend right now."

Carrie flashed her surprise and stared at the hand for a moment before cautiously reaching out and taking it."

"Come on. Let's go tell my mother," Stormy said, flashing his excitement and giving her a slight tug to have her follow. "You'll really like our house," Stormy said as they swam off. "My mother is an amazing gardener and there are flowers everywhere, and you can borrow any of my books if you want. I even have an advanced copy of the Night Flyer, although the Translator's performance is far better."

Carrie blinked in surprise and then in happiness. "You do?! I heard about it, but I haven't watched it yet."

Stormy nodded. "You'll like it, I think. The villain's a lot like your father. A normal person who does the wrong things for the right reasons, but ultimately does the right thing and earns his honor back."

Marsee and Clear Seas watched them both swim off until they were out of sight, and she smiled at the friendship forming. When she looked back at Clear Seas, he motioned for her to follow him, so she did.

When they were alone in a quiet place in the garden, he stopped. His mask dropped, and a sigh rippled across his skin as his gaze took in the handful of badges she still carried. "So, how do you want to do this?"

"Do what?" she asked, confused.

"My arrest. I just admitted to a crime," he replied. "And by my observations, you're in command of the Guard right now."

She snorted and looked down at the badges in her hand, then considered what Clear Seas had admitted to. "I heard nothing," she said and chuckled at his expression. "Clear, if you don't trust someone else to take over for you, I'm certainly not going to remove you and put one of them in power. You've admitted on several occasions what you did was wrong, promised to do better, and Carrie accepted your reparations, as do I. I see no need for this to go before the Council."

"I really don't understand you," he said, shaking his head.

She laughed and lifted the badges in her paw. "Join the club. I'm not even sure how I'm going to explain this or where my audacity to do so came from."

"Probably from your sister," he replied as hints of humor flickered on his skin.

"You're probably not wrong there," she chuckled. "The Hue-mans have absolutely no respect for rank and authority."

"They voted your father back in," he countered.

"They did, but that's because they respect *him*, not his rank. I think that's because Papa treats them as equals and rarely goes against their wishes unless it would conflict with the Charter, and I've seen him struggle with that decision. It often goes against his beliefs about what's moral and right. Take the decision against Nazari, for example. From our perspective, it was wrong, but from the Hue-man's perspective, they were preventing genocide. I've spoken to Councilor Kai about the genocide that happened to her people. They were forced onto lands that were infertile and barren, and then the government came in and took their children from them because they deemed them incapable of adequately providing for them. They prevented them from practicing their religion or even speaking their language. It was a way of eradicating a culture in only a single generation, and the Hue-mans didn't know us well enough at the time to know if that's what we intended or not. My father has had to walk carefully between our two cultures and has chosen to be their translator and mentor, not their ruler, which they've come to respect, just as your people have come to respect you."

He shook his head. "They have no reason to respect me, not anymore."

"Of course they do. If they didn't, they wouldn't have voted you back in."

"And that fact completely baffles me. I failed them badly."

"Tell me, Senior Councilor, before this past year, would you have ever stood before your Council and admitted to anyone that you were wrong?"

He shook his head. "No. As my father once told me, Senior Councilors don't make mistakes. We adjust our decisions when new information is presented. The authority that comes with the position requires that the people believe we are infallible and worthy of their trust."

"Do you know the moment my father became a Senior Councilor? It wasn't when my sister appointed him. It was the moment he found out that my mother had torn up the leash that the Council had ordered my sister to wear. He had direct orders from Tabor and a majority of the Council behind her, yet he disobeyed those orders. Only a few hours before, Little Flower had asked him to remove the leash, and he said no. He wasn't willing then to disobey a direct order from his Senior Councilor, even though he knew it was wrong. It may have been the smallest act of treason in the universe, but to my sister, it was everything, just as your apologies to Crystal and Carrie meant everything to them. The people don't want rulers. They want leaders, and they want a leader like you, one capable of admitting when they're wrong and one who can change directions and do what needs to be done to correct those mistakes. I believe you meant every word you said to Carrie, that you will do everything in your power to make your life worth the honor of his sacrifice."

"I give you my oath," he replied. "And I thank you for your trust."

She nodded. "Well, I should probably get back before my shadows come looking for me. They're probably pacing now as it is. They didn't like the idea of me going off without them, but…" she shrugged.

He nodded with understanding. "Before you go, I want to thank you for today, for your wonderful speech, which I apparently need to watch a few more times, and your song, both in public, and here. You should know we don't share this part of ourselves with off-worlders. Our song…"

"I already know," she interrupted. "Why do you think I sang that song earlier? I knew you couldn't grieve the way you needed to because it was being publicized. That was the best translation I could come up with for your song of life."

He gasped. "None of my people would dare to bring it up with an off-worlder."

"But I'm not an off-worlder anymore, am I?"

He flashed his surprise and then chuckled. "No. I suppose you're not. You're our beloved Translator and Leviathan Slayer, a seer of harm and a guard of our honor."

She tilted her head at the phrasing, but without another word, she turned and swam off.

A few minutes later, she climbed into one of the waiting shuttles and had the pilot drop her off at the rear of the Council Building. It wasn't where she planned to meet up with her guards again, but she knew it wouldn't be long before they found her. The guards by the door flashed the silver and purple but then caught sight of the badges in her hand. She ignored their astonishment and made her way down to Stinger's office.

To her surprise, the outer office was completely empty, but when she checked Stinger's office, she found him looking out his window. "I wondered how long it would take you to get here."

She snorted. "As if you didn't have people watching me the entire time."

He turned. "All of Command was watching you, including your private conversation with Clear Seas."

She nodded, not aware they'd been watching that, but honestly not surprised. "I'm guessing if Clear Seas knew what was going on, that you did, too?"

He sighed and nodded. "I don't know how much you know of our planet's history, but we were...much like the Hue-mans not too long ago. Our last war was only a few years before your ship landed here. I may have authority granted by the Charter, but I do not have authority, not in the way the other Senior Guards do. In many districts, I still swim dark. We were playing the long game, giving people time to change and for our culture to shift with exposure to the other species. With each generation, we've improved, but obviously, we still have a lot of work left to do."

"Recognizing the problem is the first step in fixing it," she replied.

Stinger's skin flashed with astonishment and confusion. "You're not relieving me of duty?"

"I didn't say that." Marsee held up the badges in her hand. "I can't say if your culture is better or worse than mine, but twenty-four of your guards chose to add to the pain of a grieving child rather than offer assistance. Tell me truthfully. What would you have done?

Would you have turned your back on her, too, just like every other child you've turned your back on over the years? Or would you have set your grief and beliefs aside and held out a hand to a grieving child, like Red Fin did? Like an Honor Guard should?"

He didn't answer, although his wildly conflicting emotions said everything.

She waited, her gaze locked on him until he looked away. "That's what I thought."

She set the badges down on the desk. "Your oath was to the people, before yourself, your family, your Guard, and your Council. Your intentions might have been in the right place, but you still broke your oath, and it was enough that Snapper Fish didn't dare to come to you or anyone else in the Guard for help. You are as much responsible for those crimes as he was because you allowed them to happen. The Council has chosen not to punish you for those crimes simply because they don't know who else to trust, just as I just did with Clear Seas, but I wonder if you're ready to be the kind of Honor Guard this world needs right now."

A sigh rippled across his skin, and he ripped the badge off his harness and stared down at it for a long time, rubbing his thumb across his name. "I've tried over the years to live up to the ideals of this badge, but you're right. My honor has been broken and the light snuffed out with every innocent person harmed by my inaction. I fully intend to do everything in my power to right those wrongs, but I don't have the right to wear this anymore. How can I lead when I have no light to shine the way?" He swam over to the desk, set his badge on top of the pile, and swam out.

She sighed, scratched the back of her neck, and followed after, not having a clue what she was supposed to do now.

She found Avery and Aris waiting for her in the outer office.

"How long have you been here?" she asked.

"The whole time," he replied.

She sighed and nodded. "So now what?"

"Now, we go collect your sister," he replied.

"I meant about Stinger. Is there anything I need to do there?"

He snorted. "No. Senior Honor Guard Red Fin will take care of the paperwork when he's back from the burial."

She flicked her ears back in surprise. Red Fin wasn't anywhere close to being next in line for rank if he had turned down his promotion.

He chuckled at her expression. "You promoted Red Fin the moment you awarded him that cloak, just as you informed the people Stormy will be their next Senior once he's old enough. Every person in Command today saw them prove you right, and you named Red Fin again only moments ago. He's the only one among their guard you trust, the one you set as an example of how an Honor Guard should act, and because of that, he's the only one the people and the Guard will accept as Senior."

She groaned. "I really need to stop doing that."

"Doing what?" Aris asked.

"Promoting people without realizing it," she replied.

Both guards chuckled with amusement.

"Well, you seem to have no problems demoting people," Avery said.

"True," she replied, then shrugged. "Well, accidental or otherwise, in this, I fully agree. Now come on, let's go find my sister and cub and something to eat. I'm starving."

4 9

ELLIE: GRUBBY PAWS

By the time the state funeral happened, Ellie felt like she knew each of the honored dead personally. While natural disasters were unavoidable, it had been a long time since there had been a mass casualty event of this magnitude, on any of the worlds, and it was all that was on the news. Snapper Fish's death was a big part of the conversation, considering the clemency he'd just received from the Senior Council. Many were not convinced he should be given honors after what he'd done, but Clear Seas had ordered it.

The entire funeral was broadcast live on all of the news channels, and Ellie set an alarm so she wouldn't miss any of it. Due to the delay in transmission and the different lengths of the days, the first moments of the ceremony started very early, hours before the suns were up on Saber.

When the doors of the council chamber opened, and Marsee swam out at the head of the Honor Guard, Ellie whooped and cheered. "Yes! That's my girl!"

The noise must have woken Jer and Myra as they both appeared a few moments later.

"Marsee's leading the Honor Guard?" Myra said, jaw dropped as she stood by the door.

"Marsee outranks everyone on that planet, Myra. I thought you knew that. Besides, Honor Guard Tanner gave her life to save Marsee, and Temperate was her friend. If Marsee hadn't been out there, I would have sent Little Flower a message to thwack her for me."

"Yeah, but one of those pilots kidnapped her. She's honoring him?" Myra asked as she and Jer made their way over to the couch to watch.

"Yes. To do otherwise would be dishonorable. It's honestly the only way Snapper Fish would have been able to regain his honor, at least in the eyes of the Water Sprites."

The press was just as surprised, and they spent a considerable amount of time discussing it, eventually going so far as to track down Kendra for her take on it.

She was trotting down a hall when they caught up to her.

"Senior Honor Guard, if you have a moment, please," the reporter called out.

Kendra stopped and raised a brow, likely surprised to be asked in the first place. She rarely gave interviews as security updates almost always came filtered through the Council.

The press quickly caught up to her. "Thank you, Ma'am. We're curious about your take on Marsee Chenzira leading the Honor Guard for the state funeral on the Water World."

Ellie snorted, and even Jer chuckled. She knew Kendra well enough to recognize that the Senior Honor Guard was decidedly annoyed to be stopped when it should have been obvious she was busy, only to be asked such a stupid question.

"Honor Guard Tanner gave her life to protect Marsee. I would expect no less from any honor guard." With that, Kendra turned and started walking away.

The reporter was stunned for a second and then chased after. "Ma'am... Are you saying that Marsee joined the Guard?"

Kendra huffed and stopped again. "No, she has not officially joined the Guard, but she *is* an Honor Guard. She's intelligent and fierce, and her honor is not in question. She nearly gave her life to stop Rip Current and save the others, and she was awarded the Leviathan Cloak for that act, a cloak historically only ever awarded to those who have died in service, as will be awarded today. As the only *living* Leviathan Slayer, it's both fitting and proper that she be at the head of the Honor Guard. Now, if you'll excuse me..." Kendra didn't wait for a reply as she spun and strode away.

The reporter didn't back off.

Ellie had to give them props for having the courage to press their luck.

"Just for confirmation, you're promoting her to Honor Guard?"

Just like she could award rank, honorary or otherwise, to anyone in or out of her Guild, so too could any of the Seniors.

Kendra turned with enough fierceness on her expression to make the reporter startle. "Let me be perfectly clear. Not only is Marsee an Honor Guard, but if she chose the Guard over the Guild, I would immediately promote her and place her as my second."

Ellie chuckled at both Kendra's attitude and the reporter's stunned expression, which matched Jer's and Myra's. It didn't surprise her, though. Marsee did have the heart of an Honor Guard, and if she could lead the Guild, she could easily lead the Guard.

Kendra obviously recognized the unasked question. "The honor of the Guard has been severely tarnished by Rip Current and his followers, but as I already stated, *her* honor is not in question. She's proven that to me time and time again." Kendra turned and strode away again without elaborating.

This time, the reporter didn't chase after Kendra but turned back to face her camera. "Well, there you have it, direct from the mouth of the Senior Honor Guard..."

Jer sighed. "I honestly don't know if that will help her case or hurt it."

Ellie frowned, wondering the same. "Well, Kendra's right. Her honor's not in question. That's a big part of the reason I claimed her. I wanted someone I could trust at the head of my guild, but I might just have to have a conversation with Kendra about trying to steal my protege."

Jer chuckled and tilted his head at her. "You know, I'm honestly not sure who would win that fight now that you're healed up, and I've seen what Kendra can do on more than one occasion."

Ellie purred at the compliment. She needed that burst of self-esteem.

Once the caskets were unloaded, the next several hours were fairly uneventful as the broadcasters explained who arrived to honor the dead — if they knew.

When Clear Seas and his family showed up, she sobbed. Myra climbed onto the bed with her to console her.

Jer, far more used to controlling his emotions, had his tucked tightly behind his mask. The only indication of his grief was a heavy sigh he let out as Temperate's mother placed her hands on the casket and began to cry.

What came next made them all stop. Even the press was silent.

Marsee's voice wasn't trained, but it was beautiful nonetheless because of the emotion she poured into it. When the others joined in, Ellie's fur stood up on end. There were a number of Sprite singers in the Guild, but she knew they only ever sang the other species' songs and understood why. She'd spoken at length with Trench about it when she took over the Guild, but she'd never heard them sing like this. Harmonies and counter melodies wove around Marsee like a beautiful tapestry, and she knew it was something she'd never forget.

Myra started crying next to her, and she hugged her friend, surprised that Myra was reacting. She didn't know the dead or Temperate. "My children wrote that song for me after I lost Marsee's litter-mate," Myra explained after the song was done, wiping the tears away.

The cameras caught Marsee struggling with her control as Clear Seas led his family away, and the broadcasters spent some time talking about Marsee and her relationship with them. They even brought up her first original book, The Adventures of Super Stormy, and downloads of that flew off the servers.

Ellie chuckled. Marsee was good for the Guild in more ways than one.

At exactly eleven local time, Marsee began the slow procession to the council chamber, and she executed every step flawlessly as if she'd done it her entire life.

I wonder how many hours she practiced, Ellie thought.

As she marched, the press split the screen to show both the slow procession and inside the council chamber, and they watched the religious ceremony with curiosity.

But even she was surprised when Marsee gave the speech. She'd expected Clear Seas to do that, as had the broadcasters. Less than a year before, the thought of standing in front of a crowd had terrified Marsee. It had been all Ellie could do at the time to prepare her to translate for her sister. She'd tried to have her give an interview once, but Marsee had completely frozen and been useless for two days afterwards. But now, Marsee spoke like she'd been giving speeches her entire life. She couldn't find a single hint of hesitation as Marsee began, and her pride for her protege bloomed in her heart.

"Who are you, and what have you done with my daughter?" Myra asked.

Ellie shushed her, not wanting to miss a single word.

When Stormy stood and flashed his skin as bright as he could, and the crowd followed his lead, Ellie cheered again. "Yes! You show'em, Stormy! Make your brother proud!"

Marsee's expression of pride was enough to tell Ellie that it had been entirely unplanned, and whether that was the end of the speech or not, Marsee clearly knew not to mess with perfection. She wasn't just trying to comfort a few grieving families. She was trying to save the Consortium and heal five planets' worth of grieving and shocked people. With every grieving family, she gave them exactly what they needed to heal.

Ellie sobbed when Stormy floated up to receive the cloak, which dangled off him, far too big for his tiny body. That image would be burned into her brain, and she decided to have a still framed and sent to Clear Seas. But even she'd been surprised when Marsee publicly forgave Snapper Fish and restored his honor, and it wasn't lip service either. She could tell that Marsee meant it.

When she found out that Snapper had saved Marsee by his actions, Ellie forgave him too and sent a message to his daughter.

The ending, though, was absolute perfection. Whether Marsee had improvised it after Stormy's impromptu addition to the ceremony or not, Stormy had picked up on her subtle instructions, and it had worked far better than anyone could have hoped for. Broadcasters later reported that Sprites from the ceremony had left, light still on, and had flown to other communities until Temperate's light had made it around their entire world. As word of that made it to the other planets, people started putting candles in their windows or turning on lights over their doors, and within hours of the funeral, Temperate's light had made it around all five planets.

"Now, can I talk?" Myra teased as the procession left the building.

"Not right now. I'm basking in the pride I'm feeling for *my* protege," Ellie said as she leaned back in the bed, closed her eyes, and sighed with happiness. After a moment, though, she opened her eyes and grinned at her friends.

Jer looked equally proud, but Myra looked stunned.

Ellie indicated Myra could speak, but nothing came out. "What's the matter, Myra? Cat got your tongue?" She just loved that Hue-man expression.

"Seriously, Ellie, Who are you, and what have you done with my daughter?" Myra asked again. "First math, now this?"

"I just helped her find what was always there to begin with. She did the rest."

"She was never good at speeches. The very idea of speaking in front of a crowd of people would put her into panic for days. But this…I can't believe it!"

To be fair, Marsee had surprised her there, too, but she'd never admit it to anyone. "I don't know why you're so surprised. Look who she has for examples: the most amazing Senior Guild Master the worlds have *ever* seen…"

Jer rolled his eyes. "You're the *only* Senior Guild Master the worlds have ever seen."

She grinned and continued. "And two parents and an uncle that exemplify living their lives with honor, and a partner and mate that can chew up and spit out Senior Councilors and Master Healers for breakfast. She's earned the titles of Translator, Leviathan Slayer, Guild Master, and now Honor Guard. She's saved the Consortium and Guild from economic collapse and defeated the biggest supervillain we've seen in millennia, and with one speech likely healed it too, or at least began the process. You'd better get used to the new and improved Marsee because she's not your little kitten anymore. When we weren't paying attention, she went and grew up."

Jer pinned his ears back and growled. "She will *always* be my little kitten."

Ellie smiled at him, but it shifted to a frown as a thought occurred. "Although...I may have made one rather large mistake."

"You? Make a mistake?" Myra scoffed. "I find that hard to believe."

"I know, right? But if she keeps growing like this, Senior Guild Master won't be nearly big enough to keep her busy. Maybe we could join *all* the Guilds together..."

"No. You have far too much power as it is," Jer replied.

"Well, don't come crawling back to me when she gets bored and decides to reorganize the Council someday," Ellie replied, only half joking.

Marsee had exceeded all expectations. Then again, the universe had thrown everything at her this past month, and somehow, she'd managed to survive and claw back stronger than ever, whereas Ellie just wanted to curl up in Marsee's cave and hide.

They watched until Marsee and the others flew off, and then some of the commentary that followed before shutting off the broadcast.

"Well, I'm just glad nothing happened," Myra said. "I was afraid someone would attack."

Jer frowned. "They would get no benefit from attacking a public funeral, and if the comment boards are any indication, Marsee's performance today may have gone a long way towards stopping another attack."

"I just hope there aren't more unintended consequences," Ellie said.

"As do I," Jer replied, and with a heavy sigh, he stood and walked out.

Myra sighed as well after Jer was gone and turned back to her. "*You* need to take a nap."

"Yes, ma'am," Ellie replied, curling up on the bed as ordered.

Myra snorted and followed out after Jer.

She wasn't even remotely tired, as Myra had obviously guessed, so the moment Myra left, she sat back up and pulled out her tablet. Then, after some consideration, she fired off a message to Kendra.

> You need to keep your grubby paws off of my protege. She was mine first, and I'm not sharing.

A response came back from the Senior Honor Guard almost immediately, and it made her howl with laughter.

> Perhaps you should have thought of that before putting your grubby paws all over mine.

She was still trying to figure out an appropriately snarky reply when another message came in, one that made her flick her ears back in astonishment.

> However, if you're interested in a trade, let me know. For some strange reason, mine won't stop grinning like a fool, no matter how much I growl at him, and I can't have that. It's decidedly bad for my reputation.

She wasn't sure what surprised her more, the idea that Quinn might be serious about a relationship or the fact that she was seriously considering taking Kendra up on the offer.

50

A BREWING STORM

The only thing keeping his skin blank was decades of training, but underneath, he was boiling red. He'd lost everything this past week: friends, family, and now his very lucrative and high-status career. Word was already spreading based on the looks and flashes of disgust he was getting from the other guards as he swam back to his suite in the Guard Complex.

He growled when he placed his hand on the scanner outside the building, and it flashed a dark blue 'Access Denied.'

"I'm sorry, sir, but your access has been revoked," a voice said over the comms.

He growled under his breath but kept his voice calm. "I would like to request an escort to pack up my belongings."

There was a lengthy pause. "Your request has been denied," the voice replied. "Your belongings will be delivered to your new residence. Please return your gear to the armory."

A flicker of annoyance escaped his control before he ripped his gear off and threw everything but his tablet at the door as hard as he could, hoping it would get damaged in the process. If they wanted it so badly, they could get it themselves.

He swam off, lost in thought until he decided he'd better find out where he was living now. He scowled when he realized nothing had been assigned to him yet, and with a state-sponsored holiday, he wouldn't be able to find anyone to assign him a new residence until morning. It was the last straw. Fury rose up in him, needing a target.

A moment later, the universe presented that target to him.

Motion caught his eye, and he scowled as he watched Marsee, laughing at something as she swam out of the rear door of the Council Building, followed by her two shadows. Both guards scowled in his direction, and he realized he'd let his control slip and his anger show on his skin.

Avery said something, and Marsee looked in his direction. Avery said something else, and her entire demeanor changed. She went from laughing to vicious in a heartbeat.

He turned and swam off, knowing that if he tried anything, her two shadows would kill him first and not bother asking questions.

He was far more convinced that Rip had been right about her and her power-hungry family than he had ever been before, but the question was, what could he do about it? He knew several people who had worked with Rip that hadn't been culled yet, and as he swam away, the rough details of a plan began to form.

He had information that would be very interesting to the right sources. If he played his cards right, he would bring down that power-hungry brat, along with her entire family and the rest of the Senior Council, and regain his place of honor in the next administration.

If protecting the Consortium from the likes of them is not honoring my oath, then I don't know what is.

He turned back around and saw Marsee and her guards swimming off in the other direction. They'd clearly dismissed the threat he posed. He grinned wickedly at them.

I hope you know how to play Rando-Tat, Little Kitten, because I'm calling your bluff. You may have superior forces, but you've shown your cards, and I will make you regret ever putting your pieces into play.

ABOUT THE PAWTHOR

Laura Napoli was born and raised in northern Vermont and continues to make the area her home. When not spending her time on the warm clicky box (computer) writing or waiting eagerly for a review, she is the caregiver to four heating cats who provide her with heat, massage, acu-paw-ture, and purr-therapy in exchange for pets and catnip treaties.

PUBLICATIONS

- The Tails of Little Flower
- The Pride of Little Flower
- The Whiskers of Hope
- The Paws of Hope
- Saber's Instinct
- Saber's Guard
- Saber's Guild

COMING SOON

- Saber's Secret